The History Ga

GIANTS
AND
DRAGONS

BJ Cross

Typeset in Dante MT Std and Loved by the King

Cover illustrations by Marion Walker

Editing, design and publishing by UK Book Publishing

UK Book Publishing is a trading name of Consilience Media

www.ukbookpublishing.com

ISBN: 978-1-910223-02-4

In loving memory of Harry, Donald, Jenny and George.

Forever in our memories.

Reunited in our imagination.

FOREWORD

On the shelves of the libraries of every country in the world lies an entire section dedicated to history: the history of the country itself as well as the history of the world that has often helped to shape it. History is engrained into the memories of every school child in every classroom, whether it comes from the written word or from the story telling of those who have passed down the tales from generation to generation.

But imagine if the books on the shelves did not represent reality or the stories told did not quite reflect what really happened. Imagine if the world's history could be changed and no-one realise. What if entire episodes of what has shaped a civilisation, its science and its beliefs could be wiped from the history books without anyone being aware?

Tucked away in the leafy countryside of England, the keepers of the world's history work hard to make sure that this never happens. They are selected and entrusted to ensure that the events that shaped the world remain unchanged and properly recorded for all to enjoy in the future.

But even the most experienced of history keepers sometimes need a helping hand, and sometimes from the most unexpected quarter…

CHAPTER ONE

The alarm was persistent but Jack kept his eyes firmly shut. Although today was a School day, he made a quick assessment that in the last days before half term, a few extra minutes in bed would probably go unnoticed.

The light was just creeping through the heavy dark blue curtains and Jack was able to bear the repeat alarm for the next minute but, as designed, it became increasingly louder and Jack's arm appeared from under the duvet and banged down on the top. It stopped immediately. He opened one eye and then the other and, at that point, he remembered!

For today was not just any day, not just a School day just before half term when everyone was excited about the holidays, but today was the day that he would have the opportunity of impressing the love of his life, JJ Buccannan. Whilst her real name was Jennifer Jane, no-one ever called her that and she was known to family and friends as JJ. Even the thought of her brought a warm feeling to his very soul. Of course Jack knew that JJ was blissfully unaware of his devotion but, even at the very grown up age of 13, Jack understood the importance of making an impression when trying to get JJ to notice him.

Today, Jack knew, he would be making that impression. What he did not, nor could not know, was that today would be the start of a great journey that would mean it was not just JJ Buccannan who would eventually be impressed.

However, before his greatest hour arrived, he knew that there were more mundane matters to attend to. He had to pack for his journey home to Bolivia for starters, trying to remember what the South American weather would be like at this time of year. The next thing was to get washed, dressed, down to breakfast and then taking his place on the Introductor Rota. He was not sure what he had done to deserve that in the last few days of term but he knew it was important to those he was due to meet.

Jack tried to contain his excitement at the thought of seeing his parents again. It had been six weeks since he was last in Bolivia and he knew that many things had changed since he was last there, as his parents had written and spoken to him by telephone about the flowers and the greenery and the feasts and the celebrations.

He knew that in 1 day, 4 hours and 30 minutes he would again be at Heathrow with his sister, Rosie, trying to dodge the unaccompanied minor representative, as they waited for their long flight home. Jack appreciated that they were lucky to be going home for half term. It was a long way but he knew that his mother and father would make the very most of the time that they had. They would walk and fish and play… he smiled with excitement and flicked on his radio to listen to the School music station. 'Walking on sunshine' was playing and it was one of his favourites; he turned it up a little and started his packing whilst dancing round the room. Not entirely cool but there was no-one else watching.

He paused as he danced past the mirror on one foot waving his arms in the air – he licked his hand and tried to flatten down his fair hair which was sticking up at right angles and then stopped to view himself from front and back in the mirror. His shoulders were broad for his age and he knew that he was almost the tallest in his class. He was grateful for his mother's height but his father's strength and agility.

The song finished and, deciding that he could pack later in the day whilst rehearsing for his moment of glory, Jack was washed and dressed in his neatly pressed School uniform within 10 minutes. He paused to listen to the news before heading towards the dining room for breakfast. The news was fed through from Radio Four and always sounded so very serious but it was important that he kept up with what was going on in the outside world and so Jack sat on his bed and listened. It was not a cheerful bulletin: floods in India and Pakistan, fires in Australia.

The news over, Jack headed out of his room towards the dining room. He said good morning in a very loud and cheerful voice to a number of friends who were looking very bleary eyed on their way to breakfast; they grunted a response and Jack laughed. Everyone always said that he was much too cheerful first thing in the morning and today he was going to be unbearable and he did not mind.

He walked through the corridors filled with framed paintings and etchings, sculptures and abstract art. Jack always saw something different every time he went through these corridors and always stopped to admire at least one or two. He paused in front of one, a large painting of a border collie dog crouched low as they do before they are about to round up the sheep. Next to it was a small card that read 'Rosie Simmons – Charlie'. He did not really know where his sister got her artistic talent, it certainly had not been inherited by him.

Jack crossed the huge hall and skipped down the stairs to the dining room. He joined the queue for hot food and picked up a tray, spotting his sister sat alone on one of the refectory benches, tucking into scrambled egg on toast. She looked up and smiled and, realising no-one else was watching, stuck her tongue out in a way that only 11 year olds can perfect.

Jack glanced around and there was still no-one, so he reciprocated by sticking his tongue out even further, and then proceeded to touch his nose with the tip – he knew that he could do that and Rosie couldn't. She grimaced back at him, knowing that he had won that particular battle, and he laughed quietly.

Rosie smiled with that wide eyed look which said 'you are about to pay for that'. However, Jack had no idea what she was talking about until he turned back to the queue and his heart missed a beat. There, two in front and looking straight at him, was JJ Buccannan. She stood tall and slim, her beautiful dark hair shone under the lights of the dining room and her dusky skin glowed as if she were not real. Dark eyes smiled at him without her lips moving but then her lips slowly broke into a smile as she saw him. Jack was not sure if that was out of sympathy having seen this juvenile exchange with his sister.

Jack could feel himself starting to blush and it felt as if it was starting from his toes all the way to the top of his head. He made a small waving gesture at JJ to acknowledge that she was there and tried a tentative smile. To his surprise, her smile widened, equally as tentatively. She waved back.

The embarrassing silence was interrupted when the two boys between them in the queue for breakfast started to engage JJ in conversation and she turned away and started listening politely, flicking back her long dark hair with her left hand and laughing delicately as they recounted tales of their recent footballing competition. Jack knew that if he wanted to he could have boasted about his tries and his recent exploits on the rugby team but he had been brought up not to boast and so he slipped into the background and just admired from a distance.

Jack went off the idea of having hot food that morning and overtook JJ and his two competitors for her affection as they were chatting and laughing, and moved across to the cold section and selected some cereal, milk and a large Danish pastry, and took his tray and moved down the tables and, seeing no-one he knew, sat down next to his sister.

'I see she is still impressed by the football boys,' said Rosie quietly, and Jack knew that in any game of sticky out tongue, that comment would trump even one that was a foot long. His sister certainly knew how to kick a boy when he was down. But instead of rising to the bait, he knew that what annoyed his sister the most was if she was simply ignored, and that's what he did.

Instead of replying, Jack turned his attention to his breakfast and was just in the process of stuffing a large piece of Danish pastry into his mouth, probably larger than he had intended, and certainly larger than his mother would have been impressed with, had she been sat opposite, when he became aware of a figure standing in front of him. Looking up, it was all he could do not to spit out his large morsel of food in shock when he realised that the tall dark elfin-like figure in front of him, was JJ Buccannan. He thought perhaps he was dreaming but his sister kicked him sharply under the table and he knew then it was real.

'May I sit down?' she asked politely, and Jack could sense that his dear sister was about to say something highly inappropriate to the effect that there was no room, and he kicked her equally as sharply.

'Of course,' Rosie said, not flinching but smiling, as she moved round to allow JJ to sit between them.

Jack knew deep down that Rosie had his best interests at heart but, nevertheless, at this particular moment in time, he rather wished that she was somewhere else. Alaska would have been his preference, but Siberia would have come a close second. However, he was stuck with his sister, sat at the table with the most beautiful and funny girl that Jack had ever met, and he would just have to make the most of it.

JJ started to delicately eat her boiled egg and looked up under long dark eyelashes, and said quietly to Jack, 'I am really looking forward to your talk this afternoon,' and Jack felt as if someone had grabbed him around his chest and had sucked all of the air out of him. The thought that JJ Buccannan was looking forward to something that he, Jack Simmons, was going to be doing, was simply too much to ask for. He thought for a short time that he might still be asleep and dreaming, back in his room, so he closed his eyes briefly and opened them again but she was still there.

Rosie looked up and, with a smile that Jack knew only meant trouble, she said, 'Of course it is not as exciting as the football finals.'

JJ paused for a second, smiled kindly at Rosie as if she were her naughty younger sister and then said, 'Anyone can play football, but there aren't many people I know who have travelled to the places that you have travelled to and I am really looking forward to hearing about your latest adventures and seeing your pictures.'

Jack glanced at his sister with an expression which clearly said 'So there!' and he proceeded to break his Danish pastry into very small pieces and eat them delicately, as his mother had taught him. He could almost hear her voice in his ears, saying, 'Manners, Jack. That is what will most impress a girl, next to a sense of humour.'

However, before the conversation could progress any further, Jack glanced at the clock on the far wall of the dining room and realised, to his horror, that his Introductor duties started in 5 minutes and he knew that it would probably take him that long to run to the grand hall to meet the guests. He drank his orange juice quickly and got to his feet.

He said, in his politest voice, 'JJ, I do hope that you will excuse me, and I must apologise as this must look very rude, but I am on the Introductor Rota this morning and my guests arrive in 5 minutes.'

JJ looked up with a smile that could light a room, and said, 'Good luck with that one, Jack. Introductor Rota at this time of the day is going to be great fun!'

With that, Jack strode from the dining room, knowing that he was leaving his great love in the hands of his 11 year old sister, and he knew that there was every chance that by the end of breakfast, JJ Buccannan would never speak to him again. He glanced over his shoulder and Rosie smiled sweetly at him. He smiled back with a smile that said, in terms that only brother and sister would understand, 'If you mess this up, it's war.' Jack had no idea how much he would need his sister in the next few days; but hindsight is a wonderful thing, as his father always said.

Jack walked calmly from the dining room and, as soon as he was at the top of the stairs, and although it was strictly against the rules, he broke into a run, down the long wooden panelled corridors, out through the east gate, across the terraces and in through the south gate, before he could slow to a moderate pace, wipe the small beads of sweat from his forehead and compose his breathing. It was 2 minutes to 9 o'clock and Introductor Rota was due to start at 9am precisely.

As he crossed the grand hall, with its enormous windows and paintings, and across to the main School entrance, he could see the receptionist sat politely behind her desk, hair worn in a traditional bun, spectacles on her nose and a fountain pen in her hand. She had a slightly troubled look on her face and Jack knew already that it was going to be one of those mornings. He smiled at her and raised a hand to say 'I am here'. She smiled back with a look that said 'good luck with this one' and glanced over into the corner of the reception area.

Jack could see, sat over in the corner, three people. He knew immediately that these were his guests that day – through instinct and experience. It was probably husband and wife and son, although in this day and age Jack did not want to make any assumptions. The mother was a middle-aged lady, smartly turned out, with a floral dress, pearls and shoes that were not too high but were, nevertheless, quite elegant. It was the sort of outfit that his mother would probably wear and he approved. He approved of most of his mother's wardrobe, with the exception of a few notable items that his father had acquired on a recent trip to Japan, which made her look a little bit like an extra from Lord of the Rings, although he had not yet been brave enough to tell her that.

The father, on the other hand, whilst obviously wearing quite an expensive suit, looked crumpled and slightly harassed. He was sat clutching two bags and was clearly doing something important on one of his phones. Jack raised an eyebrow and glanced towards the receptionist who smiled back with the smile he had seen a hundred times before which said 'I have tried without success'.

Jack turned back to his guests and studied the young man sat between the two adults. He was about 10 and Jack knew very little about his background, other than the fact that he was looking to join the School and had already passed many of the selection processes before being invited on an Introductor day. He was sat quietly between his parents, looking a little as if he didn't want to be there with them and, equally, very excited. He was clutching a small bag which Jack hoped contained, as instructed, a change of clothes and his wash bag. It was a feeling that Jack remembered well and he suddenly felt great sympathy towards the young man.

Jack glanced in the hallway mirror, adjusted his tie, patted down his hair again, which, by this stage, was sticking up at an unusual angle on account of him running halfway across the School grounds to make sure he was on time. He took a deep breath and walked towards the party of three.

'Mr and Mrs Bailey-Knox?' he asked politely, and, without looking up, the father said, 'That's us.' The young man sat next to him rolled his eyes slightly in embarrassment that his father could not even look up from his telephone to greet this person who had come to introduce himself, and Jack winked quickly at him, as if to say that it was not a problem, and, if Jack was honest, increasingly common.

His mother, on the other hand, smiled broadly, stood up and held out her right hand. 'Hello,' she said, 'I'm Mrs Bailey-Knox. You must be Jack, it's very nice to meet you. This is my son, Sam, and my husband, Mr Bailey-Knox.'

'Hello,' grunted Mr Bailey-Knox, again without looking up, but Sam got to his feet, and firmly shook Jack's outstretched hand and looked Jack straight in the eye.

Mrs Bailey-Knox looked embarrassed. 'I'm very pleased to meet you, Jack. Thank you for taking the time to show us around the School. I am really sorry if this is disturbing your day.'

'Not at all,' said Jack, with his fingers crossed behind his back. 'It's always a pleasure to introduce potential new students to the School. I will try and do my very best to answer any questions and show you as much of the School as I am able to in the time that we have. However, before we start our tour, I will have to ask you, Mr Bailey-Knox, to leave your phones and any computer and communication equipment that you might have, with our receptionist.'

That caught the attention of Mr Bailey-Knox, who looked up sharply and said, 'I have already had this conversation with the receptionist. I'll carry them with me.'

'I'm afraid...' Jack started to say, but was cut off immediately by Mr Bailey-Knox getting to his feet and saying, 'It's absolutely fine, I will carry it with me, I will not be leaving my computers and my phones with a complete stranger. Now show me the way and let's get on with this tour. I am a very busy man.'

If Jack had a pound for every time that he heard that from a father of a hopeful pupil, he would undoubtedly be a rather rich man by this stage. He was always amazed that the fathers (and generally it was the fathers, as the mothers, no matter how busy, were always much too polite to argue) would refuse this request and, indeed, it indicated how little they knew about the establishment that they were hoping to send their son or daughter to. They appeared to know nothing of School or its ethos and, most importantly, its rules.

However, Jack knew from experience that arguing was futile and they would just have to learn the hard way. Mr Bailey-Knox gathered up his bags of computers and telephones and the three of them headed towards the large door at the far end of the great hall.

They walked past the pictures of past students: politicians, athletes, actors and actresses, chefs and astronauts. Jack tried hard not to smile as they approached the One Metre Line prior to the entrance and he glanced across at Mrs Bailey-Knox, who smiled in an apologetic way, almost in anticipation of what was about to happen next. She clearly knew slightly more about the School than her husband did.

Jack, Sam and Mrs Bailey-Knox crossed the One Metre Line without incident, but Mr Bailey-Knox came to an immediate halt with a loud thud, as if he had just walked straight into a large pane of glass. He bounced back in astonishment and said, in a loud voice, 'What the hell was that?'

'Gerald!' said Mrs Bailey-Knox. 'Your language please.'

'Never mind my language,' said Mr Bailey-Knox, 'I want to know exactly what just happened. I've been hit by something. You, child, was that you?'

He looked across at Jack in an accusatory way, and it was at this stage that Sam stepped forward, 'Dad, I have been trying to explain to you for some time now that this is not an ordinary School. They do not allow computers, mobile telephones or any similar equipment within the grounds. The School is founded on the philosophy of going back to basics and teaching children how to play and interact and learn through books and research, and, because of that, no one, including visitors, can bring computer equipment or phones onto the School premises.'

Jack thought that he probably could not have put it better himself. Mr Bailey-Knox looked at his son in some astonishment and said, 'I thought that had to be a wind up.'

'No Sir,' said Jack, stepping in to the conversation. 'Your son is absolutely right; the Gates Institute, although founded by the generosity of Bill Gates and his estate, represents the complete opposite of everything that Mr Gates stood for when he built his Microsoft empire. Even he realised, as he got older, that what he had created was a world where no one talked to each other anymore, where everything was done via the internet and electronically, and he wanted to put back into society those parts that he felt that he had taken out. He therefore created the Gates Institute in most countries in the world.'

Mr Bailey-Knox looked slightly astonished and said, 'You mean *the* Bill Gates? The founder of Microsoft?'

'Yes, Mr Bailey-Knox, that Bill Gates.'

'Well, presumably, it's like any other School, we can just pay for our son to attend,' and, at that stage, Mrs Bailey-Knox raised her eyebrows in frustration.

'No, Mr Bailey-Knox,' explained Jack, ' the School is non fee-paying and pupils are here by invitation only. It is totally funded by the Gates estate and by industry.'

'But if it's not fee-paying, how have you managed to produce two Prime Ministers, contemporary artists, inventors, chefs, actors, scientists, gold medal winning athletes and of course the footballers, in such a short space of time?' Mr Bailey-Knox asked, in a fairly accusatory way.

Jack took a deep breath and said, 'It's because the School finds the best in people. It doesn't just look for academic excellence, it looks for people who are willing to keep going until they find what they are best at. The School believes that everybody is good at something and they want to encourage pupils to come with an open mind and the intention to find that one good thing in life that they will excel at.'

Mr Bailey-Knox looked around the hall and said, 'This is a wind up, right? Come on, where are the cameras? You two had me well and truly stitched up. Right, well I think we'd better go home, as we are clearly not going to get very far here.'

Jack turned back to face the portraits lining the walls around them. He pointed at the picture closest to them: 'James Cathcart, son of a dustman, he now owns two restaurants with Michelin Stars. I think that means the food is very good.'

'Very,' grunted Mr Bailey-Knox. He followed Jack's gaze to the next picture.

'Katie Harris, the first woman to walk on the moon, brought up by her mother single-handedly, she used to stack shelves in the supermarket at night to pay to bring Katie up. Katie left here, got a first class honours degree and MA in quantum physics and a place on the new NASA space programme. She comes back every year to tell us about it. We even get to try her old space suit on.' Jack was not sure if Mr Bailey-Knox was starting to take interest or not – his face remained blank.

Jack moved on to the next picture along: 'Kit Brady, the fastest man in the world over 5000 metres, son of parents who fled the troubles in Kenya and arrived in England with absolutely nothing. When Kit arrived at School he had been sharing a bedroom with four brothers at home; it took him weeks to get used to having his own room here and he still comes back every sports day if he can.'

There was a pause and eventually Jack said: 'None of these parents could afford to send their children to private school. They studied here for free because the School recognised their belief in their talents.'

'Yes but it is easy with sportsmen, what about the politicians?'

asked Mr Bailey-Knox defiantly. 'Their parents must have gone to Eton even if they did not.'

Out of the corner of his eye Jack saw Sam smile wryly; he had obviously done his homework even if his father had not.

Sam took up the story; he pointed to a picture of the last Prime Minister: 'Kevin Edwards; his Mum served the school dinners at his primary school, no-one in the family went to Eton or probably even knew where it was. Kevin is the most talented pianist and peace maker, he could make anyone do anything. He worked so hard and won a place at Oxford. He went on to become the country's most popular and longest serving Prime Minister.'

Mr Bailey-Knox was momentarily stunned into silence. It was not clear if this was because his son appeared to be more well informed than he did or because of what he had just heard.

Sam looked up at his father and put a hand on his forearm. He said, 'This is very important to me, Dad. I would like to have a look around. Please.' He looked with pleading eyes at his father.

'OK then, but I am still keeping my computer equipment,' and with that Mr Bailey-Knox attempted a second assault on the only barrier between him and the entrance to the School of his son's dreams.

This time, he approached it like a rugby player into the scrum, head down, shoulders forward. Jack winced, even before impact, as Mr Bailey-Knox ran headlong into a solid but completely invisible barrier. He bounced off with such force that he landed in a heap two foot from where impact had occurred. His hair was ruffled, his eyes were wild and the contents of his pockets were spread across the carpet of the main hall.

Jack could count at least three telephones and he suspected that that was probably not the entire haul. Mr Bailey-Knox got to his feet and snarled at Jack. 'Whatever that is, switch it off now!'

Jack put on his most apologetic face and looked Mr Bailey-

Knox in the eyes. 'I'm afraid, Sir, that I have no control over NED.'

'What,' said Mr Bailey-Knox, getting redder in the face by the second, 'in hell's name, is NED?'

There was a small exclamation from Mrs Bailey-Knox, who said, for the second time in as many minutes, 'Language, Gerald!'

'Neutralising Electronic Detector,' said Jack. 'NED, for short. It can detect, sense, and then immobilise or neutralise any form of communication equipment such as computers and phones, or, alternatively, just put up a barrier so that those carrying it can't get through.'

'That's absolutely impossible,' said Mr Bailey-Knox. 'Not even the military have a system like this.'

Jack looked at him sympathetically and said, 'I can assure you, Sir, that the military do have this system and, indeed, it was they who donated it to the School.'

'What kind of School is this?!?!?' screamed Mr Bailey-Knox at the top of his voice. 'You can't possibly operate without computer equipment, without mobile telephones.'

'Oh, Sir,' said Jack. 'We do have telephones, but we have landline telephones. These are ones that you have to dial, with your fingers, like in the olden days.' He demonstrated in the air with his finger.

Mr Bailey-Knox's mouth was gaping open in astonishment, and he quickly gathered himself together, he shook his head, as if to bring himself back to reality, and pulled himself up to his full height.

'Now look here you little...' he said, as he took a step towards Jack. Jack took a step backwards and it was too late before Mr Bailey-Knox realised that Jack had stepped back across the One Metre Line and, with a sickening 'thud' Mr Bailey-Knox hit the invisible barrier for the third time.

'Right, that's it,' he said, 'we're going home.' Mr Bailey-Knox started to gather up his things and turned towards the entrance door through which they had originally come. Neither his wife nor his son moved an inch, but they just watched him as he stalked back across the hall, obviously believing that the two of them were following.

Mr Bailey-Knox stopped in his tracks and turned round very slowly. He looked as his wife and son. 'I thought,' he said, 'we were going.'

It was at that stage that Mrs Bailey-Knox looked up at her husband and a very hard look crossed her face. 'No, Gerald, you said *you* were going, but *we* are staying. This has been Sam's dream for as long as I can remember and I am *not* having your stupidity over a few mobile telephones for a matter of hours ruin any chance he has of coming here. So, if you would like to go out and wait for us in the car, that's not a problem, but Sam and I will be continuing with Jack. The choice is yours.' And, with that, she turned on her heel and started to follow Jack towards the rear door.

Mr Bailey-Knox turned back and stalked across the hall and got as far as the entrance before his steps shortened and his pace slowed. It was clear to Jack that he was mulling over in his mind whether to carry out his threat to leave, and the implications that this had, both for his continued happy home life and, indeed, his son's future.

Finally, common sense got the better of him and, just as Mrs Bailey-Knox and Sam were about to cross the One Metre Line, a voice behind them said, 'Err, I'd like to check in two laptops and three telephones please.' Without moving their heads, Sam and Jack glanced at each other with a little smile, which went undetected by either parent who were, at that stage, glaring at each other. The glares finally turned to a somewhat sheepish look on the face of Mr Bailey-Knox and an expression on the face of his wife which, roughly translated, said 'I think you will find that was the right decision.'

Electronic equipment was checked through with the ultra-efficient secretary/receptionist. Before they moved off, Jack asked for a final time, 'Now, I just want to make sure neither of you have anything on you which would prevent us from getting through?'

Sam and his mother shook their heads and Mr Bailey-Knox said, very solemnly, 'Absolutely not.'

'In that case,' said Jack, 'let the tour begin.'

They walked back across the hall to the One Metre Line. Sam and his mother were a little tentative, having seen the vigour with which Mr Bailey-Knox had hit the invisible barrier, and they put out their hands to ensure that there was nothing to prevent them walking across the line. It appeared that they had passed the test and they stepped tentatively across.

Mr Bailey-Knox, on the other hand, had clearly decided that he had now passed the test, and strode purposefully towards the invisible line, and, with a loud 'thud' hit the barrier for a fourth time, and crashed backwards. By this stage, his face was what can only be described as beetroot.

'You told me,' he said at the top of his voice, 'that if I handed in my phones and computers, I could get through.'

'No,' said Jack, 'I told you that if you handed in all communication equipment, you could get through. What else do you have on you?'

'Nothing,' said Mr Bailey-Knox. 'Absolutely nothing.'

Jack folded his arms and looked critically at the large man crumpled at his feet. 'I don't suppose you are a journalist, are you?' asked Jack.

'A journalist!' Mr Bailey-Knox almost choked at the suggestion, and Jack assumed, from his response, that the answer was probably, no.

'I will have you know, young man, that I am one of the

country's finest lawyers.'

At this point, Sam raised his eyebrows as if this was something he had heard many times before.

'And, what's more, I have not, and never have been, a journalist. And, even if I were, how would that affect my ability to get through this ridiculous system?'

'NED not only detects communication equipment, but it also has inbuilt software which allows it to detect journalists.'

Mr Bailey-Knox roared with laughter. 'That is the most stupid thing that I have ever heard,' he said. 'How can a piece of software possibly detect what people do for a living?'

'Well it does,' said Jack. 'And I have seen it work. Apparently, following the scandal at News Corporation and the potential damage that this did to the Murdoch family, Mr Murdoch commissioned the design of a system which can detect a journalist.'

It was at this stage that curiosity got the better of Sam; 'Why?' he asked.

'Well,' said Jack. 'The scandal at News Corporation involved their journalists hacking into people's telephones and pretending to be people that they were not in order to get a good story. The Murdoch family were so embarrassed by this behaviour that they wanted to ensure that journalism was now always on a level playing field and that if people were talking to a journalist, or meeting with one, they should always know that. They commissioned the design of this system.'

Mr Bailey-Knox scoffed again, 'Oh, let me guess. It can smell them?'

'No,' said Jack, 'It's to do with the brain patterns and the pheromones put out by somebody who is trying to be somebody else.'

'Right,' said Mr Bailey-Knox. 'So, walking into this room, you are saying that we are X-rayed, scanned and interpreted by a piece of software...'

'Yes,' said Jack, 'that would be about right. It does get it wrong sometimes. For instance, one or two of the parents are members of the Special Intelligence Service, and NED has unfortunately mistaken them for journalists and barred entry. But, luckily, they have always seen the funny side.'

'And what,' said Mr Bailey-Knox, as the colour of his face started to return to normal, 'would be the problem about a journalist coming in, in any event?'

'Well,' said Jack, 'the School is very private. There are those who think there is some form of brainwashing that goes on; there are others who appear to believe that we have created our own Hogwarts and practise magic. In fact, all we want is privacy to get on with our studies and our interests without living in fear that an undercover journalist will try and infiltrate the School and print stories which would be unhelpful to everybody.'

'Well,' said Mr Bailey-Knox, as he got to his feet, 'I am not a journalist. I do not have any phones or computers on me. So, why will it not let me through?'

Jack thought for a minute. 'Do you possess a Bluetooth ear piece?'

'Well, yes, of course I do,' said Mr Bailey-Knox. 'I'm a lawyer. I spend my life on the telephone, I have always got it on me.'

'That would be it, then,' said Jack. 'I'm terribly sorry to trouble you, but if I could take that off you and check it in, then I don't think that you will have a further problem.'

Mr Bailey-Knox tentatively took out the small Bluetooth device from his pocket and passed it across to Jack, who examined it. 'I think this will be the problem,' he said. 'Try putting your hand across the line.'

Mr Bailey-Knox approached the One Metre Line much more tentatively this time and his outstretched hand wavered near the place that he had hit the invisible barrier only a matter of minutes earlier. There appeared to be nothing there. He moved a little closer and pointed a foot. That also appeared to hit nothing. Eventually he moved his entire body across the invisible line.

'I'm through!' he said, triumphantly.

'Excellent,' said Jack, 'I'll be back in two minutes,' and off he trotted, back to the reception desk to check in the offending piece of equipment.

When he got to the desk, Lucinda, the secretary/receptionist, was smiling broadly. 'Let me guess,' she said. 'Yet another little gadget that he forget he had?'

Jack raised his eyes in sympathy and said, 'You did ask him when they checked in, if they had any phones?'

She said, 'Of course I did. The mother and son co-operated immediately but the father refused to hand over his kit. I did explain in very clear terms that he would not be able to get into the School whilst he had computers about his person, but I'm sure that he thought that I was joking.'

'Don't they always,' said Jack. 'Still, it was very funny to watch.' And, with that he bounded back towards where he had left his three guests.

Mr Bailey-Knox was now looking like the cat who had got the cream, as he had managed to negotiate his way through NED; and Mrs Bailey-Knox was looking very pleased with herself, as Jack suspected that this was the first time in some years that she had put her foot down with her domineering husband. As for Sam, he just looked relieved and pleased to be there and he smiled broadly at Jack.

'Right,' said Jack. 'Shall we begin?'

One hundred miles away, anxious faces peered out through the tinted windows at the valley below. 'The mist is closing in,' said a woman's voice. 'If it continues at this pace we will be engulfed within days.'

Despite the number of other people in the room, no-one else said a thing. They just continued to stare at the mist as it swirled and turned, dancing across the fields and hedges, curling its eerie tendrils around everything in its path.

A large bird of prey let out a high pitched cry as it appeared out of the mist, looking like a prehistoric creature, wings outstretched. It flew over the building and the ten pair of eyes watched it from behind the glass. It hovered for a moment and then folded back its wings and headed down to collect prey from the field, appearing within minutes with a small rodent in its beak.

'In this mist it was something of a sitting duck,' said one of the ten. 'I know how it feels.' No-one responded.

They walked through the large oak door and into the main corridor. The windows running along the back of the corridor were floor to ceiling and gave the most magnificent views out across the School grounds.

Jack heard a sharp intake of breath as his guests took in what lay before them. It was a common reaction, but one that Jack never grew tired of. He was very proud of his School and very proud of the history and the achievements of its former pupils, and he wanted others to be proud of it as well.

Once the guests had taken a few minutes to take in the views in front of them, Jack asked them all to follow him, and they turned left into the corridor. As they walked along, out through the windows, the Bailey-Knoxs could see what appeared to be endless playing fields with teams of children competing in a variety of sport, some of which were obvious, like football and rugby, and others, not so obvious.

'What on earth are they playing?' asked Mrs Bailey-Knox, pointing to one group of children.

Jack pressed his nose up against the glass and said, 'I'm not entirely sure. Today is the trials of all the new games that the children have invented and whichever one wins will become a School sport for next year.'

'Why would children invent games?' asked Sam.

'Well,' said Jack, 'the School's view is that there is too much pressure put on children these days to be good at conventional sports, like football, rugby, cricket, netball and hockey. All are very good sports, but they are sports that need quite good eye-hand-ball coordination, and a lot of children simply don't have this. Instead of sidelining them, or them being the people who never get picked for anybody's team, they are encouraged to create their own games, playing to their strengths. For instance, people who don't have good eye-hand-ball coordination will often have great strength or balance or the powers to problem-solve, and if you combine some of those into a game and you have enough people who want to play, then the School will encourage you to play it. We'll need to get down a bit closer. We'll have a look and ask them about the rules.'

'So, how big are the grounds?' asked Sam.

'In total, about 100 acres. But a lot of that is forest and woodland and also lakes and rivers.'

Mr Bailey-Knox raised his eyebrows and said, 'Well that sounds like a health and safety risk before we even start.'

Jack looked carefully at Mr Bailey-Knox, not wanting to provoke a second outrage, but equally understanding his concerns about health and safety, bearing in mind that he was a lawyer.

'At School,' said Jack, 'we are encouraged to take responsibility for our own health and safety, and all of the parents recognise when their sons or daughters join the School that accidents happen and, when they do, the proper way to deal with it is not through the courts or through seeking compensation, but to understand how it happened and try and stop it happening again.'

Mr Bailey-Knox snorted loudly but, this time, through his clear belief that he had much more superior knowledge.

'Well,' he said. 'That's very commendable. However, unfortunately, the law says otherwise and it would be impossible for the School to write into any contract the fact that they take no responsibility for any death or personal injury of a student whilst on their premises. Not even they can flout the law and I can tell you, young Master Jack, that it is outlawed in British law to write any such clause into a contract. It would simply be null and void. That's what the Unfair Contract Terms Act says.'

Again, Jack thought carefully before responding, not wanting to provoke a man who now clearly felt that he had superior knowledge, but it was important if his son were to be accepted into the School that he understood.

'Sir, I know that you are a very knowledgeable and well respected lawyer, but you would never have had cause to examine in any detail the changes to the Unfair Contract Terms Act which came into law in 2011. They were not publicised and, unless you had cause to go back and look at that particular Act of Parliament, then you would never know that it was there.'

Mr Bailey-Knox looked at Jack out of the corner of his eye, knowing that, given that Jack appeared to have been correct on a number of occasions, even in the short time that they had known one another, that there was no reason to suspect that he was not correct in this regard as well, and, therefore, rather than embarrass himself further, he decided that outright contradiction was probably not the best policy.

'What,' he said, 'does this amendment say?'

'It says that it is legal for the School to exclude death and personal injury in respect of any student at the School and that there will be no right for any parent or any other person to take legal action as a result of any accident that occurs.'

'Nonsense!' said Mr Bailey-Knox, unable to contain himself. 'Such an amendment would have attracted a furore from the popular press. It would be *outrageous* to prevent a parent from suing in these circumstances.'

Jack looked at him and said, 'The School organises policies for each child so, in the event that they suffer an accident or injury, which means that they need support, then the insurance company will arrange this insurance. However, they take the view that if a child is badly injured or, indeed, dies, then no amount of money is going to compensate the parents for that loss. What the School pledges to do is to understand how an accident has happened and to do all that it can to prevent it from happening again.'

'Well, that's easy for you to say,' said Mr Bailey-Knox. 'What if it was your brother or sister who died?'

As they walked along the corridor, Jack slowly came to a halt, and turned back to Mr Bailey-Knox. He said, very quietly, 'I did lose my brother and no amount of money would bring him back, or help with the feelings of loss of not knowing him as I was growing up. I was only six months old when the accident happened but I think of him every day.'

His eyes locked with those of Mr Bailey-Knox and they both realised that the conversation was at its natural end, and Jack turned back to start the tour in earnest.

Their first port of call was to the indoor exercise areas. There were squash courts, badminton courts, table-tennis tables, snooker tables, and gymnastic equipment. There was also a Fives court, a netball court, indoor 5-a-side football court and two large rooms which had padded floors and Jack explained that these were for martial arts, in which he was soon to achieve his black belt in Judo.

As they entered another imposing long room with windows down one side, looking out onto yet more playing fields, Sam's eyes lit up. Hanging in neat rows along one end of the room were what appeared to be white straitjackets, and the floor was covered with a series of long thin carpets with a line denoting the half-way point of each of them.

Mrs Bailey-Knox turned to her son and said with a smile, 'Now this is what you have been waiting and hoping for.'

'Do you enjoy fencing?' asked Jack.

'Fanatical,' came back Sam's response, as he felt the carpets and drew his fingers along the lines of the jackets.

'Find one your size. I'm sure that we can find you a fencing partner for 10 minutes,' said Jack.

A look of astonishment crossed Sam's face, as he thought that perhaps Jack was joking, but Jack nodded. 'It's all part of the Introductor day. You have the chance to try out our facilities as much as us getting to know you.' And, without any further word of encouragement, Sam had selected his size and was half way into it when the door at the far corner opened and in came two students, already kitted up and ready to go. They were wearing their full masks and it was therefore almost impossible to tell their age or, indeed, whether they were girls or boys.

Behind them, followed what Sam presumed to be the tutor or, indeed, the referee. But, whoever she was, she strode purposefully across to where Sam, his parents and Jack were standing and held out her right hand.

'Hello. I am Elisa di Francisca,' she said in a soft Italian accent.

Sam's eyes widened in astonishment. 'Not *the* Elisa di Francisca?' he said in amazement. 'As in the London 2012 Olympic gold medallist?'

'It certainly is,' she smiled. 'And, you must be Sam Bailey-

Knox, Berkshire Under 10s champion.'

This time, Sam really was astonished. 'But, how... ?'

She smiled. 'We make it our business to know who would like to attend the School and I thought that you might possibly want to come and see our facilities on your tour around. I was unsure about your size and height and so I selected two of our best fencers in your age category. Perhaps if you could just stand closer to them?'

The two stood next to Sam, and Elisa pointed to one of them, who was closer in size and height to Sam and the other stood back.

'En garde,' said Elisa.

The two fencers executed the traditional sporting salute to one another and took up their 'en garde' positions. Jack noticed immediately that both of them were left-handed and assumed that this was the reason that Elisa had selected this person to challenge Sam, although, when he looked again, he realised that both of Sam's potential competitors were left-handed.

Of course, he thought to himself, if Elisa knew that Sam was the Berkshire Under 10s champion, then she would, indeed, know that he was also left-handed and, as he understood it, it was quite difficult to fence against a left-hander. Although he also understood, from Rosie droning on to him over the years, as a left-hander, that the world's top fencers were all left-handed, due to the wiring of the brain which meant that there was a shorter distance to go from the right-hand side of the brain to the left hand and, because of this, left-handed people generally had much faster reactions.

Jack was fascinated as he watched the two competitors move up and down the narrow carpet in front of him. They did not step to the side but always moved either forwards or backwards to lunge at their opponent or to step back quickly when they could see a lunge coming.

Although fencing was not his sport, he did know that on every occasion when the tip of the foil touched the opponent in a certain area of their body, this counted for points, and, therefore, the name of the game was to avoid being touched. But the speed at which the two of them were moving up and down the designated area, it was hard to understand how they could keep track.

Jack was truly impressed by Sam's agility, although it was only because he had seen him start from that end that he knew which one was him fighting, otherwise, it would have been impossible to distinguish between the two, as they were of similar size and height and it seemed to Jack that they were equally able fighters.

There was no beeping and so Jack assumed that this was just a warm up, for Miss di Francisca to see how well Sam fenced. When she called time on the match, the two saluted each other in the normal sportsman-like fashion and they both removed their helmets.

'Very impressive, Mr Bailey-Knox. We'll make a national champion of you yet,' she said, without a hint of jest.

'And, as for you, young lady,' she said, as she turned to Sam's opponent as she took off her mask and her dark hair came tumbling out, 'you need to sort your footwork out and practise using your balancing arm more to give you better stability. Sorry, my apologies to both of you, I haven't made a formal introduction. Sam Bailey-Knox, this is Rosie Simmons, the National Under 12s girls champion, and sister of young Jack there, who I'm sure has failed to tell you that he is the National Under 15s Judo champion. So, all in all, the Simmons family are not generally to be messed with on any level, are they young Jack?'

Jack smiled as Sam took off his white jacket and his gloves and held out his hand to Rosie. 'It's a pleasure to meet you, Rosie Simmons. You fence like a champion.'

'I had to learn one sport that I could beat my brother at,' she said, 'otherwise he really would be insufferable!'

Elisa pointed to the door at the back of the room. 'Sam, if you would like to go and freshen up, Rosie will show you where the boys' changing rooms are. I'm not sure if you have brought any clean clothes.'

Mrs Bailey-Knox stepped forward and said, 'We saw on the instructions that it said to bring a number of changes of clothes, so here they are Sam, help yourself to whatever you want, and please exercise some common sense when dressing.' Sam raised his eyes in embarrassment.

Jack looked at his sister. 'Rosie, when Sam is finished, could you bring him along to the vegetable garden?'

'Will do,' said Rosie, and disappeared off with Sam in the direction of the changing rooms.

Sam showered and changed and emerged from the boys' changing rooms to find Rosie sitting on the wall outside wearing her School uniform, which was a pretty candy-striped dress, traditionally cut down to the knees. It struck Sam that if this were his current school, then the girls would be hitching their skirts up to just below their bottoms and he thought how much better the style that Rosie was now wearing was; it was just so much more lady like.

'Right,' she said, jumping off the wall. 'I'd better get you to the vegetable garden.'

Sam walked beside her as they passed out through the grand doors at the end of the corridor, back into the grounds of the School. Below them, Sam could see a huge maze, cut from 10 foot hedges. 'Wow!' he said. 'Is that for real?'

'It's great, isn't it,' she said. 'It's one of my favourites. Every year they change the layout a bit and the student who finds his way out in the shortest space of time wins the Maze Cup.'

'So, how long have you been at the School?' asked Sam, as they walked along the outer edges of the maze, it now towering above their heads.

'Two years,' she said.

'Do you enjoy it?' asked Sam. At which point, Rosie came to a complete stop and turned to face him.

'You are joking?' she said. 'What is there not to *love* about a School that gives you freedom to play, to pursue any talent that you might have and introduces you to some of the most amazing people in the world.'

'Were you always a fencer – is that how you got into the School?' asked Sam as they walked down through walled gardens and enormous vegetable plots.

Rosie laughed out loud. 'I had never picked up a foil in my life before I came here. I was a typical little sister under the shadow of her older brother. I was quite good at netball, and I love to paint and cook but there was nothing that made me stand out. Until I came here.'

Sam stopped to inspect some bamboo wigwams with tiny plants at the bottom.

'Runner beans,' said Rosie and smiled.

'So how did you find out you were so good?' asked Sam, genuinely very interested that Rosie had gone from a standing start to national under 12 champion in two years.

'When you come to the School the first term is, well, it is a bit different. You get to try everything. You cook, you ride horses, play instruments, dance, invent and design things, learn to shoot, swim, play every sport known to man, to act and direct, to speak in public, solve problems, be a leader... you just do everything until they find something you are good at.'

'But,' said Sam, even hesitating to mention it, 'what if you are not good at anything.'

Rosie stopped dead in her tracks for a second time, turned and looked at him.

'You must never, ever say that again or you will never get into the School. EVERYONE has something that they are good at, without exception; it just takes time to find it and that's what the School does.' She looked quite scarily serious and Sam realised she was not joking at all.

'You see that girl over there,' Rosie nodded in the direction of a beautiful dark skinned and raven haired girl of about 13 who was raking over one of the flowerbeds. 'That is JJ Buccannan; Jack is completely in love with her.'

'Understandable,' smiled Sam and winked at Rosie.

'What would you say she was good at, just looking at her?' Rosie smiled back in a way that Sam knew meant he was not going to get this but he went along anyway.

'Tall, beautiful, got to be a dancer who works as a clothes designer and model in her spare time,' he said triumphantly.

'Close,' said Rosie. 'She is a crack shot, a champion archer and in her spare time she invents things as she is a brilliant mathematician and great at physics. She is also a taekwondo champion.'

Sam whistled quietly under his breath. At that point JJ looked up and smiled and waved at Rosie and Rosie waved back. 'You see', said Rosie. 'You made an assumption that because she is an attractive girl she must be a model; the School tries to change those assumptions.'

'Is my father right?' asked Sam. 'Do you have more chance of coming here if your parents have money?'

Rosie smiled; it was a question she was often asked and one that she loved to answer.

'Jack and I are very lucky – our Dad has a job which takes him to lots of countries around the world and he is still married to our Mum, but we are the exception here. Many of the children who come here are not as privileged as us, they may have only been brought up by one parent, their parents may have very little. They do not get to travel or have days out when they are away from School. You don't need money to come to the School, you need talent and, more importantly, a desire to find it.'

They both looked across at JJ. She saw them and waved, smiling broadly. 'JJ is an inspiration to all of us. Her parents died when she was very young; she goes to different aunts and uncles during the holidays, but never complains, is always smiling and always trying to make something more of what she has.'

They moved on towards the pig sheds, just as Rosie spotted her brother and Sam's parents there.

'But don't you miss your parents?' asked Sam. 'The School is boarding only, isn't it?'

'Yes,' said Rosie. 'And, no, I don't miss my parents. Well, maybe a little bit. But they live in Bolivia and that's a long way away and I would have to go to a boarding School anyway.'

'B-o-l-i-v-i-a! Wow!' said Sam and then paused. '...Where's that?'

'South America. My Dad is a diplomat, so he gets sent all over the world.'

'But, what about computers and mobile telephones? Don't you miss those?'

'Well, at first I did,' she said, 'because I didn't really know anything else. I grew up in an age with computers and mobile telephones but once you come here you realise how much more there is to life, the joy of playing games with your friends, making things up, having to think for yourself. You meet kids on the outside who just don't know how to do that anymore. All the School tries to do is take us back before the computer was invented, to when children used to play in the streets with their football or in the woods. When no one watched television, and everyone went to the cinema on a Saturday morning.'

'You have a cinema?'

'Oh yes. We have a very good cinema. We are only allowed to use it on Saturday mornings. We can have popcorn and ice cream and watch all the latest films. After all, there is a great deal of difference between making sure we enjoy our childhood and turning us into social misfits who haven't even seen every single one of the *Harry Potter* films at least three times.'

'How often do you see your parents?' asked Sam.

'Every long holiday, and the spring half term break is always 10 days and, if we are very, very good, then we get to go home for that as well.'

'So you will be going home soon then?' said Sam.

'Yes, that's right; tomorrow, Jack and I fly out to Bolivia to see our parents for ten days, and I can't wait!'

'Bolivia. Wow! I only get to go to boring places like Barbados. Don't get me wrong, it's a lovely place and a beautiful island but, once you've seen it, there's not much else to do except play in a pool and swim in the sea.'

'I know,' said Rosie. 'Jack and I have been to Barbados and it was very nice, but a little bit boring.'

'What's the best place you've ever been to?' asked Sam.

'Oh, the Galapagos Islands,' said Rosie.

'Where?'

'They are a bunch of islands to the, wait a minute, *'Never-Eat-Shredded-Wheat'*, west of Equa... Equa...'

'Ecuador?' asked Sam.

'Yes. Ecuador. You can swim with the seals and the turtles and the sharks, and none of them are interested in you because they have had lots to eat already. My brother, Jack, is giving a talk tonight to the whole School, all about our visit there.'

'Wow!' said Sam.

'You say that a lot,' said Rosie.

'Say what?'

'Wow!'

'Well, there's not really another word that can sum up this amazing place,' he said. 'But how come your brother gets to give a talk to the whole School? Is that a punishment?'

Rosie laughed. 'No. We have a public speaking competition every year and, this year, the topic was 'places I have travelled to'. He's been through a series of rounds and was selected by all of the students as the person to give the half term talk to all the seniors and juniors. He's going to use all the photographs from our trip and there is a really great one of me swimming next to a turtle.'

'But, how can you show photographs if you are not allowed any communication equipment?' asked Sam. 'Surely you would normally do that through a computer?'

'Not at the School you don't,' laughed Rosie. 'Jack has had to have all of the photographs converted into slides and then, with special dispensation, we get to use the School's projector.'

'Wow!' said Sam.

Down in the vegetable garden, Jack arrived with Mr and Mrs Bailey-Knox, just as the students had finished weeding the winter cabbages that they had planted last year for harvesting in the following spring.

'When did they plant those?' asked Mr Bailey-Knox, with genuine curiosity. 'Surely the frost and the snows of winter will kill them all?'

'Apparently not,' said Jack. 'They don't grow a great deal between planting and early spring, but when they do grow, they grow vigorously and are ready to harvest before the cabbage white butterfly arrives. We also have heated greenhouses, where we can continue to grow fruit and vegetables throughout the winter and also to plant up seedlings, ready for next spring. We have already cultivated our own rose and several different varieties of tomatoes and cucumbers.'

At that moment Rosie and Sam appeared at the entrance to the vegetable gardens. Jack saw Rosie point in their direction, and then shake hands with Sam in a very grown up way. She waved to her brother and then disappeared off in the direction that she had come from.

Sam was smiling broadly. 'Some girl, your sister'. Jack glanced at him side-ways. 'I am sure she is charming, as long as you are not related to her,' he said.

'I would have loved to have brothers and sisters,' said Sam wistfully. 'But I think Mum and Dad gave up after me. Too busy for more children.'

'Well,' said Jack, 'at least they recognised that rather than having more but not having the time to give them; that would probably be worse. Anyway, I can sell you my sister for a very reasonable sum...'

'I will tell her that you said that!' said Sam. 'That is, if I see her again.' He sounded a bit sad at the thought of not seeing her again.

'She is like a bad penny, she keeps popping up so don't worry, I am quite sure that you will see her again.' And with that they rejoined Sam's parents who were inspecting the vegetables with some admiration.

Jack led Mr and Mrs Bailey-Knox and Sam down through acres of orchards, vegetable plots, greenhouses and hothouses. Amongst them were children of various ages from the School, hoeing, tending, pruning and watering.

'Shouldn't they be in lessons?' asked Mrs Bailey-Knox.

'They are,' said Jack. 'At the School, we concentrate not only on the basics but also on natural sciences so, as well as home economics, where we can learn how to cook, we also learn how to grow the food and to look after it. Many of the people that you see on the television as gardeners and chefs, developed their interests here. Many of them had never even seen a garden before they arrived at the School.'

They moved down through the fruit gardens towards what appeared to be animal shelters and, as they drew closer, they could hear the squealing of piglets. Jack reached the wall surrounding the enclosure and jumped up onto a piece of wood which was next to it so that he could look over.

'Come up here,' he said to Sam, and Sam jumped up next to him, and as they put their heads over the wall, they were greeted with the wonderful sight of a mother Gloucester Old Spot pig and her ten piglets, all sucking greedily at her teats.

'Wow,' said Sam, not for the first time. 'That's amazing! Who looks after these?'

'We do,' said Jack. 'It's part of our curriculum. I was on pigs last week and I love them. They don't smell at all, like people say they do, and they are really clever.' Jack made a chirping noise and the mother pig lifted her head from its bed of straw and almost appeared to acknowledge Jack with a wink.

'See, she remembers me.'

They walked down past the pig pens and towards a paddock. As they came round the corner, Jack pointed to a young girl on horseback who was being led round the paddock on a long rein. 'You can learn to ride horses if you want to, but if you do, you have to learn to look after them as well and clean out their stables and groom them. I don't like horses very much, personally, but there are lots of the children who do.'

'But what do you do when School has finished?' asked Sam. 'If you don't have computers, then how do you keep in touch with your friends who aren't at the School, and how do you keep up with the news and play games?'

Jack looked at him and smiled. It was not the first time he had been asked that question and it probably wouldn't be the last. 'Well,' he said, 'we are encouraged to use our imagination and to play.'

Sam looked at him quizzically and raised an eyebrow. 'But how can you play without a computer?'

Jack said, 'Do your parents tell stories of when they were forced to make their own fun… and they were allowed to roam free and go to the playground, and how all of that has changed?'

'Oh yes,' said Sam raising his eyebrows. 'All the time.'

'Well,' said Jack. 'The idea behind the School is that we should try and get back to those days so that we are all free to play without fear or worry and to use our imagination.'

Sam said, 'But where do you do this? I can see that you look after the animals and you can learn to ride and grow vegetables and play sports, but what about real playing?'

Jack smiled and lowered his voice. 'Follow me,' he said, and he shouted back to Mr and Mrs Bailey-Knox. 'We will be back in 15 minutes, have a good look round,' and with that they ran out ahead of Mr and Mrs Bailey-Knox, who were strolling past the pigs with Mrs Bailey-Knox pinching the end of her nose to try and keep the smell out.

'My mother does make a fuss,' said Sam quietly.

'That's what mothers do,' said Jack.

Jack almost broke into a trot and Sam followed as they headed towards a large piece of woodland. It was very thickly planted and impossible to see through the branches but, rather than stopping at the boundary, Jack ran straight in and Sam, without hesitation, followed him. And then he stopped dead.

Inside was the most amazing adventure course that Sam had ever seen, built up into the trees with platforms and rope bridges, little tree houses and swings. Underneath all of it lay a large net, presumably to catch anybody who lost their grip whilst running across a rope bridge at 20 feet.

Balancing on the ropes and ladders were children of all ages. There was a whizz overhead and a young girl came flying down a piece of rope holding onto a piece of wood, squealing with delight. There was no pushing or shoving and everywhere Sam looked children were helping one another to climb onto the equipment or offering words of encouragement. There was laughter and excitement all around.

Jack kept walking past the adventure course and out into a slightly less wooded area. They could see small shelters had been built from wood and canvas and ropes and sat about 10 feet away was a group of children listening intently to someone that Sam could not see because there was a tree in the way. He stepped forward and gasped. There, standing in front of the children was a tall, shaven headed black gentleman, dressed in a brightly coloured robe and leaning on a large spear like object which appeared to be exactly the same height as him.

The man turned and smiled at Jack and Sam and gestured to them to come and join the others. Sam looked tentatively at Jack who nodded and they moved over and sat cross legged in front of this amazing man.

'Good morning gentleman, my name is Elias and I am a Masai Warrior, originally from Tanzania, the Ngorongoro Crater. I am here to pass on a few tips about living in the bush and what to do when a wild animal attacks.'

He turned back to the rest of the group. 'Now,' he said earnestly, 'the buffalo...' On a small tripod he had a series of large pictures of animals and he pulled out the buffalo picture and put it to the front. 'It may look just like a large domestic cow but it is the second biggest killer of humans in Africa. What do you think the first is?'

'Lions!' came one response.

'No,' said Elias softly.

'Tigers,' said another.

'Luckily for us, there are no tigers in Africa,' smiled Elias in a very patient way and everyone laughed.

'I will tell you,' he said, crouching down in a conspiratorial way so that the children all needed to move their heads slightly closer to listen. 'It is the hippopotamus.' There was a gasp of disbelief from the children but Elias continued: 'It may feed on grass but it has enormous teeth and if you get between it and its baby on land then it will do all it can to protect it and if that means biting you in half then it will.' There was a sharp intake of breath as everyone examined the hippopotamus picture that Elias held up – showing the teeth in all their glory.

'The buffalo on the other hand will use its horns to try and skew you,' and with that Elias reached back and produced the most enormous pair of buffalo horns and put them on a rock in front of him. There were low whistles of astonishment at the size.

'So if a buffalo charges at you what would you do?' asked Elias and almost in unison the whole group said: 'Run!'

'No!' said Elias, 'A buffalo can run twice as fast as you and if you run it would have a perfect view of your ribs and your kidneys and plenty of time to position its horns just right... What you need to do is lie completely flat on the ground with your arms stretched out in front of you, like you were trying to be a long snake. That way the buffalo cannot get its horns underneath you to skew you. Let's demonstrate.'

Elias gestured to a young boy from the group to come out and he lay completely flat on his back with his arms stretched out. 'Face down young man, otherwise you will just get trampled.' He rolled over. 'Bring your arms so they cover your ears and the back of the head. Now, bring those horns over.' Two boys carried over the horns. 'You see,' said Elias, 'if you are that flat to the ground the buffalo cannot get its horns under you.' And sure enough, Elias was completely correct.

'I am sure that you will not find many buffalo in England,' he smiled. 'But you never know with global warming...'

A young boy from the back of the class raised his hand. 'Excuse me, Mr Elias,' he said timidly, 'but my mum told me that the Masai kill lions; have you killed a lion?'

Elias looked at the group of children and took a deep breath. 'You must understand, children that when I was your age the world was a different place. For us, the only way to be men was to kill a lion. Today, the Masai have changed their beliefs, recognising the importance of preservation over tradition. But when I was a child... it was quite different, we are the guardians of the lion.'

The children appeared to huddle closer to hear the dark secrets that Elias had to tell. He leant back on his stick and took a deep breath.

'A lion is very clever,' he said in a low voice. 'It looks for weakness and then tries to exploit it. As Masai we must use this to our advantage and so when we are seeking the lion, we pretend, we pretend to be injured so that the lion will be deceived. We will wrap our cloth around our fighting arm and pretend that we have been injured. Like this...' Elias stood up and wrapped a spare piece of multi coloured cloth around his right arm. 'But what we hide,' said the Masai with a smile, 'is that under our cloaks we have our spear, ready to meet with the lion when it finally makes its move.' And from his cloak he brought up his spear with a sudden jerk and there was sharp intake of breath from the children gathered around him.

There was a silence as the children took in what Elias had told them.

After a few minutes Jack looked at Sam and smiled, then spoke quietly. 'We had better carry on with the tour,' he said getting to his feet. 'Thank you, Elias, that was really interesting and I hope to come and hear more.'

'I am here all week, young man and I look forward to welcoming you back. We still have elephants and more lions to deal with.'

Jack and Sam shook Elias's hand and retreated quietly from the makeshift classroom.

'That is amazing,' said Sam. 'Do you have people like that coming very often?'

'All the time,' said Jack. 'We have polar explorers,

mountaineers, we even had the Chief Scout, a few months ago. That was AMAZING. Now, let me show you the camp.'

They moved down towards the lakeside and Sam could see a series of small tents pitched by the waterside. 'We mainly use this at weekends,' said Jack. 'We are allowed to camp out and cook our own food and learn about the stars and survival techniques. I learned how to light fires without matches last week, just like the cavemen did. But my Dad made me this amazing little gadget which I always keep on me.'

Out of his pocket he produced a small metal object. 'Dad designed this for me and a man in Bolivia made it up. I call it a 'glorch'. On the front is a small solar panel which charges it. Then there is a small magnifying glass,' he pulled that out, 'brilliant for starting fires if the sun is shining because you can intensify the sun's rays and light a piece of paper. Then it has a small torch which is driven by the solar panel – it does not last forever but great in an emergency. Then there is a small pair of pliers and two different types of screwdriver and then this little thing,' Jack picked it out with his fingers, 'will create sparks so you can use it to light a fire if the sun is not in the sky.'

'Wow, your Dad is very clever,' said Sam. 'I can't imagine mine ever coming up with something like that.' This was not something that Jack was going to disagree with, having actually met Sam's father...

They started walking back through the trees and there were rope swings and nets.

'But all of this is just amazing!' said Sam. 'I've never seen anything like it!'

Jack said, 'It helps us to make up games and pretend that we are on a desert island, rescuing our friends from the jaws of sharks, to play cowboys and Indians or Tarzan. My sister does a brilliant Tarzan impersonation from that top platform.'

'Don't you mean Jane?' said Sam.

Jack looked at him and said, 'You've met my sister. What do you think?'

'I think she'd make a very nice Jane but I can see that sometimes she might want to be Tarzan as well,' he said diplomatically.

Jack smiled. It was clear that Sam had got the measure of his sister already.

'But when do you do normal lessons, maths and things like that?' asked Sam.

'We start early and we finish late, but in between we always have plenty of time outside, whether that be sport or gardening or learning about buffalo. We work hard and play hard, which is what our motto means,' Jack said without the hint of complaint.

'But how do you keep up with things going on outside School?' asked Sam.

'We are allowed to watch the news on the television at 6pm, before dinner, and as for keeping in touch, we write letters to our friends or telephone them using the landline telephones that are in the main School house,' said Jack.

'Gosh!' said Sam. 'Write, with real paper?'

'Oh yes,' said Jack. 'And we are not allowed to use biros, so we have to use fountain pens and if any of the teachers can walk behind you and not pick out your fountain pen from your hand because you are gripping it too hard, then you're in trouble! We are taught about how to write properly and politely, how to accept invitations and to write to say that we are sorry because something horrible has happened.'

'I wish I could do that,' said Sam.

'Well, perhaps,' said Jack, 'if you come to the School, you will be able to.'

'But I don't really know how I am ever going to get into the School,' said Sam. 'My Dad thinks that you can just buy everything but you said that the School is free. So, what do I have to do in order to be admitted?'

'Well,' said Jack, 'once you have been today and if you decide that this is somewhere that you would like to go to school, then the next stage is that you can then come for a week to spend time with us and do as many lessons as you can, to see if you like it. Some children don't like being away from their parents during the term time and so it is not for everybody.'

'Are there any day people who come to the School?' asked Sam.

'No,' said Jack. 'It was decided a long time ago that it would be best to have all of the children here to play and to interact and to socialise and if you have some people who are day people or weekly boarders, then that means that we would look at them as being a bit different, and the idea is for everybody to be the same and to have the same opportunities. Do you think that you would mind being away from your Mum and Dad?'

Sam looked back at Jack with an expression that didn't need to say anything other than, 'What do you think?' But, instead, he was very diplomatic and said, 'I am sure that I could cope.'

'So, what other tests would I have to do?' asked Sam.

'Oh,' said Jack. 'They will test your imagination, how you play, how keen you are to learn other skills and then, at the end of the week, both the students and the teachers get together to decide whether or not someone should be allowed to enrol.'

'Do you have to be really clever?' asked Sam. 'I'm quite clever but not really clever, and Dad thinks this is a School where they only take real brain boxes and I don't have a chance.'

Jack stopped and looked Sam in the eye. 'Your father is wrong. The School does not want to fill its classrooms with brain boxes. What it wants is children who have vivid imaginations, who can cooperate, who understand about playing fair and having a go at new things. Often, being really clever is a disadvantage and not an advantage. Of course you are expected to be able to pass your GCSEs with reasonable grades, but they are not looking for people who will only get A* for every subject. The School will talk to your existing teachers, they will talk to your friends and your neighbours to find out what sort of person you really are, and if they think that you are the type of person who would do well in the School, then you will be invited to join from September.'

Sam sat down on one of the tree trunks which formed the base of a huge wooden ship, built amongst the forest playground. 'I don't think I've ever wanted anything more,' he said. 'And I didn't really realise that, until right this minute.'

'Well, if you can beat my sister at fencing, then you get my vote,' joked Jack. 'Come on, we'd better go and find the grown-ups and get on with the tour, or I'll be in trouble, and not for the first time.'

They laughed and ran out of the woodland, just as Mr and Mrs Bailey-Knox were approaching.

'Are you boys having fun?' asked Mr Bailey-Knox, in his friendliest voice.

'Yes Sir,' said Jack. 'I think that your son would fit in very well at the School and I wish you all the best with the application.'

'By the way, I keep meaning to ask, where do you live?' Jack asked Sam. 'Is it nearby?'

'Not really,' said Sam. 'We live in a little village which is miles from anywhere and it's really hard to get around unless Mum and Dad want to drive me there, and they never really have the time, and we don't have any buses. So, sometimes, it's quite hard for me to see my friends. That's why Mum and Dad thought coming to the School would be a really good idea.'

'I know what you mean,' said Jack. 'My Aunt lives in a village a bit like that. Mum says it would drive her mad to live so far from everything, but she seems to like it.'

'Where's that?' asked Sam.

'Oh, you won't know,' said Jack. 'Auntie Issie always jokes and says that there's a cloaking device over the village so nobody knows where it is.'

Sam laughed and said, 'That's what my Mum and Dad say about our village.'

'Really,' said Jack. 'What's that called?'

'Brighthaven,' said Sam.

'That's it. Brighthaven. That's where my Auntie Issie lives. What a small world. Do you know her?'

'We don't know that many people as we have not lived there for very long. Do you know where in the village she lives?' asked Sam, now intrigued with the co-incidence.

'A thatched cottage,' was all Jack was able to remember.

'There are lots of those,' said Sam. 'Everyone seems to have a straw roof in our village.' They chatted as they walked back though the School grounds towards the main reception.

They were just passing one of the playing fields and Mrs Bailey-Knox hesitated on the side lines. There were two teams on the pitch, made up of girls and boys; the pitch was divided into lots of small squares and each child was standing in a square. Although there was a ball it was not being kicked or thrown but simply passed back and forward in what appeared to be an orderly fashion but the children were watching intently.

'What are they playing?' asked Mrs Bailey-Knox, genuinely interested.

'I have no idea,' said Jack. 'Let's wait until they have a break and ask them. And with that a whistle went and the children on the pitch relaxed. They were all ages and shapes and sizes. Tall and slim, short and round, some with glasses, one with a hearing aid and one boy in a wheelchair. Jack waved to a girl he clearly knew.

'Daisy, what are you playing?' he asked.

Daisy laughed. 'This is our entry into the School Games, it

is called Chessball and it is like chess but using a ball to move around rather than actual chess pieces and is much faster; we are just finalising the rules ready for the competition. Everyone who plays has a very good methodical mind but they do not have to be sports people; we don't move that much but when we do it sometimes has to be with some force!'

'That is fantastic,' said Mrs Bailey-Knox. 'I wish they had something like that when I was at school, I probably would have been quite good at it.' Sam smiled broadly; that was the first time he thought he had ever heard his mother talk about school.

'Daisy is very good at inventing games,' said Jack and Daisy looked embarrassed. 'She has just invented a board game which is going to be in the shops at Christmas, but I can't tell you about it because it is a secret.'

Mrs Bailey-Knox looked at Daisy, who was not very tall and had thick rimmed glasses and a stocky build. 'Well done, Daisy, you are a credit to the School and to girls everywhere.'

They carried on walking back through the grounds and Sam was chattering incessantly to his mother '...And then there was a Masai Warrior in the woods...' he said.

'Please don't exaggerate, Sam,' said Mr Bailey-Knox. 'That is not very likely is it, it was probably just a staff member dressed up...' He was looking behind him as he was saying this and as he turned back he stopped abruptly as stood right in his path was Elias, spear in hand.

'Good morning, Sir,' said Elias politely. 'I just wanted to wish your son every success in his application to the School. He has the look of a warrior and it would be a pleasure to instruct him when I am next here.' And with that Elias winked at Sam, smiled at Jack and the rest of the group and then ran like the wind back to the woods.

Sam looked at his father and simply raised an eyebrow and Mr Bailey-Knox said nothing further but turned and continued walking in the direction of the main reception.

'I had better show you the classrooms,' said Jack, almost as an afterthought.

'Well,' said Mr Bailey-Knox, almost to himself. 'For one moment I thought that perhaps no proper school work was actually done here.' His wife nudged him in the ribs.

'Final warning, Gerald,' she hissed at him.

They turned left down a long path heading towards a large modern building on the far edge of the playing fields. It was glass and metal and very modern. As they approached the doors they opened automatically and they were faced with a large directory in front of them, pointing to various classrooms. There were the obvious ones for biology, chemistry and general classrooms but there was also 'cookery', 'dance' and 'music'.

'What would anyone like to see?' asked Jack. 'I suggest that we go and see one of the standard classrooms and then perhaps the dance studios?'

'As Sam is not going to be doing dance,' said Mr Bailey-Knox straight away, 'there would be little point.'

'Ah, but he will be,' said Jack with a smile. 'We all have to try our hand at every element of music and dance to see if we have a talent.'

'Rubbish,' said Mr Bailey-Knox as he dodged another elbow in the ribs from his wife as they walked round a corner to find what appeared to be an entire football team lining the corridor leading down to a large door which announced in bold letters: 'Dance studio'. There were about 12 of them and they were dressed in shorts and football shirts and bare feet, no shoes. They all smiled knowingly at Jack as they spotted him.

'Gentlemen,' said Jack. 'Good morning to you.' The boys nodded back, not in the slightest bit embarassed. 'This is Sam who is interested in joining the School. Would you object if we sat in for five minutes on your class?' The boys shook their heads nonchalantly.

At that stage the door to the studio was thrown open and there stood possibly the most famous English dancer that had lived in the modern era, the beautiful Darcy Bussell. Although long retired from dancing she had dedicated her life to nurturing talent amongst the young and this included helping out the School in finding those with true talent. 'Come on then, boys,' she smiled and the whole corridor lit up.

'I don't believe it,' said Mr Bailey-Knox, his mouth wide open and for once speechless.

'Don't gape, Gerald,' said Mrs Bailey-Knox as she breezed past him and headed for the dance studio. Jack and Ms Bussell were deep in conversation as he was obviously seeking her approval for them to visit the class and as Mrs Bailey-Knox approached Ms Bussell extended a slender but beautiful hand. 'Mrs Bailey-Knox,' she said. 'It would be a pleasure to show you what goes on in our School. I am so glad you are so interested in sending Sam,' and she ruffled Sam's hair as he went past. Mr Bailey-Knox followed in almost a trance and looked quite disappointed that his hair had not also been ruffled. However, when Ms Bussell extended a hand to him, Jack truly thought that Mr Bailey-Knox would expire with admiration.

The boys assembled in the dance studio. It had a flexible wooden floor which had clearly been trodden by many feet, and panoramic views out over the School grounds. At one end stood Darcy Bussell and at the other stood the boys, feet apart, shoulders back, straight backs. 'Now,' she said, 'I will watch whilst I ask a friend of mine to take you through a few moves.' She looked towards the door and as it swung open the Cuban ballet dancer Carlos Acosta stepped in. This time it was Mrs Bailey-Knox who took a sharp intake of breath. Although also retired now, his finely tuned body looked as young as the days he had danced. He smiled broadly at the assembled football team.

'Gentlemen,' he said in a soft Cuban accent. 'Follow me,' and instead of a classic ballet track starting in the background, the smooth tones of Adele's James Bond theme 'Skyfall' started through the sound system and Mr Acosta led the boys around the room doing spins and jetes, jumps and pirouettes. All of the boys tried really hard; there was no embarrassment or joking around but just a desire to do the best that they could.

Jack could see Sam's feet tapping to the music as the boys moved around the room and as they went past for the second time Carlos Acosta reached down and whisked him to his feet. 'You have a very good sense of rhythm, young man,' he said. 'Try a pirouette like this,' and with that Mr Acosta executed the most perfect pirouette on the spot, head spinning round and round to the same spot that he was focussing on, no noise as he turned.

Sam looked at the other boys who were watching Carlos Acosta with interest and not making fun. He took a deep breath and tried to emulate what he had seen the great Carlos Acosta do in front of him, and all in all it was not bad. Not quite on the spot and his leg was nowhere near as high as the great man, but he did not fall over.

Mr Acosta moved forward and said gently, 'Again, but this time slower,' and as Sam turned he could feel his leg being turned slightly, his chin being kept up. He did it again, better this time. Then again, and again until he almost fell over with giddiness.

From the corner came a hand clap and Darcy Bussell applauded his efforts wholeheartedly. 'Well done, Sam. Not only did you overcome the natural embarrassment of dancing what some may think is a girl's dance,' she glanced at his father, 'but you have real talent. I look forward to seeing you at the School in the future.'

'Likewise,' said Carlos Acosta and smiled at him like a proud father. 'You have real talent, young man. Strength, balance, grace and accuracy. I look forward to welcoming you back.'

Sam looked embarrassed but his parents were both beaming from ear to ear, each admiring their respective heroes and delighted that their son had impressed. Jack got up and smiled at the tutors as he ushered his visitors from the dance studio; they nodded and smiled back and he knew immediately that their vote would have been cast in favour of Sam's admission to the School.

As they wandered down the corridors past the classrooms his visitors were remarkably quiet. However, he felt that he should continue the tour as professionally as he could. 'This,' he said opening one of the doors to the classrooms, 'is where we study.'

The desks were very old fashioned, being wooden and with a lid that lifted to store books inside. There were ink wells and ridges to keep pens and pencils. At the front of the class there was a large blackboard with chalk. Mr and Mrs Bailey-Knox both looked on in wonder, the classroom looking just as it had when they had been at school many years ago.

'But where are the computers?' asked Mr Bailey-Knox. Sam raised his eyes to the heavens as if to say 'Has my father listened to nothing I have said'. Jack was very patient.

'Teaching methods are very traditional here. We have to read the books and do the sums without the help of computers and programmes that will do it for you or precis the book you are reading. We have libraries where we have to learn to research rather than just press a computer key and it is all done for you.'

'Well what a waste of time,' said Mr Bailey Knox. 'In computers you can do it in half the time.'

'Well,' said Jack patiently. 'It is not actually you doing it, it is a computer doing it and so you risk a whole generation not knowing how to research or calculate sums. So if the computers stop you don't know how to do it. It is bit like map reading. Everyone uses their phones and their sat nav but when they stop no-one has a clue where they are.'

'Let me guess,' said Mr Bailey-Knox. 'Map reading is on the

curriculum as well.'

'That's right,' said Jack. 'We do the three peaks challenge with a map and a compass; it is fantastic fun.' Mr Bailey-Knox looked at him, not sure if Jack was being serious enough. It was completely alien in the current days of technological advance to consider a bunch of 12 year olds running around the three peaks, something not even he had dared to do.

They walked along the long corridor with the ceiling to floor windows, out past the One Metre Line and into the main entrance hall. This time there were many more pupils milling around and Jack smiled to himself. 'Sam, see that bell?' he asked Sam in hushed tones. 'See what happens when you ring it,' and he gestured towards the bell with his head. Sam hesitated but Jack looked at him with widened eyes and nodded again in the direction of the bell.

Sam looked around nervously and then eventually walked up to the bell and grasping the small piece of rope that hung down from it, he gingerly rang it.

It was if the whole of the hall has stopped in their tracks the moment they heard the sound. Children who had been scurrying across the Great Hall deep in thought turned and smiled at Sam. Children who had crossed the One Metre Line and were heading out into the School came scurrying back, laughing. They all gathered around Sam and his bell and Sam looked slightly nervously at them, wondering exactly what it was they were about to do to him. Sam saw his father start to move towards his son with concern but Jack had put out a hand to restrain him.

Then suddenly it started, from the back of the assembled children of all ages, a low hum. It spread, this time with lighter harmonies and the children started to sway, a couple of them started to snap their fingers in time to the melody; it was not in English but sounded as if it had African origins. They sang their hearts out, each child smiling and laughing and looking at Sam in a way that told him they truly were very happy. It was infectious; even Sam started to snap his fingers and sway and the children gestured for him to join in. He stood alongside one or two of the boys who he thought were probably his age and their voices as deep as his and started to imitate their sounds and rhythm. The boys were delighted and placed their arms on his shoulders and Sam placed his on theirs and they started to sway together.

The song got louder and louder and then, as abruptly as it had started, it stopped. There was a slight pause and then all of the children burst out laughing and started clapping. Those around joined in too. The boys and girls all moved across one by one to shake Sam's hand and then they disappeared about their day as if nothing had happened. Sam was left standing in the Great Hall looking stunned and slightly bemused. He looked at Jack. 'What was that all about?' he asked.

'That was this month's School song,' said Jack. 'We learned it from Elias who you met earlier. It is sung by the Masai during celebrations. Every month we learn a new song and we have to be prepared to sing it anywhere. It helps us to really learn and enjoy it. Well done though,' he smiled at Sam, 'I can see that you really enjoyed that. I think you will like it here.'

When the singing had stopped Mr Bailey-Knox had gone ahead and was meticulously checking all of his computers and telephones, dictating machines and Bluetooth connectors to ensure that they were in exactly the same condition as they had been when he had begrudgingly handed them over some hours previously. He grunted and put them away into his bag, which seemed to indicate that all was in order.

'Well then, Master Jack. It just remains for me to thank you for your time today. I think that Sam really enjoyed himself, so thank you. Come to think of it, I had a few memorable moments as well...'

Jack shook Mr Bailey-Knox's hand in a very grown up fashion.

'My pleasure, Mr Bailey-Knox. We look forward to welcoming Sam at the School if he passes the entrance test.'

'Well, of course he will,' said Mr Bailey-Knox, somewhat indignantly, and, behind him, Sam's eyebrows were raised and he looked to the rafters in exasperation.

'No pressure, then,' he mumbled under his breath.

His mother patted Sam's shoulder in a familiar and understanding way and just said, 'What will be, will be, Sam,' and she leant across and shook Jack's hand. 'Thank you, Jack, that was a really good morning. Everyone here looks so happy, and that's all I could ever ask for Sam.'

Jack turned to Sam and shook his hand. He squeezed it and said, 'Until the next time, Sam Bailey-Knox.'

'Until the next time,' said Sam, and they disappeared out through the main door, out into the real world full of computers and mobile telephones. A world that Sam suddenly understood had forgotten how to play.

The Oval Office in the White House is usually the quiet sanctuary of the President of the USA. But on this day it was anything but calm. There were people moving in and out every few minutes, carrying laptops and books, large boxes and maps.

The President looked at his wife and daughters who were sat quietly in a corner. 'I want you to leave Washington now on Air Force One,' he said. 'I am not prepared to debate it.' His youngest daughter started to cry.

'I am frightened, Daddy,' she sniffed. 'Will we see you again?'

The President walked round from behind his desk and picked her up in his arms. 'I promise, my pumpkin, that we will all be together again very quickly. We have the finest brains working on this and we will find a solution.' He tried to sound as convincing as he could, but in his heart of hearts he did not feel as confident as he sounded.

But if he could not convince his family, how could he persuade a whole country that he had the situation under control? They desperately needed a breakthrough and time was running out.

CHAPTER TWO

Jack looked at his watch and realised that his presentation was in about four and a half hours and he hadn't yet rehearsed.

He ran out through the back entrance to the main hall and across the terraces. He was half way across when a stern voice shouted to him from an upstairs window, 'Master Jack, no running, it indicates urgency and therefore inefficiency.'

Jack pulled up to a fast walk without even glancing up. 'Sorry, Mr Warren,' he said, and stopped and looked up at the elderly, bespectacled man leaning out of the second floor window. It would be fair to say that he was not as clean cut as some of the other tutors and could have the occasional look of madness about him, but he was one of Jack's favourite teachers. One who did not beat about the bush when he had something to say.

'Well,' he said. 'How did the Introductor morning go?'

'Very nice,' said Jack. 'Someone I'd be happy to have in the School.'

'I understand,' said Donald Warren, smiling very slightly, 'that his father was, shall we say, less than cooperative about the School rules.'

Jack looked down at his feet; Mr Warren knew everything. 'I just don't think he understood, Sir. I don't think he knew much about the School when he arrived but, hopefully, we have put him right on that one.'

'Well, thankfully,' said Mr Warren, 'we shall choose the children and not the parents. Otherwise, if that were the case, the School would probably be fairly empty at the moment.'

Jack smiled to himself. He was very familiar with Mr Warren's views on the problems with society, which he blamed entirely on the parenting skills, or rather a lack of them.

Mr Warren's view was that society had become too obsessed with pushing forward their children to make them bigger and better and more educated and the top of their class. Jack could not help but agree with this, based on his experience from his friends outside School. Half terms and holidays had become a competition between parents to see who could do the biggest and the best entertainment for their children, and many of Jack's friends outside of the School were now so obsessed with the next great electronic device that that was all they thought about.

Jack heaved a sigh of relief that he and Rosie were both lucky enough to be at the School. Just because he was there, it didn't mean automatic entry for Rosie; she had to persuade the School in the same way as he had that she had an open mind, was prepared to play and experiment, took an interest in society and was prepared to try anything to find what in life she was really good at. She had found that in her fencing and was now destined to be champion. Without the School she would never have even known she had that talent. The School's philosophy was that every person has something that they are very good at and that is where their house motto came from, which is 'Everyone has a Talent'.

Jack got back to his room and was thankful for the fact that this was the day before term ended and so there were very few lessons. He looked at his watch again. Four hours to go and time for him to practise and rehearse his talk to the School, and look again at the pictures that he had chosen; he could not bear the thought of eating lunch as that would undoubtedly interfere with his butterflies.

As much as he told himself that he was not nervous, Jack knew that he was. Not least because this was his big chance to impress JJ Buccannan, and it also gave him the opportunity to show the rest of his fellow students and his friends, just how much fun he has when he is on holiday with his parents. That was something which was very close to the ideals and teachings of the School, but Jack knew that there were many students for whom, although they enjoyed play and socialising and fun when at the School, all of that stopped the moment they got home as their parents were so wrapped up in their own lives and their own careers that they didn't have the attention and the time. For those parents who did not have careers, their children often did the best at the School. What they did not have in wealth, they had in imagination, fun and support.

Jack knew that many of his friends prayed for the start of term time, rather than the start of holiday time and that today, being the day before holiday started, would be a difficult time for a lot of them who would, if given a choice, probably prefer to stay at the School.

Of course, he had always been very lucky. Jack's father had a job which took him around the world and so they got to see many wonderful places and have many experiences. He knew that not all of the children would have that opportunity. Some, because their parents simply could not afford it, and others, because their parents just were not interested in that type of holiday.

He felt that whatever the reason they were unable to enjoy wonderful and exciting holidays, it was his job to share his experiences with the rest of the School so that even if they weren't able to go on these holidays themselves, they would at least have the chance to look at his photographs and listen to his description of what it was like to spend three weeks in the Galapagos Islands.

He looked through the slides one by one and remembered as if it was yesterday what it had felt like, smelt like and sounded like. These extraordinary creatures, on islands miles from nowhere, creatures which had either swum or flown there and developed over thousands of years to deal with the conditions that they faced.

His father had explained to him how Charles Darwin, many years ago, had come to the islands and had observed the same creatures and from what he saw he had written a book which had changed biology forever. Jack had talked to his biology teacher, Professor Mufflin, at length on his return, sharing his pictures with him and understanding more what Charles Darwin had said in his famous book 'On the Origin of Species'. Professor Mufflin had explained that Darwin was able to see that birds, finches in fact, had evolved over time to have different beaks to eat different types of food.

Professor Mufflin had explained that not everyone believed this, that there were many, particularly in America called 'Creationists' who believed that God had created everything and that it was important that we respected other people's religions. However, Jack could tell that Professor Mufflin, as a scientist, preferred Charles Darwin's views.

Whatever the truth, it did not detract from the most amazing sights that he had seen when he had been there and Jack was always happy to keep an open mind on these matters.

Jack rehearsed for three hours until he was word perfect and then checked his notes and slides for a final time. He looked in the mirror, straightened his tie, patted down his hair again and took a deep breath. He then pulled open the door to his room and headed off to set up ready for his big moment. He breathed quickly, trying to forget that there were likely to be many people there.

As he walked through School he watched as his friends and colleagues muddled past, often deep in conversation or in some cases singing, or dragging a musical instrument behind them. Around the notice board there was a gaggle of students all waiting for something to be pinned up and Jack stopped for a moment to see what it was. After a minute or so the Head of Games strode out of the staffroom and pinned a big notice to the board which read 'Next Term's New Game is: Chessball' and a big cheer went up from the small crowd gathered. There were a few disappointed faces but they knew they would have a chance again next term.

Jack looked over and caught Daisy's eye; she waved and he waved back. He knew that she was yet another member of School that the whole world would know about one day and he was proud to call her his friend.

He moved on through the building until he came to the double doors to the main theatre. Outside the posters announced that the winner of the public speaking competition, Jack Simmons, would be giving that afternoon's lecture. He felt a swell of pride reading his name and he knew his father in particular was very proud of him.

The main stage in the School's theatre appeared to Jack to be absolutely enormous. He climbed the stairs to the top and walked across and adjusted his lectern and, again, tested the remote control for the slides that he was going to be showing throughout his talk. It all seemed to be working perfectly, but he tested it again, just in case.

He could feel the butterflies starting in his stomach, wondering if anybody would come and listen to his talk. Whilst it wasn't compulsory for students, he knew that the teachers would expect most people to attend, and he really hoped that his friends and his colleagues would want to come and listen to him.

It had been a long, hard slog to get to this stage, with various rounds of the competitions, to decide who would have the honour of presenting the half term lecture, and he had been very proud to have been chosen.

He remembered when he telephoned his mother and father

the evening that he won to let them know. They had been so
proud of him. The students were allowed one telephone call a
week (two if their parents were separated), which was from a
booth in the central foyer and it was always such a delight to hear
his parents' voices. Sometimes they would hold up the telephone
so that he could hear the sea or the birds in the trees and he
would delight in telling them everything that had happened that
week and they would tell him what had been happening back in
Bolivia.

Jack had concluded that there was nothing further he could
do. He knew what he was going to be saying, word for word,
and had rehearsed it so many times now, he could almost say it
backwards, but not quite.

He stepped back from the lectern and watched, as one by one
the students started to arrive and fill up the seats in the theatre,
mainly from the back, which is what all young people do, he had
concluded.

His heart missed a beat, though, as he saw the familiar frame
of JJ Buccannan walk through the bottom door and take a seat
right at the front. She looked up and smiled at him and he could
feel his colour changing to beetroot and hoped she couldn't see
from where she was sitting.

'Good luck!' she mouthed to him, and smiled, and he smiled
back in a slightly wobbly fashion.

'Thanks,' he managed to mouth and then looked as if he
was seriously studying his notes again, so as not to appear too
embarrassed.

He looked up to see Rosie arriving with a number of her
friends and they all sat in the third row and stared at him with big
smiles on their faces. Although she was never prepared to admit
it, Rosie had been extremely proud of her big brother when Jack
had been chosen to give the half term lecture. She had been even
more pleased when he had selected pictures which had her in

them.

Jack had even allowed her to take one of them out because she said that it was not her best and as Rosie had always been something of a poser to the camera, he did not want to run the risk of incurring her wrath by including a picture that she was not happy with.

The whisper of voices started to get louder as the theatre filled up further, and then, as the clock approached 5 minutes to 5, it became clear that there was hardly a spare seat in the house. The students started to sit down the stairs and a number were standing around the back. Jack had never seen the theatre so packed before and he felt the butterflies starting again in his stomach.

He heard a deep cough from the edge of the stage and looked across to see Mr Warren, his spectacles on his head at this stage, waiting in the wings, ready to introduce him. Mr Warren nodded and raised his eyebrows in Jack's direction, which he understood to mean, 'Was everything OK and was he ready to go?' Jack nodded back and thought, 'It's now or never,' and out onto the stage strode Mr Warren, pulling his glasses down onto his face as he did so.

'Ladies and Gentlemen,' said Mr Warren. 'Welcome to the theatre and welcome to this afternoon's lecture, to be given by Jack Simmons, the winner of this term's public speaking competition. Before I hand the stage over to Jack, just a word of warning to remind all of you travelling this half term, to collect tickets and passports from the Bursar's office by 8pm this evening and anyone having difficulties with their travel arrangements, please see me or the Bursar. If I don't have the opportunity, then I just want to wish you all a very happy half term holiday.'

A slight groan went up around the room, presumably from those students who would in fact prefer to stay at the School.

'And I wanted to say how much we look forward to

welcoming you back after half term. With no further ado, I hand you across to Jack Simmons, who is going to enthral you with tales in his talk entitled…' he stuttered slightly. 'Entitled… I'm so sorry, Master Simmons, I have completely forgotten what you are going to be talking about.'

Jack looked at Mr Warren, who was looking at him in a slightly strange manner, and Jack stepped forward to the lectern. 'Yes, of course, Mr Warren. I am going to be talking to you today about my adventures in…' Jack paused. A knotted feeling started at the bottom of his stomach and he realised that he could not remember what he was supposed to be talking about.

In true ad lib fashion, he said quickly, 'I am going to be talking about the most wonderful adventure holiday that I had with my parents and sister last year.'

Jack saw one of Rosie's friends nudge her at that reference to her, and she giggled.

Jack looked down at his notes quickly to remind himself of exactly what he would be talking about as his memory had gone completely blank.

To his horror, and as if it was some bad dream, when he looked at the sheets of paper in front of him, they, too, were completely blank. 'This must be some sort of joke,' he thought. And, immediately he tried to work out how somebody could come in and replace his notes when he had been looking at them only minutes earlier. 'It just wasn't possible,' he thought. 'There must be a mistake,' and he turned over the pages again and again, and all of them were completely blank.

'The slides,' he thought. 'The slides will tell me. If I can see the slides, I can remember what I am supposed to be talking about,' and he hit the remote control for the first slide. The stage lit up and he turned to point at the slide, happy in the knowledge that he would now have his memory jogged and could carry on.

As he turned to the slide, the pit in his stomach got even

bigger, as he stared at a completely blank screen. He looked at Mr Warren and out across the darkened theatre.

'I'm terribly sorry,' he said. 'There appears to be a technical fault with the slides. I just need to check, as they seem to be out of order.'

There were a few giggles and a couple of slow hand claps in the theatre but Jack ignored them and ran to the carousel where the slides were all lined up, ready to be displayed onto the wall behind him. He picked them out, one by one, and, one by one, they were completely blank.

He walked slowly back to the stage with every thought running through his mind at a hundred miles an hour. He simply could not remember what he was supposed to be speaking about and it was clear that Mr Warren couldn't remember either. His notes were blank, his slides were blank. He could, of course, just tell everybody that this is what had happened and risk ridicule and humiliation in front of JJ Buccannan, or he could do what his father had always taught him to do, which was to improvise.

He stepped onto the stage with confidence and charisma and turned to face his audience.

'Ladies and Gentleman, as it seems we have a few technical difficulties and as I cannot possibly give my talk without the photographs, it is time to go to Plan B. 'Life in the Arctic Circle'.'

For 45 minutes, Jack enthralled his audience with stories of narwhals and seal kicking (a game invented by the Inuits (who used to be called Eskimos) to while away the long days during the winter). It did not involve actual kicking of seals but rigging up a pretend seal which the Inuits have to kick with their feet. He even rigged up his own seal kicking demonstration in a matter of minutes and attempted a couple of kicks, counting his lucky stars that he had just started karate as well as his beloved Judo.

Jack talked about the hunting of the polar bears and how each family was entitled to kill a certain number but how the families were now selling those licences to the rich Americans to hunt.

He talked about the soapstone carvings and the skill required and how you could buy them cheaply in the villages but if you tried to buy them outside of the Arctic Circle, how much they cost.

He explained the life of a mother polar bear and how she dug into the snow and stayed there for many, many months, bringing up her cubs, and emerged into the light, desperate for food.

He talked about the pack ice and the damage it could do to the hulls of boats, and he finished with his impersonation of the call of a humpback whale, to loud and rapturous applause from everyone in the theatre.

Jack glanced towards the side of the stage and saw Mr Warren there, wiping his brow, with an expression that simply said 'phew,' and Jack knew that he had saved the day, despite the difficult start.

He received the applause graciously and the thanks and congratulations of Mr Warren, and a number of students came and surrounded him to ask him more questions about the ice and the snow and the polar bears and was it really true that a polar bear could stand 12 feet tall on its hind legs? Jack confirmed that it was true, that males could stand that tall and that if you travelled in the Arctic, your guide always had a rifle as well as a hand gun, in case the polar bear knocked the rifle from your hand.

Jack saw, out of the corner of his eye, JJ Buccannan approaching, together with his sister, and he took a deep breath as he very much expected his sister to be justifiably upset with him for not showing photographs in which she was included. But, instead, she threw her arms around him and gave him a big hug and said, 'Well done, Jack, that was brilliant.'

'You're not upset then?' he asked. 'That I had to change what I was talking about.'

'Did you?' she asked in real surprise.

As Jack couldn't actually remember what he was supposed to have been talking about, but could just remember that there were pictures that included her, he decided not to pursue this any further for the time being. But there was definitely something very strange going on.

What's more, he was happy to take the praise because JJ Buccannan also appeared to share his sister's view that his talk had been the most amazing thing that she had heard in a long time.

Jack made a mental note that having pictures didn't necessarily tell the whole story and he was very glad of the praise, as he felt sure that the couple of minutes before he had started his talk on the Arctic had probably taken its toll and taken at least three years off his life.

As the students started to disappear off to prepare for their travels home, Mr Warren approached Jack. He looked at him quizzically and said, 'What happened to your slides?'

'I don't know,' said Jack. 'My slides had gone and my notes had gone. I can't actually remember what I was supposed to be talking about.'

Mr Warren pushed his glasses onto the top of his head and said, 'No, Jack, neither can I.'

'And...' said Jack, 'my sister can't even remember that I was supposed to have been talking about something else, and neither does JJ Buccannan, and I told them both.'

Mr Warren sucked his teeth for a few minutes. 'Very curious,' he said. 'Do you feel unwell?'

'No,' said Jack. 'I feel fine.'

'And when was the last time you saw your notes or your slides?'

Jack said, 'Two minutes before you came and started introducing me. There is no way that anybody could have swapped them. Perhaps if we could remember what I was supposed to be talking about, then that will jog our memories.'

'I know!' exclaimed Mr Warren. 'It was on the letter that you wrote to me, advising me of the title. Come with me, Jack.'

Jack picked up his blank notes and a couple of the blank slides and followed, as Mr Warren strode purposefully through the corridors, down into the teaching section, in through his office door and started ferreting around on his rather untidy main desk.

'Here,' he said. 'Here it is. It says: Dear Mr Warren, I am pleased to advise you the title I have chosen for the end of term lecture is...' and Mr Warren stopped. He said, 'It's blank.'

'Blank,' said Jack. 'It... it can't be. It was written with a fountain pen.'

He took the piece of paper and examined it carefully. It was indeed entirely blank in exactly the space where the title of his lecture should have been.

'Is this some sort of joke, Master Simmons?'

'No, Sir,' said Jack. 'I just don't know what has happened!'

'Come on, think,' said Mr Warren. 'You must be able to remember what you were going to speak on. It must have been in relation to a holiday. That's what you always speak on.'

'I just can't remember, Sir.'

'Right,' said Mr Warren. 'Let's start eliminating things. I want you to come with me to the sick bay. Let's have you checked out to make sure that there is actually nothing physically wrong with you.'

'If there was something wrong with me, Sir, you would have it as well as you can't remember what I was supposed to be speaking about, and the paper wouldn't be blank.'

'OK, good point,' said Mr Warren. 'We'll both go. We'll both go to the sick bay.'

After almost two hours of poking and prodding, scans and
X-rays (the rules on computers not applying to the sick bay area
of the School, which was considered to be much too important
to deprive the students of up-to-date technology), Dr Beale
confirmed that there did not appear to be anything physically or
mentally wrong with either Jack or Mr Warren and he had, in his
medical opinion, after many, many years of practice in Harley
Street, 'Absolutely no idea what had happened'.

They thanked him for his honesty and left the sick bay, none
the wiser.

At that stage, Mr Warren's pager bleeped and he looked at it
with raised eyebrows. 'I've got to go, Master Simmons, it appears
there might be a problem with travel arrangements. I'll have
to give this some serious thought and see if I can come up with
a sensible explanation for the events of this afternoon. What I
suggest you do is go back and pack, ready for your trip back to
Bolivia tomorrow.'

As Jack walked from the sick bay back towards his room, he
encountered a number of students, all of whom had clearly been
at his lecture. They patted him on the back and congratulated
him. 'That was brilliant!' 'Well done, mate!' 'Can I come on
your next holiday?' were just some of the comments that he was
receiving from his fellow students.

It was clear that he had not completely failed, but he knew
in the back of his mind that he had not delivered the lecture that
he was supposed to and he couldn't understand why. How could
everything be blank?

He got back to his room and pulled out his case from under
the bed and started packing, ready for his trip tomorrow. Going
over and over it in his mind Jack tried to remember what he was
supposed to have been talking about. He had just about managed
to sit on his case to get the locks shut when there was a knock at
the door. 'Come in,' said Jack.

The door opened and a familiar bespectacled head popped itself round the door and looked at Jack with a smile, as Jack sat astride his suitcase trying to shut it.

'It seems I came at the right time,' said Mr Warren. 'But I am afraid, rather than good news, I am bringing some slightly bad news, and, in view of the troubles you have already experienced today, I didn't want you to hear this from anybody else.'

Mr Warren's forehead was furrowed with deep lines and he looked very concerned.

Jack leapt up immediately, thinking that perhaps he had finally worked out why neither of them could remember what Jack's lecture was supposed to be about, but Mr Warren shook his head, as if reading his mind, and said: 'I wanted you to be the first to know, Master Simmons, but today might just not be your day at all.'

Jack looked at him suspiciously and, without invitation, Mr Warren continued, 'We've just had word that all flights out of the United Kingdom have been cancelled with immediate effect and the situation is not likely to get any better for at least four to five days.'

The grim reality of what Mr Warren had just said sank quickly into the pit of Jack's stomach. 'No flights?' he said. 'Why?'

'Well, it's all to do with a big volcano in Iceland called Eyjafjallajökull. Every ten years or so it erupts, churning out volcanic ash and despite technology moving on so quickly, and we can send space ships and satellites to Mars, I'm afraid it appears that it is impossible for our aircraft to fly though volcanic ash without running the risk of crashing.'

'You're absolutely sure?' said Jack. 'There is no chance at all that we will be going home?'

'I'm afraid not, Master Simmons.'

'But, what will we do?' said Jack. 'We can't stay at the School, I suppose, because all the teachers will be wanting their own holidays.'

Mr Warren sat on Jack's bed and pushed his glasses back. He said, 'We are just looking at the logistics now, but it seems unlikely that the School will be able to stay open as staff have just got other commitments. So, we think it is likely that we are going to have to start looking at your emergency contacts and half term arrangements. What do you normally do at half terms?' he asked Jack.

'Well, it depends,' said Jack. 'Sometimes, if it is a long half term holiday, we fly back to see Mum and Dad, but other times we go away somewhere with my Aunt.'

'Does your Aunt not live in this country?' asked Mr Warren.

'Oh yes, she lives in Berkshire. But we always go away somewhere, rather than stay in her house because she says it's just too small for growing children, and so she always organises something special for us, like going to the seaside or the mountains, and last year we went to the Lake District and that was really fun. But I don't expect she will be able to organise something on this short notice, and she may not even be there at all. What will happen if there is nowhere for us to go?'

Mr Warren stood up from the bed and patted him on the back and said, 'Don't you worry, my boy, there will be somewhere. But, first things first, we'd best let your parents know and then see if we can get in touch with your Aunt. I assume that all her details will be on your file. Do you have more than one Aunt?'

'Yes,' said Jack,' but the other one lives in Australia and so won't be much good.'

'Right, so what's the name of the Aunt in England?'

'Auntie Issie,' said Jack with a wry smile.

'Right, Aunt Issie it is. Leave me to make a few calls and I'll let you know when things have been arranged and then perhaps you might like to ring your parents directly. Normal rules on weekly calls will obviously be relaxed, and, Master Simmons, I am sorry, I know how much you were looking forward to this holiday. It must be a real disappointment to you.'

Jack looked up at Mr Warren and smiled. 'A wise man is one who knows the things he can't change,' said Jack.

'Well, that's a very grown up expression for someone so young,' said Mr Warren.

Jack smiled. 'Sometimes you have to be grown up, that's what Dad says, and today it's my turn to be grown up. I know that Rosie is going to be very upset that we won't be going home, so I have to be strong for her. I do hope that Auntie Issie can have us. She's as mad as anything and makes us both laugh.'

'Is there an Uncle Issie?'

'Oh, yes,' said Jack. His eyes lit up. 'Uncle Stanley. He's a whizz at Latin and Greek and he's really good when we go and visit old buildings because he can translate all of the inscriptions and I wish that I was as good as he was.'

'Well,' said Mr Warren. 'Keep studying hard and one day you will be just as good. You've got such a flair for languages.'

'Yes,' said Jack. 'I think I get that from Dad. Should I unpack my suitcase?'

'No,' said Mr Warren. 'But perhaps you might like to have a look at the contents, as spending ten days in England might not be quite the same as ten days in Bolivia, although, that said, it may be that the dust cloud will lift sooner than we think and we can get you on a flight home as soon as possible. So, on second thoughts, pack for all eventualities.'

'I'd better go and break the news to Rosie,' said Jack, pulling himself up to his full height and trying to make himself look as old and important as possible.

'Your parents would be very proud,' said Mr Warren, and he left Jack's room, closing the door quietly behind him.

CHAPTER THREE

The large room was slightly darkened and on one wall stood
a huge bank of LCD display screens. Each one of them had a
different picture. In the centre of the room was an enormous
screen and the picture on it was one that no person in the western
world could fail to recognise. As the lights in the room were
turned down it was difficult to see who else was there, but the
person on the screen was clearly talking to somebody.

'And you are absolutely sure?' said the figure on the big
screen. 'We have no idea at all?'

A woman's voice spoke up from the darkened room, 'No, Mr
President, I'm afraid we don't. We have used every resource at
our disposal. We still have no idea what they are planning.'

The President looked down at the papers in front of him.
'Well, you've tried your hardest. We've come up with nothing
else from this end, so I guess we just have to hope that somebody
finds the answer, or things are just going to get worse.'

At that stage, there was a low vibration that could be heard
in the room, and it was clear that it was coming from someone's
mobile telephone, placed on a desk in the darkened room.
The woman's voice said, 'I'm so terribly sorry, Mr President. I
know this may seem terribly rude, but I do need to take this.
It's my nephew's school on the line and, in light of the current
difficulties, I want to ensure that everything is as it should be.'

'Perfectly understood, Issie,' said the President of the United
States. 'Please take it, and I hope that all is well. We are just about
finished here anyway and I will speak to you all at the same time

tomorrow, unless you have any further news for me before then. God Bless and good evening to all of you.'

There was a murmuring from the seven or eight people in the room. 'Good evening, Mr President.'

The screen flickered and, rather than going blank, there then appeared a second picture, this time not of the President of the United States, but the UK's very own Prime Minister, Amy Jones.

'How did he take the news?' she asked.

'As well as can be expected,' came a male voice from the back of the darkened room.

'No pressure, guys,' said Amy Jones, with a smile. 'But the buck really does stop with you. You know that whatever resources you need, whatever brain power, you just have to ask, but, as I understand it, it's not quite as simple as that.'

'If only,' came a voice from the dark.

'Just keep me informed,' she said. 'No doubt we will speak later.' And the screen went blank. The darkened room was lit momentarily as someone exited, mobile phone pressed to their ear.

Once outside in the corridor, Issie was better able to respond to the person on the other end of her call and was listening intently with a number of 'Hmms' and 'Yes' and 'Of course'. She was a lady in her fifties, dark hair cut into a neat bob, jeans and a sweatshirt with a picture of an animal on it.

The phone call was short but it appeared to be satisfactory and Issie made her way back into the room, putting on the lights as she did. Sat in a semicircle of chairs in an auditorium style were seven others. They all looked very worried and tired.

'Everything alright, Issie?' asked the man at the end.

'Nothing I can't deal with, but just unfortunate timing,' said Issie, slipping the mobile phone into her pocket. 'I'm afraid I'm going to have to go to Bristol tomorrow. I shouldn't be too long.'

'You could probably do with a break,' said the man on the

end, tilting back his chair and placing his large boots on the table. 'You look exhausted.'

'I fear,' she said, 'that things are going to get a whole lot worse before they get better.'

She gestured to the bank of LCD screens. 'Max, anything coming up at all?' she asked of the man sat observing the screens keenly.

'Nothing,' Max said without even turning, such was his concentration.

'Well,' she said. 'Keep at it. Something has got to turn up, it always does.'

'But it's never been this long or this close to the wire,' said a woman with wild blonde hair tied under a scarf, her ripped jeans flapping around as she moved.

'I know, Angela,' said Issie. 'But we are doing everything that we possibly can and, our hard work has to pay off.'

'Ever the optimist,' said Alfie, sat poring over large books in front of him, with a wry smile.

'Someone has to be,' said Issie, 'with earthquakes, wildfires and floods, we now have volcanoes and fog. We need to stop it now...' It was said more out of hope than anything else and Issie pulled out a chair, fired up the computer in front of her and plonked down in front of it. 'Right, time for work...' she said with real determination.

The gates of the School opened automatically as the dark blue Land Rover Defender approached. It was slightly dirtier than Auntie Issie would have liked but, frankly, cleaning the car was low on her list of priorities at the current time.

She drove up past the main School buildings and took a right turn towards the boarding houses. There were many children milling around, some looking a little confused, others looking happier than she would have expected given the cancellation of their holiday plans. She glanced in her rear view mirror and through the cage, between the rear seats and the vast boot of the Land Rover, she could see two small brown, white and black faces looking at her with excitement.

'Oh, I expect you two know where you are, don't you. Now try not to leap over everybody or poo on the lawns or dig up anything that the gardeners have put in.'

The two dogs just continued to look forward with their tongues hanging out and ears upright in expectation and, as Auntie Issie's attention was focused again on the road in front of them, the two dogs glanced towards each other in what could only be described as a wry smile.

Whilst it would seem to the untrained eye that driving into the School was exceptionally easy, Auntie Issie knew that as the car had approached the gates, her vehicle had been scanned and compared to DVLC records. Her face would have been photographed and compared to those held on file for her, and whilst it may appear that she was about to drive through the most beautiful tunnel of roses and hedge, she knew that in fact this was a complete vehicle scanner, which would have ensured that there was no one else in the car other than the dogs, who she had already declared as attending.

The dogs knew that they were being scanned and there was a brief whine from both of them because they could feel the electronic eye pass over their bodies. But they knew, as dogs do, that this was all for their own good and that of their young charges.

Whilst the School may not allow any form of communication electronics amongst the students, it did not stop them from using it to their full advantage to ensure the complete safety of its students. The philosophy of the School was to create happy, interactive and quizzical children, but there was also an obligation to keep them very safe.

As Auntie Issie drove up towards the boarding house that she knew her nephew and niece lived in, she could see two slightly forlorn figures sat outside on a large suitcase. As she got closer, she realised that in fact Rosie was not only not in her School uniform but was already wearing the Princess dress that she loved so much. From a very young age, Rosie had always jumped at the chance to wear her Princess dresses, whether it be walking down Bristol High Street, through an airport or, indeed, as had happened last year, whilst ascending to 2,000 feet in a hot air balloon at the Bristol Balloon Festival.

As she had got older, they had all presumed that this would be something that perhaps she might grow out of, but, instead, she just chose slightly more sophisticated Princess dresses, and whilst she was not able to wear them on a daily basis whilst at the School, Auntie Issie knew that whilst staying with her they would be a regular feature, unless, of course, she was practising her fencing, in which case she tended to be a little more practical.

Jack, on the other hand, was wearing his smart School blazer and a pair of grey trousers and a white shirt. He looked quite the young man. Auntie Issie was amazed how much they had changed every time she saw them.

They saw her vehicle and leapt to their feet and started running down the road towards it, jumping to one side as Auntie Issie pulled up at the kerb, ready to put the suitcase straight into the back.

She switched off the engine and jumped down onto the pavement and gave them both a big hug. 'I'm so sorry,' she said. 'You must be so disappointed.'

'Well,' said Jack. 'We were but then we heard we were coming to stay with you, so it had a happy ending.'

Auntie Issie laughed and said: 'You may not think that after 10 days.'

Jack looked up. 'We may be able to go if the volcano stops.'

'I know,' she said. 'We'll keep an eye on it but plan for all eventualities. I presume you have your passports?'

'We are already chipped and scanned,' said Rosie. 'We don't need passports anymore.'

Auntie Issie laughed. She had forgotten how much technology had moved on in the last few years and good old fashioned passports in their leather holders were no longer required. A small implant, coupled with an iris scan, was all that was needed these days.

'Well,' she said, 'just in case you were too disappointed at the thought of having to spend time with your elderly Aunt, I have brought along two friends to help you cheer up.'

Auntie Issie looked at them and smiled and they realised instantly what she meant and ran to the back of the Land Rover, opening it wide, at which point two boisterous tri-colour Border Collies leapt out at both of them, pinning them to the ground and licking their faces all over.

'I think they are pleased to see you,' said Auntie Issie. 'Now, I'm not sure that this suitcase is big enough,' she said with an element of sarcasm in her voice. 'You're sure it was just 10 days you were staying for?'

Jack laughed. 'Well, in case we do go to Bolivia, we have brought our summer clothes. And then there was the judo clothes and Rosie's fencing ones.'

'And another two Princess dresses,' piped up Rosie.

'Obviously,' said Auntie Issie.

'And wellingtons and raincoats, and ...'

'OK,' said Auntie Issie, 'I think I get the picture. Let's see if we can manhandle this into the back of the car and the dogs can sit on top of it.'

'Oh, can't they sit with us?' pleaded Jack and Rosie.

'I don't think that that would be a very good idea. You know what Charlie is like in the car. The moment another vehicle goes past, he starts to bark at it and he will ruin your lovely outfit, Rosie, and your very smart jacket, Jack. And, besides which, if we have an accident and they are not tied down, then they will go through the windscreen, and that will be the end of them. So it's best if they stay behind the grill.

'Now, I can't remember what the rules are but I have borrowed a couple of car seats off our neighbours. I hope to goodness you fit in them. I'm a bit out of touch with things like this and thank goodness they remembered just as I was driving off, otherwise I would have been driving you home in the back with the dogs.'

Jack and Rosie laughed. 'We don't need a car seat anymore,' said Jack proudly. 'We are too old and too tall.' They opened up the door to the back seats and Jack looked in amazement to see two bright pink car seats. 'You are not serious?' he said. 'You wanted me to sit in a pink car seat?'

'It was either that or nothing,' said Auntie Issie. 'If you can squeeze in next to it no problem but otherwise you might have to sit in it.'

Jack sighed deeply and pulled himself up into the rear seats between the two pink car seats and started to clip himself in.

At that stage, at the top of the steps to the boarding house, appeared Mr Warren. 'You two buckle yourselves in, I'll just go and have a word with Mr Warren,' said Auntie Issie, and she disappeared up the steps.

They talked in hushed voices for a few minutes and Auntie Issie then appeared in the driver's seat. She was not a tall woman and seeing her sat in the driving seat of this enormous commercial Land Rover always made Jack laugh.

'Right,' she said. 'All sorted. Let's be on our way.'

The journey back to Auntie Issie's house took about two

hours. It was motorway at first, but then beautiful rolling countryside, which would have looked even nicer if it hadn't been pouring with rain, with thunder and lightning and mist and fog. Jack couldn't really remember such an awful day of weather and it really summed up the last few days. Forked lightning shot down from the sky, appearing to hit the tops of hills and trees, loud rumbles of thunder came in across the hill tops, which almost made the car shake. Jack could hear a whimpering from the back of the car, and he knew that no matter how big and brave Molly and Charlie were, they did not like thunder and lightning at all.

'Don't be such babies,' said Auntie Issie, in a semi harsh way, and both dogs cuddled up together right at the back of the car with their ears down flat.

'You are supposed to be roughty toughty sheepdogs and I don't remember the job description being 'roughty toughty sheepdogs except if it is thunder and lightning'.'

As they left the motorway and headed out into the countryside, it started to get foggier and Jack shivered involuntarily, as if someone had just walked over his grave. 'What very funny weather,' he said to Auntie Issie, who glanced at him in the rear view mirror.

'Yes,' she said, 'it's been a bit strange for a while, but I am sure it will be fine when we get home.' And, just as she said this, they turned left to climb up towards Brighthaven and came out of the fog into the most wonderful sunshine.

'How did you do that?' said Rosie.

'Magic,' said Auntie Issie with a smile.

Jack and Rosie looked at her with slightly open mouths. 'I'm only joking,' she said. 'It's just that I know from when I left this morning that the fog started half way down the hill and I suspected it was probably the same. A lucky guess.'

At the top of the hill, Auntie Issie turned right into a much narrower lane. There were no road signs and no road markings, but Jack knew that this was Lavender Lane. Mum and Dad had always cursed every time they tried to find Lavender Lane in the past because of the lack of signs and the fact that anyone you stopped, never knew where Brighthaven was, never mind Lavender Lane.

Jack always remembered it because of the triangle of grass with the tree on that had been planted for the Queen's Silver Wedding Anniversary, and once he had found the triangle, he always knew that he could find Auntie Issie's house. They drove slowly now down the narrow lane.

'Are the cows in the field?' asked Jack.

'Yes,' said Auntie Issie. 'All the Highland cows and last year's babies are there waiting for you.' And, as she said that, the most enormous pair of horns appeared over the gate and in between them was a long shaggy fringe. 'See,' she said. 'They've come to greet you.'

Poking out from next to the huge woolly Highland cow was a pretty little brown face. There were no horns and the baby stood close to its mother and was only a fraction of its size. It peered curiously at Jack and Rosie as they went past in the Land Rover.

There were not a lot of houses in Lavender Lane. Seven to be precise, and although Jack and Rosie had visited on many occasions, it was only for a day or normally for a few hours to see Auntie Issie and perhaps have lunch or tea with her. They had never stayed for longer than that and Jack was looking forward to knowing a bit more about the 7 houses and the people who lived in them.

His mother had always said that Lavender Lane was called 'the Mafia of Brighthaven', as it was set apart from the rest of the village, notoriously difficult to find, and his mother claimed that those living in Lavender Lane, including her dear sister, in some way controlled what the rest of the village did. Jack had always rather taken this with a pinch of salt, but there had to be some positives to not going home to Bolivia for the holidays, and he made himself a pact that he was going to find out a little bit more about the people and why his mother referred to them as 'the Mafia'.

They passed a house on the left hand side with a beautifully tended garden and carried on for about 200 metres and pulled in, in front of an oak garage.

'This is new from the last time we were here?' asked Jack.

'Yes,' said Auntie Issie, 'I suppose it must be. We finally gave up on the old garage when Uncle Stanley backed his car into the doors and we couldn't open them again.'

Jack and Rosie laughed. Poor Uncle Stanley got the blame for most things, it seemed, but not in a nasty way, in a light hearted and funny way. They both knew that Auntie Issie adored Uncle Stanley, who was a very clever and kind man and, despite her bossiness, everybody knew that Uncle Stanley was really in charge of the household, but always made it look as if it was Auntie Issie, to make her feel better.

They unloaded their enormous suitcase and the dogs and went in through the new garden gate. 'Wow,' said Rosie. 'Your garden looks so pretty.'

'Thanks,' said Auntie Issie. 'It's just coming to life after a very hard winter. The daffodils and crocus are particularly good this year, and I'll take you up to Spray Wood so that you can see the bluebells later on.'

'Where is Uncle Stanley?' asked Jack.

'Oh, he had to go and do some shopping. We didn't really have much to eat that would be of interest to either of you two, so I sent him down to Waitrose to see what he could find. I have already spoken to your mother about your latest eating habits and I know, Jack, that you don't eat any meat, except lamb. Don't worry, Rosie, we've got plenty of olives in for you, as I know that they are your favourite.'

Just as she said that, they heard a car pull up and a door slam, and through the garden gate came Stanley Culpepper. Jack could tell that he had not only been sent down into Oldbury to buy the groceries, but he had also been instructed by Auntie Issie to have a haircut, as it was neatly clipped and cut and had clearly just been done.

'Nice hair,' said Jack, with a smile.

'Don't start,' said Uncle Stanley giving him a hug. 'You've only just got here! But thank you. I hope you approve. Auntie Issie seemed to think that it was terribly important that I should have short hair for your arrival,' he said as he gave them both a hug.

'My goodness, look at the size of that suitcase,' he said, as he saw what Auntie Issie and Jack were trying to drag down the garden path.

'Come on, out of the way. Let me take that. Why don't you go and help with the shopping baskets, and please make sure that the dogs don't get their noses in first. There is plenty in there that would interest them.'

Jack and Rosie ran back to the cars and, sure enough, sat in the boot with their noses in the bags, were Charlie and Molly.

'Out,' said Jack, and both of them sat bolt upright as if butter wouldn't melt in their little canine mouths. 'Garden. Both of you,' he said in a very authoritative way, and both dogs jumped out and went back through the garden gate, which Jack firmly shut behind them.

When all of the bags were unloaded and things for the fridge were safely put away, Auntie Issie said, 'Right, who would like a nice cold drink and a slice of one of my Victoria sponges?' and both Jack and Rosie grinned in unison.

Rosie said, 'I think I might enjoy this holiday.'

'Let's sit outside,' said Auntie Issie. 'The sun's warm enough.' And they pulled up the chairs by the oak table, overlooking the garden and across the valley for uninterrupted views of the

Berkshire countryside.

'I'm afraid that I'm not quite sure what time I'm going to have off over the next ten days,' said Auntie Issie. 'That's the bad news. But the good news is that Uncle Stanley might have a little more time. But, between us and the Kentons, we should be able to make sure that you've got something to do for most days.'

'Are the Kentons the people who live half way down the lane?' asked Jack.

'Yes, that's right. They've got three children: Daisy, Florence and Daniel. Daisy is a bit older, Florence is probably about your age, Jack, and Daniel is about the same age as Rosie. The children are going down to Devon for the first week of the holidays with their mother but will be back for the last few days, if you are still here. Now, before that, tell me all about the School. Jack, I hear that you were chosen to give the half term lecture. That's fantastic! We'll have to celebrate that. It's an amazing achievement. And, Rosie, how is your fencing coming along?'

'It's OK,' she said.

Jack laughed. 'OK? What she hasn't said is that there is no one in the School who can beat her now.'

'Unless Sam comes to the School,' said Rosie. 'He was very good, and also left handed.'

'Yes, I did notice that,' said Jack.

'Sam?' asked Uncle Stanley.

'Oh, Jack was on the Introductor rota yesterday and a very nice boy called Sam was being shown around. He had an awful Dad but, despite that, Sam was very, very nice.'

'Rosie, that's rather rude,' said Auntie Issie.

'But, sadly, the truth,' said Jack. 'The sort that can't be bothered to look up to say hello because he is too busy with his telephone. He thinks he knows everything and thinks that he can buy his way into the School.'

'Ah,' said Auntie Issie. 'Well, I can understand your

reluctance. When will Sam join?'

'In September, if he passes the induction week. It's really weird though,' said Jack, 'because, apparently, he lives in Brighthaven.'

'Does he?' said Auntie Issie. 'Let me guess. You describe the mother. I assume there was a mother?'

'Oh yes,' said Jack. 'Um, a pleasant lady, in her late 40s, floral dress, smart shoes, not too high, politely spoken. That is, compared with her husband, who, despite having an expensive suit, looked crumpled and harassed, and he is a lawyer, apparently.'

'Ah,' said Auntie Issie. 'Mr and Mrs Bailey-Knox.'

'You know them?' asked Jack, in astonishment.

'Well, know of them,' said Auntie Issie. 'Mr Bailey-Knox made himself quite unpopular in the village by buying a house and immediately wanting to knock it down and build a much bigger one at the bottom of the garden. He came around to our way of thinking in the end, but it did take some time.'

Jack laughed. 'So does that mean that Sam doesn't live very far away?' he said with some excitement.

'That's right,' said Auntie Issie. 'They live in the centre of the village so it will probably take you about 10 to 15 minutes to walk across the footpaths. You could take the dogs.'

'Fantastic,' said Jack.

'And, I've got somebody to fence with,' said Rosie.

'Well, that's on the basis that they are there. Don't forget it is holiday time and they might have gone away somewhere.'

Jack looked at his Aunt and tilted his head on one side. 'They don't look like the 'going away' kind.'

'Enough said,' said Auntie Issie. 'Now, another piece of sponge, Jack?' and she cut and placed a piece on his plate before waiting for an answer. 'We'll go and call on them on our way back from Spray Wood.'

Uncle Stanley asked, 'So what's happening to the rest of the students who live abroad, now that there aren't any flights?'

'Oh,' said Rosie. 'Many are going to Aunts and Uncles, like we are. Others are going to stay with other pupils. What's happening to JJ, Jack?' asked Rosie, sounding almost concerned. 'She often goes to stay with her aunt and uncle in Hong Kong, doesn't she?'

'Yes,' said Jack. 'But I didn't really have a chance to speak to her before we left, so I don't know what's happening and where she is going to stay.'

'JJ?' asked Auntie Issie, raising one eyebrow.

'Jack's girlfriend,' said Rosie, mischievously.

'She is not!' said Jack.

'Only because you are too shy to ask her,' said Rosie.

'She wouldn't be interested in someone like me,' said Jack. 'I don't play football.'

'That's where you are wrong,' said Rosie. 'Because she told me she found you much more interesting than all the other boys because you are clever and you make her laugh.'

'That sounds familiar,' said Auntie Issie, looking towards her husband. 'I first met Uncle Stanley when we were in Africa and we were with a big group. Someone asked me what women like most about men and I said 'A sense of humour, good manners, and intelligence' and it seems to me, Jack, that you probably have all three of those, so, clearly, JJ has very good taste.'

Jack smiled. 'Well, there's always the second half of term,' he said.

Jack looked up to catch a glance between his Aunt and Uncle, which was difficult to read, but one which made him feel slightly nervous.

'Now, Jack, tell me about your talk,' said Auntie Issie.

'Well,' said Jack, 'it was really weird because I had written this great talk about our last trip to the Galapagos.'

Jack jolted. 'Oh my goodness, I can remember,' he said.

'What do you mean?' said Auntie Issie.

'Well, it's a long story,' said Jack. 'But, I was supposed to be doing a talk and I had done all my slides, I had rehearsed, and I had had the topic approved, but when it actually came to it, I couldn't remember what I was supposed to be talking about! And, the really weird thing is that Rosie couldn't remember either, and neither could Mr Warren. So we went back to look at the memo that Mr Warren had given me to approve the topic, and it was blank!'

Jack said this in a voice that made it sound as if he simply didn't believe what had gone on, and he realised that, having told the story, it did sound rather incredible.

Uncle Stanley leant forward and smiled gently, 'But you can remember now what it was about?'

'Yes,' said Jack.

'And what about the slides?' asked Uncle Stanley. 'Where are they?'

'They'll be in my bag,' he said. 'I put them in there thinking I might have a look at them over the holiday to try and work out why they were all blank.'

'Well, let's get them out,' said Uncle Stanley.

Jack scurried up to his room and pulled open the suitcase and rummaged around in the bottom for a few seconds, and eventually found the box with the slides. He ran down the stairs, closely followed by Charlie, who was sticking to him as if they were attached by a piece of string. Jack placed them on the dining table and everybody came in from the garden and sat down on the dining chairs. This left the two end chairs vacant, as there were only four of them and the table took six. As if they had heard Jack thinking about this, in unison, Molly and Charlie both climbed up onto the seats at either end of the table and sat upright.

Jack and Rosie started to giggle and Jack said, 'I know Charlie used to do that but I didn't know that Molly had learned it as well.'

Auntie Issie sighed. 'Yes, sadly it's not a habit we have been able to get them out of or, indeed, have tried too hard, but we do have to remember when we have polite company to discourage the dogs from doing it, as people find it a bit off-putting.'

Jack took the lid off the box and five pairs of eyes watched him doing it. He lifted out the first slide and held it up to the light and there, in front of him, was his favourite photograph of him and Rosie under water, next to a turtle that was lying on the bottom of the sea.

'But how did that happen?' asked Jack, and grabbed for the next one.

The next one was of a large land iguana with a slightly bloody nose. He reached for the next one, an albatross taking off from the cliff top. As he pulled each one out, every one had a familiar picture on it and every one was in the order in which he had placed them to give his lecture.

'But, that's crazy,' said Jack. 'They had all gone. They were all blank, weren't they, Rosie, you were there?'

'Yes,' said Rosie. 'But perhaps you had put the wrong slides in?'

'I didn't,' said Jack. 'I put all of these slides in and I had my lecture notes, and all the words had disappeared.'

Jack saw that glance again between Auntie Issie and Uncle Stanley and the hairs on the back of his neck stood up a fraction.

Auntie Issie laughed and said, 'Well, at least you've got them back and I'm sure that there's a really sensible explanation. Just one that none of us can think of at the moment. It was probably your friends playing a practical joke because they were jealous that you had won the competition.'

'If it was, I'll kill them!' said Jack.

'So, what did you do?' asked Uncle Stanley. 'If your slides were blank and your paper blank, how could you give the lecture?'

Jack smiled and said, 'I just had to improvise, like Dad taught me, and I gave a talk on the Inuits in the Arctic and did the best display possible of seal kicking.'

Auntie Issie's eyes widened.

'No, not that kind of seal kicking, Auntie Issie. Not actual seals. It's what all the young Inuits do to keep themselves occupied in the long winter months. They hang something up and you have to kick at it with your feet.'

'Obviously,' said Auntie Issie. 'I knew that.' And everybody laughed.

'Well, why don't you two go and unpack and then perhaps we can go for a walk and take the dogs with us. Uncle Stanley's got some business to attend to this afternoon, but he can join us later on. And before you ask, there is more cake.'

'Hurrah,' said Rosie.

Auntie Issie's cakes were infamous in the family and it had long been joked about that she could make a cake out of almost anything. Any type of fruit, vegetable, chocolate, even lavender, which was everybody's favourite.

Jack and Rosie raced each other up the stairs, closely followed by Charlie and Molly, who ran into their room and leapt onto their beds. Molly on Rosie's and Charlie on Jack's. They settled themselves down to watch as Jack and Rosie started to unpack their things.

'Will you be putting something more sensible on to go for a walk?' asked Jack, eyeing Rosie's Princess dress. 'We wouldn't like everybody to think that you were completely mad.'

'I'll wear what I like,' she said indignantly.

'I know you will, Rosie, but we are in the country and you'll rip it or get it dirty and then Mum will be cross. Why don't you put your jeans on and you can put the Princess dress on later on when we have supper?'

'I suppose you're right,' she said, and started rummaging through her bags for her smart new jeans and sweatshirt. Molly had her head practically in the case and gently with her teeth, pulled out a very pretty blue and white striped sweatshirt. Molly pulled it a bit more until it started easing itself out from underneath the rest of the clothes.

Rosie laughed. She said, 'I think Molly wants me to wear this one.'

Downstairs, Auntie Issie and Uncle Stanley made another cup of tea in silence, with the occasional glance at one another.

'What time will you go up the road?' asked Auntie Issie.

'Oh, in about an hour,' said Uncle Stanley. 'We have another update with the top man which shouldn't take too long as we are no further forward than we were yesterday.'

'How are the indicator signs? Are things deteriorating?' asked Auntie Issie.

'Oh, about the same as yesterday,' said Uncle Stanley, as he poured milk into the tea. 'The volcano is still erupting at full strength; the flood water in Pakistan is shortly to reach record levels; the fires in Australia are no closer to being under control than they were yesterday. What was the weather like, heading down to Bristol?'

'As you would expect,' said Auntie Issie. 'Overcast, foggy, miserable. I haven't seen it this bad since 1983.'

'I don't think,' said Uncle Stanley, 'that we have ever come this close before. When did the fog start improving?'

'Oh, the bottom of Finchbill,' said Auntie Issie. 'Just as we turned off the road to Needage we broke through the fog.'

She glanced out of the window and down into the valley below them where the B994 ran through; although they couldn't see the road from the house, what they could see was the bank of fog nestled in the base of the valley.

'It hasn't come any closer,' said Uncle Stanley. 'But it's

definitely closing in.'

'Do you think there's anything to Jack's problem with his talk?' asked Auntie Issie.

'No,' said Uncle Stanley. 'Just his classmates playing a practical joke on him.'

'But,' said Auntie Issie, 'we know that we are living in the only place in the world where we are protected, so if it was connected, then that might explain why Jack can't remember it when he is in Bristol but can remember it when he is here.'

'I fear, darling, that it's just an unfortunate coincidence,' said Uncle Stanley. 'But we mustn't close our minds to any possible angle. Right, I will tell Cameron and just see if there is anything that he can pull up that might be a connection.'

They heard footsteps coming down the stairs and glanced at each other again, as if to remind themselves that the topic was not to be discussed in front of the children.

Auntie Issie nodded very slightly, 'Right, well you'd better get that second cake out, hadn't you,' she said in a light, bright tone. 'Under the glass cake stand behind the television,' she said, knowing the look on her husband's face which said 'I've got no idea where it is'.

Jack returned with the cake, clutching the plate in both hands. 'How is 441?' he asked as he placed it down on the table between them. 'Will we be able to go on it while we are here?'

'You have a very good memory Jack,' said Uncle Stanley. '441 is now moored in the Isle of Wight and Angela and Alfie go out on it whenever they can, so there is a chance we could arrange something.' He glanced at Auntie Issie who smiled thinly.

'Yes of course,' she said. 'What a great idea'.

Jack knew that there was definitely something that they were not telling him.

'Who is 441?' asked Rosie. 'Is it a prisoner?' Everyone laughed.

'441 is the World War Two rescue launch that was restored by

Alfie and Angela who live in the house opposite,' Uncle Stanley nodded his head in their general direction of their house. 'When the Queen had her Diamond Jubilee in 2012, 441 was in the Royal Pageant representing the RAF Museum and flying the RAF Royal Standard.'

'I remember,' said Jack. 'We went to watch it with Mum and Dad and it was really, really wet. We waved and cheered as 441 went past and took lots of pictures.'

'I don't remember,' said Rosie forlornly.

'You were only five' said Jack. 'Well, almost six. Still quite young really. You could not see over the wall so Dad had to put you on his shoulders.'

'Well,' said Auntie Issie. 'After the pageant, 441 went to its new home in the Isle of Wight and Alfie and Angela go and sail on her as much as they can. With those huge 300 horse power engines, they can travel pretty quickly to anywhere they want to get to!'

'And did Alfie replace the fake guns on the back with real ones?' asked Jack with a mischievous smile. 'He always said that no-one would notice after a while.'

'You do have a good memory!' said Uncle Stanley. 'To my knowledge they are still replicas but you can never tell with Alfie!'

'I will have to ask him when I see him,' said Jack with a smile and he stretched across to have just one more small piece of cake.

Outside the central control room, Uncle Stanley swiped the door with his card, placed his hand on the fingerprint lock and gazed directly at the retina scan, which identified him, and the door slid open.

The room was a hive of activity.

Ella, the archaeologist, had huge maps out over the table, poring over them with a large magnifying glass. Cameron sat behind a large pile of military books.

In one corner, with her head in her hands, was Angela. She looked up as Uncle Stanley came in. 'That bad?' asked Uncle Stanley.

'No, just resting my eyes. If I have to look at one more art exhibition on this blasted computer, I swear I am going to throw it out of the window.'

'Nothing?' asked Uncle Stanley.

'Not a dicky-bird,' she said. 'Everything absolutely as it should be.'

'Ella?' asked Uncle Stanley.

'Same,' she said. 'No historical sites have disappeared. Everyone is still reporting exactly what they should be.'

'Where's Max?'

'Oh, he's just on the phone in the other room, checking around the archives of all the universities. There are no philosophers missing, no attempt to re-write any text.'

Uncle Stanley turned to the tall man, sat across from Angela. 'Adam, anything? Anything in the world of farming?'

'No,' said Adam. 'I thought perhaps I was onto something earlier as Farming Today was running a story on milk yields and a suggestion that selective breeding wasn't working, but it seems a bit of a dead end. But I'll keep at it. What time are we on with the President?'

'Two o'clock,' said Uncle Stanley. 'It's likely to be a short conversation at this rate.'

The door opened again and in came Alfie with a tray with tea. 'Oh, hi Stanley,' he said. 'I didn't realise you were here, I'll make you a cup now.'

'Don't worry,' said Uncle Stanley. 'I've just had one. I guess it's too much to ask that you've had any luck at all?'

'Zilch,' said Alfie. 'No unexplained car crashes or plane crashes. There was the crash in Nevada with the World War II plane, but absolutely nothing to link it to the problem.'

'Are Alice and Michael here?' asked Uncle Stanley.

'They've both been here since 4 o'clock this morning. I sent them off to their respective homes for a couple of hours' sleep because they were simply no use to us in that state,' said Cameron. 'They'll be back before the President's briefing.' He turned to Uncle Stanley and said, 'I don't suppose anything has occurred to either of you two?'

Uncle Stanley knew that in the back of his mind there was something that he needed to talk to Cameron about but, for the time being, this had slipped his mind. He concluded it couldn't have been important and sat himself down in front of one of the computer screens, ready to start trailing through any indications that anything had changed in relation to Greek and Roman history.

His heart had a sinking feeling that he could not remember having had for some time, and as he looked out of the window and saw the fog approaching up from the valley, he knew that time was not on their side. If they managed to pull it out of the bag on this occasion, it would have been the closest that they had ever come.

Back at Rose Cottage, Auntie Issie was gazing into the fridge in the kitchen, wondering what she could possibly feed her niece and nephew for lunch, when the phone rang. She answered it and a voice at the end, which sounded relatively young, asked if it would be at all possible to speak to Rosie Simmons. Auntie Issie didn't recognise the voice but she could tell it was that of a young man and she asked politely, 'Could I ask who is calling?'

'Could you tell her that it's Sam, and I wondered if she would like to fence with me this afternoon?'

Auntie Issie smiled to herself and said, 'I presume from that, young Sam, that you don't mean putting up a partition around your house?'

'Certainly not!' said the young voice at the other end. 'I mean fighting with her.'

'One moment,' said Auntie Issie, 'I'll go and find her and see if she is available for fighting.'

She put the phone down and called to Rosie, 'Rosie, there's a young man on the telephone called Sam, who would like to know if you would like to come and fight him.' There was a scrambling as she heard Rosie thundering down the stairs and, before she knew it, the phone had been snatched from her hand and Rosie was talking directly to Sam.

'Sam! Where are you? How did you know I was here?'

'Hello, Rosie. I gave Jack my details before I left yesterday and he sent me an email when he got to your Auntie's house to tell me you were staying in the village and how to contact you. He knew you would be very upset about not seeing your parents.' Rosie was quietly touched by her brother's thoughtfulness but equally knew it was a good way of getting her out of his hair!

'Well it seems that we are both staying in the same village for half term and I was very bored and wondered if you wanted to have a bit of practice?' continued Sam.

Rosie sighed, 'I'd love to, but I haven't brought all of the equipment home. I have not brought my foil.'

'Don't worry,' said Sam. 'We've got everything here and we can use the village hall, apparently, because there's nobody using it this afternoon, so we'll have plenty of space.'

'That would be fantastic,' said Rosie. 'But, how do I find you?'

Auntie Issie was hovering nearby, still contemplating what to give them for lunch. She whispered, 'Don't worry, I'll take you. I have to go down into Oldbury today.'

'That's great,' said Rosie. 'What time?'

'How about two o'clock?'

Auntie Issie heard this through the receiver. She was conscious that they had an update with the President at two o'clock and she whispered back, 'two thirty?'

'Two thirty,' said Rosie. 'Is that all right?'

'That's fantastic,' said Sam. 'I look forward to seeing you then.'

Rosie smiled and put the phone down. 'I'm going to go upstairs and sort out my kit,' she said, and disappeared.

Passing her on the stairs was Jack, who appeared in the kitchen. 'Auntie Issie, did I just hear you say you had to go into Oldbury this afternoon?'

'That's right,' said Auntie Issie. 'There are a few things I need to do.'

'Is there a library in Oldbury?' he asked.

Auntie Issie looked quizzically and said, 'Yes, of course there is. It's down by the canal. But you can use our computers to look anything up, Jack.'

'Would you mind if I came with you and you dropped me at the library whilst you went shopping?' Jack said. 'I just want to see some pictures in a reference book and I would rather see it in person.'

'No, not at all,' she said. 'Is there anything in particular that you are looking for?'

Jack gazed at her for a few seconds and said, 'I am not really sure but I will know when I see it,' and they left it at that.

'Well,' said Auntie Issie, 'I do have a library card somewhere if you want to get anything out. I will dig it out when we have had an early lunch, so lunch can go down before Rosie starts fencing.'

Auntie Issie reached further into the back of the fridge and found some ham and, together with the cheese her husband had just bought, and the fresh bread, would probably manage a lunch for the three of them and she set it out in the spring sunshine.

They ate their ham and cheese sandwiches and Auntie Issie had also managed to find a couple of bags of crisps in the back of the cupboard that she had hidden from Uncle Stanley, on the basis that he liked crisps too much but they didn't agree with his waistline.

No sooner had they finished eating, Rosie raced upstairs and came down with a long thin bag, which was almost as big as she was.

'What on earth is in there?' asked Auntie Issie.

'This is all my protective equipment,' she said. 'I need it so that I can fight Sam properly.'

Auntie Issie said, 'I'm not entirely sure that I approve of you fighting a boy. Surely he must be much stronger than you are.'

Rosie bristled in a way that Auntie Issie recognised immediately as being very similar to her mother, Auntie Issie's sister Grace, and Auntie Issie smiled to herself.

'In fencing you don't have to be strong, you have to be clever and agile and I could beat Sam any day of the week,' Rosie said, and dropped the long thin bag at Auntie Issie's feet.

'Well, I'm glad to hear it,' said Auntie Issie. 'I wouldn't like to think that any niece of mine was going to be second best to a mere boy.'

Jack appeared and he had his coat on and he had a small folder in his hand. 'Rosie,' he said, 'will you have a mobile phone with you, so that I can call you?'

Rosie looked at him quizzically, 'Yes,' she said, 'I have the holiday phone that Mum and Dad give us to use when we are not at the School.'

'Is that the same number as always?' he asked.

'Yes,' she said. 'I haven't changed it.'

'So, if I was to ring you when I was in Oldbury with a question, then you would be able to answer it?'

'Obviously,' she said.

'Good. Well, I'm going to the library because Auntie Issie's going to drop me off, so if I ring you there with a question, then please try and answer your phone, no matter where you are in the fight with Sam. Promise me.'

'I promise,' said Rosie.

'I will be fifteen minutes,' said Auntie Issie. 'I just need to pop down to Lavender Lane House to drop some things off with Cameron. Will you be OK?' Jack and Rosie nodded in unison.

The Land Rover pulled up outside Sam's parents' house and Rosie got out, as did Auntie Issie. She went into the house to say hello to Sam's mother briefly. As the door opened Sam came running out but checked himself straight away, aware that he should not look too keen. Jack jumped out and shook Sam's hand firmly, in a very grown up fashion. 'Great to see you again so soon and thanks so much for this, Rosie will be much happier knowing she has someone to fence with.'

'I am really pleased too,' said Sam. 'Thanks so much for your email; I was not sure if you would know how to send one being at the School.'

'Don't worry,' said Jack. 'I know my way around a computer. Now try not to damage her or I will have my parents to answer to!' and with that Jack jumped back into the Land Rover, buckled himself into his seatbelt, not a pink car seat to be seen. He was quite keen to get under way as soon as possible and was relieved when Auntie Issie appeared and got into the driver's seat.

Sam looked genuinely pleased to see Rosie and the two of them disappeared through the cottage gate chatting away.

'He seems a nice young lad,' said Auntie Issie. 'Does he go to the School?'

'Not yet,' said Jack. 'But I would be very, very surprised if he doesn't get into the School. I really liked him and I think he will do really well.'

'Good,' said Auntie Issie. 'You need good, solid people like Sam and I am delighted that he and Rosie have a common interest as that will really help me over the next week. Right, let's get down to the library then.'

As they set off, the road dropped down the hill and within five minutes they were into the thick fog that they had experienced on the way to Brighthaven.

'Is it always like this?' asked Jack.

'Not always, but we just go through periods of fog every few years,' said Auntie Issie, trying hard not to show any emotion. 'I am sure it will get better.' Although she said it, she did not really mean it. She had just had a difficult conversation with the President and they were now having to plan for the worst if they could not find the answer in the next day or so. Her heart was beating faster than it ever had and she tried not to let the worry show on her face. Jack glanced at her and somehow Auntie Issie knew that he suspected something was wrong.

The library in Oldbury was indeed down by the canal, where there were lots of swans and people feeding them. It was quite a modern building with glass, making it light and airy.

Auntie Issie pulled up outside and said, 'Are you absolutely sure you'll be fine?'

'Auntie Issie, please stop fussing,' said Jack. 'I don't want to take any books out, I just want to look at something for a reference.'

'Is there anything that I can help you with?' she said. 'Surely you could look that up on Google?'

'I could,' he said. 'But I prefer to look it up in books if you don't mind. It will help me with my studies when we go back to School.'

Auntie Issie shrugged, pressed £10 into his hand and said, 'Take this in case there are any problems and also take Uncle Stanley's mobile telephone,' and she pressed this into his hand as well. 'Uncle Stanley's phone is quite a basic one because he doesn't really know how to use them and he keeps dialling all his friends by mistake. So, all you need to do is to push up the top and then dial the number. Have you got Rosie's number?'

'Yes,' said Jack. 'I have written it down on my pad. If I need to ring her, I will.'

'Don't forget, they get very funny about noise in the library.'

'Auntie Issie, I know about libraries.'

'OK, well I just thought I'd mention it. I'm going to go to Waitrose and I'll probably be about three quarters of an hour. If there are any problems, I'll call you, but let's arrange that we will meet outside the library at half past three.'

'Half past three,' said Jack, 'unless I hear from you beforehand.'

He jumped out of the Land Rover and walked towards the library. He went in through the turnstile and walked along the rows looking for a specific section. He had forgotten now nice public libraries could be with all the books there in front of you. Of course, they had a fantastic library at School, but it was very much geared towards School studies and not general topics and novels that would appeal to grown ups.

He moved quickly through the sections until he got to Geography and started to study the books which were almost floor to ceiling. As he was doing this, Jack suddenly realised that he could not remember specifically what he was looking for. Jack sat down at a desk and opened up his folder. He remembered that before he had left Lavender Lane, he had written on the folder where he had been the previous year on holiday with his father and what the subject of the talk he was due to give at School had been. As he opened up the file, the page in front of him jumped out but was completely blank.

Jack had anticipated this and, for this reason, he pulled out Uncle Stanley's telephone, flipped open the top and rang his sister's number. It rang for quite a long time and Jack was about to curse and stop ringing when, eventually, a voice answered. It was very, very out of breath and it was Rosie.

'Huh, huh, is that you, Jack?'

'Yes, Rosie, it's me. Are you all right?'

'Huh, I'm fine, but he's just beaten me and I need to get him back.'

'Well I'm glad you're having a good time. I need to ask you something.'

'Huh, as long as I don't need to speak too much,' she said.

'You don't need to speak, Rosie, but you need to think. I want you to tell me where we went on holiday last year with Mum and Dad and what my talk was going to be at School.'

'Huh, that's easy,' she said. 'It was going to be all about the Galapagos Islands and all the lovely animals that we found there and the turtles that we swam with and Darwin's finches and how everything on the Islands either swam there or flew there.'

Jack wrote this down immediately on his pad. He looked away and started to talk to Rosie again. 'You're absolutely sure?' he said. 'Because sitting here, I have never heard of the Galapagos Islands.'

'Huh. Jack, you must be mad. It is the most amazing place in the world.'

Jack glanced down at the pad on which he had written the words Galapagos Islands and, to his absolute amazement, the words had disappeared.

'Rosie, I need you to keep talking to me.'

At that stage, somebody from a few feet across from Jack said, 'Shhhhsh,' and an Assistant immediately came rushing up and said, 'I'm sorry, young man, but you can't use mobile phones in here.'

'Thank you,' said Jack, 'I'm very sorry, but this is very important,' and he placed the receiver to his ear and said, 'Rosie, I'm just going to go quiet for a moment but what you need to know is that here I cannot remember what you tell me for more than a couple of seconds. What I'm now going to do is I'm going to go and check in the Geography books to see what we have.'

Rosie said, 'Don't forget that Charles Darwin wrote a book called 'Voyage of the Beagle' which was all about his time in the Galapagos Islands.'

'Of course,' said Jack. 'Keep talking to me, Rosie. I won't say anything here so that I don't get into trouble for talking, but you need to just keep telling me what I'm looking for.'

'SSSHHH,' said the library assistant as she moved towards Jack.

'Are you sick?' asked Rosie.

'No, I'm not sick, but there is just something really weird going on.' And Jack started to run towards geography.

He started moving toward the non fiction and said to the Assistant who had told him to be quiet, 'I'm looking for Charles Darwin's book, 'Voyage of the Beagle'. Can you tell me where I will find it?'

The assistant looked back at him blankly. 'I'm sorry, young man, I have not heard of the author Charles Darwin. Are you sure that you've got the right name?'

Rosie could hear this through the receiver. 'Jack, I can't believe that she's just said that! Who doesn't know who Charles Darwin is?'

'Please look,' said Jack. 'I just need to double-check.'

He moved behind the Assistant as they walked down the lines of books towards where somebody with the surname starting 'D' would have been found and, sure enough, there was no reference to Charles Darwin.

'OK,' said Jack. 'I want you to tell me if you have any books on the...' and he hesitated... 'Rosie, what was the name of the place that we went to?'

'The Galapagos Islands,' she said.

'The Galapagos Islands,' repeated Jack to the Assistant.

The Assistant looked at Jack blankly, 'The where?'

He said, 'Can we just look?' and he followed her again all the way down to the Geography section. They looked and there was nothing there.

'I'm sorry, young man. Again, I've not heard of this place. Is it possible that it's from a fictional book?'

'Could you just check your computers?' asked Jack, and they walked back towards her desk. She entered the search term 'Galapagos' and nothing came back.

'Put in 'Charles Darwin',' he said. Again there was nothing.

'I'm sorry,' she said.

On the end of the telephone, Rosie was saying, 'Jack, Jack! What is going on? I can't believe they don't know who Charles Darwin is and the Galapagos Islands. We've been there!'

'It's all right, Rosie,' said Jack. 'I'm going to be back soon. We're going to pick you up on the way through and so can you and Sam be ready, please. I think we need to talk to Uncle Stanley and Auntie Issie as soon as possible. I want you to remember this because I don't think that I will do by the time I get back to Lavender Lane. I want you to remember that at the library in Oldbury, they do not know who Charles Darwin is or the Galapagos Islands. Promise me you will remember. Tell Sam.'

'I'll tell him now. Don't be long, will you,' she said. 'This is really serious.'

'Right,' said the Assistant, 'that is it, give me the phone please, young man,' and she moved towards him with the air of authority. Jack jumped back and just as he did a figure stepped between him and the library assistant. Jack thought that perhaps he must be dreaming, or hallucinating. He closed his eyes and opened them again. But there, in a pair of jeans and a sweatshirt, dark skin glowing and looking as beautiful as ever, was JJ Buccannan.

'I must apologise for my friend,' she was saying to the assistant. 'He has been separated from his parents because of the volcano and they just managed to get through by telephone. I am sure you understand it is very important for him to speak to them.' The face of the library assistant softened.

'Oh how awful, poor lad,' she said with sympathy. 'I fully understand. But people in here like to have peace and quiet so you do need to keep noise down.'

'We understand,' said JJ politely. 'We were just going, weren't we, Jack?' she said smiling at Jack. It was all he could do to nod back and with that she took him by the arm and led him out of the library.

'What was all that about?' JJ asked as they got out onto the pavement. 'You looked white as a sheet.' They sat down on the bench outside and watched the swans.

'I don't know,' said Jack forlornly. 'There is something very strange going on and I know it is important but I can't remember what it is.'

'Are you ill?' asked JJ with real concern.

'No, not at all, I just know that there is something important I need to remember and I can't.'

'Do you want me to call someone for you?' asked JJ.

'No, my Auntie Issie will be here in a moment to pick me up. How come you are in Oldbury anyway?' asked Jack.

'My other Aunt and Uncle live here, so I was always coming to stay with them for half term. It's OK, a bit boring really because I do not know anyone because they all go to the local school. But I am going to do some horse riding and my aunt has promised to take me shopping in London.'

Jack watched the swans jumping for the bread being thrown to them. Then he sat upright.

'Are you doing anything this afternoon?' he said. 'It is just that you were at my half term talk and you saw everything that happened.'

'Your talk was amazing,' said JJ.

'But do you remember that at the start my slides did not work and my notes were blank?' asked Jack anxiously.

'Of course, but we all thought that was part of the show, to make it look like you were making something up on the spur of the moment, so it looked even more impressive.'

'I don't know what happened but I know there is something really scary going on and I might need some help. What are you doing now?' asked Jack.

'My Aunt and Uncle are both at work so I was just doing some shopping and would then go home later on. My cousin will be there and will cook me some supper,' said JJ who did not look that enthusiastic at the prospect.

'Come and have supper with us,' said Jack suddenly. 'I know my Aunt and Uncle won't mind, but I really need you to tell them what happened on the day of the talk as they think I was fooling around.'

JJ looked at Jack and tilted her head on one side; she smiled slightly and after a couple of seconds she said, 'I would love to. Can I use your phone to call my Aunt and let her know?'

Jack handed her the phone and she started to laugh. 'Don't say a word, it is my Uncle's; he is not very good with technology,' Jack said as JJ flicked up the top and worked out how to dial the number.

Having secured her Aunt's permission to have supper with Jack, JJ and Jack sat side by side on the bench outside the library waiting for Auntie Issie.

'Do you have any other brothers or sisters?' asked Jack. 'I can always lend you Rosie – I could let you have her for a good price.' JJ laughed.

'No,' she said. 'Just me...' She looked a little sad.

'Do you live with lots of different Aunts and Uncles or one in particular?' asked Jack as he clutched his folder and kept an eye on the traffic.

'I live with various aunts and uncles away from School, whoever can take me really.' She looked down at her feet, slightly sadly.

'But they must all be very proud of you?' asked Jack with a little bit of surprise. He wanted to say 'because you are beautiful, clever and the most brilliant archer' but was much too shy.

'I guess...' she said and just as she was about to go on, Jack spotted his Aunt's car approaching. It was such a huge tank of a vehicle it was quite hard to miss in fact.

'Here she is.' Jack grabbed JJ's arm and raced to the edge of the pavement. As his Aunt drew up Jack said, 'Auntie Issie, this is JJ, she is from the School and she is going to help me with something important this afternoon, I hope that is OK? Oh, and I also asked if she wanted to have supper...' Jack glanced at his Aunt with that 'this is really important' look and she knew immediately what he meant.

'Of course JJ, very nice to meet you at last, you are very welcome indeed.' Auntie Issie smiled warmly and shook JJ's hand. Jack glanced at her again with a look that said 'thanks' and the two of them jumped into the back of the Land Rover.

'Did you find what you were looking for?' asked Auntie Issie.

'Yes, I think so, or rather should I say that I didn't find what I was looking for,' said Jack.

'And can I ask what it was?' asked Auntie Issie.

'You can but I won't be able to answer because I can't remember,' said Jack. 'But I know someone who will. I told Rosie that we would pick her up on the way through. I hope that was all right.'

'Yes, of course,' said Auntie Issie. 'That's what I'd intended doing anyway.'

He said, 'Do you mind if Sam comes too, just to spend a little time with us this evening? I think he gets a bit bored at home.'

'We are going to have quite a party,' said Auntie Issie. 'But anything that keeps the two of you occupied is fine by me,' she said.

The journey back to Brighthaven was even more interesting than it had been on the way from School. The fog was even thicker than before and this time, as Auntie Issie turned off the main road to climb up to the village, the fog still lay thick around them until they were almost at the top. Auntie Issie was looking out of the window more than before and shaking her head as they passed out into bright sunshine. As they did, Auntie Issie seemed to accelerate the Land Rover down the lanes heading towards Sam's house; they pulled up outside and Auntie Issie applied the handbrake.

Sam's Mum came out when she saw the Land Rover pull up. Jack got out of the vehicle and moved towards her and held out his hand. 'How very nice to see you again,' he said.

'You too, Jack,' she said. 'I'm so sorry that we were a little disruptive when we visited the School.'

Jack smiled. 'Please don't worry. We see that all the time and it made me smile a great deal. I do like Sam and I do genuinely hope that he comes to the School because I think that we could be quite good friends.'

Mrs Bailey-Knox smiled back and said, 'Well, if it's any consolation, he said exactly the same thing about you and Rosie. They have had a lovely afternoon, fencing to within an inch of their lives. They are both pretty tired but I have made sure that they have had lots of water and although they are a bit red-faced, I think that they will be fine, provided they get to sit down for half an hour.'

Jack smiled and said, 'Rosie is a little bit like Auntie Issie's dog, Molly; she doesn't know when to stop or when she is exhausted.'

'No,' said Mrs Bailey-Knox. 'But I suspect that that's what will make her an Olympic fencer.'

'I've no doubt,' said Jack. 'And Sam isn't too bad either.'

'I know,' she said. 'We were so delighted when he discovered that he had such an aptitude for the sport. Anyway, I hope that your judo is coming on well.'

'Yes,' said Jack. 'I love that too, although it's a little bit harder to try and find people to fight in Brighthaven.'

'I don't know,' she said. 'You haven't tried yet.'

'No, that's perfectly true. We've only been here for half a day,' he said.

At that point, Rosie and Sam appeared around the corner, very red-faced, but smiling. Sam followed, carrying her large bag and a bottle of water.

Auntie Issie said, 'We had better get these two in the car before they fall over. I'll drop Sam back a little later.'

As Rosie walked round to the back door of the vehicle and pulled herself up she exclaimed with excitement as she discovered that JJ was sitting in the back. 'What are you doing here?' she said with genuine interest and surprise.

'I ran into your brother in the library in Oldbury. He invited me home for tea.' Rosie looked at her brother with that smug look and raised eyebrows. He scowled back out of sight of JJ 'come on'. He said, 'We have work to do.'

Something in the back of Rosie's brain stirred and she felt sure that she was supposed to tell Jack something but could not remember what. Like the thickening fog around them, she felt as if her brain was a little hazy. She put it down to exhaustion.

Rosie jumped into the back of the Land Rover and Sam followed. He leaned across and shook JJ's hand. 'Hello, I am Sam,' he said. 'I think I saw you at School the other day when I was being shown around.'

'Hello Sam, yes I remember, I was raking the gardens and you came around with Rosie. I assume you are hoping to come to the School?'

'Really hoping,' said Sam slightly sadly, as he realised it was what he wanted most in the world.

And, with that, Auntie Issie started it up and headed back towards Lavender Lane. In the car, Auntie Issie said, 'I just have to pop down to Cameron's house, who lives at the end of Lavender Lane, for about half an hour or so. We were supposed to have a call at 2 o'clock this afternoon but it got postponed, and it's going to take place in about half an hour. Will you four be all right on your own in the house?'

Jack looked at her with that 'What do you think?' question.

Auntie Issie smiled. 'I'm sorry, I keep forgetting that you are no longer five and three and that you are quite grown up now, but I thought I'd ask anyway.'

'We'll be fine,' said Jack. He was sure that there was something important he needed to do but he could not quite remember what.

They turned down into Lavender Lane and Auntie Issie pointed out the large house with the big sign, 'Lavender Lane House' outside it. 'That's where I'm going to be if there are any problems and I'll have the mobile as well. But I'll drop the four of you off and give you a cold drink and you can sit in the garden and play with the dogs until we get back.'

'No problem at all,' said Jack, and the warm March sun was still shining, which was a surprise to everybody really.

Auntie Issie dropped them all off, rooted in the fridge for some cold drinks and glasses, placed them all on the kitchen table and then turned the Land Rover round and headed back towards Lavender Lane House.

CHAPTER FOUR

The four of them grabbed a cold drink and went into the garden and sat at the oak garden table and looked out across the amazing view that Auntie Issie and Uncle Stanley had from the back of their garden. It was across fields and hills and although it was slightly marred by the mist in the centre of the valley, it was, nevertheless, beautiful.

'The fog was really bad coming back,' said Jack. 'You could hardly see where you were going, but up here it seems fine.'

Sam said, 'It's been like that for the last few weeks. Everywhere seems to have the mist and it seems to be getting higher and higher. We joke and say that Brighthaven will never get it because we are closest to God.'

'But it is really weird,' chipped in Rosie. 'It is almost like the fog gets into your head as well, and makes you forget. I am sure that there are things that I am supposed to remember but I can't remember what it is...' She looked at the other three and felt sure that they did not quite understand what she was talking about but they looked at her sympathetically.

Just at that point a grey squirrel dropped out of the branch of the lilac tree and landed on the lawn directly in front of them, on all fours with a very startled look on its face. Its little ears were perked up and the small tufts on the top quivered as it watched them closely, completely still. Its mouth then appeared to drop open. Rosie let out a laugh and then Molly spotted the small furry creature on the lawn and the chase began.

The squirrel ran up the tree and Molly was in hot pursuit. She launched herself at the bottom of the tree, trying to climb it like the squirrel but obviously not being as agile or as small. When she realised she could not follow she started to bark at the bottom of the tree and the squirrel scurried up the trunk and along the topmost branch. At that point, with nowhere left to go, the squirrel stopped and looked down at Molly, who by this stage was on her hind legs barking wildly.

'Molly be quiet!' said Jack with the authority he had heard his aunt and uncle use. Molly's ears flattened on her head and she lay down on the grass looking forlorn. 'You will never catch it,' he said sternly and Molly's head drooped even further. Then Jack smiled and snapped his fingers and Molly came bounding over to have her head stroked.

'Do we get red squirrels in England?' asked Rosie as she slurped her drink loudly and her brother raised an eyebrow in the same way that he had seen his mother do.

'Excuse me,' said Rosie quietly and glanced across at Sam in embarrassment.

'Apparently,' said Sam very knowledgeably, 'grey squirrels have evolved so that they wake up much earlier from hibernation and so they go out and nick all the food, which means that when the red squirrels wake up, there is nothing for them to eat, so they starve to death. Because of that, there are only a few places in England where they still survive, although you get them in Scotland because they don't have many grey squirrels.'

'That sounds really mean,' said Rosie. 'Why can't they all live together nicely and then we could have them both in the garden for Molly to chase.' With that Molly raised her head with ears alert at the thought she may be required for something. Rosie laughed. 'Not yet Molly, but one day when I am Prime Minister I will change it all.'

Jack sighed. 'Rosie, no matter how terrible, it is nature, it is called survival of the fittest and the red squirrels have adapted that way. You can't change nature can you?'

'Not according to that American man on the television,' said JJ. 'The politician who they think will be the next President, he said that we were all created by God... I am really surprised that no-one has mentioned Darwin's finches to him and his theory of evolution.'

Jack's heart missed a beat as he realised just how clever JJ was; he would certainly have to up his game if he wanted to impress her... and as he gazed at her admiringly he realised that what JJ was saying was absolutely right. In the big race to be the next President of the United States and live in the White House a new politician had come from nowhere, who was a 'creationist' and had persuaded many people that his theory was correct, that we were all created by God and that nature had no hand in it at all. He realised that not one person though seemed to have mentioned Charles Darwin or his theory of evolution, certainly not in the articles he had read or the news reports he had seen.

'Jack,' said Rosie almost absent-mindedly. 'You asked me to remind you about something.'

'Did I?' said Jack, distracted by the thought of America.

'Yes. You've asked me to remind you that you wanted to give a talk about the Galapagos Islands and Charles Darwin and that when you went to the library, you couldn't find any reference to it.'

'Did I?' asked Jack.

'Yes,' she said. 'You said that when you got back to Brighthaven you wouldn't remember what had happened in the library.'

He said, 'I don't.'

'You said that you wouldn't remember that you asked about books on the Galapagos Islands and books on Charles Darwin and they didn't have any at all.'

It was at this stage that Jack looked across Sam's shoulder, at the squirrel still sitting in the tree and he leapt to his feet. 'Oh my goodness!' he shouted with an exclamation, leaping to his feet and almost knocking over his drink.

'What's wrong?' asked Sam also leaping to his feet, looking around him, thinking they were under some sort of attack.

'There is something very weird going on,' said Jack. 'I think it has to do with Charles Darwin and the Galapagos Islands.'

'I don't like it,' said Rosie. 'I'm frightened.'

Jack put a comforting hand on her shoulder. 'Don't be frightened, Rosie,' he said. 'It is nothing to be scared of, but just something very odd that I think we need to tell Auntie Issie about.'

'Right,' said Jack. 'We need to find Auntie Issie and Uncle Stanley.' Molly and Charlie leapt to their feet at the sound of their master's name.

'You two have to stay here.' They both lay down, heads on their paws, ears flat. 'I mean it!' The dogs appeared to sink even lower and looked down at the floor.

'Right,' said Jack, running towards the back gate. 'They are only just down at the end of Lavender Lane. We need to go and tell them that there is something very weird going on and I think it is all to do with Charles Darwin and the disappearance of the Galapagos Islands.'

All four children ran to the garden gate. Rosie pulled it open but before she could secure it with the two dogs shut in the garden, Charlie had already pushed his way through and Molly followed quickly.

'We don't have time to put them away,' said Jack. 'The grownups need to know what's going on. This is really serious.' And he started running in the direction of Lavender Lane House. The other three followed and Charlie and Molly started to run too, quickly overtaking the children and almost leading the way. It took about three minutes to run down to Lavender Lane House and turn in between the two big hedges and across the gravel drive.

They all slowed and stopped in front of the large front door and Jack knocked on it. There was no answer. He knocked louder and still no answer.

'I know there're here,' he said. 'That's what Auntie Issie said.'

'Let's go around the back,' said Sam.

'Isn't that a bit rude?' asked Rosie. 'We don't really know these people at all. We can't go snooping round their house.'

Jack pointed to the mist that was by now only a few hundred metres away from the house. 'I can't help but think that that mist is going to engulf all of us very soon,' he said. 'And I think that we know something that's very important. I think we could at least try. What's the worst that's going to happen? We'll just get told off.'

'I agree,' said JJ, and they opened the gate which led into a garden area. In the middle of the garden was a swimming pool. This was completely fenced and, on the opposite side to where Jack, Sam and Rosie were stood, they could see another gate. Jack ran up, pulled back the bolt and pulled the gate open. Charlie and Molly went straight through without waiting to be invited.

What they could not see was that inside Lavender Lane House a small red light started to flash and after a few seconds a hand moved up and switched it off. The hand then picked up the telephone next to the light. 'Problem?' said a man's voice.

As the children came round the side of the house, Jack suddenly ducked down below the window ledge and the others followed instinctively.

'What's wrong?' whispered Sam.

'Look at the windows,' said Jack, quietly. 'They are reflective. I can see myself in them, which means that the people inside can probably see us.'

'Oh my gosh!' said Rosie. 'Why would the people living here

want that when they've got such a lovely view and sun all day? And, why are they such a funny colour?'

'Keep your voice down,' said Jack. 'The window's open slightly over there and whoever is inside might hear us.'

Rosie whispered, 'Well, I thought it was Auntie Issie and Uncle Stanley who were inside.'

'I'm not so sure anymore,' said Jack. 'I'm not really sure what to think, but I know that we ought to crawl along and see if we can hear anything. I bet you're glad you haven't got a Princess dress on now,' he said to Rosie, looking at her in her tracksuit bottoms.

She poked out her tongue at him and all four of them started to crawl along the grass underneath the window ledge, closely followed by the two dogs, who obviously thought that this was now a great game. As they got closer to the open window, they could hear voices but it was hard to make out what was being said, so they crawled even closer.

A voice that they didn't recognise could be heard coming from inside. 'And we really have no idea?' he was saying in a very strong American accent.

'No, Mr President, I'm afraid not. The mist is getting closer and we have had our researchers working on this day and night since it started and I'm afraid that we are no further forward.'

Jack recognised that voice as being Uncle Stanley. He wasn't sure who this 'Mr President' chap was that he was talking to but that was definitely Uncle Stanley's voice in the conversation.

All four of the children exchanged glances and settled themselves down below the window sill where they couldn't be seen, to listen to the rest of the conversation. Charlie lay on Jack's feet and Molly on Rosie's.

Whilst Jack knew that it was rude to listen to other people's conversations if you weren't taking part in it, somehow he knew that this was important.

A lady's voice joined the conversation and this was a voice that Jack thought he did recognise, and it was not the voice of Auntie Issie. 'Mr President, this team have been fantastic over many, many years, and have averted so many disasters, I can't tell you. We are all as disappointed as you are that on this occasion it looks likely that they are not going to be able to stop the mist finally engulfing Lavender Lane. Once that happens we don't know what will happen but judging by the recent natural disasters we can only assume that this will get worse.'

There was a deep sigh from the man that they called 'Mr President'. 'I know that you have all done everything you possibly could, it just seems these guys are cleverer than us and have covered their tracks too much this time. It seems that there is nothing that we can find anywhere that tells us what they intend to change in history. I'm very grateful to you all. I know how much hard work you have put into this, but I guess I'm going to have to brief the citizens of the United States of America and prepare them for the worst.'

The lady's voice that Jack thought he recognised, chipped in at that stage. She said, 'Yes, I too will have to prepare to tell the British people what is happening. The mist is approaching so rapidly now, I think that it's going to be a matter of hours and so I will stand by to do the broadcast at the same time as you, Mr President. I never thought I would say that evil has won but I guess it had to happen in the end sooner or later. We have done all we possibly can to find out what part of history is changing and we have not succeeded.'

It was at this point that Jack leapt to his feet from beneath the window before any of the others could pull him back down again. As his head appeared in the window, silhouetted against the light, everybody in the room turned round as they heard Jack bang into the open window.

'I know,' he shouted. 'I know what's happening.'

Jack looked down into the room; the floor was much lower than he had anticipated and it was quite a drop from the window down to the people below. He recognised a few faces – his aunt and uncle, and Alfie and Angela Parker who lived opposite, who they have met a few times. There was also Adam, whose children he had played with a few times when he had visited for the afternoon.

There was a stunned silence from within the room, and Jack's eyes moved from the people that were facing him to the large video screen on the wall, where, looking back at him was a very distinguished looking gentleman whose face he instantly recognised. This was, Jack believed, the President of the United States. What was more, the President appeared to be watching him.

'And, who is this?' asked the American gentleman, in a kindly way, as if he was talking to a grandchild.

Most of the people in the room looked at each other and shrugged their shoulders as they had no idea at all who the young man stood before them was.

'This is my nephew, Mr President,' said Auntie Issie. She shuffled forward, looking slightly embarrassed. 'He and his sister are staying with us as they were unable to fly home to be with their parents for the holiday.' She said it in a slightly exasperated way and Jack knew that he was probably in a bit of trouble.

'Are you on your own, young man?' asked the American President.

'No Sir, I've got my sister with me,' and Rosie stepped into view.

'And Sam,' said Rosie.

'As in Sam Bailey-Knox?' asked Cameron.

'Yes Sir, as in Sam Bailey-Knox.' And, at that point, Sam lifted himself up from his crouched position beneath the window frame.

'Anyone else?' asked the President looking more incredulous at the appearance of three children at a time of great national concern.

JJ stood up shyly and flicked back her dark hair. The President looked at her quizzically as if to say 'anyone else'?

'Just Molly and Charlie,' said Jack.

'There are six children outside the window?' asked the President.

'Oh no, Sir, they're not children, they're dogs.' At which point Molly and Charlie appeared at the window with their front paws resting on the window ledge. Because Charlie was a lot bigger than Molly, who was still only three, she could only just reach the window ledge, but her nose and ears were enough for the President to realise that Jack had not been joking when he'd said that there were also two dogs.

The lady on the screen, who did not appear to be in the same location as the President, but was nevertheless watching intently what was going on, now spoke.

'Well, young man. Do you have a name?' she asked Jack.

'Yes, Madam,' he said in his politest voice. 'I'm called Jack and you're the Prime Minister, aren't you?'

'I am indeed, young Jack, and I am afraid that your Aunt and Uncle and all of the people here in this room are all trying to deal with something really, really serious and important and I know that you are probably bored in the holidays but we do need to try and finish what we were talking about as quickly as possible. So if I could ask you all to go home, and you need to remember that you must not discuss with anybody what you've seen here today.'

'But...' said Jack. As he opened his mouth to say something, the President held up his hand to stop him.

'Jack, this is very, very important. Please, we must finish our work.'

Rosie pushed herself to the front of the group of children. 'But

Mr President, I know that you're really important and all that, but Jack knows what's going on.'

The President smiled in a kind, fatherly way, as if he was indulging a small child who had asked for more sweets from the shop.

'My dear girl,' he said. 'We have the finest brains who have been working on this for weeks and still they have no idea what is happening and, with the greatest of respect to young Master Jack, he cannot possibly even understand what we are discussing, never mind know what the answer is.'

Sam stepped forward at this stage, 'Well, with the greatest of respect, Sir, you're wrong. I know you run a big country and everything, and you do a lot of good things, but I think you should just hear what my friend has to say.'

Auntie Issie stepped forward and held up a hand to tell the children to be quiet. She turned to the screen and addressed the President directly. 'Mr President, even if my nephew does know what is going on, you understand the implications… If he is the one who discovers it, then he is the only one who can put it right.'

Jack, Rosie, JJ and Sam looked at one another. Even the dogs exchanged glances.

'Issie,' said the President. 'If this young man knows what is going on, he may just be about to save the planet.'

'But, Sir,' she said. 'Even if he is right, and the Gate opens, he is a child.'

The President paused for a moment. 'I appreciate all that you are saying, Issie, but at the moment he is our only hope. Master Jack, rather than address this through the window, could I suggest that you come round and into the room.'

'Only if we can all come,' said Jack.

The Prime Minister spoke, 'I think we could probably leave the dogs outside.' At which point Molly and Charlie's ears flattened on their heads.

'No,' said Jack, 'we all come,' and their ears perked up again.

'I'll go round and fetch them,' said Cameron. 'Come back round where you started and meet me by the front door,' he said to the children and disappeared out through the large steel door at the back of the room.

Jack, Rosie, JJ and Sam ran back through the gardens of the house, opening and closing the gates behind them and waited patiently by the front door, Charlie and Molly sitting at their feet. Cameron opened the large door to Lavender Lane House and looked down at them all. Without a word he held open the door and they all traipsed in; Jack led the way and Molly brought up the rear.

Inside it seemed like a normal house with a corridor and many pictures of Cameron in military uniform. About halfway down the corridor was a door and Cameron pulled it open and it appeared to lead down to a cellar.

The children exchanged glances as this did not look as if it belonged to the house that they had been outside – it looked much too modern and secret. It crossed their mind that they were about to be placed in a cupboard and left there until the grown-ups had finished their conversation. Charlie moved to the front of the pack and stepped through the doorway; he sniffed with his nose very close to the ground and, having much better eyesight in the darkness, he soon ascertained that there was no danger and he looked back over his shoulder. He gave a short, sharp bark and then led the way down the staircase. The children and Molly followed.

They walked down a steel staircase and at the bottom was a large steel door. Cameron put his hand on it and put his eye up to the hole in the middle. A computer voice said, 'Fingerprint and retina scan complete. Welcome Cameron,' and the door clicked open. The children exchanged nervous glances again.

Behind the steel door was a room with carpet and a small

kitchenette and chairs. On the other side of the room was a second steel door. Cameron approached it and went through the same process again. The voice said again, 'Fingerprint and retina scan complete. Welcome Cameron.' There was a click and the door opened. The stairs led up again into the room that they had seen from the window and in it, everyone was stood where the children had left them.

Sam turned to Jack and said, 'Wow, look at this! It's like something out of James Bond. It's so secure.'

'Not that secure,' said Jack, 'if you can walk round the back and climb in through the window.'

Cameron heard this and tried hard not to smile. 'We don't usually have the windows open, but it was very hard to detect how far up the valley the mist had come because of the tinting on the windows,' he said with a smile. 'Alarms had already gone off, telling us that you were there, and you would not have been able to get any further into the room, as there is a magnetic force field around the room. Also,' he said, 'a team of SAS soldiers were in the garden with their weapons trained on you, but, as you were children, they didn't think it appropriate to shoot.'

'There was no-one else out there,' said Jack with an air of authority.

'I'll show you.' Cameron walked Jack to the open window and they looked out. Cameron raised his voice slightly and said, 'Bravo One, stand up please,' and, mysteriously, from what appeared to be a hedge line stood the figure of a man dressed in camouflage. A man wielding a large rifle. 'Bravo Two,' said Cameron, and further down the hedge line emerged a second figure. 'Bravo Three.' From the tree at the end of the garden, a man's face appeared, camouflaged, of course, and he, too, was carrying a large rifle.

Jack's mouth dropped slightly. 'You weren't joking.'

'No, Jack, I wasn't joking. And the four of you were extremely lucky.'

Sam turned back and the man on the screen was still there. He wasn't sure if this was live and whether or not he could actually be heard by the President of the United States, but before he could ask the question, the President spoke.

'Master Jack,' he said. 'I understand that you believe that you know what the problem is.' He looked directly at Jack. Rosie, JJ and Sam instinctively moved up and stood closer to him.

'Sir, before I tell you, could you please explain what's going on here?'

The Prime Minister, who was on the second screen, interrupted, 'We're not really sure that we have the time for this, Jack. If we don't stop this thing now, then no amount of explanation is going to help us.'

'But,' he said, turning back to the President, 'I heard what my Auntie said about me being the only one who could help and I really just want to understand what I'm letting myself in for. You won't know this, Mr President, but my parents have already lost one son and if I am to do something dangerous, then I need to do it knowing exactly what I will be letting myself in for. It's not that I'm frightened, it's just that I have my sister to consider.'

Rosie stood closer.

'I understand entirely, Jack,' said the President, 'and I commend you for your thoughtfulness to others. It will take us a matter of minutes to explain what is going on and I feel it is only fair to do so in the circumstances. Issie, he is your nephew, I think that that task should fall to you.'

'Sit down,' said Auntie Issie. The children looked around and found themselves the nearest seat and Molly lay down at Jack's feet, but Charlie attempted to climb up into a seat himself, something that he normally did at home.

'Charlie!' said Auntie Issie, and he looked at her, realising that perhaps this was not the appropriate time and climbed down off the chair and settled right up against Rosie's legs.

'You know that we have always joked that Brighthaven has some kind of cloaking device over it, because nobody ever knows where it is?' She looked at Jack.

'Yes,' said Jack. 'That's always been a joke for as long as I can remember.'

'Well,' said Auntie Issie. 'It's not really a joke, it's reality. You see Brighthaven is a very special place because it's the only place in the world where the History Keepers live.'

'History Keepers?' said all four children at the same time, eyes wide.

'Who are they?' asked Rosie.

'You are looking at them, well most of them,' said Auntie Issie gesturing to the people in the room. 'Beneath the foundations of the Lane are the archives and records of absolutely everything that has happened in the world since records began.'

'The residents of Lavender Lane have, for many centuries, guarded the archives. Although the fact that they should live in Lavender Lane always appears to be a coincidence, it is nothing of the sort,' she said. 'The first thing that they must have is a knowledge and interest in key areas: arts, history, military, archaeology, philosophy, ancient civilisations, farming, parenting, teaching, law, sports. But knowledge is not enough. There are lots of very many clever and well read people in the world. But, to live in Lavender Lane, they must also have what outsiders would refer to as a 'sixth sense'.'

'What's one of those?' asked JJ.

'Well,' said Angela. 'Does it happen to you that sometimes you are thinking about something and another person starts talking about that very same subject?'

Cameron then said, 'You dream about something and then it comes true, or you wish hard enough for something and it happens?'

Jack looked up. 'Sometimes, yes. Sometimes it does.'

'Well,' said Auntie Issie. 'It's not magic. This is not Harry Potter. We don't have wands and cast spells and have magic schools, but we are just able to feel things and sense things and almost predict things sometimes without it being too specific. As you get older, you will meet people in life who are very good at predicting who is going to come first in a race, for instance.'

'What else,' asked Rosie. 'How else can we tell?'

'Well,' said Uncle Stanley. 'These people love animals and animals love them.'

Jack could feel Charlie and Molly snuggling up closer to his legs. 'OK,' he said. 'I think I understand about that, so you have clever people with a sixth sense who like animals and look after the archives. But why is it that we have the President of the United States on a video screen and also our Prime Minister?'

The President interrupted. 'The million dollar question,' he said gently.

Uncle Stanley stepped forward. 'The History Keepers are here to make sure that history is not changed. Because if it is then Lavender Lane will eventually be engulfed by the mist and Evil will take over the archives. History will be changed any way that they want it to be changed and life as we know it will change forever.'

There was a stunned silence in the room as the children took in the enormity of what they were being told. Jack closed his gaping mouth. He could not think of anything to say. It was JJ who was thinking sensibly:

'But how can anyone change history?' It was a reasonable question.

The grown-ups looked at one another and Auntie Issie stepped forward. 'Everyone who lives in this area knows that during the time of Oliver Cromwell the village of Brighthaven was a Roundhead village and across the fields in Saddleworth, they were Cavalier, so there was always great competition and difficulty between them. However, what they don't know is that the problem was a lot deeper than that. Lavender Lane had twin brothers who were History Keepers. Everyone thought that they were Roundheads but in fact one of them secretly became a Cavalier and moved to Saddleworth. He was less interested in guarding the secrets of history and more interested in trying to change it.' Auntie Issie paused; it was clearly a difficult thing for them all to understand, even after so long.

'He was a clever man and knew that for every positive there was a negative, so that if we had a positive Gate into history, he must be able to find the negative Gate. It took him a while to find it and we don't know how he did it, but he did. In the same way as Lavender Lane built up the History Keepers, Saddleworth built up the Destroyers, who go back through the negative Gate and try and change something important.'

'But how can you tell?' asked Sam. 'Can't they just start doing things and you would not know?'

Uncle Stanley perched on the side of the desk: 'Luckily for us we start to get signs. We get floods and volcanoes, drought and fires. That tells us that something is happening and then we have to use our skill and knowledge in trying to work out what they have done.'

'Does this happen a lot then?' asked Rosie, her eyes wide with disbelief.

'They take time to plan what they will change and they are clever. They won't do something massive which will quickly become obvious, they change something that will not have an immediate effect and we have to use all of our resources to work out what it is. We probably have a couple of serious attempts every year, but we have never got this close before.' Auntie Issie suddenly looked very tired.

'But why can't they just come up here and use your Gate?'

asked JJ.

Cameron smiled; he recognised a bright girl when he saw one. 'They hate animals which is why Lavender Lane and the whole of Brighthaven is filled with animals. We all have dogs and cats and there are cattle in the fields. But slowly with the mist, they drive all the animals inside. Even this morning we had to move the highland cows from the field as they were too wet and cold. The more the days go by and we do not unlock what they are doing the mist gets thicker and colder until eventually we are overtaken by it and they will be in. It has never happened so we do not know how it will work in practice but we do know that it will be the end of the world as we know it.'

Sam laughed. 'But with all of those security guys out there,' he pointed out of the window, 'and the might of the USA, it must be easy to stop a few people getting into Lavender Lane?'

'If only it were that easy,' said Uncle Stanley, 'but the problem is we do not know what they look like or who they are, so we would not know who to stop. When we realise what they are doing, the person who guesses it is permitted to enter through the Gate and has to stop history being changed.'

'Has anyone failed?' asked Jack.

'No, Jack, in all the hundreds of years we have managed to guess what they are doing and go back in time and stop it. But this time we don't even know what it is they have done.'

Jack looked at his Aunt and Uncle and turned to look at his little sister. He looked thoughtful and concerned. Charlie and Molly sat upright and alert. Charlie whined a little and Jack patted his head and flicked Molly's ears the way she liked. He stood up to his full height and walked towards the screen where the kindly gentleman was watching him intently.

'Mr President,' he nodded to the screen and turned to the smaller screen, 'Prime Minister,' and nodded to Amy Jones. 'Two years ago I went to the Galapagos Islands on holiday with my family – Rosie included.' He gestured back towards his sister. 'I am sure, being very eminent and clever people that you will know that this was where Charles Darwin was when he discovered his theory of evolution. Everything on the island either swam there or flew there. However, I have discovered that all references to the Galapagos Islands have disappeared from the library, together with all mention of Charles Darwin. When I am not in Lavender Lane I cannot remember this holiday. I was due to do a talk at the School all about the trip and all my slides were blank as were my notes. I could not remember what I was due to talk about. So I think that the history that is changing is that Charles Darwin is not going to find the Galapagos Islands and is never going to publish his book...'

Uncle Stanley put his head in his hands. 'I knew there was something I had to remember!' Auntie Issie put her hand on his shoulder. 'Don't worry darling, they are getting close, it is even starting to affect us.'

It was at that stage that a large red telephone on the desk in front of them started to ring. Auntie Issie picked it up and a voice at the other end said something.

Auntie Issie looked at the President and the Prime Minister and took a deep breath. 'That was Alfie... the Gate is open.'

'Praise the Lord,' said the President. 'Thank you, Jack, you are a very brave young man. Now we have little time, I will leave you to prepare. And good luck.' The screen went blank.

'Your country is very proud of you, Jack,' said the Prime Minister. 'Safe journey,' and her screen also went blank.

Everyone in the room looked at one another. Jack, Rosie, JJ and Sam weren't entirely sure why they were looking at each other in that way but it seemed that the occasion called for it.

'What happens now?' asked Jack.

Auntie Issie started packing up the things on her desk. 'We must get to the Gate as quickly as possible. Just to make sure,' she said.

Cameron picked up the telephone closest to him. He didn't dial a number but someone was obviously at the other end. 'All parties exiting now, please hold your fire.' Jack realised that he must have been talking to the hidden guards in the garden who had so nearly stopped him, Rosie, JJ and Sam in their tracks, and, with Angela leading the way, they all traipsed up the spiral staircase, back into the main part of the house, out through Cameron's front door and, in almost a run, they set off down Lavender Lane in the direction of Angela's house.

Charlie and Molly trotted along at the heels of Rosie and Jack, their heads down, ears alert. As they passed the first house, which belonged to the two professors Max and Ella, Max shouted to the open window, 'Ella, come at once, the Gate is open.'

They moved past Adam's bungalow, empty as Amelia and the children were away. Adam ran ahead and knocked on the front door of Michael and Martha's as the rest of the party was passing. Michael came to the door and understood immediately. 'Martha, get your coat,' he said.

It was at that stage that Alice appeared from the cottage behind Michael and Martha's, wheeling the bin, ready for the next day's collection. She saw the entourage as it marched down Lavender Lane and, knowing immediately what was happening, fell in behind the last of the troop.

And so it was that the Keepers of this ancient and secret Gate strode on down Lavender Lane, past Rose Cottage and eventually arriving at Alfie and Angela's house, Homegarth. Its thatch gleamed yellow in the sunshine and although they could see the mist making its way up the hill towards Lavender Lane, its advance appeared to have stopped completely. They passed what appeared to be the front door of Homegarth, which was never normally used for visitors, other than to filter out those who truly knew Lavender Lane from those who pretended to, and round to the back door.

The stable door at the back led into the large kitchen. The top of the door was open and the bottom part closed and bolted. Angela leaned over and unbolted it and they poured in one by one. Jack noticed immediately that most of the room was taken up by a large Aga. He knew that Auntie Issie had always wanted an Aga, but there was not really much room in her small cottage, and now he understood why. But this was no time to discuss the furnishings of the houses and it quickly became clear that they weren't stopping in the kitchen anyway. They all filed past the Aga and through into the room behind, which had an enormous fireplace, but no fire, and a large model of a steam train on the windowsill.

There were three doors to this room, the one they had come through, one in the far left hand corner, which clearly led through to another room, and the one which now stood directly in front of them, to the right of the fireplace.

This door was not completely shut; it was slightly ajar and radiating out from the edges of the doorframe was the brightest light that Jack had ever seen. It was so bright that it was unnatural.

'It's definitely open,' came a voice from behind them, and Jack spun round to see Angela's husband Alfie stood behind them, propped up on the gap between the kitchen and this room, studying the door intently.

'Have you opened it further?' asked Auntie Issie, as she stepped closer to the door and examined around its edges.

'Not yet,' said Alfie. 'I wanted to wait for you to arrive, as I needed to understand why it had opened.' He looked again at the group in front of him and blinked. 'What are the children doing here?' he asked earnestly.

'Jack opened it,' said Rosie very proudly. 'He guessed what was going on when nobody else could.'

Alfie looked at his wife, Angela. 'Is this right?' he asked.

'I'm afraid so,' said Angela.

Jack stepped forward. 'They explained it to me and I knew what I was doing,' he said with authority but looking more nervous than he sounded.

Adam stepped forward. 'We cannot allow a child to try and close the Gate,' he said solemnly.

Jack stepped forward. 'Could people please stop talking about us as if we were not here and stop referring to me as 'a child',' he said. 'I am 13. I also know that I am the only person who can go through the Gate because I was the one to solve the puzzle, and so unless I have misunderstood that explanation, you can complain as much as you want about the fact that I am younger than you, but you will still not be able to get through the Gate.'

'Well said, young man,' said Michael. 'Well, we had better check and ensure that the Gate is definitely open then,' and they all turned back to inspect the door in Alfie and Angela's dining room.

They all stared as a bright light came out from under the door and got brighter as Alfie pulled it open a little more and then suddenly light shone from all around the edges, and it was so bright and intense that it reflected off the faces of everybody stood in the room, turning them a pale yellow colour.

'Is that the Gate?' asked Jack, although it wasn't really a question that he needed to ask, but he felt that he ought to in front of his friends and his sister.

Alfie stepped forward and felt his way around the edge of the door. 'It is indeed,' he said, sighing in a resigned way.

'Is it stuck?' asked Rosie.

'No,' said Alfie. 'It's just that the light is so bright, I don't want to open it fully until we know that we want to use it, but I also need to check that there is nothing blocking it or holding it back for when we do need to move.'

Jack turned to his Aunt. 'Auntie Issie, have you been through the Gate?'

Auntie Issie smiled. 'You've got to promise not to tell your mother, but, yes, many times, Jack.'

'What happens when you get through the Gate? Is it like being on another planet?' he asked.

'Well, not quite,' said Auntie Issie. 'The Gate will take you back to the time period that the Destroyers are trying to change.'

Rosie looked up. 'So, there'll be real people there?'

'Yes,' said Auntie Issie. 'Real people but just from the past.'

'And, is everything else from the past?' asked Jack.

Uncle Stanley stepped forward. 'It's just like you have been transported back to the days when Charles Darwin was sailing through the Galapagos Islands.'

Jack's eyes widened. 'So it might open into the sea then?'

Angela laughed. 'No, Jack, it won't open into the sea. The Gate is very sensible. It will open up somewhere where it knows that you can make a difference.'

Sam stepped forward and frowned. 'So, Jack would then have to try and stop whatever was going to happen so that history won't be changed. Is that right?'

Alfie looked up from the Gate and smiled. 'You've got it in one,' he said. 'Evil is at work and they are already fairly advanced in their plans. That's why we have so many natural disasters and that's why the mist is so far up the hill. They are very close to achieving a change in history which will be catastrophic to all of us. Jack needs to find them and find what they are doing and stop them.'

Rosie slumped down on the seat in front of her. 'But he's only 13. How could he do all that on his own?'

Auntie Issie sighed. 'That brings me back to my point in the first place. We just can't let Jack go through the Gate. He's too young. And, what's more, my sister will kill me.'

Jack looked up at his Aunt and he had a very serious grown up expression. 'Auntie Issie, from what you are telling me, if we don't do it, then there will be no world as we know it and Mum can be as cross as she likes but none of us will be around to appreciate it.'

'Can't fault the logic,' said Adam.

'But why can't somebody else go?' asked Rosie, almost in desperation. 'Why does it have to be my brother?'

Jack went and sat next to his sister. 'We knew the rules, Rosie, and you don't need to worry about me. I will be absolutely fine.'

'But I want to go with you,' she said.

'That's just not possible. You can't go everywhere with me.' Jack looked at his sister and smiled. 'Sometimes, Rosie, we just have to do the right thing.'

'But I want to come with you,' she said mournfully.

'I know you do, but you can't and that is the end of it.' He tried to sound like his father when he was saying no to something.

'But it's just not fair,' said Rosie, turning to the grown-ups in the room. 'Why would this silly Gate thing only let one person through. Why won't it let us through too?'

Alfie came and sat next to her on the other side. 'It's a question we've often asked ourselves,' he said. 'But it seems to be the Gate's way of stopping everybody coming through, that it will only let through the people who know what the problem is and have worked it out for themselves.'

'But if we all stand together,' said Rosie, 'we would be like one grown-up and perhaps it wouldn't notice.'

Everybody laughed. 'You are definitely your mother's daughter,' said Angela. 'Ever logical.'

It was at this point that Sam stepped forward. 'Can I ask,' he said, 'what do you mean by 'close the Gate'? How would Jack do that?'

'Right,' said Angela, 'I am putting the kettle on. We are going to have a cup of tea and we are going to have a full and frank discussion about this,' and off she marched in the direction of the enormous Aga, opened the lid and plonked the large kettle full of water on top of it.

The men went from room to room, collecting chairs and stools and big cushions, until eventually there were enough for everyone to sit on. When all the tea was served, together with biscuits covered with thick chocolate, Rosie looked at them all and asked:

'But how will he know how to act and to dress, and how will he know who he'll meet?'

'Well,' said Adam, sitting down in front of her. 'It sounds to me as if the problem is going to come either before Darwin gets to the Galapagos Islands or whilst he is there. As you and Jack have already been to the Galapagos Islands, it sounds like Jack has probably got a head start because he knows what to expect, which is probably more animals than there were when you visited. However, when Darwin went to the Galapagos, he was doing a big trip on the Beagle and they stopped at many places before they reached the Islands, and so there is always a chance that the Gate will take Jack somewhere different.'

'Will there be any clues?' asked Jack, genuinely interested.

'Sadly not. I'm afraid you have to try and work it out when you get there,' said Adam.

'But as for what you wear,' said Angela. 'That's where we can help. And I think that now you know all the secrets of the Gate, it's about time that we took you to the History Keeper archives, where we can try and find out as much as we can before you go through the Gate.'

'But,' said Jack, 'won't the mist be up to the hill by that stage? Won't you all be engulfed?'

'No,' said Auntie Issie. 'Because the Gate is open now, this gives us a little bit more time. Once you go through then time stands still here but until you do we have a few hours perhaps, but enough time to look at the archives and to look upstairs and see what we might have that you could wear.'

The children all looked at each other 'You mean you have dressing up things upstairs?' asked Sam, his eyes wide.

'Yes, of sorts,' said Angela. 'Not quite dressing up but the ability to dress people in the right thing so that they won't stick out too much. Sometimes we've got it wrong, of course, but most of the time we get it right.'

'Oh yes,' said Alfie. 'Like arriving in the centre of London in brightly coloured Victorian clothes on the day that everyone was in mourning for the death of Queen Victoria. I remember that one well.'

'You dealt with that admirably,' said Angela. 'It's amazing what a black cape can do in the circumstances,' and everybody laughed.

Jack looked around the room and realised that this was a very important job that these people did day in and day out. They showed no fear or worry but just calmness and a desire to sort out a problem, and he admired that in them.

'Are we all allowed in the archives?' he asked. 'Or is it just me again?'

'No,' said Auntie Issie, 'you can all come.' She glanced at the dogs. 'Except for those two, they tend to chase the Collectors so they are banned.' Molly and Charlie lay with their heads on their paws and did not try and protest this time. They knew that it would be a long, long time before they were let back into the archives.

'Are the archives back at the big house?' asked JJ.

'Well, it extends that far,' said Alfie. 'But we access them through our garden.'

'Wow!' said Sam. 'It must be huge!'

'It is,' said Alfie. 'If anyone wants to build anything in this

area, they always have to apply to the local RAF base, RAF
Welbridge, for permission to build. Everybody thinks that that's
because RAF Welbridge have lots of secret bunkers with nuclear
weapons in, but, in fact, it's just to prevent anyone digging down
into the archives or building over the top of one of the ventilation
shafts. Luckily, when the archives were built they were so
enormous that no new building work will be needed for many
centuries.'

Angela stood up, brushed the biscuit crumbs off her skirt
and turned towards the back door. She led the way out and one
by one they followed through the big wooden door into their
garden. As they stepped into the garden, it was shaped like a
small amphitheatre so that the ground outside the house was
mostly higher than the house itself. They went up some steps
and across the lawns. In front of them was quite a big swimming
pool.

'Wow!' said JJ. 'That's fantastic!'

'You'll have to come back when the weather is warmer,' said
Angela. 'We always love it if people use the pool.'

Past the summer house and running along to the left was a
large, tall hedge. At the end of the hedge, there was a series of
what looked like beach huts. They were different colours and
different sizes and Angela pulled open the door into the first
beach hut that they came to. 'Follow me,' she said.

Jack stuck his head in and it appeared to be a garden shed.
There were rows of shelves with pots and gardening forks and
compost. Before he had even moved inside, Angela had already
stepped through a door at the back of the shed into the next one.
Jack followed. This, too, looked like a potting shed but, as Jack
stepped through, he could feel a tingling from his head to his
toes. Not serious, but like a scanner had just been passed over
him.

A softly spoken voice appeared to come from nowhere. 'Jack

Simmons. Age 13. Passport number 37249283. Height 4ft 11ins. Weight...'

Angela interrupted. 'Skip data,' she said.

'Data skipped,' said the voice.

Jack looked at Angela, who smiled. 'He is reading your passport chip,' she said.

'Who is 'He'?' asked Jack.

'Well, you know that you have Ned at school? Just think of him as his brother, only on a much bigger scale and much more fearsome.'

Alfie stepped in behind Jack. 'In fact,' he said, 'we call him 'Big Ned'. Don't we, Big Ned?'

'Affirmative,' said the quietly spoken voice. 'Welcome Angela. Welcome Alfie. Will you commit Jack George Simmons to pass or should he be annihilated?'

Jack's eyes widened, and he looked at Alfie and Angela. 'He is joking, right?'

'No annihilation required, thank you Big Ned. Jack George Simmons is a friend and authorised to enter.'

'Thank you, Alfie.'

Behind them, they could hear the others coming up the path and Rosie was the first to enter. 'Rosie Grace Simmons. Passport number 567...'

'Thank you, Big Ned,' said Angela. 'Rosie Simmons authorised to enter the archives.'

'Affirmative,' said Big Ned.

'Now,' said Alfie, 'your two friends we will have to hear all of the details about because we don't know them very well, and you will appreciate that we cannot let Destroyers into the archives.'

'But they are not Destroyers,' said Rosie.

'We know that, Rosie, but it's not really our decision. Just let them go through the checks.' Alfie put a comforting hand on her shouder.

They watched as both of their friends walked through the scanner and Big Ned read both of their details. JJ was first. She stood in the middle of the shed as Big Ned scanned her. She stood stock still and looked rather frightened.

'Jennifer Jane Buccannan,' it said and read out her identification number. And then Big Ned stopped. 'Jennifer Jane Buccannan,' it said again, and read out the identification number. It had done this four times by the time that Auntie Issie and Uncle Stanley started exchanging slightly worried glances.

Jack suspected that Big Ned could read not only the passport identification numbers but could read other things for those trying to enter the archives, and it suddenly occurred to him that he knew very little about JJ and her family, and whether perhaps she had been born into an Evil family. He thought about it for a second and then discounted it almost immediately. There was no way that someone so beautiful and clever and gifted could be tainted with Evil. And, just as he was thinking this, Big Ned pronounced, 'Authorisation complete. Jennifer Jane Buccannan, you may proceed.'

Jack heard his Aunt exhale slightly from behind him and realised that she, too, had been quite worried by the length of the process.

JJ stepped towards them and said, 'Thank goodness. I thought I was about to be shot or something!'

Uncle Stanley laughed. 'Don't worry, Big Ned is much more subtle than that,' and they all looked at him with wide eyes. 'Only joking,' he said, and yet, somehow, Jack suspected he probably wasn't joking at all.

When Sam's turn came, he looked a little apprehensive. 'What if I don't pass?' he said.

Angela smiled and said, 'Don't worry, your end will be very painless.'

Sam's eyes widened.

'I'm only joking,' she said. 'He won't have any problems at all. I know your parents and, despite your Dad, I know that you will have no problem getting through.'

Sam stood still as he was scanned. 'Access granted,' said Big Ned.

'Well,' she said, 'you'd better follow me.'

By this stage, Angela, Auntie Issie, Uncle Stanley, Alfie and the four children were all gathered at the end of the third shed. It wasn't a very big shed, and so they were stood close to one another, the adults shoulder to shoulder.

'What now?' asked Jack.

'Everyone stand away from the edges,' said Alfie, and they all put their hands by their sides. 'Now, please don't be alarmed, nothing here is going to hurt you, it just might be a little… different.' At that stage, the wooden walls surrounding the shed suddenly turned to metal and all four children could feel themselves falling as if they were in a large lift.

Jack put his hand on his sister's shoulder to steady her as the shed appeared to be moving at a very fast rate in a downwards direction. He was convinced that they would crash at the bottom, as if they were in some terrible horror film. But, in fact, the shed slowed and eventually came to a gentle halt and the 'wall' behind Alfie suddenly opened as if it was a door.

'Welcome to the archives,' said Alfie. 'Now, please remember, don't touch anything and please be alert to the Collectors – search and find robots that will come up behind you, looking for records, as they are very quiet and they can be a little startling.'

'Robots!' said Jack. 'In Brighthaven?'

Auntie Issie smiled. 'You really are in for a few surprises today.'

They stepped out on to what appeared to be a platform suspended in the most enormous room that Jack had ever seen. In fact the word 'room' didn't really describe it. It was like 300 football pitches, all laid end to end and side to side, and it went on for as far as the eye could see. On every shelf were books and scriptures and documents. All four children stood with their mouths open, as they surveyed the scene below them.

As they looked out across the vast library, there suddenly appeared in front of them a small flat box with antennae, three of them, and what appeared to be two grabbing hands at the front. Jack realised it was not suspended on anything, but appeared to be hovering in mid air.

'Welcome Angela. Welcome Alfie. Welcome Issie. Welcome Stanley,' it said in a monotone voice. 'And welcome to your guests, Jack, Rosie, Sam and JJ.'

'Welcome Transfer One,' said Alfie. 'Today we require a copy of *Voyage of the Beagle* by Charles Darwin and any other books and archives that you may have in relation to Charles Darwin. However, priority for *Voyage of the Beagle*.'

'Thank you, Alfie. I will be with you momentarily.' And with that, Transfer One disappeared in a downwards direction.

The children looked over the edge of the balcony and could see below them, Transfer One, and what appeared to be many of his brothers and sisters, scooting around the archives below them. 'That is amazing,' said Jack, and before Jack could even draw a breath, Transfer One appeared in front of them and in his two grabbing arms, was a pristine copy of a book entitled 'Voyage of the Beagle'.

'As requested, Alfie. The rest of the archives will be following.' And, as he said that, up to Transfer One's left appeared an identical version of Transfer One, with a number 'Two' written on it, carrying another book and, one by one, until there was a line of about 100 Transfer robots, all clutching books of varying sizes.

'That is amazing!' said Sam. 'It must have taken them about 30 seconds!'

Alfie reached over and took the *Voyage of the Beagle* from Transfer One's mechanical arms. As he gripped hold of the book, Transfer One released the book into Alfie's hand.

'Have you ever dropped it?' asked Rosie.

Alfie smiled. 'If I did, there would be another Transfer directly below who would pick it up in milliseconds before it hit the floor,' said Alfie with a degree of certainty.

The long line of Collectors would have taken forever to dispense their books to the waiting arms of the four children and four adults. However, with one whistle from Alfie and his pointing in the direction of a large door, the Collectors immediately started moving in single file in that direction.

At that point, the lift behind them opened and out poured what seemed to be all of the residents of Lavender Lane: Adam, Alice, Cameron, his wife Caitlin, Michael and Martha, Ella and Max and finally Benjamin and Melissa. Without instruction they all headed immediately in the direction of the door that Alfie had pointed the Collectors towards.

Alfie got to it first and opened it into an enormous great room. There were many tables with beautifully ornate desk lamps and comfortable chairs and coffee making facilities and a machine dispensing chocolate and crisps.

Everybody else seemed to know what to do and they immediately took up their position on one of the desks or selected their more comfy chairs in the reading area. And then, as if it was completely coordinated, although Jack wasn't sure how it could have been, the Collectors started to assemble the books into piles in front of each person until, one by one, each of them had dropped its precious cargo and headed out back through the door and disappeared into the vastness.

This left only the four children standing with Alfie and Angela, Auntie Issie and Uncle Stanley, but even the four grown-ups moved quickly to select a desk or comfy chair and indicated to one of the children to follow each of them.

'What are we doing now?' asked Jack.

'Well,' said Auntie Issie, 'all of the books that the Collectors have brought to us have some reference to Charles Darwin and, in particular, the *Voyage of the Beagle*. Most important of them is this,' and she held up a smallish book, entitled '*Voyage of the Beagle*'. 'This is the voyage in Darwin's own words, tracking their entire circumnavigation of various continents. What we need to do is to read these and try and understand exactly where Evil will try and stop him. The fact that the Galapagos Islands disappeared from everybody's references outside of Lavender Lane, would indicate that it was either before or whilst Darwin was there and all we can do is hazard a guess at this stage.'

She opened up the *Voyage of the Beagle* and turned to the chapter entitled 'Galapagos Archipelago' and she started to read.

Jack was stood there, not entirely sure what purpose he was serving and Auntie Issie looked up and realised that the children were really not able to add much at this stage. She snapped her fingers twice and Transfer One appeared through the door like a faithful dog.

'Transfer One, replicate four copies of *Voyage of the Beagle* as soon as you can, please,' and Transfer One disappeared back out through the door into the vastness and reappeared in a matter of minutes, carrying four identical books, which were carefully placed down on the table in front of Auntie Issie.

'Thank you, Transfer One. Right, here you are children,' said Auntie Issie. 'I would like you to start at Chapter 17, Jack, and the other three I would like you to start at the three chapters before, Rosie; Chapter 16, JJ; Chapter 15 and Sam; Chapter 14. See if there is any idea or indication as to what Evil are up to. I will get you some refreshments now. Hot chocolate for everybody?'

Four faces lit up and Auntie Issie knew that she didn't have to wait for a response. She went over to the machine and came back with four steaming mugs of hot chocolate and a bar of Cadburys Dairy Milk for each of them.

Jack by this stage was starting to get slightly concerned. 'Auntie Issie,' he said, 'I thought that we had problems with the urgency and that if I don't go through the Gate quickly that Evil will overtake us.'

Auntie Issie smiled. 'You are absolutely right, Jack, but we do have a window for a couple of hours. The mist would have stopped advancing up the valley, which means it's not going to get any further at the moment until you have gone through the Gate. At that stage, time will stand still here until you return. It will seem as if you have been away for days but in fact you would only have been gone a matter of minutes. It is important that we spend this time trying to prepare you as much as we can in this limited window.'

Jack laughed. 'That's what my Dad always says, the six 'Ps'. 'Prior preparation and planning prevents...' He hesitated, as he knew that the next word was a rude one and didn't want to use it in front of Auntie Issie, so, instead, he skipped it and said, 'Poor performance.'

'That's only five 'Ps', Jack,' said Rosie.

Alfie laughed from behind them and said, 'Very diplomatic, young man.'

There was then silence in the room as each of them settled down in front of the book that they had been allocated and the children, with their hot chocolate, started to read through what was, essentially, quite a grown-up text, but most of it could be understood.

It talked about creatures they had never heard of and experiments and scientific theories, but it was possible to follow exactly what Charles Darwin was doing and where. He had arrived in the Galapagos in April 1835. He explained what the various islands looked like and whether they were volcanic, whether they had vegetation and he described in great detail the extraordinary landscape and amazing animals that he had found when he had first arrived. He was not the first to find the islands – buccaneers and whalers had visited them long before he did, and on Charles Island there was even a small settlement of a few hundred people living five miles inland.

Because all the islands had been formed from volcanic activity, it meant that any creature that was on them had either swam there or flown there, apart from the goats and pigs brought in by those living on Charles Island. Because these birds and animals were trapped on the islands, it meant that they were able to evolve in a way that made it much easier for someone like Charles Darwin to notice the changes.

Although not quite the latest *Harry Potter* book, all four children found themselves very interested indeed in the words of Charles Darwin.

Occasionally, someone would get up and make themselves a coffee or get something from the machine, or go out to the loo, which was situated at the back of this enormous room.

Because some of the words were quite big, Jack was skipping across them, which meant that he was reading much faster and it wasn't until he got to page 514 that he suddenly exclaimed. Everybody in the room, without exception, looked up.

'I think I might have it,' he said. 'On 8 October 1835, Charles Darwin and some of the crew were left on James Island, whilst the ship went off to find fresh water,' he said. 'What if, when Charles Darwin got off, something happened to him or to his ship which puts him in danger?'

The adults were still looking at him, and Jack assumed that because nobody had shot him down in flames, that perhaps this wasn't such a stupid suggestion.

'Which page?' asked Auntie Issie.

Jack replied, '514.'

'I think you may be on to something,' said Angela. 'Well done, Jack.'

Alfie raised his voice, 'Transfer One,' and Transfer One appeared obediently at the doorway. 'Another 10 copies of *Voyage of the Beagle* please. Quick as you can.' Transfer One reappeared in a matter of minutes, balancing 10 copies of this precious cargo and proceeded to distribute it to all of those who didn't have a copy.

Cameron, who was the military man, pushed back his seat. 'If there was going to be a time to attack, then this would have been the time that Darwin was most vulnerable if he didn't have his ship. If I was planning an attack, that would certainly have been my plan.'

Uncle Stanley looked around at everybody. 'Is everybody in agreement then, that this is our best shot in terms of where the Gate will open?' And everybody nodded. 'Right. Angela, Caitlin, Martha and Alice, we need some authentic clothing, the best that we've got, please.'

'Melissa, Ella and Max, we need a presentation in 20 minutes on what the boat looks like, what Charles Darwin looks like and a briefing on what to expect on this particular Island.' They both nodded and disappeared off. 'Benjamin, Cameron and Michael, we need a knapsack with equipment he might need.' They nodded and headed for the exit.

'Jack, you and the others go with Angela, please.'

With that, the children followed Angela and the other ladies back into the lift. It went up as quickly as it had descended and in a matter of minutes they were emerging out through the sheds in Alfie and Angela's garden.

Jack looked back and, from the outside, it just looked like a set of garden sheds. It was impossible to tell that beneath them lay such an amazing library filled with robots!

He wondered at first whether perhaps he had just simply

imagined it but when he turned to his sister and two friends, all of them had an amazed look on their faces, which told him that he was not dreaming at all, but had simply stumbled into a world that he had not known existed.

They headed off back down the garden path towards Alfie and Angela's house and when they walked in through the door, instead of going through to the kitchen, Angela ushered them upstairs and down a long corridor. There was a room at the end which appeared to be locked and Angela took out a large key and turned it in the rather ancient lock and it made a very loud clunking noise. She pushed open the wooden door and walked in. She gestured to all of them to follow her and the four children walked through the door with Alice coming up behind them.

For the second time in an hour, the children stopped and stared in amazement. In front of them there were rows and rows of clothing. There were bales of cloth of every different type of colour and threads and buttons and sewing machines. Down one side there were sewing machines and ironing boards.

'Right,' said Angela, 'we'd better get going, hadn't we. First things first, where's my tape measure?' And, with that, she grabbed a tape measure and started to measure all of Jack's dimensions: his height, his waist, his chest.

'Now,' she said. 'That one, that one and that one,' and pointed to three bales of cloth which Alice immediately picked up.

Angela then started moving down the lines of clothing on the rails and the four children followed her.

'Wow!' said JJ. 'This is amazing. Look at this beautiful dress.' And she pulled one out of the rails.

'Please make sure you put it back where you found it,' said Angela. 'This may look like chaos, but it is in fact quite ordered. That's an Elizabethan evening gown and very expensive. Now, the problem is, Jack,' she said, 'I'm not sure what we've got in your size but we will have a look anyway.' And the children followed her down what appeared to be miles and miles of the most amazing clothes that they had ever seen. There were pirates' outfits, army uniforms, safari outfits and the most beautiful dresses.

'Right, here we are,' said Angela. 'Go over there into the changing rooms and try these on. There are a few pairs of trousers which will hopefully fit you, and these shoes and this jacket.' She started handing out clothes and shoes from the piles and Jack's outstretched arms were almost overladen in a matter of minutes. 'Alice, Caitlin and Martha will run you up a few tops to wear,' Angela said, to no-one in particular.

Angela almost ran back towards the door and leant over and switched on the computer in the corner of the room. She waited a few minutes and hit a couple of keys and the printer next to it sparked into life. There was the usual clicking and whirring and the printer erupted into life. She picked up the pieces of paper as they came off and on each of them was a drawing of boys of Jack's age in unusual dress, which Jack took to be from the time of Charles Darwin. They wore trousers in a darker colour and lighter coloured tunic shirts with a form of tie and slightly more formal jackets.

'Right,' she said. 'Almost there.'

It was at that stage that Martha appeared with Caitlin and the two of them took a bundle of cloth each and a drawing and all three started to lay out the fabric to cut it quickly and expertly and then to sit down behind sewing machines and start to sew.

JJ asked, politely, 'Is there anything that I can do?'

'That's very kind,' said Alice. 'If you could possibly sew some buttons onto this piece, that would be very helpful. The buttons are there. Could you use the black ones?'

Rosie asked the same question of Martha and she, too, was given some sewing work and both she and JJ looked at Sam. 'I'm not proud,' he said. 'Is there anything that I can do?' And Auntie

Issie laughed. 'Yes, of course, Sam. Here are some buttons, if you could sew these on as well. There's a needle and thread over there. Do you know how to thread the needle?'

'Of course I do,' he said. 'I may be a boy, but I'm not stupid.' And Rosie giggled.

Jack then emerged from the changing rooms, wearing his brogue like trousers, with a short jacket over his T-shirt.

'Perfect,' said Angela as she settled back behind her sewing machine and it sprang into life under her expert guidance.

Jack looked at the three seamstresses beavering away as three shirts quickly took shape. It was clear that this was something they had done many times before. Jack studied them carefully. Eventually he said, 'You are making me more than one shirt. Am I going to be there for a long time?'

Auntie Issie arrived in the room to hear her nephew ask what was in fact a very relevant question. She laughed. 'It's hard to tell at this stage, Jack, but best to be prepared. You'll need one to wear now, though, and it's almost finished. It's probably slightly more Vivienne Westwood than Versace, but it will have to do,' and with that Angela threw the first one in Jack's direction. He disappeared back into the changing room, emerging a minute later wearing the entire outfit, including his shoes.

'You'll do,' said Auntie Issie. 'Now, let's just find a jumper for cold weather and a bag to put a few essentials into.'

'I know this may sound a stupid question,' said Jack. 'But how will I know when it's time to come home?'

Auntie Issie looked up. 'It's not a stupid question, Jack. The Gate will open in exactly the same place as you came through it. You will see the same bright light you can see through the Gate downstairs and you need to walk towards it. There is one rule that you need to know: it is forbidden to bring back through the gate anything that you did not take with you; if you try you will not get through.'

'But what if the bright light doesn't come?' asked Jack. 'Will I be stuck there forever?'

Auntie Issie exchanged glances with Angela, and Angela answered. 'The truth is, Jack, we don't know the answer to that because nobody has ever failed. We have always managed to stop Evil in its tracks and the Gate has always opened to let us back.'

'OK,' said Jack, and went back to thinking quietly to himself.

It was at that stage that they all heard a gentle sobbing and, looking around, it appeared to be coming from Rosie. She had her back to most people and was diligently sewing on her buttons but with big round tears falling onto the material as she sewed.

Auntie Issie went to get up to go and comfort her but Jack held up his hand to stop her. 'I'll go,' he said, and he went across and sat down next to his sister, putting his arm around her shoulders.

'Don't worry, Rosie,' he said. 'I will be fine. I'll come back and, if I don't you can guarantee that I'll come back and haunt you.' And she laughed through her sobs.

'But it's not fair,' she said. 'You shouldn't have to do this on your own.'

'I know, but life's not fair, as we always remind ourselves. I'll do everything I can to come home, but I don't want you being sad whilst I am away and I will ask Sam for a full report. Is that understood?' He looked his sister in the eye and tipped her face up to meet his gaze fully. 'Is that a deal?' he asked and Rosie nodded tentatively.

Downstairs in the kitchen, Michael, Cameron, Benjamin and Melissa were arriving clutching books and computers, notebooks and pens, cakes and packets of biscuits. They all had the same frowns on their faces.

Adam arrived and as he strode through the door and took off his scarf, he said, 'The mist has started to creep forward. It's almost time.'

They all exchanged glances, and, with that, they heard footsteps on the wooden stairs, coming towards them, and Jack emerged through the kitchen door. He had on shoes that looked as if he had been wearing them for some time and which had been washed in the sea many times, smart brogue trousers, a smart shirt with a loose darker tie and an over-jacket.

The Keepers smiled involuntarily at the same time, as he looked so much the part that they almost forgot the immense danger that he was about to place himself into.

'Don't forget your watch,' said Alfie, pointing at Jack's left wrist. 'You need to take off anything that indicates you are from a different time.'

Jack glanced at his sister and hesitated but slowly started to take his watch off. 'I'll look after it, Jack,' she said, and held out her hand. She knew that the watch meant a lot to Jack, as it had been his brother Harry's, and he had cherished it from the moment his parents had given it to him. Whilst it had needed a few running repairs over the years, it still kept good time and always felt to Jack as if it was some connection with the brother that he had never really known.

Instead of giving it to his sister, Jack handed it over to his Auntie Issie. 'If I do not come back, Rosie can have it,' he said without emotion. He saw Rosie's lip start to tremble and looked at her with raised eyebrows and she stopped immediately.

Jack looked down at the dining table, which was by now full of biscuits and cakes and cups of tea, and his eyes widened. 'I'm starving,' he said, and started to help himself, and everybody else took his lead, suddenly forgetting that there was a national emergency to be dealt with.

As Jack was filling his plate, Melissa and Uncle Stanley were setting up a computer and Angela was moving all of the pictures and knick-knacks from the large wall in the dining room so that they could project onto it.

'Right,' said Benjamin, 'we don't have much time, as the mist is moving closer. Here's what we've got in the limited time we've had.' He pressed a button and projected up onto the wall was a picture of a large ship. It had three enormous masts, each with many sails and a large mast pointing forward from the front of the ship. Rows of portholes could be seen along its middle. It appeared to be enormous. It flew two flags – a pendant flag from the very top of the biggest mast in the middle – this was white with a red cross; the second flag had the red cross but in one corner the union jack that was more familiar to Jack.

'This,' said Cameron, stepping into the presentation, 'is the HMS Beagle. It should be easily recognisable, not least because it will have its name written down the side, but, otherwise, its distinguishing features are the three masts and the flags that it is flying. We know that on the 8 October 1835 the Beagle left Darwin, the stand-in surgeon Mr Bynoe and their servants on James Island for a week whilst the ship went to refill with water, and so it may be that when you pass through the Gate, you can't actually see the ship at all. Don't worry if this is the case; it will be back, hopefully.'

Rosie and Jack exchanged glances.

There was a click and the next slide appeared on the wall. 'This is Charles Darwin. This is an illustration from the *Voyage of the Beagle*. Therefore, we can only assume that it is a good likeness. He was only 26 at the time of the voyage and therefore a very young man. Other likenesses that we have found from other reference books are also here.' Cameron flashed up a number of other images on the screen, which all looked fairly similar.

'There was a total crew of 76 and the Captain was Commander Robert Fitzroy. Charles Darwin was the second choice of naturalist and at the time was a failing medicine student.' Another picture flashed up on the screen. 'The original surgeon on board was Robert McCormick but he departed in Rio in 1832 and was replaced by a Mr Bynoe. In addition there were carpenters, royal marines, armourers, clerks, a quarter master and an artist.'

'Wow,' said Jack. 'Will I have to remember all of their names?'

'I would not worry about that too much Jack, but if you could recognise the captain that might be helpful,' said Uncle Stanley. 'I doubt that you will be taken straight to the Beagle but you are likely to be on the island itself. I think that your cover story should be that you have arrived on a whaling ship.'

'Whaling,' exclaimed Rosie, 'that's terrible.'

'I know Rosie,' said Uncle Stanley. 'But we do know that there were Spaniards in the area who were whaling and so we need to give you a good cover story. The island that we think you will be on is James Island, which is mainly volcanic with some vegetation and some of the tallest trees amongst all the islands.'

The children gasped as a large picture of a land iguana was blasted onto the wall in front of them.

'That looks like a giant dragon!' said Jack.

'No, it's just the way the picture is,' said Benjamin. 'In fact, they are only about this big,' and he gestured with his hands to show something which was probably no more than a foot long.

Rosie said, 'I remember them from when we went with Mum and Dad. They were all over the rocks, and they were in the water as well.'

'Yes, but they are slightly different,' said Uncle Stanley. 'They are the water iguanas,' and he put up a picture. 'They look very similar, but neither will hurt you.'

'Is there anything on the island that will hurt me?' asked Jack.

'No, no large mammals except tortoises, no dogs or cats or bears. There are some snakes but they are pretty harmless.

Remember, anything on the Galapagos Islands either swam there or flew there and they are all of normal size, so anything else you see is not real.' Uncle Stanley paused.

Jack looked round the room and the Keepers were looking down, either at their food or at their finger nails or at their toes.

'What do you mean 'not real'?' asked Jack suspiciously.

Auntie Issie sighed loudly. 'Well,' she said. 'As if things weren't difficult enough, Evil does all it can to prevent us from undoing the damage that they are trying to inflict and they do this by making things look bigger to frighten you.'

'So, a bit like a Disney theme park, really,' said Jack, and laughed, and the Keepers also laughed nervously.

'Something like that,' said Alfie.

Sam piped up, between bites of biscuit, 'So, how will Jack know which island he is on? Are there some animals that are on more than one Island?'

'Yes,' said Uncle Stanley. 'There are. But it's really only important for him to know if he is on James Island, because if the boat isn't there, then he knows it will be coming back and that Charles Darwin is on the island somewhere.'

'What about food?' asked JJ.

Uncle Stanley smiled. 'I'm afraid there aren't going to be any McDonalds' on the Island. We can send you with some energy bars and a bottle of water, but, after that, you are on your own. Your travelling bag will be packed with as many things that will help you to survive, but which will not, if you are caught and stopped, give any indication that you are from a different time.'

Alfie brought forward the bag and opened it up. Jack smiled. 'You are just like Q from James Bond, aren't you?'

Alfie smiled back at that comparison. 'I guess so,' he said. 'I just don't have any exploding jumpsuits or cars that can go in the water.'

Jack took the bag and looked inside; there was a container

with water, and containers with what looked like chopped up bits of Mars Bar, and energy food. There was also a little jar with tablets in.

'What are those?' asked Jack.

'They are water purifying tablets,' said Alfie. 'First of all, you mustn't drink salt water, but if you find other water which is not salt water, then you must always put one of these in to make sure that it kills any bugs. There are matches, a needle and thread, and a small first aid kit. Everything has been taken out of its wrappers but it should be self explanatory. There is an old fashioned set of binoculars and also some fishing wire.'

Jack picked out a few things and looked at them in detail. 'That's fine,' he said.

Angela came forward and helped to reassemble everything back into the bag. 'Bear in mind, Jack, that you must not bring anything back that does not belong in this time zone, so no bag full of mementoes when you come back.' She smiled at Jack and Jack smiled back.

'OK, so my plans of seashells and musket balls are out of the window, then?'

'Probably,' she said, and smiled again.

'So, let me sum up,' said Jack, in a very grown up voice, which made Rosie smile. 'I am going through a Gate in time. I don't know where I'm going to end up, and I don't know if I can get back. I am going to encounter things that may or may not be real. I don't know which island I am going to be on, or what animals are there, and I don't even know if Charles Darwin will be there when I get there. Is that an accurate summary?'

He looked up at all of the pairs of eyes watching him with deep, deep concern.

'Oh, do come on,' he said. 'Have a little faith. I may only be 13 but right now it looks to me as if I am the only chance you and the rest of the world have got.'

He turned and looked at Auntie Issie. 'Will I have to kill anyone?'

Melissa almost choked on her tea at that point.

Auntie Issie looked him straight in the eye and said, 'I certainly hope not, Jack, but you just have to do whatever it takes to make sure that Charles Darwin leaves that island unharmed.'

'So,' said Jack, putting on his best Sean Connery accent. 'I have a licence to kill.'

Michael had his head in his hands at that stage, as he wasn't entirely sure if Jack was taking this seriously, or whether they had just authorised a 13 year old child to maim and kill in the interests of protecting history.

'What will happen to the mist when I am gone?' asked Jack.

'It will hardly move at all,' said Angela. 'Time will stand still. It will only start to move again at speed if you are unsuccessful in stopping Evil.'

'So you will know then,' said Jack, 'if I'm coming back or not?'

Auntie Issie put her arm around his shoulder, 'You'll be coming back, Jack. You have my word.'

JJ stepped forward and put her hands on Jack's shoulders. 'I know you'll be coming back, Jack. You're my hero,' and she gave him a kiss on the cheek.

Jack was slightly stunned for a moment and, as JJ moved past him to take her seat back on the bench along the wall, Jack exchanged glances with Sam to the effect that if he died now, it would all be worth it.

'Right then,' said Jack. 'Well we can't stand around here talking can we? I guess it's time to open the Gate.'

There was a small whimper from under the bench and Jack looked down to see that Charlie and Molly had been hiding themselves behind the legs of everyone, listening to all that had gone on. Two little heads pointed out now as if to say goodbye.

Jack bent down. 'Don't worry you two, I'll be back soon.'

They both flattened their ears. 'And I promise,' he said, 'lots of ball games when I return.' Their ears perked up immediately.

'Come on then,' said Jack, looking up at the assembled masses. 'To quote my Mother, "I hate long goodbyes".'

'It's not goodbye,' said Auntie Issie. 'Goodbye means forever.'

Jack sneaked two more biscuits off the plate and slipped one into his pocket and ate the other. 'Right,' he said, 'I guess we'd better go.'

Everybody else hesitated and Rosie slipped her hand into his. JJ and Sam exchanged glances and stood up and, reluctantly, the adults followed. One by one they moved through from the kitchen table and through the door into the dining room where the Gate was located. The room was empty except for a small table and two chairs, and it struck Jack as strange that such a large room should have so little furniture in it.

'Why don't you use this room?' he asked Angela, in a way that suggested that his forthcoming fate did not bother him at all.

'We used to,' she said. 'But because the Gate is located in here, strangers and visitors to Lavender Lane would come for dinner or to stay and used to complain that they could feel as if there was some sort of spirit in here.'

'What, you mean like a ghost?' asked Rosie.

'Yes, that's right, Rosie. Just like a ghost. It must be something to do with the Gate, and so we just stopped using it. We've got another, bigger dining room through those two doors, and if we have lots of people for supper, we normally use that instead.' Angela nodded her head in the direction of the other part of the house.

'So it's haunted?' asked Sam.

'Yes,' said Angela. 'In a manner of speaking, I suppose it is. But in a nice way, not in a horrible way.'

Molly and Charlie stuck close to Jack's legs as they walked through to the dining room and they all stood in front of the

Gate and looked at the bright light coming from around the edges of the door.

'So, when you open it,' asked Jack, 'is it going to be that bright? Will I be able to see where I'm going?'

Alfie stepped forward. 'At the moment, all the light is concentrated round the edges because we've got the door shut,' he said. 'As we open it up, it will be less bright, so you will be able to see where you are going and you'll quickly work out which way is up, if you know what I mean?'

Jack looked round and everybody was now in the room. At the front stood the other three children and the two dogs, and behind them stood all of the other History Keepers. They were stood side by side, almost as if they were in a Church. They all looked solemn, even slightly upset. Some could not look directly at him. They knew that this was such a huge thing to ask someone who was only 13 but they were helpless to step in to help.

Auntie Issie stepped forward. She put her hand on Jack's shoulder. 'You don't have to do this, Jack.'

He turned and gazed into her eyes. They reminded him so much of his beloved mother. His heart ached that she was not able to see him now and wish him luck but he knew in his bones that he would be returning. 'Yes I do, Auntie Issie, and you know that I do,' he said. 'But thank you for being concerned.'

'I am just rehearsing what to tell my sister,' said Auntie Issie.

'Does she know about the Gate?' asked Jack.

'No, she knows nothing of the Gate,' said Auntie Issie. 'It is a hard thing to bring up in conversation. She just thinks we are bit eccentric… Right, so you've got your bag?' Auntie Issie changed the subject like any good lawyer.

Jack tapped his rucksack, strung over his neck and shoulder. 'I've got it all,' he said. 'And a few extra biscuits to keep me going…'

The other three children involuntarily held hands in a line and Charlie whined very gently.

'Now, come on, Charlie,' said Auntie Issie. 'It's bad enough for the rest of us without you starting,' and Charlie flattened his ears and nuzzled into Jack even closer.

'He'll be fine,' said Auntie Issie, rather unconvincingly.

Molly put her ears down at that stage as if to say, 'I'm really not sure about this,' and stepped closer to Jack.

'Right,' said Alfie. 'Hold on to the dogs. I'm going to open the Gate now. I'm going to pull it back so it's fully open. You will feel a slightly strange sensation because we are essentially crossing time. It will make your legs feel a little bit wobbly and it'll make you feel a bit light headed, so don't worry.'

'It just gets better,' said Jack in jest as he stepped forward.

'We will hold the dogs,' offered Rosie and caught hold of Charlie's collar. JJ reached down and caught hold of Molly's.

Alfie took hold of the handle of the Gate and slowly pulled it back and as he did so the light got brighter. But as he pulled it further, the light became less intense, but nevertheless filled the whole room, and Jack could feel his legs starting to wobble and his head a little lighter. Suddenly there was a rush of wind that came out from the Gate, as if he was stood on the seaside with the wind blowing in his face as the waves crashed. He smiled at Auntie Issie and with a deliberate stride, stepped towards the Gate and walked straight through it.

Jack could hear the 'whooshing' noise in his ears and over the noise of the wind, he heard his sister's voice shout, 'Jack!' and suddenly the light had gone.

In Angela's former dining room, the grown-ups stood and looked at each other in astonishment! 'How did that happen?'

asked Ella.

Auntie Issie sat down. 'I have no idea, but I've got an awful lot of explaining to do.'

They all gazed at the Gate and Alfie moved forward to close it.

'But,' said Uncle Stanley. 'How did they do that?'

Auntie Issie replied, 'The Gate has many mysteries and this one we'll never be able to answer. Still, at least they will all be together and can look after each other.'

What Jack was not aware of was that as he had stepped through the Gate, his sister and their two friends and two anxious Border Collies, had jumped through after him.

CHAPTER FIVE

Jack opened his eyes, having involuntarily shut them as he stepped through the Gate. The light had gone and, instead, he was looking at what appeared to be the inside of a cave. He was just focusing his eyes on his new surroundings when he heard a movement behind him and jumped.

He span round and there, in front of him, were his sister, Sam and JJ. 'What the ...' he said. It was only then that he looked down and saw Molly and Charlie looking slightly bemused, but, nevertheless, pleased to see him. They wagged their tails.

'How did you get through the Gate?' he asked in absolute astonishment.

'We don't know,' said Rosie. 'We just ran and it didn't try and stop us.'

'Well,' said Jack. 'Let's hope we don't meet too many people. We could probably explain me away but four of us and two dogs on an island that has no dogs...' He stopped himself and realised that he was sounding very ungrateful.

'Come here, all of you,' he said, and they all had a group hug. 'Thank you,' he said. 'Thank you for being there for me. I was so frightened, but I didn't want to let it show.'

'We know,' said Rosie. 'That's why we came. We even bought more biscuits.' She held up a large bag, with what appeared to be the entire contents of a biscuit tin inside.

'So, you had this planned,' said Jack.

'Well,' said Rosie, glancing at JJ and Sam, 'when you were upstairs having your costume fitted...'

'Outfit,' said Jack. 'It's an outfit, not a costume, the idea being that I would blend in with whoever I met. Fat chance now!'

'We agreed that if we could, we were going to come with you, so we borrowed some clothes.' Rosie held up a small cloth bag and pulled out a few neutral clothes, more in keeping with those that Jack was wearing. 'I brought the biscuits... and the remains of Angela's Christmas cake' – she held up the third bag with an entire fruitcake inside.

'And, what will the dogs be eating?' asked Jack. 'We can't give them fruit cake, it will be poisonous.'

The dogs looked at each other, as if to say that they had probably not thought about that but biscuits would do fine.

'Oh, we'll find them something,' said Jack. 'Spit roast iguana is probably quite good at this time of year. First things first, we need to try and find our way out of this cave. Let's just stop for a moment and listen to what we can hear.'

They all stopped and, faintly in the background, they could hear the sound of the sea.

'OK,' said Jack. 'So it sounds like we are near the sea. The question is, how do we get out of this cave?' He looked at his sister and their friends in a rather accusing fashion. There was no answer.

'Well, I know two people who have got much better sight, sound and smell than we have.' He looked down at the two dogs. 'OK you two, do you want to go out?' Their ears perked up. 'That's the good news,' he said. 'The bad news is that you need to find the way for us.'

Charlie tilted his head on one side, but Molly stood up immediately and started sniffing at the floor. 'Good girl,' said Jack. 'Now find the way out.' And, immediately, the two dogs started sniffing around the edges of the walls. Their eyesight was so much better than the children's.

'Now, you three, stay exactly where you are,' he said. 'We

don't want to get lost in the caves, but the dogs will find us.'

The children stood still as the dogs sniffed and pawed and got further and further away, until, eventually, slowly, they faded from view, but the children could still hear them snuffling, but it got fainter and fainter. The four children stood in silence in the middle of the cave.

'Would anyone like a biscuit?' asked Rosie.

'I think we'd better save them,' said Sam. 'Until we know if we can get food or not.'

They stood for what seemed like ages, and then, eventually, they heard the patter of canine feet on the cave floor, and the two dogs bounded into view. They both sat down, and Molly looked up and said, in what Auntie Issie always called her part human language, 'Ow Oo Ow.'

Jack laughed. 'This is normally the stage that Uncle Stanley says, 'What? Three children down a mineshaft?' and we all laugh. But I guess, on this occasion, it really is what she's saying – four children trapped in a cave!'

'Hopefully,' said Sam, 'she's saying 'I've found a way out'.'

'I think that's exactly what she's saying,' said Rosie.

'Come on, you three, let's go,' said Jack, and the dogs turned immediately and started heading back in the same direction they had come from. 'Not too fast,' Jack called after them. 'We need to be able to see you.'

'They don't understand,' said JJ.

'They do,' said Jack. 'They are clever dogs. Now walk carefully, we don't know what's on the floor or if it's slippery, or slimy. Stick together please. Make sure that you can touch one another at all times.'

And they moved slowly, dogs in front, towards the entrance to the caves. The sound of the sea started to get louder and louder and slowly they made their way through tunnels, until, suddenly, the dogs came to an abrupt halt, and they lowered themselves to a crouch, ears back and flat on their heads, which is what they did when they were frightened or apprehensive.

'What is it?' whispered Jack.

They could just about make out at the end of the tunnel that this was now daylight, but between them and the natural light, there appeared to be living things lying on the floor to the cave. They were quite large in size and, as Jack strained his eyes to see, they appeared to be quite rounded. Charlie let out a low growl. 'Be quiet,' said Jack. 'We don't want to frighten whatever it is.'

They took a few paces further forward and then a few more, and then they heard the sound. It was a cry that sounded a little like something was laughing, but also very much like a donkey. They all looked at one another.

'Do you think it's real?' asked Rosie. 'We know that Evil will send things to try and confuse us.'

'I think it's a seal,' said Jack. 'Do you remember we saw them when we were in the Galapagos Islands with Mum and Dad? They used to lounge around in the sand and on the edges of the sea and they would make that noise to communicate with their babies.'

He took a few steps closer. As his eyes started to acclimatise, he could see that that was exactly what it was, lying on the path between him and the outside. In fact, there was not just one but probably five or six.

'How do we get past?' asked Rosie. 'Don't they bite?'

'I think they probably would if they thought that we were trying to interfere with their babies,' he said, pointing towards the smaller curved objects, which appeared to be lying next to their mothers.

The children stopped for a few minutes and watched as the large round shapes humped and wriggled slightly as some of their babies got closer to suckle. The dogs stayed completely still and it appeared that the seals were blissfully unaware that they were there. It helped with the roar of the sea coming through the mouth of the cave, as it meant that any noise would be muffled from inside. Jack thought that was perhaps why the seals had to shout so loudly for their babies to be heard over the roaring of the sea.

He looked carefully at the entrance to the cave and it did appear to him that there were seals completely blocking the way out. He looked carefully at them again and thought perhaps they might be sea lions, rather than seals, and he couldn't remember which way round it was because he remembered his father telling him that one of them had ears and the other didn't. However, at this moment in time, whether they had ears or not, they seemed to be blocking the way and Jack did not really have a plan.

He felt a small nudge in his back and turned round and JJ was pointing to the edge of the cave. He let his eyes focus and, as the shapes became more detailed as his eyes got used to the darkness of the cave, he could see what she was pointing to. There, running around the edge of the cave appeared to be a ledge of some kind. It wasn't clear how wide it was but it wasn't very high, but it seemed high enough to keep them away from the seals/sea lions.

As Jack started to move, the dogs immediately stood up, thinking they were going somewhere. Jack used his hand flat down to indicate 'down' and both of them dropped back down to the floor and waited for the next command. Jack moved slowly round the edge of the cave so as not to startle the seals, and felt around the edge of the ledge. It appeared to be quite a wide ledge and was about two feet off the ground. It was hard to see where it went to but it certainly seemed, from preliminary investigations, that it went round the edge of the cave and out through the tunnel entrance.

Jack put both of his hands onto the ledge and pulled himself up until he was stood looking down on the other three. The dogs were watching him, heads up, ears erect, waiting to be summoned up to the ledge.

'Stay here,' mouthed Jack, and started to move slowly up the ledge, round the side of the cave.

It was wide enough so it was unlikely that anyone would fall off; it was a little slippery, but there were a few rocks to hold on to as he made his way round. Slowly he made his way towards the natural light, with the seals down below him not appearing to notice that he was there. He got to the edge and, to his delight, the ledge continued out through the cave entrance and round to the right. It was almost as if someone had created a little fast lane into the cave, but, however it had got there, Jack was convinced it was their way out.

Jack carefully made his way back down the ledge and back towards his sister and friends who were waiting. He sat down on the edge and called them all close so that they could hear him without him having to shout.

'I think it's all right,' he said. 'It's a bit slippy so watch your footing and hold onto the wall.' He then looked at the dogs and realised that even for them jumping up to the ledge might be difficult. 'We'll have to lift the dogs up,' he said, and gestured to the two to come over. He grabbed hold of Charlie's collar and the other three took the rest of his body and, on a count of three, hoisted the full-size Border Collie up to the ledge, Charlie licking Rosie's face all the way.

Next, it was Molly's turn and she was a bit more uncertain, but seeing her beloved Charlie up on the ledge and she was still down on the cave floor, when he gave a little whimper, she practically leapt into Rosie's arms, waiting to be hoisted up to join her brother. Finally, all four children and two Border Collies were up on the ledge and Jack, out in front, started to lead the way.

Charlie tried to push forward so that he would be in the front, but Jack signalled to him to stay back. He didn't want them to

run into another creature or for Charlie to be so startled that he
started to bark.

'Heel,' said Jack quietly, and Charlie understood that
command and tucked in behind Jack's feet as he made his way
along the ledge.

It was starting to get lighter and Jack was just beginning to
think that they had made it out of the cave when there was an
exclamation from his sister and she stumbled behind him. She
fell forward and Jack managed to grab her on the way down, just
as her legs started to disappear over the edge of the ledge. Below
her were the seals, oblivious to their human guests. Everyone
stopped and pulled Rosie back up to stop her falling on top of the
seals.

'Are you hurt?' whispered Jack.

'No,' she said. 'I just tripped over my feet. I'm fine,' and
Charlie gave her a lick on the face for good measure.

Jack looked down and the seals still didn't appear to have
noticed them. The children all stood up again and they moved
their way slowly round the edge and out into what was warm
sunshine.

The ledge turned sharply round the corner and Jack followed
it round, glancing out across the beautiful blue sea, and, as he
turned his attention back to the path in front of him, his heart
almost stopped as he saw what lay in his path. Because, there in
front of him, probably four times his size, was what appeared to
be the most enormous dragon-like creature sat on the path.

Its body was covered in scales and it had long sharp claws and
almost a spiny crest down its back. The only thing missing was
the fire breath.

Jack inhaled sharply and, as the others saw what was in front
of them, JJ let out a small squeal but the Collies lay down with
their ears back and didn't utter a sound.

'Oh my goodness, what is that?' exclaimed Sam. The creature

in front of them didn't move.

'It's a dragon,' exclaimed Rosie.

Jack held back his hand to stop them all from rushing forward. 'I don't think it's real,' he said. 'I don't think the dogs can see it.'

The four children looked down at the dogs, who were lying at their feet, ears back but not concerned.

'I think it's Evil making everything look bigger to frighten us.'

'Rosie, we've been here, haven't we? We know the iguanas don't grow as big as dragons this big. Everybody hold hands and think really positive thoughts. Think of good things.'

They each grabbed each other's hands and Jack noticed that JJ's was the hand closest to him. He squeezed tight. They all closed their eyes and when they opened them again, in front of them the dragon stood as large as before.

'We need to say it out loud,' said Jack. 'Think of something good you have done…'

'I made my Aunt some sandwiches for lunch today,' said JJ. 'Does that count?' Jack sneaked a glance out of one corner of his screwed up eyes and the dragon appeared to have got a little smaller.

'Excellent,' said Jack. 'I helped Uncle Stanley clean out the chickens earlier.' He hesitated; it was earlier but it seemed an age away. He sneaked a look, the dragon looked half its original size now.

'I let Sam win the first two bouts at the School so he would feel welcome,' blurted out Rosie and the dragon reduced in size again. Rosie looked at Sam out of the corner of her eye and he smiled.

'I let Rosie win the last two bouts,' he said with a smile. The children all opened their eyes at once and suddenly stood in front of them was not a dragon, but a small iguana, no more than a foot long. It was at that stage that the dogs saw it properly. Charlie got up to move to encourage it away. 'Stay,' said Jack, and Charlie lay down again.

The iguana looked almost prehistoric with a scaly face that looked like a Dr Who monster, and long claws for grasping onto the rock. It looked at them and blinked and walked off back up the path. They all let out a collective sigh of relief.

'Evil is quite powerful,' said Sam, 'if he can make us see things that don't exist.'

'I think it existed,' said JJ. 'But it just looked much bigger than it should have and perhaps that is all they can do to frighten us.'

'I hope so,' said Rosie nervously.

They carried on walking up the ledge until it joined the main part of the top of the outcrop that was overlooking the sea, and which housed the seals underneath in their special cave. The rock was very strange. It was blackish/grey and looked a bit like those strange stones that Mum had used to get off rough bits of skin when he was younger. It was then that Jack remembered that, of course, all of the islands had been made when a volcano had erupted and so what they were standing on must be lava from the volcano, which had flowed down to the sea and had then turned to rock.

The landscape certainly didn't look like Cornwall, and was very bare, with very few trees or vegetation near the shoreline. As Jack looked around, he could see hundreds and possibly thousands of small iguanas, either lying on the rocks in the sun or heading down towards the water's edge. As he looked in the water, he could see little heads bobbing around as they swam.

Rosie could see where he was watching. 'They must be the sea iguanas,' said Rosie. 'Do you remember Dad telling us about them, that there were two types, one that stayed on the land and one that went in the water?'

'You were listening then?' said Jack.

'Of course I was,' she said. 'I always listen to Dad.'

Jack raised an eyebrow, as if to say, 'I don't think so,' but didn't think now was the time or the place for an argument with his baby sister.

They carried on walking across the black rocks until they got to a more sandy area. 'Let's sit down,' said Jack. 'And have a look at exactly where we are and make a plan.'

'I'm thirsty,' said Rosie.

Jack opened up the water bottle that Auntie Issie had given him. 'One sip each, please. This was supposed to last me and now there are four of us.' He looked at the dogs, who turned their heads to one side, tongues hanging out. 'OK,' he said. 'Six of us. It's not going to last very long unless we can find a water supply.'

They sat on the sand and Rosie got out the big plastic bag of biscuits and handed one to everybody, and half each to the dogs.

'Right,' said Jack. 'Rosie and JJ, I want you to stay here with the two dogs and Sam and I are going to go out in opposite directions along the shoreline to see if we can find anything. There has to be water on the island somewhere because, although there are few mammals, even birds need water to drink, and I don't think the island is very big.'

He looked at Sam's clothes. 'You had better change into some of those clothes you brought with you,' he said, and then he ferreted around in his little pack, given to him by Benjamin, and came out with his glorch.

Sam's eyes widened. 'What are you going to do with that?'

He said, 'I'm going to chop off the bottom half of your Chinos to make them look like longer shorts. At least from a distance, you might look like somebody from the right century.'

He then turned to his sister and JJ. 'Do what you can,' he said. 'But, given those colours, I don't think we're fooling anyone that either of you were born in this century.'

'There aren't exactly many people around,' said Rosie. 'How will anyone know?'

'Expect the unexpected,' said Jack. 'We don't know who's here and we don't want to give the game away before we even start. The best thing we can do is to find somewhere to camp, where you two and the dogs can stay safely whilst Sam and I try and find out what's going on.'

'Right, Sam,' said Jack. 'I want you to walk at this pace and count to 1000 and then turn round and retrace your steps in the sand. Remember that if you see anything out of the ordinary, like a large creature, it's a mirage and it's not real, and don't forget that there are no mammals on the island except the seals and tortoises, other than these two hounds.' He pointed at Charlie and Molly. 'So, there is nothing that will hurt you. Are you happy?'

Sam nodded.

'Agreed,' said Jack. 'Right, see you in 20 minutes then.'

'Right, girls,' Jack turned back towards Rosie and JJ. 'You have the water and you are allowed one sip each, please. Sam and I will have a sip before we go. Do not let the dogs run off under any circumstances.'

The dogs flattened their ears, as if to say: 'As if we would,' but Jack felt that it was important to say it anyway. He took a sip from the water bottle and Sam did the same.

As Jack strode off in one direction and Sam strode off in another, Rosie got out the water bottle. She hesitated to look out to sea and just before she took the top off, suddenly a strange black and white bird appeared on the sand in front of her.

'How beautiful,' said JJ, and just as she did, a second bird appeared, and then a third, until, suddenly, they were surrounded by about 20 of them. 'Is this for real?' said JJ.

The birds started hopping towards them and tapping at the water bottle. Rosie thought for a moment, and then laughed. 'They are for real,' she said. 'They are mocking birds. They are after the water,' she said. 'It's important that we don't give

them any, otherwise we'll never get rid of them,' and she firmly
tightened the screw top on the water bottle and hid it underneath
her cardigan. 'They'll get bored,' she said, and they sat and
waited. The mocking birds sat on the beach and watched them,
determined that they weren't going to go. Rosie looked at JJ and
then looked at Charlie. With a small flick of her head, Charlie
caught the instruction immediately and leapt to his feet, and the
mocking birds took off immediately, in a big cloud of white and
black feathers.

Jack set out across the volcanic rock. It was shiny black with
little holes everywhere. It looked more like the surface of the
moon than an island in the ocean, but Jack remembered from his
time on the islands with his parents that this is what most of the
islands looked like.

He assumed, from what he had read in the book that Charles
Darwin had written, that they were on James Island. The ground
towards the middle of the island was quite high and had some
cloud near the peaks, and it was a little bit greener than he
remembered from some of the islands that he had visited with his
parents. There was also no sign of the Beagle.

The shoreline was littered with seals and iguanas. There were
also the most amazing brightly coloured little blue crabs all along
the rocks down to his left. He thought that these were probably
Sally Go Lightly crabs that he had seen the last time, although he
may have got the name wrong.

As he looked further down on the rocky outcrops leading to
the sea, he could see strange birds with piercing bright eyes and
blue feet, and remembered sniggering when Dad had told him
that these were called blue footed boobies, and he watched as the
mating couples performed a ritual involving a small piece of stick,
which the male would hold and dance in front of the female to try
and attract her.

Jack reached a sandy beach and decided to drop down and

take his shoes off and walk along the sand. It had been a long time
since he had walked on sand and the heat on the soles of his feet
and the little grains of sand between his toes felt good. The sun
was beating down on his face now and it felt like an August day
in Cornwall.

Going in the opposite direction, Sam had counted to 500. He had
been going for about five minutes he thought and the terrain
was just as it was when he had set off. Black volcanic rock, dotted
with large seals and iguanas. He spotted some grass further up
from the shore and decided to head up to investigate on the basis
that if there was grass then perhaps there was water that was
keeping it damp. As he approached, he noted that there were five
large boulders on the grass and thought at the time that this was
a slightly odd place for boulders, which he would have expected
to see on the rock or in the sand. He moved towards them and,
suddenly, stopped dead in his tracks. One of the boulders lifted a
large prehistoric head with grass in the corners of its mouth and
looked at Sam in a cross between curiosity and surprise.

Sam stood stock still and his breathing became shallow.
Suddenly, the one head became five heads, as each of the boulders
appeared to spring a head and each looked more menacing than
the first.

'It's just a mirage,' said Sam out loud, although he wasn't quite
sure who he was speaking to. 'It's just a mirage.'

But the prehistoric creatures stood and watched him, neither
side looking to make any sharp move or approach the other.

Sam started to back away, very slowly at first, keeping his
eyes firmly fixed on the prehistoric creatures. Then his steps got
faster and faster and when he felt that he was a safe distance from
what he knew to be simply a trick that Evil was playing on him,

he turned on his heels and ran like the wind, back in the direction that he had come from.

As Jack walked along the sand, he got to 800. He knew that in 200 counts, he should turn round and go back to report that he had had no success in finding water or, indeed, anything else of interest. He looked at the shallow waters lapping up the sand and, as his feet were getting hotter and hotter, decided that he would cool them off in the warm shallows of the ocean.

Jack approached the water line, dipping his toe in, just to check that it was as warm as he remembered. It was warmer. He bent down and touched the water with his hands and he was not imagining it, it was like a warm bath. He kicked at the water with his foot and took a few paces back to take a running jump at the warm ocean, when a voice behind him shouted loudly: 'Stop!'

Jack almost jumped out of his skin as he spun round to see where the voice was coming from.

Stood on the rocky outcrop was a young man, probably about fifteen, with dark hair and a rounded face with smiling eyes. There was something about him that looked quite familiar to Jack, something comforting.

'I'm sorry,' said the stranger. 'I didn't mean to startle you, but I didn't want you to run into the water.'

Jack studied the boy in more detail and saw that he was wearing clothes very similar to Jack's although not quite as clean, and some parts were starting to fray.

'What's wrong with the water?' asked Jack. 'It looks and feels beautiful.'

'I will show you,' said the young man, and jumped down from the rocky outcrop onto the sand and stood alongside Jack. 'This is a favourite place for the sea creatures to come to eat,' he said. 'If you step down on them, they will sting you with their rays. You have to slide your feet into the sand and move along like this,' he said, and then demonstrated. He sunk his feet right into the sand and started to shuffle and as Jack watched in amazement, he saw round flat creatures appear in the water between the surface and the tops of his new-found friend's feet.

'What are they?' asked Jack.

'I think they have a very special name,' he said. 'But I call them the ray that stings. Watch.' He picked up a piece of hardened seaweed and poked the back gently of one of the creatures that was balancing on his foot. As Jack watched in amazement, the creature's tail flew up across its back and knocked into the seaweed.

'You see,' said the boy. 'If that was your foot, you would be in very great pain now, and even our doctor could not make it better.'

'Would it kill me?' asked Jack.

'No, it would not kill you but you would be in great pain for many months. I have seen my friends when they have trodden on the ray that stings.'

'Thank you...' said Jack. 'I don't even know your name.'

'Harold Wright,' said the young man. 'But my friends, they call me Harry for short.'

'That's easy to remember,' said Jack. 'My brother was called Harry. I am Jack,' and Jack held out his hand and shook Harry's outstretched hand firmly.

Harry looked Jack up and down and his eyes settled on Jack's clean clothes. He said, 'Which ship have you come from?' as if he did not believe that anyone so clean could have come off a ship.

Jack had to think quickly. It was clear that this young man could not think it unusual that Jack should be there, and he tried to rack his brain for what Charles Darwin had said about other boats in the area.

'I'm from a whaling boat,' he said. 'We tied up about two hours ago in that direction.' And Jack pointed back to where he had walked from.

'Which one?' asked Harry.

Jack was ashamed to say that all he could think of was the books his Dad had read him as a child. 'The Captain Moby,' he said.

'That's not one I've come across,' said Harry. 'But it is always nice to meet new people.'

'What about you, Harry? Where have you come from?' asked Jack.

'Oh, I'm with a research ship,' he said. 'We are on a five year journey and our boat has gone off in search of fresh water, so me and some of the crew and our naturalist are all camped about half an hour in that direction,' and he pointed along the coast.

'What is the name of your ship?' asked Jack, trying to look as if he was only vaguely interested but not entirely sure if he had been successful.

'The Beagle,' said Harry and smiled. 'And we have the most eccentric scientist on board. He studies everything. He shoots the little birds so that he can examine them, and he measures and writes in his little books. It is very funny to watch.'

'Oh,' said Jack. 'But I am sure that in years to come, people will be very grateful for his research.'

'I don't think so,' said Harry. 'All he seems interested in is birds and their beaks and why some animals are on one island and not the other. I don't think that this will be of use to anyone.'

Jack smiled in that knowing way that his Dad did to Jack when he knew something that Jack didn't, but didn't want to make a big point of it. 'If only you knew,' he thought, 'that you are currently making history.'

'So, who is your scientist?' Jack asked nonchalantly. 'Will he be someone I have heard of?'

'I don't think so,' said Harry. 'Apparently he was second choice but he is a nice man. His name is Mr Charles Darwin and he is eccentric, but very clever. He likes to try and teach us and I like to learn.' Jack's heart missed a beat.

'Where is he now?' asked Jack, apprehensively, hoping that they were not too late.

'Oh, he's back in camp, writing up his work from yesterday,' and as Harry said that, a shot rang out in the distance, very faintly.

Jack almost jumped out of his skin and looked around nervously. 'What was that?' he asked in horror.

'Oh, I expect that was Mr Darwin shooting his next bird to study,' said Harry in a very matter of fact way.

'He shoots them?' asked Jack. That would be so contrary to everything that Jack had learned in his short life about conservation and preservation, but he had to remember that this was more than a century beforehand, when perhaps this was the only way that scientists knew.

'Oh yes,' said Harry. 'Frequently. Would you like to meet Mr Darwin? He is always very interested to meet people from other boats. We get to see so few people on our voyage that it is always a great pleasure to meet others, and hear about their experiences.'

'I would love to,' said Jack. 'But I did say to my shipmates that I would be back with them by a certain time and if I am not back, they will worry. Can I arrange to meet you again later on and perhaps we could go and meet Mr Darwin. How long will you be staying?'

'We will be staying until our ship returns,' said Harry. 'Once it has found water.'

'So, there is no water on the island?' asked Jack, with a certain amount of alarm.

'There's plenty of water,' said Harry. 'But it is up in the hills and it is hard to bring down to the boat. We need a lot of water for our voyage and there are islands where water is easier to come by. Are you short of water too?' he asked.

Jack shook his head and said, 'No, it was just we were thirsty when we were out exploring the island and wanted to refill our water flagons.'

Harry nodded in the direction that Jack had come from, and said, 'If you follow the sea along until you find green grass between the sea and the dunes, there is a spring. You will know you're in the right place because you will find the giant tortoises eating the grass. There you can fill up your water flagons. We could not use it to fill the boat because the rocks are too jagged and we could not bring the boat in close enough. I would love to meet your friends later on, but first of all let me introduce you to Mr Darwin. Shall we say we'll meet as the sun drops to there,' and he pointed skywards on the horizon. 'At that time, I will meet you here.'

Jack remembered that the Beagle had only been there for a week and so it was important to work out how much longer they had on the island. 'How long have you been on the island?' asked Jack.

'Five days,' said Harry. 'It has been good to be on land for that long.'

Jack realised that they did not have much time but at least he had managed to find them in time and Mr Darwin appeared to still be alive.

'Until later, Master Harry,' said Jack and pretended to touch his imaginary cap.

'Until then, Master Jack,' and Harry imitated the gesture and turned and ran off in the direction of the shot.

Jack put on his shoes and started to walk back along the shore in the direction that he had left his sister and friends. He thought perhaps he had been gone for slightly longer than 20 minutes and so broke into a jog.

As he ran to the bend, he saw, to his relief, the familiar figures of Rosie and JJ, and, in front of them, was Sam, who was clearly telling them what he had found, as he was making signs with his hands as if he was explaining a big fish that he had caught. He looked out of breath and as he was telling his tale, he was holding his arms as wide as possible to indicate how big something had been. He then moved on to how tall it was and stood on tiptoe and held his arm up high to indicate that it was much, much taller than he was.

As Jack approached, none of the three of them noticed he was there, but the two dogs sat up immediately and leapt to their feet when they realised it was Jack, and ran towards him, almost bowling him over in their excitement.

Jack could tell by the expressions on the faces of his sister and friends that there was clearly something worrying them.

'What is it?' he asked in alarm.

'We think that Evil has been playing tricks again,' said Rosie. 'It tried to frighten Sam with prehistoric creatures which were taller than he was.'

'What did they look like?' asked Jack.

'Well at first,' said Sam, 'I thought that they were boulders, but, as I got closer, these huge heads, like dinosaurs, appeared.' He held out his arms as wide as he could to demonstrate the enormous size.

'Were they quite rounded?' asked Jack.

'Yes. How did you know?' Sam sounded a little hesitant.

'Did they move?' asked Jack, a small smile crossing his face.

'No,' said Sam. 'They just stood and looked at me.'

'Were they eating the grass?' asked Jack.

'How did you know that?' said Sam.

Jack started to laugh. 'I'm sorry, my friend. I don't mean to laugh at you,' he said. 'But what you have seen are one of the animals that lives on the Galapagos, that is found almost nowhere else in the world: the giant tortoise.'

'A tortoise?' said Sam. 'You mean the thing that has just frightened the life out of me and caused me to run at probably the equivalent of the speed of sound, was a tortoise?'

'A very big tortoise,' said Jack.

'And a lot of them,' said Sam.

Rosie said, wisely, 'If you didn't know, Sam, I'm sure it was very frightening. I'd forgotten that they have giant tortoises on the Galapagos. And, from your description, I thought that perhaps it was some kind of dinosaur that Evil was conjuring up.'

'But it's important,' said Jack, 'for us to know where they were, because if we find them, that's where the water source is. Was there grass there?'

'Yes,' said Sam. 'That's what the tortoises were eating.'

'Of course,' said Jack. 'Sorry, I forgot. Well, that's where we need to go to get the water.'

'How do you know that for certain?' asked Rosie.

'I met a boy on the beach,' he said and sat down on the rock next to the other three and the dogs tucked in beside him very close. He started to tell his sister and two friends all about his encounter and the fact that Mr Darwin was definitely on the island.

'I just need a sip of water,' he said. 'And then we'll go and refill the water bottle.' As he sat with the other three opposite him and started to unscrew the top of the bottle, he saw a small smile across their faces and stopped unscrewing.

'Why are you all smiling at me?' he said. And the smiles grew even larger.

'Nothing,' said Rosie. 'Tell us about Harry.'

'Well,' said Jack, as he started unscrewing again. 'Harry is part of the ship's company for the Beagle, and they are camped about 40 minutes in that direction. Harry wants to meet new people, so I have suggested that he meets me later this afternoon, just as the sun gets to a certain position on the horizon, back exactly where I met him this morning.'

As the top to the water bottle became looser, the first bird appeared on the rock.

'That's a pretty bird,' said Jack.

'Yes,' smiled Rosie, as the second one arrived and then the third, until there were probably about 20 of them surrounding the group of four friends.

'Why are these birds watching me?' asked Jack.

'Don't you remember?' said Rosie giggling. 'When we were in the Galapagos, the birds were after the water. They know that you have water, so you had better drink it quick before they try and take the bottle off you.'

Jack took a couple of swigs and then screwed the top up tightly. He looked at the two dogs, who looked a little warm. 'We're not far from water. You two, you can have your fill when we get there.'

The dogs sat upright with their tongues hanging out and ears alert. It was as if they understood.

As they started packing up their things, ready to walk back towards the spring, Sam asked, 'Why are they camped, if they have a boat?'

'Don't you remember?' said Rosie. 'The boat left them to go and find water and Charles Darwin and some of his group camped on the island until they came back.'

'I'd forgotten that,' said Sam. 'Even if I knew it in the first place.'

'He is apparently there,' said Jack. 'Shooting birds to study them.'

'No!' said JJ, with a sharp intake of breath. 'He's shooting them?'

'I know, I know,' said Jack. 'It's not what we would do nowadays but it's what they did in those days, and we can't make a fuss because we will give ourselves away. As if we are not going to give ourselves away enough with two hairy Border Collies in tow.'

Charlie and Molly put their ears flat, as if they had done something wrong. 'It's all right, you're not in trouble,' said Jack. 'It's just that you're not really supposed to be here. We can't exactly dress you as giant tortoises, and you are a bit big for iguanas, so we'll have to decide what to do, once we have found some water.'

'I'm a bit hungry, too,' said Rosie. 'And I'm a bit fed up with biscuits.'

Jack raised his eyes as if to say he knew this would happen if his younger sister came with him, but he didn't say anything. He was grateful for the company and would not have liked to have done this on his own.

'Well, why don't we see what we can get out of the sea,' said Jack. 'There have to be crabs and shrimps and loads of fish. Let's go and find a safe place by the water first and let's see what we can use to fish with. I think in my bag I've got some fishing wire or a couple of fish hooks, so perhaps we can try and catch crabs like we used to when we were children. If we can find some kindling, we can start a little fire, like the Masai taught us. There isn't much wind but the direction it's blowing, it should keep the smoke well away from the camp.' Jack stooped down and picked up some sand and watched the way the grains fell when he released them, so he knew the gentle breeze was coming from the west.

They started walking back towards where Sam had seen the giant tortoises. As they walked along the shoreline, JJ said, 'What's that in the water? It looks like a big fish but with a really square head.'

They were looking down into the sea and they gathered on the edge of the path; they saw not just one, but probably thirty of these creatures.

'Is that pretend as well?' said JJ.

'No,' said Jack. 'They are hammerhead sharks. We saw them when we were here. They get a lot of them in the Galapagos. They won't hurt us; they are after the fish.'

'How can they catch anything with big heads like that?' said Sam.

'Apparently their eye on the sides of their heads give them really good all round vision,' said Jack. 'So, it helps them to sense where they are and where the fish are.'

'They are amazing!' said JJ. 'I've never seen anything like that before in my life.'

'They are even more amazing,' said Jack, 'if you are in the water and one of them swims up to you, which is what happened to us when we were swimming with the seals.'

'Were you really scared?' said JJ.

'No,' said Jack. 'Dad had already explained to us that they are not interested in us, but they are very well fed here in the Galapagos. But still it was a bit scary.'

As they rounded the corner, they saw the green grass further up from the shoreline and there, still munching away, were the four or five boulders that Sam had seen earlier.

They tiptoed a bit closer and there they were, the most amazing, graceful prehistoric looking creatures that any of them had ever seen, with enormous great shells, which were almost six feet in length and standing at least four feet off the ground. The enormous shells glistened in the sunshine. The big heads were raised, looking at the four children and with minor alarm as they saw the two dogs trotting behind them. Jack saw them look. 'Stay,' he said to the dogs. They both lay down in the sand.

The tortoises were chomping away at the green lush grass, and seemed unworried by the presence of four children, who walked amongst them, touching their shells.

'Why are they not frightened?' asked Rosie.

'Because they don't really know what we are,' said Jack. 'They have seen so few humans before or at least not small ones!'

'But,' said JJ, 'Darwin's book says that they killed tortoises and ate them and that is why people stopped here. They also kept their meat on board the boats. So they should be frightened of us.'

'Perhaps these four haven't had that much to do with human beings,' said Jack, as he patted the largest of them. 'Now, let's try and find where this water source is.'

They followed the grass up as it became lusher and deeper.

'Shhhhsh,' said Jack. 'I can hear something.' And they all stopped, and, sure enough, there was a small trickle coming from beneath the grass.

'I think it's here,' he said. 'Molly, Charlie,' he called them over and they came directly in a big circle around the tortoises and it was unclear who was the most worried about who: the tortoises, probably never having seen a dog, and the dogs certainly never having seen anything like a giant tortoise. One of the smaller tortoises outstretched its neck to get a closer look at Molly, whose natural reaction was to snap her jaws quietly.

'Molly! That's very unfriendly,' said Jack. 'That's very naughty.'

Molly put her ears down flat, as she did whenever she heard the word 'naughty'.

'Go and say hello nicely.' And Molly approached slowly, slightly crouched.

'Not too close,' said JJ. 'We wouldn't like the tortoises to pick up any disease from the animals.'

'No, that's a good point,' said Jack. 'Molly away please. Come and help with the water.'

The children were down on their knees in the grass, trying to work out where the noise was coming from. They pulled back the grass tufts and there was a small trickle of water.

'How would we know it's safe to drink?' asked Sam.

'The dogs will soon tell us,' said Jack.

And as the fresh, clear water trickled out of the hillside and was gulped down by two very thirsty Border Collies, Jack looked up. 'There's your answer,' he said. 'But I think it would be sensible to put in one of those tablets that they gave us, just in case.' Jack rummaged in his bag and found a tablet and dropped it into the water bottle, swishing it around.

Once they had all drunk enough water and refilled the water flagon until it was brimming, they decided to make this place their camp as best they could. No one had any idea how long it would take for them to prevent Evil from stopping Mr Darwin, but as they had water and a plentiful source of food from the sea, there seemed little point in going anywhere else at the moment.

Jack went to explore by the water's edge and dropped down out of sight, over the edge of the black rock. He popped up a few minutes later. 'I've found a cave,' he said. 'That should give us some shelter and we could also light a fire in there without being seen.'

They picked up their things and one by one dropped over the edge after Jack. By the entrance to the cave, there were large boulders of rocks with huge deep rock pools, which appeared to be teeming with life. Along the shoreline there were dried pieces of seaweed and the odd stick that had been washed up, although the children were not quite sure where from, given the lack of trees around the edges of the shoreline.

Sam volunteered to go slightly more inland as he had spotted a few bigger trees, and hoped that there may be some old dried out wood that they could use for the fire, whilst the girls picked the mussels from the sides of the rock pools, split them open with a stone and took out the mussel to use as bait for bigger fish. Jack took off his knapsack and started to carefully unpack it to see what he had with him. He was delighted to see that he had some fishing line and hooks.

He set up a few crab lines in the rock pools, as they had
watched a number of enormous crabs on the bottom of the pools
but they had been too far down or too quick for them to capture
them. Also, in the open sea, he put out a couple of hooks on wires
with small pieces of mussel in the hope that something bigger
would be tempted.

Within an hour, they had four huge crabs and when Jack
pulled up the fishing line out to sea, there were about 6 little fish
that looked similar to sardines, all hanging off the hooks.

It was at this stage that Jack was extremely glad that he
had listened carefully to his father when they had been fishing,
and understood about putting animals out of their misery very
quickly, and he took the fish and the crabs back into the cave and
quickly and humanely killed them, using a large rock for the fish
and a sharp knife that he had found in his knapsack to despatch
the crabs.

It was at that point that Sam appeared with an armful of
firewood, and using the kindling and his Glorch, Jack quickly
started a small fire, using the rays of the sun at the entrance to the
cave.

Sam had taken the dogs with him in his search for firewood
and when they returned, the sight of the four large crabs lined
up along the wall was clearly something that was worrying the
collies. Charlie tried pushing one of them with his front paw and
jumping back, waiting for retaliation from the huge crab claws
at the front of the recently deceased beasts. Molly, on the other
hand, attempted an attack from the rear, leaping on top of the
dead crab and throwing it into the air with her paws, so that it
almost ended up back in the water, if Jack had not been quick
enough to grab it.

'Will somebody please give these dogs a biscuit before they
completely ruin our lunch,' he said, exasperated.

That afternoon, the children feasted on fresh crab and fish. Jack showed them how to take sharp rocks and break the crab shells to get the tender meat out and also showed them the poisonous black sack that they had to take out and not eat. He was surprised how much he remembered from his days by the seaside with Dad and was very glad that he did, otherwise they would have all gone very hungry.

Once they had finished their food and cleared away the crab shells and washed their hands in the warm salty water, they refilled their water bottle and drank their fill and ate a few more biscuits, and then all sat out in a line outside the cave in the warm afternoon sunshine, listening to the sea lapping on the rocks and the seals calling for their young.

Overhead there were so many sea birds it was impossible to count them all, ranging from small white birds that Jack thought were probably terns, to enormous long winged beasts that they all decided were probably albatross. Jack remembered that although they looked like normal seagulls from the ground, that, close up, their wingspan was about twelve feet, which was almost three times as tall as he was.

All around on the rocks were the little blue Sally Go Lightly crabs, which were beautiful and harmless, but very inquisitive. Jack looked at the sun. He said, 'I think we've probably got another two hours before I have to meet with Harry. Shall we go and explore some of the island? If we are where I think we are, there is a salt pan not far from here with flamingos on it.'

'Flamingos!' said JJ. 'They're my favourite.'

'And mine,' said Rosie. 'Will there be lots of them, like in Africa?'

'I hope so,' said Jack. 'But no promises. It's important that we go in the opposite direction to where Charles Darwin is because we don't want to be seen. Now make sure that we have a lot of water and bring the biscuits. Darwin reported that they had met quite a few Spaniards on his visit so we need to keep an eye out for them. Four children and two dogs may look very strange.'

They climbed up the rocks to the top of the cliff so that they were overlooking the sea, and walked off in the direction of the springs where the giant tortoises were still drinking and eating the grass. Beyond that, there was more vegetation but the trees took on a slightly grey look and were not very tall. They were alive with little birds.

'I think these are Darwin's finches,' said Jack. 'Look, they have different beaks to the ones at home.'

'They are very tame,' said JJ.

'That's because they are not really used to people and they don't know that we could harm them.'

Sam laughed, 'Apart from Mr Darwin, of course, who will more than likely shoot them to get a closer look.'

Jack looked wisely. 'It's called 'science', and although it sounds cruel to us, without it, we might never have known how creatures can adapt over time to fit in with their surroundings.'

Rosie looked thoughtful. 'Is that what Mr Darwin said?' she said. 'I don't want to look stupid if we meet him.'

'It's probably best not to say anything,' said Jack. 'It may be that he hasn't yet come up with his theory of evolution and we don't want to put ideas into his head.'

As they came over the top of the small hill that they were walking up, in front of them opened out the most amazing sight. It was an enormous great white circle and stood in it, only a couple of inches deep, were thousands upon thousands of pink flamingos. Jack indicated for them all to duck down and lie flat on their stomachs and look out across at the flamingos.

'Why is it so white?' asked JJ.

'That's the salt,' said Jack. 'What the islands don't know is that in years to come, people will try and mine the salt without success.'

'But what about the flamingos?' said JJ.

'Oh, they'll be disturbed,' said Jack in a matter of fact way.
'Like man disturbs everything.'

Sam turned round with his back to the flamingos and looked
out across to the sea. 'My goodness,' he said. 'Look, there's a boat.
Is that the Beagle?' Jack hoped not as it would be two days early.

They all turned round to face the same direction as Sam to
see what he was looking at and, sure enough, on the horizon, was
a large boat.

'I think I have some binoculars in my knapsack,' said Jack,
and fished them out straight away. He tried to focus them. 'No,'
he said. 'It's not the Beagle. I think it's a whaling boat.'

JJ looked in horror. 'You mean as in a boat that will catch
whales?'

'Yes,' said Jack. 'I'm afraid so, and it looks as if they have
actually got a whale that they are hauling alongside.'

'No!' exclaimed Rosie.

And, with that, the flamingos took off from the lake.

'Get down,' said Jack, and they all lay flat against the grass in
case anybody was watching.

'Sorry,' said Rosie.

'It's all right,' said Jack. 'I don't think they can see us from
here. They won't have the same glasses that we do.'

The two dogs lay alongside them and as the flamingos took
off, Charlie went to chase them, but Jack was ahead of him and
held on firmly to his collar. 'No,' he said to Charlie, and Charlie
looked at him with an expression that was probably doggy
language for 'spoilsport'.

'Well at least if Harry sees the whaling boat, then he will
think that I am definitely from there. We just need to check and
make sure we know where it's anchored in case they come in
search of fresh water at the spring.'

They watched as the whaling ship with sails fully out being

pushed along by the afternoon wind, moved along the edge of the coast, past where the spring was located, further round, out of sight.

'That's just awful,' said Rosie, as it disappeared from sight. 'That poor whale.'

Sam gazed out into the distance, and said, 'Well, at least we humans finally saw sense about hunting whales, but not until they were hunted to within an inch of extinction.' They were all silent for a few minutes. Eventually it was broken by Sam.

'So, which direction is Mr Darwin's camp?' he asked.

'That direction,' said Jack, pointing.

'Well, whilst we are this high up,' said Sam, 'why don't we walk along and see if we can use your binoculars to try and work out what's going on? It would be useful to know how many people are there and what they are doing, bearing in mind we've got no idea what Evil will try and do to Mr Darwin whilst we are here.'

'Good idea,' said Jack. 'Is everybody up for that?' And the dogs leapt to their feet immediately. 'Well, I know you two would be. Rosie, are you all right to go on?'

'Of course,' she said.

'Me too,' said JJ.

And they started moving further along from the salt rim and round the corner towards the Darwin encampment.

The first sign that they had that they were getting close was the smoke coming from the camp fires, and as they crept across the landscape and settled themselves into a position that they could look down onto the camp, they could make out the people down below. There were probably about twenty in total. Some were sat down cleaning what appeared to be muskets, others were cooking and, set to one side of the camp, was a smaller tent and outside sat at a desk was a gentleman in a hat. He appeared to be studying samples on a desk in front of him and every so often writing in the journal that he had.

He had a roundish face, with blondish hair and was wearing a pristine white shirt which was quite full and flowing, but neatly tucked into his britches. He also had on a dark cravat and a waistcoat. He looked deep in concentration.

'Oh my goodness!' said Jack, 'I think that's Charles Darwin, and I think that's him writing the *Voyage of the Beagle.*'

Even to Rosie, this historical fact was not lost and the children sat and stared for some minutes. They were actually watching a piece of history.

Suddenly, there was a shot that rang out and all of them jumped and the dogs were about to let out a bark, when Jack and Rosie grabbed them both and all but sat on them to stop them from making a noise.

'What was that?' said Sam.

'I suspect that that was somebody collecting one of Mr Darwin's samples,' said Jack. 'Either that or they were hunting for supper.'

'I think they've got supper already,' said Sam, with the end of his lip curled up, which indicated that he was not very impressed. And when Jack looked through the glasses, he realised that he was right. For there, cooking over the fire, appeared to be a very large giant tortoise.

'Oh my goodness,' said Jack. 'That is just awful!'

Each of the children looked through the glasses in turn.

'How could they?' said JJ. 'They are so beautiful.'

'That's horrid!' said Rosie, as she looked. 'And all those poor tortoises that are in that compound, do you think they are all going to be eaten as well?'

Six pairs of eyes fell on the compound with tortoises. 'Not if I can help it,' said Sam, and went to stand up.

Jack pulled him down. 'Don't be silly, Sam. This is not the time to rescue tortoises. We are here to stop one of the greatest scientists the world has ever known from being stopped in his tracks.'

Rosie looked at him. 'Do you mean murdered?'

'I don't know what I mean,' said Jack. 'But Evil has something planned to stop Charles Darwin from publishing his theory. We just need to work out what that is.'

'What's that?' said JJ, pointing past the camp and towards the sea.

Jack couldn't see anything with his naked eye and so lifted the small binoculars up to have a closer look. 'You've got good eyesight,' he said, and then remembered that as she was one of the country's finest young shots, it was more likely than not that she would have better eyesight than he did.

'There,' she said pointing. 'There seems to be a small boat.'

Jack focused the binoculars, and, sure enough, there, on the sea was a small rowing boat with probably four or five men inside.

'I expect they are just fishing or setting traps for lobsters or crabs,' said Jack.

'Let me look,' said Sam, and Jack passed the glasses across. 'I would be surprised to see people going fishing wearing cutlasses and daggers,' he said, and passed the binoculars back to Jack.

'My goodness, you're right,' he said, passing the binoculars across to the girls for them to have a look. 'And they seem to be heading towards the camp,' said Jack.

Sam thought about this for a moment. 'But there are only five of them,' he said. 'And over 20 people at camp. There's no way they are going to attack the camp with those numbers.'

Jack turned the glasses back to the camp and realised that Sam was, of course, right – that although there were a number of cooks and bottle washers, there was clearly a large number of crew at the campsite and it would be a hard job for five men, even with cutlasses, to overwhelm them.

It was at that stage that all four children stopped exactly where they were, as a strange hissing sound came from behind them. They all looked at each other and turned together to see where the noise was coming from.

The dogs were still lying still at their feet, looking in the direction of the sea and they didn't appear to have heard the sound. As the children turned together, Rosie let out a scream and the flamingos took off across the lake for a second time that day.

'What the…' said Sam, because, there, behind them, as tall as they were and as wide, was the most enormous snake. 'Oh my goodness!' shouted Sam as the snake flicked its tongue in and out, almost as if it was counting the number of small children it was about to eat.

The dogs leapt to their feet and turned to face the children. They had the expression on their faces as if to say, 'What's all the fuss about?'

Rosie was about to start running down the hill when Jack grabbed her hand. 'It's not real,' he said. 'Look, the dogs can't see it, it's not real. It's just Evil playing tricks on us.'

Charlie stood with his body straight, the hair on the back of his neck standing up slightly, as he pointed with his nose towards the grass just behind the children. Molly looked to see where Charlie was pointing and she, too, adopted the same pose. They both seemed to be pointing towards the bottom of where this giant snake was sat, looking menacingly at the children.

'I think,' said Jack, 'that there's a real snake there, but Evil is just making it look ten times bigger.'

The snake lunged forward and Rosie screamed again. If the flamingos had not been flying around already they would have taken off for the third time.

Jack picked up his binoculars and quickly looked down towards the camp and realised that those in the camp had probably heard the screams and were looking up in the direction of the hillside on which they were all stood. Even the men in the boat had stopped rowing and were looking towards where the screams had come from.

'Right,' said Jack. 'Everybody close their eyes and think of something really good that they have done in their lives. Something you've done to help someone else or where you've been kind. Sam, you first. Say it out loud.'

'I help the little old lady who lives next door to us to unload her shopping from the car every week.'

Jack opened his eyes a little way and the snake appeared to have got smaller.

'JJ?'

'I helped rescue a hedgehog from the side of the road last week,' she said. 'I put it in a box with some water and some dog food and we made it better.'

The snake shrunk even further.

'Rosie?'

Rosie squeezed her eyes really tight and held her brother's hand even tighter. 'I didn't tell JJ that Jack is in love with her,' she said, and JJ's eyes flew open. Jack could feel himself getting redder and redder, but it worked and the snake halved in size. JJ shot a glance at Jack, who just kept looking at the snake, even though he knew that she was watching him.

It came to Jack and his mind went blank. He knew that he had done many kind things in his life but now, on the spot, when it really mattered, he couldn't remember any of them. There was a few seconds' silence.

'Jack, come on,' said Rosie. 'What have you done?' And Jack could feel Charlie nuzzling his leg. He looked down and Charlie lifted up his paw and looked at it.

'I know, I know!' said Jack. 'I took a thorn out of Charlie's paw when we had been on a walk.'

They all opened their eyes and the snake had all but disappeared. And then they saw something move in the grass and the dogs started to chase it.

'Stop!' said Jack. He could not remember if the snakes on the Galapagos Islands used poison or whether they constricted their prey, and now was not the time to find out. 'We have to move quickly,' said Jack. 'They have seen us at the camp and will be wondering who we are.'

'Look!' said Sam. 'They are rowing back, the men with the cutlasses.'

'Does that mean we've stopped it?' said Rosie.

'No, I don't think so,' said Jack. 'They look pretty determined. Whatever it is, we need to find them and find what they are doing.'

He looked up into the sky. 'Right, we need to move,' he said. 'I'm due to be meeting Harry at the spring soon. I can't be late.'

And, with that, they turned on their heels and started to run back in the direction of the spring as fast as they could. Down through the small bushes and trees they ran, not looking back. On to the sand and finally across the black rocks to the safety of their cave. Only once they were all there, dogs included, did they stop and sink down to the ground. They all drank greedily from the water bottle and poured some into a shallow rock for the dogs to drink.

'That was a bit scary,' said Rosie, and they all laughed nervously.

'Just a bit,' said Sam. 'Evil knows just how to frighten us, doesn't it.'

Jack said: 'But remember, it can't conjure things up, it has to make something which already exists bigger, and if the dogs can't see it or aren't frightened by it, then it is not likely to be real.'

'Unless it's a giant tortoise,' said Rosie, and Sam shot her a look and then ruffled her hair.

'I'll get you for that, Rosie Simmons,' he said.

Back at the cave, they all sat with their backs to the walls in the warm evening sunshine.

'We haven't even got any weapons,' said Sam.

'But we could make some,' suggested JJ, and everyone looked at her in a way that said 'don't be silly, we haven't got anything to make weapons from'.

'We have string and fishing wire. There's wood. We have a penknife. We've been to the School, we're supposed to know what to do in situations like this. We've had the Masai come in and tell us about it.'

'Well,' said Sam, 'technically speaking, I don't go to the School yet, so perhaps I can be excused from this one.' He smiled to let them all know that he was only joking, but that he hadn't had the benefit of a Masai upbringing in recent years.

'Anyway,' said Rosie, 'that nice Masai man was only talking about killing lions and I don't think we've got any lions on the island. I don't think he meant for us to make weapons to attack people with.'

Jack looked thoughtful. 'If the Masai have to defend themselves they will use weapons,' he said. 'And we are not here to attack anybody but just to defend Mr Darwin to make sure that he is not hurt, or, worse still, killed, and that Evil wins. Remember,' he said, 'if we don't succeed, then we will probably never go back.'

He could see Rosie's bottom lip start to tremble slightly at the thought, and Charlie put his head on her lap.

'Come on Rosie, we're not having any of that nonsense. You decided to follow me, so you have to be brave about this,' he said in his most authoritative voice that made him sound most like Dad, but even more like Mum.

Jack turned to JJ, trying not to let the embarrassment of Rosie's revelations cloud his judgment. 'JJ,' he said, 'that's a great idea. Can I put you in charge of weapons? Quick as you can, please, I think I'll be meeting Harry very soon.'

'Don't you trust him?' said Sam.

'Of course I trust him,' he said. 'But I just don't know who his friends are, and if the men with cutlasses are heading this way, we need to be prepared. Now, make something that you two can usefully use; JJ and I can take care of ourselves,' and he smiled at JJ.

'But I thought that you were a good shot and we don't have any guns,' Sam said.

JJ smiled. 'I am quite good with a bow and arrow.'

Jack looked at her and raised his eyebrows as if to say, 'You might as well tell them the rest now'.

'Oh, and I probably didn't mention that I am the Under 13s World Taekwondo champion.'

'Wow!' said Sam. 'You mean where you kick people in the head for fun?'

JJ smiled. 'Yeah,' she said, 'I guess that's about the long and short of it.'

The two dogs exchanged glances as if they had completely understood the last conversation, and you could see them almost making a mental note not to stand too close to JJ if she was cross.

'Wow!' said Sam. 'That is impressive.'

Rosie stepped forward, as if not to be outdone. 'I can use a bow and arrow, too,' she said.

'Well, that settles it,' said Jack. 'Bows and arrows might be a bit difficult but any sharp spears, swords – well whatever you can manage, really, in the time available.'

'Ok,' said Sam. 'We're on it. Rosie, you come with me. Let's go and find some wood. JJ, do you want to search the shoreline for anything that we can improvise with?'

JJ picked up a few remains of the crabs where they had smashed them with the hammers, and some of the parts were extremely sharp. 'Well,' she said, 'we can start with these.'

'I'll help you,' said Jack. 'And I'll keep an eye out for Harry.'

Together they searched the shore just outside the cave and managed to find a number of sharp shells and small bits of coral, all of which would be quite sharp if jabbed at someone. They had just concluded that they probably had enough to make a few decent weapons when Jack looked up to see a small figure wandering along the shoreline in the general direction of the spring.

He looked towards the cave to make sure that Rosie and Sam had returned, to find them sat there stripping bark off small branches and making sharp tips with the penknife.

'JJ,' he said, 'he's here. Go up into the cave and give these to the others and see what you can do with them. Keep the dogs quiet and I'll be back as soon as I can.'

JJ stepped back behind the rocks so that Harry could not see her, but she crouched and watched as Jack strode purposefully along the beach to meet his new-found friend.

As Jack approached, Harry saw him and waved and broke into a trot towards him. As he got closer, he held out his right arm. 'Master Jack,' he said, 'how lovely to see you again.'

'The same to you, Master Harry,' Jack smiled, and they shook hands like proper grown-ups.

'How has your day been?' he asked.

'Enjoyable,' said Jack. 'It is good to have some time away from the boat.' He fibbed slightly, his fingers crossed behind his back so it would not count.

'I agree,' said Harry. 'It is so infrequent that I cannot remember the last time that I have had this much time to myself. Did you hear all the commotion up on the hillside this afternoon?' he asked, pointing in the general direction that Jack and the other three had been. 'We thought at first it was some sort of raiding party.'

'Where from?' said Jack.

Harry pointed up towards the hills. 'There are supposed to be some savages living further up into the rainforest,' he said. 'I have never seen them myself, but I have heard of their existence.'

'What are they supposed to look like?' asked Jack.

'They have black faces and arms,' said Harry. 'And big white teeth, and apparently they eat people.'

Jack raised his eyebrows. Cannibalism was certainly nothing that had been mentioned to him during his stay, and he wondered if this was just an assumption on the part of those who had travelled widely, that anyone who had coloured skin would behave like some of the ancient tribes of Africa, where they did, indeed, eat each other and shrink heads.

'Did you get a good look at them?' asked Jack.

'No,' said Harry. 'They were too far away and by the time we climbed the hills where they were, they were long gone, but there were strange tracks in the sand.'

They started walking back along the shoreline towards Darwin's camp. Harry kicked his bare feet through the sand and from time to time would bend down and pick up beautiful shells or jump into the water and pull out small living creatures, like sea cucumbers, or spiny sea urchins. He seemed keen to show Jack his vast knowledge of the creatures of the land and sea.

'How do you know so much?' asked Jack.

'I have been travelling the world with the great Mr Darwin,' said Harry proudly. 'He has been trying to teach me as we have sailed from island to island and country to country. Some of it is very complicated but some of it I understand and I always try and be interested. I watch how Mr Darwin draws his pictures and the labels that he gives, particularly to the little birds that he has been capturing. He looks at their beaks and makes careful note of what they eat and what they do. Do you want to swim?' he said.

'Of course,' said Jack, and without further invitation he

stripped off his trousers and top, and they both ran into the sea.

'Over there,' said Harry, 'you see all the blue footed boobies diving into the water? That means that there are lots of fish.'

The water was beautifully warm, like a bath, and the two of them swam out to where the blue footed boobies were dive-bombing into the water. Just before they hit the water, they would fold back their wings so that they were as sleek as possible before diving down through the ocean to find their fish.

Jack was swimming along, looking under water, his eyes open. The saltiness of the sea stung a little but it soon subsided, and the pain was worth it for the most amazing sights of tropical fish of all shapes and sizes.

Just as he was watching two huge, brightly coloured blue fish swim past right in front of him, something nudged him from the right. Jack spun round in the water, thinking that perhaps it was Harry playing tricks on him. Then he realised that Harry was ahead of him in the water. Something nudged him again and Jack spun again and this time he saw what it was. A huge sea lion, swimming round and round Jack like a corkscrew. Jack's heart missed a beat and then he realised that the sea lion was just playing with him. Jack started to mimic every move the sea lion made and the sea lion responded.

In the water ahead of him, Jack saw Harry stop and change direction and come back towards Jack and the sea lion. He thought at first that Harry was concerned, but in fact Harry just wanted to join in, and the two of them frolicked and twisted and turned in the warm ocean water with their new friend.

Eventually, Jack's lungs felt as if they would burst and he broke through the surface of the water, laughing and spluttering, closely followed by Harry.

'That was just such fun,' said Jack.

Harry spluttered through a mouthful of salt water, 'I think she liked you.'

'How do you know it's a 'she',' said Jack.

Harry laughed, 'You'd soon know if it was one of the boy sea lions. They are about twice the size and they would rather bite you than play with you because they would think that you were trying to move in on their girl.' And just as Harry said that, there was a loud noise from the rocks to the left of them that sounded a little like a monkey but was very deep throated, and, on the edge of the rock, stood the most enormous sea lion that Jack had ever seen.

'You see what I mean,' said Harry. 'I think we'd better leave our new friend to herself.'

The sea lion had obviously heard it as well and, with a flick of the tail, she disappeared back towards where her 'beach master' was waiting to take her back under his protective care.

They swam for a bit longer, their eyes constantly looking down at the fish and the creatures of the sea. Harry pointed, excitedly, to a large rock at the bottom of the sea bed and Jack looked at him with some surprise, as although it was a nicely rounded rock, it didn't appear to be anything of significance. Harry gestured, 'follow me' and they took a deep breath and swam down toward the rock.

It was only as they got closer that Jack realised that what he had mistaken for a rock was in fact a sea turtle and, as they approached, a head poked tentatively out to see what was causing the water to be disturbed. It looked carefully at Jack and Harry and decided that they were not predators, and carefully pulled its head back into its shell and went back to sleep.

As they were watching the sea turtle, all of a sudden small rockets started raining down on them from the surface of the water. Creatures travelling so fast, surrounded by a pocket of air. The first one missed Jack by inches and he jumped back in the water. He tried to focus his eyes on what it was that was raining down on them, thinking perhaps it was some sort of meteorite storm. But when he saw, he almost laughed out loud, because what was being propelled through the water with such speed were in fact the blue footed boobies that they had been in search of in the first place.

Jack looked around and, to his left, saw immediately why the boobies were so attracted to this area. A huge shoal of fish, swimming this way, then that, altogether and then suddenly dispersing as a blue footed booby landed headfirst in amongst them, reappearing with a fish every time.

Jack and Harry played and watched the boobies and the fish for a while until Jack's skin started to wrinkle a little and the water suddenly didn't feel as warm. He gestured his head towards the shoreline and Harry nodded and the two of them set off swimming back to where they had left their clothes on the secluded beach.

They sat out on the sand and dried off in the late afternoon sun. Jack could see Harry looking at him slightly strangely and he worked out that it appeared to be Jack's underpants that were perplexing his new-found friend.

'What strange undergarments you wear,' Harry said.

Jack hoped that Harry did not want to inspect them even closer, as the Marks and Spencer's label probably would have been one step too far.

'They were a present,' said Jack, 'from a very far away land. They are not very comfortable, but they were the only clothes that I had that were clean.' And, at that stage, Jack decided it was probably best to put the rest of his clothes back on before Harry wanted a closer inspection.

'Tell me about yourself, Master Jack,' said Harry, as he pulled on his somewhat more raggedy clothing. 'Do you have brothers and sisters?'

'I have one,' and then he hesitated. 'No, I have two. One brother and one sister. My brother died when I was very young.'

'I'm very sorry, Master Jack,' said Harry. 'That must have been very sad for you.'

'I was very young,' said Jack. 'I didn't really remember him, but I know a lot about him.'

'What do you know?' asked Harry.

'Well, he shares a name with you. He was called Harry, he was very outgoing, he loved his drama, he loved to play soldiers with Dad, he had just started drama school.'

'How was he taken from you?' asked Harry, genuinely interested.

Jack was about to explain that it was a car crash on the A303, but realised that that would probably mean very little to Harry, and wondered how he could best express it, that would not give away the fact that he was from a time hundreds of years in the future.

'A carriage hit him,' he said. 'It caused such injuries that they were unable to save him. He was 10 years old.'

'I would have liked to have known him,' said Harry thoughtfully.

'I have a sister as well. She is called Rosie, and, well, she is a very nice sister, but it's not quite the same as having a brother. I can't beat her up, like I could beat up a brother. If I did, Mum would get really cross with me. I'm not even allowed to practise my judo on her.'

Harry turned his head to one side to indicate that he didn't really understand what Jack had just said. 'Judo?'

'Ah,' said Jack. 'It's an ancient martial art that means 'gentle way' and I learnt it when I was very young.'

'Can you show me?' asked Harry.

Jack did not need any encouragement whatsoever to demonstrate his judo skills and he came a little closer to Harry and quickly slipped his leg behind Harry's left leg and pulled him backwards, pinning him to the floor.

'Whoa,' said Harry. 'This is the skill that you call 'judo'? Show me again.' For half an hour they practised throws in the warm sunshine of a faraway land. They laughed out loud, not having anyone to disturb them, and Jack was very surprised how quickly Harry picked up the basics. By the end of half an hour, Harry had almost landed a couple of throws that Jack simply didn't see coming.

'Anyway, Master Jack,' said Harry, standing up after their latest rough and tumble in the sand. 'I was supposed to be taking you to camp to introduce you. We had better go, before it gets dark and we are mistaken for intruders.'

CHAPTER SIX

Rosie and Sam had managed to fashion their own fencing foils out of bits of tree and were attempting to fine-tune their fencing skills outside the cave's entrance. JJ was watching on from the safety of a rock, which was slightly elevated and meant that she was in no danger of being poked in the eye by the makeshift implements. She looked at her own weapons – short weapons with sharp pieces of shell and crab claw, enough to be able to do some damage if attacked.

She looked up as the fight was in full swing. 'Please don't hurt yourselves,' she said. 'My first aid is not that good!'

The two dogs were lying spread-eagled in the sun, having feasted on crabmeat and fish. JJ stood up and the dogs immediately raised their heads.

'It's all right, you two,' she said. 'I'm not going far. I'm just going to look in the rock pool behind you.' They put their heads down again.

JJ scrambled over the rocks and watched as all the little Sally Go Lightly crabs scattered when they saw her shadow over them. She dropped down to the beach below, out of sight of Rosie and Sam, as they continued their epic duel with their handmade weapons. She found a little rock pool and perched herself on the edge and watched the little crabs scurrying around on the bottom and the anemones opening and closing whenever they thought it was safe to do so. Little fish darted from rock to rock and right at the bottom was a sea cucumber, which looked pretty revolting, but Jack had assured JJ that it was completely harmless and, indeed, tasted quite nice.

She looked up the beach towards where Jack had disappeared with his new-found friend, Harry, and wondered how long it would be before he reappeared and, indeed, what they would do if he didn't. She didn't feel frightened, but just a little apprehensive. After all, it had only been a few hours ago, it seemed, since she had been stood in the library at Oldbury, trying to stop the Librarian from confiscating Jack's telephone.

She took a sharp intake of breath as she suddenly realised that perhaps her family might be missing her, and wondering what she would tell them as and when they returned, but somehow it didn't really seem that important at the moment.

She could see Jack's tracks in the sand where he had passed an hour or so beforehand, and in the far distance she could make out the campfires which presumably came from the Darwin camp.

It was not yet dark, or, indeed, threatening to get dark, but JJ knew that there was probably not that much more light left in the day and she hoped that Jack would be back before it was night.

She wriggled her toes in the warm waters of the rock pool and brushed back her long dark hair from her face. Leaning back on the rock to catch the full rays of the sun, she had no idea that approaching her from behind was a complete stranger. So quiet were his steps in bare feet across the rocks, not even his breath could be heard. By the time that JJ noticed that the Sally Go Lightly crabs were scuttling away in the shadow that was not hers, it was too late, and she felt a large hand clasp her mouth and in it was some sort of rag that smelled vaguely sweet. And then it all went black.

Outside the cave, Rosie and Sam had exhausted themselves with their swashbuckling. Sam had gone back up to the spring to replenish the water supplies and the two dogs had gone with him. Rosie was lying exhausted outside the mouth of the cave, trying to catch her breath. But she was not so tired as to realise that she had not seen JJ for at least 10 minutes. She then heard a sound and sat bolt upright.

'JJ, is that you?'

There was no reply.

Rosie jumped up onto the rock where she had last seen JJ and looked down. There was no sign of her. Rosie jumped down off the rock and ran round the outside, looking in the sea for her friend. There was no sign of JJ's dark hair bobbing around in the water, cooling herself down.

She could see the tracks of her brother leading up to his meeting place with Harry, but they were only his. And then she saw them. Big footprints in the sand, running around the edge of the rock. They were much too big to be Jack's, Sam's or, indeed, JJ's, and they were fresh. The waves had not yet swept over them.

Rosie immediately took up a defensive pose. She had no weapon in her hand but she could deliver a fairly good kick if she needed to. She listened, but could hear nothing. She looked up and in the distance she could see Sam making his way across the volcanic rock on the top of the entrance to the cave. She started to run towards him. She practically bolted up the rocks until she was standing directly in his eye-line. He could obviously see the panic in her face and started to run towards her, the dogs following.

'What's wrong?' he shouted, from a distance.

'It's JJ,' she said. 'She's gone!'

'What do you mean, 'gone'?'

Rosie was close to tears. 'She was on the rocks and then she had gone, and there are great big footprints, like a giant.'

'Rosie, calm down,' he said. 'Now you're sure it's not just Evil playing tricks?'

'Come and see,' she said. 'Quickly, come and see.' And the two of them bounded back down to the rocks and the footprints.

'There,' said Rosie, pointing at the enormous footprints in the sand. 'I'm not imagining it.'

Sam whistled. 'My goodness,' he said. 'That is a giant, and the footprints are quite deep, as if he was carrying something.'

'We need to follow him,' said Rosie. 'We need to get JJ back.'

The dogs sat upright, with their ears alert, as if to say that they agreed entirely and were prepared to set off.

'Wait,' said Sam. 'Let's think about this. Jack is off, trying to find out what is going on at Darwin's camp, and if we are not here when he gets back, he is going to be very worried.'

'Well, we could write him a note,' said Rosie.

'With what?' said Sam. 'We are not in the middle of Bamshire now, Rosie. We are on an island.'

'We will just have to use our brains then,' said Rosie, and started running back towards the cave.

She picked up her makeshift weapon and kicked the fire until she found a piece of charcoal. It was still a little bit warm and she dropped it in surprise, but then found a piece of cloth, wrapped it around it and started to write on the wall of the cave.

'But we don't even know what the time is,' she said.

'Well, how long would you say Jack's been gone?' asked Sam.

'About an hour?' Rosie thought.

'OK, let's start with that. 'One hour after you left, JJ taken by–' by what?' Sam asked questioningly.

'By unknown man? Unseen? So he knows that we don't know what this person looks like.'

'OK, 'unseen man with big feet heading'...' Sam looked at Rosie. 'We don't even know which direction they were heading.'

'The dogs will know,' said Sam, and they rushed back to the site of the footprints with Molly and Charlie.

'Find them,' said Sam.

The dogs both sat down and looked at him with their heads sideways, their ears alert.

'I'm not sure it works with Border Collies,' said Rosie. 'They are more used to rounding things up than search and rescue.'

'But they like to play games,' said Sam. 'So let's make it a game.'

He looked behind him and said out loud, 'Where's JJ?'

This time the dogs were up on all four feet. 'Where's JJ?' said Sam again, and then pointed at the footprints in the sand. 'Where's JJ, Charlie?' Charlie looked at him and then put his nose to the ground and started sniffing.

'Come on, Charlie! Where's JJ?' said Rosie, joining in.

Molly, too, started to sniff and paw at the ground, and, as if in unison, the two dogs set off, following the trail of footprints until they stopped as the kidnapper had reached the rock. It was now that they would know if Charlie and Molly really could follow the scent. They did not even break stride. They both leapt up the rock face, heading in the same direction, which would take them past the spring and heading up into the hills.

'Right,' said Sam. 'You follow the two dogs, I'll go and finish the message to Jack, and catch you up.'

'Bring the weapons,' said Rosie. 'Also bring the water and knapsack.'

'Will do,' shouted Sam, as he was running away from Rosie, back down towards the cave.

Sam picked the charcoal and thought for a few seconds; he needed something quick, but that gave Jack all the information. He hesitated for a moment and then, on the wall, wrote, '*JJ taken by unseen person. M&S, C&M chasing. Heading to hills 1 hr after U left,*' and he picked up his makeshift weapons and headed off up the hill after Rosie and the dogs.

Jack and Harry tracked along the shoreline until Jack could see the smoke from the campfires billowing up, and he knew they must be close.

'Will Mr Darwin not mind if you bring a stranger into camp?' asked Jack.

'No,' said Harry. 'He likes to meet different people. He knows that we are not the only people journeying in this part of the world, and he wants to hear about other people's exploits and the animals that they have come across and hear the stories they have to tell. There are a lot of Spanish but not many English. He will be very pleased to see you. Some of the other men on the ship are not as receptive to visitors, but Mr Darwin is the only one who matters and if he welcomes you, then everybody else has to welcome you.'

'You like him, don't you?' said Jack.

'I do,' said Harry. 'He is such a clever man. I hope that in many years to come, he will be remembered.'

'You have no idea how much,' thought Jack.

As they approached the camp, he could see the tents up. They were positioned slightly above them and Harry caught Jack's arm and pulled him down into the grass. 'Something isn't right,' whispered Harry. 'There aren't enough people there, and Mr Darwin always sits outside at his desk at this time of day.'

The camp was all but deserted, except for a couple of men who were sat with their backs to where Jack and Harry were watching from their viewpoint.

'I can't see their faces,' said Harry. 'But I don't think they are part of our group. Their clothes look wrong.' And with that, one of the men stood up and appeared to be looking exactly in their direction. The two boys ducked their heads down quickly, so as not to be seen.

'I don't know him,' said Harry. 'He doesn't belong to our camp. Where is Mr Darwin?'

As they carefully lifted their heads from the grass, they watched as the two strangers walked across to one of the larger tents and pulled out a young boy, probably not much older than Harry. His hands were bound and he had a piece of material tied tightly round his mouth so that he couldn't speak. He was dragged out and literally thrown down in front of the third man, who was clearly in charge.

'Now boy,' said the man in a loud voice, so clearly that Jack and Harry could hear it from where they were lying. 'I'm going to ask you again, where are they?'

One of the three captors reached down and untied the piece of cloth, tied round the poor boy's mouth.

'Oh my gosh!' hissed Harry. 'That's Covington!'

'It's like I told you, Mister,' said Covington. 'They all go out during the day, collecting samples. They are normally back by now but today they're not, and I don't know why.'

The ringleader picked Covington up by the front of his soiled shirt and looked him clearly in the eyes. He then almost lifted him off his feet and flung him to the ground to his right.

Jack felt Harry twitch, as if he was going to get up and even the score right there and then, and he put his hand on his arm. 'We can do nothing at the moment, Master Harry. Is it right that Mr Darwin would have been back by now?'

'Yes,' said Harry. 'Like clockwork. He's always back. The only time he's not is if he finds something really interesting and wants to keep watching it or catch it, or, indeed, shoot it.'

Jack always flinched when Harry mentioned shooting things, as it seemed so out of keeping with everything that Charles Darwin stood for, but he was slowly starting to understand that this must have been the only way of getting a good, up-close look at these creatures. Mr Darwin did not have the cameras and long lenses and films that Jack now took for granted.

'So, he might be somewhere on the island?' said Jack,

hopefully. 'Would he have gone alone?'

Harry thought about it. 'No, not normally. Normally he would take one or two of the boys from the camp. We all take it in turns because we like to accompany Mr Darwin. I wonder how many people they left in camp?'

And as he said that, the captors moved to another tent and pulled out another bound and gagged forlorn soul and went through the same procedure of demanding to know where Mr Darwin was. He got the same answer and received the same fate of being thrust to the ground like a ragdoll.

'We need to warn him,' said Jack. 'You must have some idea of where he was going today?'

Harry thought for a moment and chewed his bottom lip as he thought hard as to where his mentor may have gone on his expedition.

'The finches,' he said. 'I'm sure he was going to see the finches. There is a group of trees further up the hill with a mound next to it. Mr Darwin likes to hide behind the mound and try and observe the finches from there. He likes to see what they are doing with their beaks.'

'Do you know how to get there?' asked Jack. 'And do you think that they can see the camp from where they are?'

'No, they definitely can't see the camp,' said Harry. 'I have been there many times and there is no clear view of the camp. They will either be there or on their way back and if they come back, then I fear for Mr Darwin's safety. Those men, they don't look as if they want to ask questions about animals and plants. They look very threatening.'

'Right,' said Jack. 'We're going to start wriggling backwards, so that we can't be seen. Which direction are the finch trees?'

Harry nodded with his head across to his right, behind the camp.

'Right,' said Jack. 'We are going to head over in that direction as soon as we are out of sight.'

They started to crawl backwards, still facing to their front to make sure that they were not being observed. Slowly they crept back, using their knees to propel their bodies. Foot by foot they descended down the hill and they were about to stop and stand up when, at the same time, their feet hit something hard and both of them had to fight hard not to exclaim loudly.

They looked round and realised that they had hit the shell of a tortoise, and this wasn't just a giant tortoise, this was a tortoise that must have been the size of a small house. Its head was inside its body but, after a few seconds, it started to emerge, like a giant dragon coming out of a cave. Although Jack knew that tortoises did not eat people, or, indeed, any kind of meat, the sheer size of the beast behind them was enough to send him and Harry scurrying backwards on their bottoms, heading back up the hill that they had just come down.

Jack was breathing deeply, as the giant head started coming towards him, and then he realised what was happening. He grabbed Harry's arm. 'Stop,' he said, and Harry tried to pull away and head back up the hill on his bottom.

Jack grabbed him again. 'Stop!' he said as loudly as he dared. 'It's not real, it's an illusion.'

'But we kicked it,' said Harry. 'It must be real.'

'No, we kicked the shell of the real tortoise, which is much, much smaller. It's an illusion. Pretend.'

Harry looked at him as if he had gone completely mad. 'I do not understand, Master Jack, these words you use.'

'Do you understand magic?' asked Jack.

Harry nodded.

'It's bad magic,' said Jack. 'Playing tricks on our mind. Here, take my hands and start thinking of good things, things that you have done, and keep thinking about them. Tell me out loud.'

'When my brother was a baby,' said Harry, 'he was choking

and my mother was not in the room. I slapped his back very hard and he stopped choking.'

Jack looked at Harry in surprise; his mother had told him an identical story from when he was a child and his brother had saved his life. Quickly he said, 'When my Grandad was ill, I went and helped him to do the gardening.'

And, as they both watched, the giant tortoise reduced in size, right before their very eyes. It went from the size of a house to the size of a car and eventually down to the size of a normal giant tortoise. Still big, but certainly not the size of a dragon.

The two of them fell back onto the grass, dropping hands as they did.

'How did you know what to do, Master Jack?' asked Harry, seriously.

'I have encountered this before,' said Jack, trying to sound as formal as his young friend. 'There is someone playing magic tricks on us and making real things appear so much bigger than they really are.'

'So, someone is watching us?' asked Harry, looking around.

'Not watching exactly,' said Jack. 'But someone knows we're here and are just trying to scare us off.'

'Well, it won't work,' said Harry, and he got to his feet. 'We have a job to do. We need to find Mr Darwin.'

And, with that, Jack got to his feet as well and they started jogging in the direction that Harry had pointed earlier.

Rosie, Sam and the dogs continued up the semi pathway, heading towards the hills. The sun was just starting to think about going to bed for the night and it was noticeably cooler.

Rosie and Sam both had their makeshift weapons in their hands and the dogs ran alongside them, looking from side to side, always on guard. Now and then, the dogs would put their noses to the ground and double check that they were going in the right direction, and then run on as if their lives depended on it. Rosie would have to call them back because she and Sam simply couldn't keep up with them, and they did not want to exhaust themselves and to drink all the water.

After about an hour, they stopped in a sheltered spot and ate a couple of biscuits and drank some water, and they were very grateful when, about 10 minutes after that, they heard the faint trickle of water and found a stream where they could refill their water bottle.

The terrain was getting much more wooded, the trees much taller and the grass longer. The trees looked sinister in the half light but they were running too hard to worry too much about them.

As they jogged on, suddenly both dogs stopped, dead still. Rosie and Sam did the same. They listened but could hear nothing, but they knew that the dogs' hearing was ten times better than theirs. And then they smelled it. They knew why the dogs had stopped, because, on the air, they could just smell ... just smell... food!

Rosie and Sam looked at each other. 'Can you smell that?' she whispered.

He nodded. 'It smells like one of my Mum's casseroles,' he said, and thought about it for a moment, and added: 'Although probably not with tortoise.' And Rosie made a face.

Charlie cocked his head to one side to indicate that he was listening to something, and Molly followed almost immediately.

Molly was about to make that funny noise that only she could make when she wanted to tell Auntie Issie and Uncle Stanley about something important, when Rosie looked at her with wide eyes, as if to say, 'Not now Molly, now is not the time to make a noise'. Molly realised immediately and flattened her ears on the top of her head and lay down in the way that dogs do when they are resting, but ready to spring. Charlie assumed the same position.

'Stay,' said Rosie, without quite knowing if that would have the necessary effect, but, as she and Sam walked past both dogs, they remained exactly in that position.

And then they heard it, very quiet, very melodic but there appeared to be some sort of singing coming from the direction of the smell of food.

Sam and Rosie looked at each other in surprise, and looked back at the dogs, whose ears went straight up and, again, Rosie gestured to the dogs with her hand to stay.

Rosie and Sam crept forward, being careful where they trod so as not to snap any branches and alert anyone that they were coming. They held their makeshift weapons in front of them.

Jack and Harry set off at a pace in the direction of the finch trees. They didn't speak much, as they were worried that other members of the gang might already be searching for Mr Darwin and his companions, and didn't want to draw attention to themselves.

They moved through the shrubs as quietly as they could, but everything was so dry that, with every footstep, it let out a loud crackle, that Jack felt sure could be heard across the other side of the Island.

As they rounded the curve of the hillside that they were on, they suddenly heard men's voices and both of them dropped flat on the floor within a second of hearing that sound. They could hear the men's voices quite clearly now, deep and gruff. 'They've got to be around here somewhere.'

Jack looked across at Harry and raised an eyebrow, as if to say,

'Do you know these people?' Harry shook his head.

'This is where the boy said,' said a man, standing so close to Jack that Jack could almost feel him breathing. Jack held his own breath, quite sure that at any moment he was going to be discovered.

The footsteps were coming closer and closer towards him and then, suddenly, they stopped and turned round and the owner of the voice started to go in the opposite direction. Jack could feel Harry breathe a sigh of relief next to him.

Although they could no longer hear the men's voices, they lay there for five or ten minutes, until they were quite sure that the coast was clear. Even then, they carefully got up on their knees to look above the grass to see if there was anyone around, and they could just see the tops of the men's heads as they disappeared down into the small valley ahead of them.

'They've got the wrong trees,' whispered Harry. 'These are not the finch trees. The finch trees are up there on the right,' he nodded with his head. And with one glance back at the two men disappearing out of sight, Jack and Harry climbed higher up the ridge to where the trees could be found.

They watched the trees intently, as they were conscious that they were moving higher up the hillside and were therefore more likely to be spotted, but the vegetation was a little thicker and seemed to screen them from watching eyes.

There did not appear to be anyone in or around the finch trees, other than the finches that Jack knew would become much more famous in years to come. They did not seem at all scared of humans and sat there in the trees, watching the boys as they approached, chattering happily.

'He isn't here,' said Harry. 'Where could he have gone?' His voice was frantic, concerned about the man who he clearly idolised. He ran from tree to tree, studying every angle, looking under every bush.

And with that, there was a small cough from behind the mound to their left. Jack and Harry jumped visibly and looked at each other. After a moment's hesitation they went opposite ways around the mound and there, lying in the grass, looking up at them, was a man who was, in many years to come, going to be one of the most famous scientists who had ever walked the earth.

'Mr Darwin, I presume,' said Jack.

'And who might be asking?' asked Mr Darwin.

At that point, he saw Harry. 'My dear Master Harry. What a great pleasure to see you. I was afraid that you, too, had been captured.' Mr Darwin still looked smart and unruffled, his large billowing shirt still pristine white, his waistcoat neat and starched.

Harry and Jack sat down on the grass next to Mr Darwin. 'You know, then,' said Jack. 'We thought perhaps that you were just up here shooting and studying the birds and didn't realise what was happening in the camp.'

'No, no,' said Mr Darwin. 'I was half way down from the finch trees when I saw the commotion in the camp. There were many assailants and they quickly overpowered our small group. I watched them being bound and gagged and interrogated as to my whereabouts. I knew that the only person who would know where to find me would be you, Harry. And so I came back to the finch trees and hoped that you would find me. I had not, however, anticipated that you would not be alone. Pray, please introduce your young friend.'

Harry almost bowed his head in acknowledgement of his rudeness. 'Mr Darwin, I am very sorry. Please allow me to introduce my friend. This is Jack. He, too, is from England and has come in on the whaling boat.'

'Has he indeed?' said Mr Darwin, studying Jack with friendly eyes. He ran his fingers through his hair in an almost nervous way and then Mr Darwin looked at Jack with a look that grown-ups give when they don't entirely believe you, and Jack decided that now was probably the best time to try and change the subject.

'Mr Darwin, you are in grave danger,' said Jack. 'There are people who have come to this island and I believe that they are intent on harming you, or at least stopping you in your research. For reasons that I can't begin to explain to you, it is important that they do not succeed. How long is it before your ship returns?'

Mr Darwin looked thoughtful. 'I'm not really sure,' he said. 'A day, maybe two. They've gone in search of fresh water and we have provisions for another week.'

Jack thought for a moment: 'I have three friends who are also on the whaling boat with me, and we are currently enjoying some rest and recuperation, and we have found a cave near to the water spring. It is very comfortable, although probably not as comfortable as your tents have been, but I think that we can keep you safe until your boat arrives.'

Harry looked at him. 'But why can't we just go back to your boat?'

'Oh,' said Jack. 'Perhaps I didn't explain clearly enough. Like you, the boat has left us on the island whilst it goes to re-supply, and do a little hunting, and we have been given some time off to explore the island. There is plenty of food with the local wildlife and we have fresh water, so we, too, are in the same position as you, in that we are trapped on the island. But for you there is a gang of men who are intent on finding you and, I fear, trying to harm you. I think that if we all try and stick together, then we have more chance of...' He searched for the right words... 'avoiding them...' he said eventually.

'My boy!' exclaimed Mr Darwin. 'What a magnificent way of putting it. Of course, survival of the fittest.'

Harry looked at Jack critically and Jack shook his head, as if to say: 'Don't ask anymore, I'll explain later.'

'Well,' said Mr Darwin. 'I must confess that I am not entirely sure how two young boys and a few of their friends can keep me out of harm's way, but if you are prepared to have me, then I am prepared to accept your generous offer of accommodation in your cave. Lead on!' he said, and lifted up the stick that he had in his right hand.

They all got to their feet and Jack looked up at the sky. 'We must hurry, it's going to be dark soon, and we need to be back in the cave.'

Charles Darwin put his hat on. 'Lead the way, my boy,' he said. 'Lead the way,' and off they set across James Island, towards the caves that would give them sanctuary.

Sam and Rosie crept closer and closer to the sound of the music. The smell of food grew stronger and Rosie could hear her tummy gurgling to remind her that it was probably about time for supper. She longed for one of Auntie Issie's spaghetti bolognaises with lashings of parmesan cheese and a big green leafy salad. She started to salivate at the thought and tried to stop her thoughts in their tracks.

Finally, as darkness started to surround them, they saw the twinkle of what appeared to be the lights of a camp fire up ahead of them. They could hear laughter and the smell of food was getting stronger.

As they came closer and closer, they could see that there appeared to be women and children sat in a circle around the campfire. They seemed to be having fun. And there, sat right in amongst them, smiling and laughing, was JJ! She was wearing what appeared to be a traditional headdress and with a beautiful multicoloured scarf around her neck. But she did not appear to be tied up and she did not seem to be upset or worried. Sam and

Rosie looked at each other in astonishment.

'Perhaps she's been drugged,' whispered Rosie.

Sam looked at her and raised an eyebrow, which probably said, 'Don't be silly,' as he was too polite to say it directly to her.

'What should we do?' asked Rosie.

'Well, I think we should just stay and watch for a while to try and work out what's going on. We don't want to go rushing in until we know if she is being held captive or not... And there are quite a lot of them,' he added.

They sat and watched. Surrounding JJ there were many men who appeared to be very tall, despite sitting down. Their skin was very dark and they were wearing what appeared to be traditional dress, which glinted in the camp fire.

Sam and Rosie made themselves comfortable in the grass and could just see over the top of the leafy fronds of the vegetation around them. They saw that there was a large pot in the middle of those who were sat around JJ, from which everyone appeared to be helping themselves to whatever was smelling so delicious.

Although JJ didn't appear to be speaking with any of the people around her, she certainly seemed to be trying to communicate through sign language and actions. Those around her were clearly amused and interested; they smiled a great deal and did not look threatening.

Sam and Rosie watched for probably half an hour, until it was almost completely dark. Suddenly, there was a whoop that appeared to come from the direction that they had come from. This was quickly followed by a squeal, first from Charlie, as if somebody had trodden on his foot, and then from Molly, in the way that she does when Charlie chews her ears if she is rude enough to try and greet somebody before he did.

'The dogs,' said Rosie, and went to get to her feet, but Sam held her arm.

'Wait,' he said. 'There are people there and we don't want to give ourselves away.'

They lay in the grass and listened. Their hearts beat very quickly and they tried hard to listen to what was going on behind them.

They waited until finally they heard the sound of something moving through the grass not far from them. They lay down flat and watched as three or four young adults walked past them in the grass, not a foot away from them. In the dark they could just make out that between them were slung two poles and, hanging down from the poles, were what looked like grain sacks, only these grain sacks were moving, and moving quite a lot.

One bundle strung between the poles looked slightly smaller than the other and, with a rising feeling of horror, Rosie realised immediately that inside these two grain sacks were Auntie Issie's beloved dogs. However, they were clearly still alive and moving about, just not barking, or, indeed, making any sound at all.

'Oh my gosh!' said Rosie. 'They are going to kill them and eat them! We have to save them!' And she went to get up.

Sam pulled her back down again. 'Don't be ridiculous, Rosie. Have you seen how many there are? Have you seen how tall they are? Let's just watch and see. If we think they are going to harm them, we'll move in and try and do the best that we can.'

The young adults moved quietly through the grass towards the camp fire. They were wearing what looked like blankets for clothes and Rosie was reminded of the Masai Warriors, but these people had different features. Not African, but, nevertheless, very distinguished with their dark skin and large frames.

The youths moved into the light of the campfire that JJ sat beside and walked to the centre of the ring and lowered the poles to the ground. The sacks continued to move and one of the youths raised a spear, as if to defend himself, but with the obvious intention that the spear was aimed at the bag of movement that was at his feet.

'No!' came a shout, and JJ jumped to her feet. 'Do not harm them,' she said loudly, although she appeared to appreciate that nobody actually spoke the same language as she did.

She came running to the centre of the circle where the two sacks were lying, and carefully unknotted the top of the smaller sack. She opened it up and pulled it down over the top of whatever was inside, and there was a loud, audible intake of breath as the head of Molly appeared over the sack.

She looked terrified and her eyes were even wider than they normally were. And then she saw JJ and let out a whine and a whinny and almost leapt into her arms.

'It's all right Molly, it's all right, you're quite safe,' said JJ, holding her close and stroking her head.

JJ gestured to the second larger sack and asked that the youths untie it. Gingerly they moved over and started to do so, a couple still with spears up. However, Charlie's reaction to being unceremoniously dumped into a corn sack and carried along on two poles, was less tolerant than Molly's. As soon as he felt the bag loosened, he leapt, like a tiger possessed, from the sack, baring his teeth and growling.

Everyone stood back in shock and spears were raised all around JJ. 'No,' JJ shouted. 'He's just frightened.' And, although they were not speaking the same language, it appeared that the message she was trying to convey had been understood, and the spears gently started to be lowered, until Charlie barked. Out of the corner of her eye, JJ could see a spear not only raised, but released, and she realised with horror that it was heading straight for Charlie's chest.

JJ heard a scream come from about 100 metres away, which she instantly recognised as being Rosie's. She, too, had seen the spear and was too far away to be able to do anything about it. Just as JJ was trying to process the scene and decide what she needed to do, she saw another movement, this time at right angles to the spear, and heading straight for it. Before she could comprehend what was happening came a movement so quick that with a leap that must have been almost twice her height, Molly had seen the danger and as if catching a ball with precision, she leapt through the air and gripped the spear tightly in her jaws and knocked it off course.

Molly and the spear landed in a heap, close to JJ's feet. As Molly hit the floor she squealed loudly to indicate that she had hurt herself. Charlie stopped snarling immediately and ran straight over to her, as she lay still on the ground. JJ also ran over and started to feel Molly all over for cuts or breaks but there was nothing. But Molly lay very still. And then Charlie started to lick Molly's face, slowly at first and then faster. Then he licked her front legs and her ears and whilst JJ started to quietly sob, convinced Molly was dead, Molly slowly lifted her head up and looked at JJ, with what was the closest to a doggy smile that JJ had ever seen.

'Good girl,' said JJ, and Molly wagged her tail in acknowledgement and jumped to her feet, slightly wobbly, obviously just stunned by the impact of hitting the ground. Charlie barked just once and sat down, standing guard over his best friend in the world.

As if the scene was not chaotic enough, it was at this stage that Rosie and Sam made an appearance, brandishing their home made weapons, backs to each other, ready to take on the world.

'Don't hurt the dogs,' shouted Rosie. 'Take us, but don't hurt the dogs.'

It was probably not the reaction that Rosie was expecting, but a small ripple of laughter could be heard from the assembled crowd, and Rosie and Sam looked slightly perplexed. They had assumed that they would be surrounded by savages, attempting to kill them and Auntie Issie's beloved dogs. But as they started to look around, they realised that the faces were smiling at them.

The spears were lowered, and everybody looked that much more relaxed.

JJ leapt into the centre with Rosie and Sam. There was no time for social niceties. The three of them formed a circle with their backs to one another and JJ said quietly, 'Don't worry. They're perfectly friendly.'

'But,' said Rosie. 'They'd captured the dogs and they were about to kill them. We saw them, we were just outside the camp.'

JJ said in a quiet, soothing voice, 'You have to remember that these people have probably never seen a dog before. They were just frightened and protective, but now they understand and I don't think that they are going to hurt us or Charlie and Molly.'

At that point, JJ knelt down on one knee and called the dogs to her. 'Come here,' she said quietly, and the two dogs rushed to her open arms and sat in front of her as she cuddled them both and made a fuss. Sam and Rosie gently lowered their makeshift weapons and looked around and realised that those surrounding them were all staring at the dogs, and they realised that of course JJ was quite right. They had never seen a dog before.

Sam and Rosie both fell to their knees and joined in with cuddling and fussing the two Collies. They could see, as they sat at leg height to their captors, that there were one or two smaller children moving their way through the legs of their parents and looking tentatively around knees to see exactly what these creatures were.

Rosie picked out one angelic looking child, who must have been two or three, with beautiful dark skin and wild hair. He was transfixed by the dogs and just couldn't take his eyes off them.

Rosie beckoned to him. 'Come closer,' she said, and the boy drew back automatically in apprehension. Rosie held out her hand and slowly but surely the small boy reached out to her until eventually his little chubby fingers were entwined in hers. Rosie tugged at his hand and he started to move away from the comfort and protection of the legs that he was cowering behind, and stepped towards the strange creatures with all their fur and long noses and big pointy ears. He had taken a few steps towards the dogs when Molly stood up suddenly from her seated position. Out of the corner of her eye, Rosie could see a few stiffening of shoulders and straightening of backs and the odd hand reached for their spear.

'It's all right,' she said gently, and put her other hand out to calm people down. 'Come on, Molly, say 'hello'.' She was not really sure who was more afraid of who, Molly of the little boy or the little boy of Molly, but whatever their fears, they slowly moved towards one another and Molly sat down in front of the small boy, her head almost as tall as he was, and, without any additional encouragement, gave him a big lick from the bottom of his face to the top. There was a short silence and Rosie was not sure how this would have been received by the boy who, until 10 minutes ago, had never seen a dog. And then, much to her relief, he let out a howl of laughter and threw his arms around Molly's neck and the two of them wrestled and licked and played as if they had been friends forever.

Charlie watched on from a short distance away and clearly decided at that stage that Molly was the centre of attention, which needed to be changed. He too stood up and everybody froze. He singled out the tallest of the captors, who appeared to have the largest of the spears, and walked up to him without a fear in the world, when his front paws were inches from the man's enormous feet, he sat down obediently and looked up into the man's face. The huge man looked towards JJ as if to say, 'What do I do?' JJ gestured with her hand to show that he should bend down and stroke Charlie under the chin, which is what he liked.

The man opened his hand and bent down towards Charlie, who cowered back slightly, seeing the enormous hand moving towards him, and JJ had to gesture again to show that he should not try and pat his head, which dogs generally don't like, but most people don't appreciate. Instead, she gestured to tickle him under the chin, and as soon as the man had found the right spot, Charlie almost sighed in happiness and leant against the man's enormous legs whilst he enjoyed all the fuss.

Sam and Rosie almost simultaneously turned to JJ and whispered, 'Who are they? Why did they take you?'

JJ smiled. She said, 'We don't appear to speak the same language, but I believe that they thought that I had been captured by you and they had come to rescue me. They are extremely friendly and peace loving, but, because of the colour of their skin, they thought that perhaps I had been taken as a slave, the same way that some of them have been in the past. I think that they saw the boats with the strange men with cutlasses off the island and assumed that I had been taken by them. They have been very kind, they have fed me.'

'Food,' said Sam. 'You've had food?'

JJ smiled. 'You're hungry?'

He said, 'I could eat a whole giant tortoise and go back for its brother.'

At this point, Rosie looked at him in absolute horror. 'You wouldn't?' she asked.

Sam smiled. 'No,' he said. 'I wouldn't. I'm just winding you up, but I am very hungry indeed.'

JJ looked at the tall man who was still stroking Charlie and pointed to Sam. She made a gesture which involved rubbing her tummy and then pointing to her mouth to show that food was required. The big man smiled. He finished stroking Charlie, much to Charlie's upset, and clapped his hands. He pointed to the three children and the two dogs and said something in his own tongue, and for a moment Rosie, Sam and JJ were not sure if that meant, 'kill them now' or 'let's feed our guests'. And, luckily for them, it appeared to be the latter.

The man gestured towards the fire and the crowds opened to form a route through to the huge ball of heat, with the great cauldron of food hanging over it and, together, the three children walked towards it with the two dogs obediently walking behind.

As they approached the fire, all three children realised just how cold it was. As they got nearer, large capes were placed around their shoulders. Their hosts gestured politely for them to sit by the fire and gratefully they sat in front of the huge burning logs and ate noisily from the bowls of food that were placed in front of them.

Indeed, it was not just them who were to be fed, but Molly and Charlie were presented with bowls of food as well. Rosie had already poked her fingers into the dog's bowls to ensure that there were no bones on which they could choke and, being satisfied that there weren't, nodded the dogs to eat as much as they wanted. They did not need a second invitation.

The dogs wolfed it down straight away and the bowls were replenished straight away.

The rest of their hosts sat cross legged on the matting which was spread out around the cauldron. They smiled and laughed and their multi-coloured clothes shone and sparkled in the light of the fires which were burning around them.

As the children looked up they would catch one or two of them staring at them, and they would look away immediately, embarrassed. There seemed more men than women and many children; no-one looked too thin or ill, just happy and friendly – now that they had got over their curiosity about the dogs.

However, there definitely seemed to be a pecking order and sat on the matting behind the cauldron, with the children, was the tallest and slightly older gentleman who was clearly their chief. He had a face which was deeply lined but very friendly and kind and a low deep voice. Not that they understood a word that he said of course, but so much could be said in gestures.

Rosie was watching him as she tucked into her fourth bowl
of the rich broth that had been served with flat breads and
vegetables. She had of course extracted a solemn promise that she
was not eating tortoise and had been assured many times that she
was not. The chief was engaged in sign language with Sam and
they appeared to be discussing how they hunted.

'The Chief reminds me so much of my granddad George,' she
said. 'Tall and kind and always wanting to help everyone.'

'Well,' said JJ, 'as he seems to have a name that I cannot
pronounce which seems to involve a certain amount of tongue
clicking, I think that that is what we should name him – George.'

At that point Sam stopped his sign language and looked up
with a smile. 'What was that?' he asked.

'We are going to call the Chief George,' said Rosie, 'because
we cannot pronounce his name.' Sam laughed and turned back
to George. He pointed at Rosie and said her name slowly. George
tried to pronounce it with limited success, coming out more
like 'Me', then he pointed to JJ and said her name; George coped
better with this one and was able to say 'JJ' quite clearly. Then
he pointed to himself. 'Sam,' said Sam proudly. 'Sam,' repeated
George.

Then Sam pointed at George and raised his eyebrows as if to
say 'and what is your name'. George smiled in an understanding
way – 'Jidmoonh'. Sam tried it a few times without success. Then
he smiled, pointed at George and said 'George'. George repeated
it back and then pointed at himself 'George' and all three children
laughed loudly.

'George,' said Rosie, 'just like my Grandad.'

Her eyes were very tired now and she leant against Charlie
who was sat close to her, and slowly she drifted off to sleep. It
had been a very long day. Charlie lay down quietly and Rosie was
lowered gently towards the ground as he did, until eventually she
lay there, head on Charlie's back, and fell into a deep sleep.

George looked at her kindly and said something to the women to his right. They got up quickly and scuttled into the blackness, returning within ten minutes. George looked at Sam and JJ and then in the direction of the sleeping Rosie. He put his hands together next to his head to indicate sleep and they nodded sleepily. He pointed at the kindly ladies and gestured for them to follow. Goerge stooped over and picked up Rosie in his arms and followed behind, with Molly and Charlie keeping guard next to him.

They came to a small round hut and there was fabric hanging from the door; the ladies pulled it back and lit up the room with a candle. There were three beds made up on the floor; piles of fabric and pillows and furs and without invitation JJ and Sam fell into their beds with a dog sandwiched on either side. Gently George lowered Rosie down into the third bed and pulled a fur blanket over her. She did not wake.

He stood up and nodded wisely. 'JJ, Saam and Me,' he said slowly, followed by words in his own language which probably meant goodnight.

'Goodnight George,' chorused Sam and JJ. As their heads hit the pillows they were instantly in a deep, deep sleep.

Jack, Harry and Mr Darwin moved along the track inland from the shore, keeping their eyes open for any unusual movements. Occasionally, they were startled by an iguana or a grazing tortoise, but eventually Jack reached the part of the stream that he recognised and they followed it down carefully and quietly towards the shoreline.

'My friends are here,' he said. 'They can help us.'

Harry looked at him quizzically. 'You have not said much about your friends.'

'There's quite a lot I haven't mentioned,' said Jack. 'But now is not the time.'

Harry just looked at him and raised his eyebrows but said nothing further.

'It is this way,' said Jack. 'We need to follow it all the way to the coast and the cave that my friends are in, is below where we can see. Let's stop here and drink from the stream before we head down.'

They each sat down on the grass in the warm evening air and drank through their cupped hands. Jack did not think it the time to mention about the tablets they should put in the water – that would have been one suggestion too far.

Jack reached into his bag and pulled out a handful of biscuits and offered them to Harry and Mr Darwin, who accepted gratefully and they ate them in silence.

It was eventually Mr Darwin who spoke, as he gazed out to sea. 'I wonder when the Beagle will be back for us?' he asked, to no-one in particular. Jack wanted to say 'the day after tomorrow' but instead studied his biscuit in the dark.

'Captain Fitzroy will be very concerned when he returns to find us gone,' went on Charles Darwin. 'He will probably think that I have led the crew members off on another adventure designed to cause him maximum irritation. However, perhaps he may even be concerned? He will have no-one to argue with about the Bible.' Jack could see that Mr Darwin was smiling.

'Do you argue?' Jack was too intrigued to hold back the question.

'We do indeed,' said Mr Darwin. 'Robert Fitzroy has very fixed ideas about the Bible and believes that everything in it is quite literal. I have been well versed in such arguments, being the son of a clergyman myself, but I feel that we should open our eyes wider for an explanation. We discuss this at length.'

'It is always helpful,' said Jack, 'to have a healthy debate about these things.'

'I agree, Master Jack,' said Mr Darwin. 'But Captain Fitzroy should know better; he is an intelligent man with a good knowledge of sciences. He should realise that our views can exist together and we do not need to argue about it.'

It was Jack's turn to smile, thinking that many, many years later, these two views would still be argued over, but again, this was probably not the time to say so. Instead he placed his hand on Mr Darwin's arm and said, 'Don't ever give up the fight, Mr Darwin.' Their eyes were locked for a few seconds in the semi darkness. 'Promise me?'

Mr Darwin thought for a moment and then placed his hand on top of Jack's. 'I promise, Master Jack, I will continue with my beliefs no matter how difficult others may find them.'

Harry looked at the sky. 'We had better move, Master Jack,' he said. 'We do not know how far behind us they are.'

With that they gathered up their belongings and started moving down the grass verge, over the rocks and quietly towards the route down to the entrance to the cave. As they got closer, Jack expected the dogs to come running out any minute and frighten everybody, but they didn't.

They reached the path and followed it round the bottom towards the shoreline until it doubled back into the cave's entrance, and still there was no sign of anyone.

Harry glanced at him as if to say, 'Where are your friends?' but Jack chose to ignore it and thought that perhaps Sam, Rosie and JJ were keeping a low profile, not knowing who Jack was bringing back to the camp. Mr Darwin walked between the two of them, single file as they picked their way across the path. It was now almost dark and they rounded the entrance to the cave and there was still darkness.

'Rosie,' he hissed. There was silence. 'Sam, JJ, Charlie, Molly. Where are you?' But there was nothing. Jack could feel panic start to set in as to where they might have gone, and exactly what his parents would do to him if he had to confess that he had managed to lose his baby sister on an island that was shortly not to exist.

'OK,' said Jack, quite loudly. 'The joke's over now guys. Come on out please. This is really serious.' Again, there was no response.

'Where are they?' Jack asked himself, and ran into the cave. It was pitch black inside. He looked around thoroughly and then started to think sensibly. 'They must have left a message,' he thought. 'Quickly, we need to get some light.' He reached into his knapsack and took out the glorch and held it up inside the cave. He could not really see much, as the light that projected from it was not great. The other two stared at him as if he had gone very mad and they looked to see where the light was coming from.

'There,' said Harry suddenly, and pointed to the wall. Sure enough, in the semi darkness, Jack saw the message on the wall for the first time. He stepped closer and read it carefully.

'This is a message from your friends,' said Mr Darwin. 'It says that they have gone inland.'

Jack read it and read it again and his heart sank. Not only had his three friends moved away from the safety and security of their cave, but his beloved JJ had been taken by persons unknown and he was not really sure if he would ever see them again.

The three of them looked intently at the wall. In fact, so intently that none of them noticed the figures creeping up behind them in the darkness, and it was not until the men were almost upon them that Jack turned. 'What the...' he said, before a sack was placed over his head and everything went dark.

CHAPTER SEVEN

Lavender Lane was a hive of activity. At Homegarth, Alfie was on the telephone to the boatyard, arranging for 441 to be lifted from its resting place in the Marina, placed on a transporter to be driven at high speed (or at least as fast as it would go, even with a police escort) to RAF Northolt. From there, he had arranged for 441 to be placed on an army transporter plane for the long flight to Ecuador.

At Lavender Lane House, Auntie Issie, Angela and Cameron stood before the large video screen, on which was displayed the face of the US President.

'I've cleared it with the Ecuadorian Government,' he said. 'The plane can land and 441 will be transported to the water's edge. I can't say they were that happy but I called in a few favours. The problem is, there is no point in telling anybody now about where it's going, because everybody has forgotten the name of the islands, including me.'

Cameron looked earnest. 'All you need to know, Mr President, is that 441 needs to be in the water. What other shipping is in the area?'

'Our investigations have shown,' said the President, 'that there are a number of cruise ships in and around the vicinity, although it appears that no one can now answer the question as to why they are there, because there are no points of interest for them to see.'

Angela chipped in at this stage, as she was dunking a biscuit into a large mug of tea. 'But cruise ships were never allowed to go to the Galapagos Islands anyway, Mr President.'

The President looked quizzically at her, as if to say: 'I've got no idea what you are talking about.' Angela remembered that, of course, anybody outside of Lavender Lane would have had erased from their memory banks, anything to do with the islands and their history.

'Sorry,' she said, as she realised what she had said. 'Do we have any control of or contacts for these cruise ships?'

Auntie Issie stepped forward. 'I know the President of Drucan,' she said. 'Does that help?'

The President smiled. 'Issie, is there anybody that you don't know?'

Auntie Issie smiled back. 'I take that as a compliment, Mr President, coming from a man of your position and standing in the world. He's an old friend and I used to work with him.'

'Let me put it this way,' said the President. 'If the President of the United States rings you up and asks you for a favour, then after much deliberation and discussion and checks about my authenticity, generally, I will get what I asked for. But it takes a long time. But, if we have a personal connection, then wheels are likely to turn more quickly.'

'My great worry,' said Cameron, 'is that there will be little left of the Galapagos unless we get to them soon, and if they disappear completely, then we have no hope of bringing the children back.'

Angela's biscuit dropped off into her tea and she uttered a rude word.

Auntie Issie slumped down onto the seat next to her. Cameron was saying what nobody else wanted to discuss, but they all knew that it was true. Time was not on their side. The mist was slowly creeping up the hill again; it had started in the last half an hour and this meant that things were not going well on the other side of the Gate. Its pace was slower than before but at this rate it would soon engulf them and once it engulfed them, they knew that it would be too late, that all trace of the Galapagos Islands would be wiped out and the history books would be re-written.

Jack woke up and opened his eyes. He shut them again quite quickly because it hurt quite a lot. He felt the back of his head and wasn't sure if perhaps somebody had hit him, or if it had just been where he had been thrown. He tried to focus and his eyes didn't seem to want to work. But, eventually, he was able to make out the dim shapes of Mr Darwin and Harry, lying in what appeared to be a tent.

The light was just starting to show through the stitching in the tent canvas and Jack could hear strange calls outside the tent, which he assumed were being made by the unusual inhabitants of the island.

Jack shifted slightly to try and prop himself up by his elbow, and a low groan came from the largest shape, which he assumed to be Mr Darwin.

Jack pulled himself up onto both of his elbows and moved slowly towards Mr Darwin, trying not to make any noise.

'Are you awake?' he asked, as quietly as possible.

'I believe so,' said Mr Darwin. 'Where is young Harry?'

'I think he's next to you,' said Jack. 'I'll just go over and check,' and he moved on his hands towards the sleeping shape that lay between them.

There was no sign of movement from Harry, and Jack moved his face as close to Harry's as possible. He could hear that he was still breathing, which was something of a relief at that stage, and he prodded him.

Harry let out a low groan. 'Shhhhsh,' said Jack. 'You must keep your voice down.'

'Where am I?' asked Harry groggily.

'In a tent somewhere,' said Jack. 'But I couldn't tell you where. Is it anywhere that you recognise?'

He could see Harry trying to focus in the same way as Jack had five minutes earlier. 'We are in our tents,' he said eventually.

The light was shining even more brightly now through the gaps in the tarpaulin, and, slowly, Jack edged his way to the wall of the tent itself and lifted up the lower part to see if he could work out what was going on outside.

In the dim light of dawn, he saw scenery that he was unfamiliar with and, more importantly, he saw the large bodies that were sat outside the tent, keeping guard. More bodies than they could hope to overcome with the three of them. His heart sank, as he knew at that stage that they had failed, that they had not prevented Evil from changing history, and that this meant that they were never likely to get home.

Jack let the tarpaulin drop down, as he realised the enormity of what he had just thought. He realised that he would never see Bolivia again, or his beloved Mum and Dad. In fact, it was unlikely that he would ever see Rosie again, as she had gone up into the hills without him. He could feel the tears starting to well up in his eyes and he pulled himself together and remembered the words of his Dad, 'It is not over until the fat lady sings,' and Jack concluded that he had definitely not heard anyone singing, never mind a fat lady, and that he was not, under any circumstances, going to give up the fight until he did.

However, it was clear that the captors had realised that their 'guests' were starting to stir, and with a large whoosh, the tarpaulin was thrown back and an enormous man stood in the dimly lit doorway. He was, without doubt, a buccaneer, with many weapons about his person and long hair. Jack pretended to be asleep and had luckily moved sufficiently far away from the tarpaulin edge for it not to be too obvious that he had been looking out onto the camp prior to his captor's arrival.

'Wake up, my beauties,' the large buccaneer said loudly. And the three of them stirred dutifully as if they had just woken, and started to sit up.

Mr Darwin looked straight at the man in the doorway. 'Who are you and what are you doing?' he asked.

'Well,' said the man. 'A direct question, I will give you a direct answer. I am a Destroyer and I am here, Mr Darwin, to ensure that you do not return on the Beagle, that you do not finish your scientific papers and that the world never hears from you again.'

Mr Darwin's bottom jaw dropped, as it was quite clear that this was not the answer that he had been expecting.

It was Jack that spoke next. 'Why? What has this scientist ever done to you?'

The Buccaneer laughed. 'Poor Master Jack, so close and yet so far. You thought that you and your little friends could prevent us from succeeding, but this is what happens when you send children to do men's work. I'll agree that you were not easily frightened by our greeting party and you quickly worked out how to reduce the size of the beast, but your people have sent children to do a man's job and you will all pay dearly for it.'

Jack glanced across at Harry, expecting him to be completely lost at this stage of the proceedings but, quite the contrary, Harry was following the conversation with some interest and a clear understanding of what was going on.

'Let the boy go,' Harry said. 'He is of no interest to you. He is not from our ship.'

The Buccaneer laughed and threw his head back to reveal his gold teeth. 'Now even I am not that naïve,' he said loudly.

'So,' said Harry. 'What will you do? Kill us all?'

The Buccaneer tilted his head on one side. 'We are not barbarians,' he said. 'We are not in the game of killing. But what we will do is repatriate you to a nice small island where no one will find you for many, many years. You will have food and water and be able to live, but Mr Darwin's theories will never be published and the course of history will be changed forever.' He laughed loudly, and the sound got louder and louder.

'Well,' the Buccaneer said, 'I just wanted to give you that news in person. I will send in some breakfast. Let's regard it as the last supper.' He laughed loudly and threw back his head as he did so. Then he backed out through the tent and let the tarpaulin drop back down.

As the three of them sat in the semi-darkness in the tent, Mr Darwin looked from one boy to the other. 'Would somebody like to tell me what's going on?' he asked eventually.

Jack and Harry glanced at one another and looked at Mr Darwin, and then looked back at one another.

'You first,' said Harry.

Jack took a deep breath and made himself as comfortable as he could, sitting on the sacks on the floor.

'Mr Darwin, this is going to be quite difficult for you to understand, but I am from the future.' He paused and Mr Darwin looked at him with a cold stare that gave nothing away.

'I know that you are on the Beagle at the request of Captain Fitzroy, as he wanted intellectual company on his long trip and for him to have a scientific person on board. I know that you are simply viewing this as a means of studying the natural history of the different countries you visit, but you have no idea of the importance of this voyage to the whole of mankind.'

Mr Darwin sat bolt upright and viewed the two boys with some scepticism. 'My dear boys,' he said, 'I am simply collecting plants and animals and birds, making notes and journal entries, and enjoying studying the natural history of these wonderful islands and this great journey.'

Harry and Jack looked at each other and exchanged knowing glances.

'In many years' time,' said Jack, 'you are going to publish
On the Origin of Species; it will be a scientific paper that takes the
world by storm because it will tell the world that species develop
by natural selection and that the fittest survives and that species
adapt to their surroundings.' Jack hoped that Professor Mufflin
would forgive his rather short hand explanation of science's most
revolutionary evolutionary theory.

Mr Darwin looked at Jack with a mixture of surprise and
incredulity. 'I think you may be confusing me with someone else,'
he said eventually. 'I am simply a scientist.'

'No, I'm not,' said Jack. 'It will take you years and years and,
to be honest, Mr Darwin, there are many of us who wondered
what on earth you had been doing between the voyage and
publishing your paper, but publish it you did in 1859 and you are
the most famous scientist that the world has ever known.'

Mr Darwin looked back and forward between them both, as
if this was some sort of joke, but, in unison, they nodded their
heads.

'He's right, Mr Darwin,' said Harry. 'You are going to
become a very famous man. But unless we free you from these
buccaneers, then that will never happen. All memory of you will
be erased from the future and, what is worse, the Galapagos
Islands will disappear forever and no-one will have the delight of
visiting this special place.'

Jack's head almost snapped round, as he turned to stare at
Harry, who, up until that moment, he had believed was simply a
travelling companion of Mr Darwin's on the Beagle.

'How...?' said Jack, as he stared at the young man next to him.

Harry laughed. 'How do I know all this?' he asked. Jack
thought for one terrible moment that Harry was indeed a
Destroyer and he had allowed him into their lives and now it was
all about to end.

Harry looked at Jack and smiled but his voice was very

serious. 'Jack, you and I have met before. You will not remember because you were very young when I passed from your world. Although I can no longer be in your world, I have found I can pass through the Gate at will to other time zones, I just cannot pass back to your world.'

Jack took an involuntary breath.

Harry continued, 'I am able to pass through the Gate but only to try and help the next person who comes in the fight against Evil. Whilst I cannot get back, I will do all that I can to ensure that you do. I promise you that.' And he held out his hands and Jack took them and squeezed them as tightly as possible.

After a few seconds the boys dropped hands. 'Right, Master Jack,' said Harry with a deep breath and in a very grown up voice. 'We need a plan.'

Rosie, Sam and JJ awoke as the sun rose above the horizon to the east of the island. They each awoke on the beautifully crafted cots with layers of hand stitched blankets and, between the three of them, lay the two dogs, exhausted from the night's activities and stuffed full of delicious meat casserole and relaxed from the hours and hours of stroking that they had endured. Since the good people of the village had taken them to their heart, Rosie had lost count of the number of times that she had seen Molly upside down with her legs in the air being stroked and nuzzled by groups of small children, intent on being able to say that they had touched a real dog.

The shelter in which they were sleeping had a cloth door and, as all three were just starting to wake and wonder where they were and recounting in their minds the memories of the night before, the cloth door was drawn back and George appeared in the doorway. He looked troubled and the children sensed this

immediately. The deep furrows on his forehead were even deeper
as he frowned at them. He carried a small tray with wooden
bowls full of something steaming, and he presented each of the
children with one and sat down on the edge of Rosie's cot.

The floor was covered in cloth as makeshift carpet and
George pulled back the carpets to expose the bare sand. As each
of the three children managed to sit upright with their legs over
the cot and started to sip the sweet, milky, chocolaty fluid from
the mugs, George started to draw in the sand in front of them.
Even the dogs sat up and watched intently.

George drew a line in the sand and, on one side, he drew
squiggly lines with fish.

'That's the sea,' said Sam. 'So this must be the land.'

He looked at George. 'Where are we?' he said, pointing
towards himself and then pointing to the map.

George nodded and pointed to a spot well inland.

JJ looked at the picture and gestured to George, as if to say,
were they up high?

George nodded again. He pointed with his stick to where
they were and gestured with his hands to show that they were up
high. He then drew a line about halfway down from where they
were towards the sea and it was wiggly.

'Is that the stream, do you think?' asked Rosie.

JJ looked at George and wondered how to ask that question
in a way that he would understand. She put her hands down as
if she was trying to cup water in her hands and bring it up to her
mouth. She did this a few times and then pointed to the wiggly
line. George nodded.

'It's the stream,' said Sam.

George then pointed to the edge of the shoreline, just below
the stream, and he pointed to each of the children.

'That was where we were,' said JJ. 'That is where the cave
is.' She pointed to each of them and to the edge of the line that

George had drawn, and he understood and nodded furiously and pointed at all three of them and pointed back to the edge of the water.

'OK,' said Sam. 'So that was where we were.'

George then drew an arc around to the right and made another cross. He then made a gesture, as if someone was shooting, but not shooting directly in front of them but shooting at something in the sky.

'That must be Mr Darwin,' said Rosie, 'shooting his birds.'

Sam took another stick and on the diagram, in the sea, just past the point that George had just drawn, he drew a basic picture of a boat with a big sail. George nodded furiously.

'Right,' said Sam. 'So this must be where the Beagle landed Mr Darwin and his crew.'

George then drew a further line around the coast, past Mr Darwin's camp. He pointed at where he had drawn the latest spot. He looked at the three children and frowned, as if to say that he didn't really know how to explain this part. He moved towards Sam, who was sat closest to him and grabbed him around his arms, so that his arms were pinned to his body, and lifted him off his feet, and pretended to walk off with him.

The children looked at George curiously, not quite understanding what he meant. George pointed again at the spot and then made out as if he had spears and was hunting towards Mr Darwin's camp. The children looked slightly confused still, and he drew a line in the water between this new camp and Mr Darwin's camp, and made actions as if to say he was rowing between the two.

'I know,' said Rosie. 'These are the people that we saw from the top. They're the buccaneers. The pirates that we thought were coming for Mr Darwin. How do we ask him about Jack?'

They all thought about this for a minute and then JJ turned to George. She counted and pointed to Sam, one, Rosie, two, her, three, and then four, she pointed back towards the cave area.

George appeared to understand what she was saying, that there was a fourth member who was missing. He nodded and he drew a line to indicate that the buccaneers had come from their camp. He showed with his line that those from the buccaneers' camp had gone first to Mr Darwin's and then on to the caves, and he then drew a big sweeping line to indicate that they had gone back.

He pointed to the children, JJ, Sam and Rosie, and then pointed to the fourth space that indicated Jack, and he then pointed back to the buccaneers' camp.

'Oh my goodness!' said Rosie, loudly. 'He's been captured!' And the two dogs leapt to their feet at the very suggestion.

Sam wanted to check, so he looked at George and, again, counted one, two, three and then pointed to the imaginary spot where Jack would be sitting. He held his hands up together, as if they were tied and pointed back towards the buccaneers' camp. George nodded.

'That's definitely it,' said Sam. 'He's definitely been taken.'

With that, all three children clambered to their feet and JJ gestured to George. 'We must go to the camp,' she said. 'We must rescue our friend,' and she pointed to the imaginary space where Jack would have been standing.

George stood and gestured for them all to sit down. He gestured for them to drink their hot cocoa and then, when they had done so, to join him outside.

George lumbered towards the entrance to the shelter. He turned back and smiled at them, as a kindly father would do, and closed the cloth curtain to the door.

Rosie, Sam and JJ downed their hot cocoa and threw back the covers, found their shoes and, in the case of Rosie and Sam, their makeshift weapons, and prepared themselves for a difficult day. When they were sure that they were all ready, they and the dogs stood as one, as they pulled back the curtain, ready to rescue Jack.

However, what lay before them was not the scene they had expected. Instead of a bare camp, with a central fire, as it had been last night, there stood in front of them rows and rows of fiercely dressed warriors. All the kindly men folk of the evening before, who had tickled the dogs and made a fuss of the children, now stood before them as warriors with bones through their noses and ears with brightly coloured blankets and spears. As the children emerged from their shelter, as one, the warriors all took their right arms and smacked them across their chests, as a salute to the children. The children glanced at one another and, as one, they reciprocated the salute.

However, it appeared that not even warriors would be moving off without a hearty breakfast inside them and, the formalities now dispensed with, they all sat down to the piping cauldrons of beans with homemade bread and fresh fruit, washed down with yet more warm chocolate milk.

As the children tucked into their second bowl of what looked a little like porridge but tasted really quite different, but was topped off with the most wonderful sweet honey that any of them had ever tasted, they all suddenly realised at the same time that the dogs appeared to be missing. Rosie practically dropped the wooden bowl from which she was eating her breakfast.

'The dogs!' she said, and went to stand up, and there was a small ripple of laughter that went amongst the warriors before her. She realised immediately that it was unlikely that the dogs would have been harmed but, nevertheless, she was worried not to have them in her sight. After all, Auntie Issie had entrusted them with her and her brother, although, whether Auntie Issie had actually realised that they would jump through the Gate and be now stuck on an island surrounded by warriors in multicoloured clothing, was another matter.

The laughter got a little louder and, before them, the warriors started to part so that there was a gap between them. Not a big gap, but a gap big enough for, say, a dog. And it was at that stage that all three children saw the dogs at the same time.

The children's mouths fell open as they saw, walking towards them, not two humble farm Border Collies ready to round up sheep, but two canine warriors, ready to defend the honour of the family. Each had a brightly coloured coat, which seemed to fit them perfectly. On their chests was a breastplate, gleaming in the morning sunshine, and on their heads a headdress which, whilst decorated with beads and feathers and placed carefully over each of their ears, did appear to be offering real protection to their heads, made of similar material to the gleaming breastplates that they were also wearing. Given that these people had never seen a dog until a few hours ago, it was clear that they had spent most of the night creating the most perfect dog armour.

JJ looked up at George and put her hands together and bowed her head in a signal that she knew meant, 'Thank you'. And then the warriors parted again and, this time, it was not the arrival of the dogs in their armour, but, instead, the women of the village came with their arms out in front of them and, draped over their arms, brightly coloured clothing, similar to that which the warriors before them were now wearing.

They moved forward until in front of each of the three children stood two of the women. One held out the clothing and each of the children took this from them. It was difficult to see exactly how it should be worn, but they should not have worried too much because, suddenly, from behind them, appeared scores of young women and older children, each eager to help to dress the three strangers. The garments were lifted onto their backs and twisted and turned and fastened, and the headdresses were placed on each of their heads and pulled and fitted until they were tight fitting and very comfortable.

The dogs sat calmly in front of them, watching their every

move. Rather than fuss and pull at their new armour, they appeared to find it quite comforting. Charlie had the occasional glance at Molly as she blew at the small beaded tassel that was hanging down a little too close to her eyes. But, all in all, both dogs were transfixed by the transformation that was happening in front of them, as the three, slightly tired and rather scruffy children were transformed before them into warriors.

Although the garments were brightly coloured, and appeared to fit them perfectly, they were still able to move their arms and their legs freely. Although it would seem at first glance that the outfits were quite heavy, in fact, once they were fitted around their bodies, they were as light as a feather.

Sam looked at the two girls, as the final adjustments were being made to his outfit. 'Wow!' he said. 'Look at you two.'

'You don't look so bad yourself,' said Rosie. 'Quite scary really.'

Charlie barked once, as if to say, 'What about us?'

Rosie bent down beside him. 'And you look fantastic too, Charlie,' she said, and he nuzzled against her face.

Not wanting to be outdone, Molly started nuzzling on the other side until, eventually, the two dogs were licking Rosie's face and succeeded in pushing her backwards, so that she lay on the ground laughing, with two Collies in full warrior regalia pinning her down and licking her.

'Auntie Issie is never going to believe this,' said Rosie.

Just as they were all admiring each other for one last time, there was a sudden shout and the dogs leapt to their feet. Running through the camp came a teenager, shouting something in his own language, and George frowned, and his eyes widened.

JJ looked at him with her arms out, palms upturned, as if to say, 'What is wrong?' And, rather than trying to explain using sign language and lines in the sand, George beckoned for her to follow him. In fact, he beckoned for all of the children to follow, and, such were the length of his legs, that the children had to jog alongside him to keep up. He moved quickly through the undergrowth until he emerged from the shrubbery onto a flat piece of land, which had the most amazing views out across the rest of the island. And as he came out into the clearing, with a clear view, George stopped dead, and uttered something which the children could only presume was some sort of expletive.

They studied the scene below them, but as they had not seen things in the light from the top of the hill, combined with their lack of knowledge and geography of the island meant that it was impossible for them to tell what was concerning George. JJ touched his arm and, again, raised her hands and shrugged her shoulders, as if to say, 'What is the problem?' George took his stick and drew a shape which the children assumed was the shape of the island. He made a small spot to show that that was where they were standing.

'So far so good,' said Sam.

He then pointed over his shoulder with his stick. 'What does that mean?' asked Rosie.

He gestured with his hand over his shoulder, as if to say that something was behind him.

'Behind us?' asked JJ.

'No, no,' said Sam. 'I think he means yesterday.'

George drew a second picture, and this time it was the same shape, but considerably smaller, and, again, he placed the dot in the middle, which is where they were standing. He pointed again at the bigger shape and gestured over his shoulder, and then at the smaller shape and pointed at the ground.

'I think I understand,' said Sam. 'Yesterday, the island looked like this, and today it is, my goodness me, reducing in the size.' The reality hit was not lost on him. The island was disappearing.

The children looked again for any signs of what George was telling them, and Rosie pointed. 'Look,' she said. 'The rocks that

were surrounding the island with the caves in, they've all gone.
The sea is almost up to the grass where the tortoises were eating.
Oh my goodness,' she said. 'Jack! Where is Jack?'

'Look,' said JJ. 'You can see the giant tortoises all moving up
inland and there appear to be lots of little creatures.'

Sam said, 'I expect that's the iguanas.'

Rosie pointed, 'And all the birds, all their nests have gone.
They are just flying around in circles above us. The island is
disappearing.'

The children all looked at one another. 'Evil, it's winning,'
said Rosie. 'The island is disappearing, they have almost won.
They've killed Mr Darwin, and Jack, we've lost Jack!' And she
started to cry.

Sam took her firmly by the shoulders and looked her in the
eye. 'Rosie, if Jack was dead, and Mr Darwin was no longer, then
the whole island would have gone, but it hasn't, which means
we've still got a chance. Now is the time to be brave, Rosie, not to
give up.' Rosie pulled herself up to her full height and wiped the
tears away with the back of her hand.

All three children turned to face George. They pointed to
where they thought that they had probably come from and then
pointed to themselves. George nodded. He pulled a small horn
from inside his multicoloured jacket, which Rosie thought looked
suspiciously as if it was made from tortoiseshell, but decided now
was not the time to take an issue with that.

The warriors appeared, each of them clutching a weapon
of some kind, a spear, a knife, a bow and arrow. Three of the
warriors moved quickly towards the children and offered to each
of them their own bow and arrow. They were beautifully crafted.
Much better than the makeshift ones that Rosie and Sam had
managed to shape the previous day, and each bow came with its
own quiver of beautifully crafted arrows. Sam and Rosie held up
their own weapons and smiled but JJ took one of the beautifully

crafted weapons. She took the bow and arrow that was offered, placed it carefully over her left shoulder and the quiver of arrows over her head and right shoulder.

Suddenly, George clapped his hands loudly and they all recognised that this meant that now was the time to move. Weapons were gathered up, including Rosie and Sam's makeshift weapons from the day before. The dogs leapt to their feet and George made a low throaty noise that seemed to indicate to everyone that it was time to move, and off down the side of the hill they set, at such a pace that the children, again, had to jog to keep up.

At a military airbase on the western side of Ecuador, the large transporter trundled to a halt and taxied to what passed as the terminal building.

Stairs were placed against the door to the cabin of the aircraft and Alfie came bounding down the steps, two at a time. As he reached the tarmac, his phone rang. He pulled it from his flying jacket, 'Hello?'

'Alfie,' said Angela. 'The islands are disappearing – you need to move fast.'

'Roger that,' said Alfie, not a man of many words, but there was not much more to be said.

A man in uniform approached him. 'Mr Parker?' he asked in good English. 'I have been placed at your disposal by the Ecuadorian Government.'

'Excellent,' said Alfie shaking his hand. 'Get this boat out of this aircraft and on the water as quick as you can, please. Or, otherwise, lives will be lost.' There was no time for social niceties but Alfie was polite when he spoke.

'Understood, Mr Parker,' said that man, and started shouting in Spanish at those around him.

'We'll get along fine,' said Alfie, looking the young man up and down and pleased that he did not need to stand on ceremony with him. He pulled his overnight bag onto his shoulder and stalked to the waiting car.

Within an hour, 441 was being gently lowered from the transporter into the water. By this time, she had assembled quite a crowd. After all, it was unlikely that many Ecuadorians had seen a World War II rescue launch in their lives and it was unlikely that they would do so again. Alfie certainly hoped not, anyway. However, despite their lack of experience in this model of craft, the precision of the Ecuadorians in lowering it into the water safely could not be faulted.

As the shining black body of the boat settled into the water, its bright white paintwork was emphasised even more than usual in the sunshine. Alfie had brought with him the cover for the rear deck, not because he thought it would be raining but because they may need it for shelter from the sun. He busied himself fixing this on as whilst the covered cabin was not large, it was big enough in ordinary circumstances – but these were not ordinary circumstances.

CHAPTER EIGHT

Jack, Mr Darwin and Harry were sat on the floor of the tent with their backs to one another. Their hands had been tied behind their backs and, just to make sure, the buccaneers had tied a rope around all three of them, so that it swirled around like a large snake, making sure that they could not even move their upper arms to try and escape.

They hadn't said anything to each other for a while, as there didn't really seem much else to say. Jack wondered how his sister, Sam and JJ were and whether they had missed him yet.

He worried that they would come out as a search party, looking for him, and, they too, would be captured. The thought was too terrible, but so, also, was the thought that none of them would ever get back to their world and that Jack had failed them and failed the History Keepers.

He knew that whenever he was feeling down, his Mother would say to him that 'a wise man is one who knows what he can change'. Normally that thought would be enough to snap Jack out of it because, very often, he would be worried or concerned about something over which he had no influence at all. But now, thinking of his Mother's words, made him feel even worse, as he knew that this was something that he did have influence over, but he had not succeeded.

He thought back to all the lessons that he had had at the School, all the people that had come in to talk to them about survival in the bush, dealing with difficult situations, being in Antarctica, in Africa, and all of those places, and yet here he was on an island and the only major predators were those with two legs and a brain that was probably smaller than his.

'So,' said Mr Darwin, making polite conversation, 'tell me again what I do with my life.'

With half a sigh, Jack started to tell him again. 'In about 20 years, you write a book called *On the Origin of Species* and this explains how the fittest survive and how species evolve, rather than perhaps being created, as many religious people believe.'

Harry chipped in. 'Of course, there are still those who believe that man was created by God, and that's not to say that they are wrong, it's just a differing view. But, personally, I have always preferred your theory.'

Mr Darwin smiled, although neither of them could have seen that, as he had his back to them.

'So,' said Jack. 'If we get out of here and manage to save you from these men, it is really important that you don't do anything for a while because, if you do, then you will change history, and that's almost as bad. So, promise me that if we rescue you, you will not rush off and write your book now?'

'I promise,' said Mr Darwin, very solemnly, although all three of them knew in their heart of hearts that it was unlikely to count for much as they were unlikely to escape.

'It's all gone very quiet out there,' said Harry. 'I thought they were supposed to be putting us in another boat, and taking us to a desert island for us to live out our days.'

'I'm not entirely sure that they were telling us the truth,' said Jack, eventually. 'There is too much at risk. If they take us to another island, we could escape and Mr Darwin could go on to write his famous book.'

'So, do you think they will just kill us?' asked Mr Darwin. He sounded genuinely alarmed.

Harry said, 'Well, you would think that if that was their intention, then they would have done this some time ago, but, instead, they have gone to great lengths to tie us all securely together. But I agree, there has not been a word from camp for some time, which is quite unusual for such uncouth men. Shall we see if we can move across to the entrance to the tent?'

'We'll all need to move at once,' said Jack. 'Otherwise we might end up pulling against each other. So if we all try and move towards the door on my count of three? One, two...' And the three of them toppled over sideways.

'If this was not so serious,' said Mr Darwin, 'it would be quite funny. Now, it's important we must all move together and it's a shuffle, rather than a jump. So, let's try again. One, two...' And, again, they all toppled over.

'OK, third time lucky,' said Mr Darwin. 'One, two...' And, this time, they moved in unison across the floor towards the entrance to the tent.

'Good,' said Mr Darwin. 'Excellent. Now one, two...' And they moved closer.

By about the third move, they had well and truly got the hang of it and, within the space of a few minutes, had managed to get across to the opening of the tent. They sat there quietly for a minute or so, to make sure that they definitely couldn't hear anything outside.

'Right,' said Jack in hushed tones. 'I'm closest to the door, so I will see if I can look out. I'm going to have to lean over and, to stop us all toppling out through the tent, the two of you will need to pull back as a counterbalance. Do you understand?' The other two whispered 'yes' as quietly as they could.

'Right,' Jack said. 'I'm going to do this gently. So I'm moving now. Can you counterbalance?' and he moved his head, and slowly reached the canvass and gently he poked it out through the gap, expecting at any stage a large man to grab him as he did so. But, as his head slowly protruded, there was no large man. In fact, there were no men at all. The camp appeared to be completely deserted.

'There's no-one here,' said Jack. 'No-one at all.'

'Can you see any signs of life, any belongings, anything personal?' asked Mr Darwin.

'No, nothing. Just the ground and the sea,' he said. 'Can't you hear the sea?'

The three of them all stopped and listened intently.

'Now you come to mention it,' said Harry. 'I can, and it sounds quite close.'

'It is,' said Jack. 'It's actually very close. I'm surprised we hadn't heard it earlier.'

'But the seas here aren't tidal,' said Mr Darwin.

'Oh,' said Jack as his heart missed a beat. 'I think I know what's happening.'

'Then tell us quickly!' said Mr Darwin.

'Too long to explain, but, essentially, if Evil succeeds, and you are 'prevented', shall we say, from writing your book, then the islands will disappear completely.'

'But what about the animals?' said Mr Darwin. 'The species that are here are nowhere else in the world. How will anybody be able to write about them? It's only because they have been trapped here on these islands, so had no choice but to develop, that I have been able to study them in such detail.'

'That's just it,' said Jack. 'Perhaps your theory will never see the light of day. Perhaps those who believe that we were created by a God will have the loudest voice. I don't know. It's my first experience with history being changed.'

'Then we must do something about it,' said Mr Darwin, with an air of authority that sounded very optimistic. However, inside Mr Darwin was very glad that neither boy could see his face, which said nothing of the sort.

The dogs ran out ahead, their multicoloured coats and beads jangling as they ran. Although Rosie thought that perhaps this might upset them, instead it seemed to spur them on, and like streaks of multicoloured mist, they raced down the slopes ahead of the matching multicoloured warriors.

Rosie was the shortest by far and was struggling a little to keep up with the main pack, but her fitness as a fencer meant that what she lacked in height, she made up for in strength and fitness. JJ's long legs meant that she was easily able to match the warriors, and she had found herself in the centre of the pack, next to Sam.

Down the rolling hills they ran and passing them, going in the opposite direction, were hundreds, if not thousands, of small creatures: land iguanas, snakes, followed by the lumbering tortoises of all sizes. They were all heading in one direction and it was in the opposite direction to Rosie, Sam and JJ. They had all seen the seas closing in around them and were following their natural instincts to get to higher ground.

Rosie looked at the coastline again, past the bright warriors as they danced down the slopes and she was quite sure that the waves had got closer, even since they had left the top of the hill.

She could feel the tears welling up in her eyes as she worried about her brother and where he was, and the thought that, because the island was being engulfed by water, perhaps Jack had not been successful in saving Mr Darwin from whatever fate Evil had in store for him.

Jack was her life and the thought of losing another brother was almost too much for her. Although she had never known Harry, as he had died before she was born, she always felt as if she had known him because her parents talked so much about him.

She stumbled slightly, as the tears welled up in her eyes and she couldn't quite see her footing on the grassy slopes, and as she struggled to regain her balance, she suddenly felt a strong arm lift her from the ground whilst still running. She looked up to see

George smiling at her as he lifted her off her feet as if she was a feather and swung her up onto his back. George made a gesture which Rosie took to mean, 'Hold tightly round my neck,' and she did as instructed, burying her head in the soft folds of his brightly coloured warrior clothes, and clung on for her life.

----

441 was being loaded up with provisions. The more that came on board the lower they sank into the water as boxes of food, filtered water, flares and blankets were loaded on board.

The Ecuadorian Government had provided Alfie with a total of five of their finest soldiers; the other four had arrived with their identical kitbags and in their smart green combat outfits. Their leader, who had met Alfie at the airport, was called Jose, and he spoke extremely good English, which was probably as well, as Alfie's Spanish was fairly non-existent, although he probably could have got by in French.

Jose looked at Alfie with his head slightly tilted to one side and in his Spanish accent he said, 'So, Mr Parker, I understand that we are going somewhere that none of us know and to carry out a rescue operation for people that don't exist.'

'Ah, that's about it,' said Alfie. 'Are your men settled? In which case, we'd best get under way.'

And, with a shrug of his shoulders, Jose muttered something very fast in Spanish and his four companions immediately set about preparing 441 to cast off from the jetty and to get under way.

Alfie moved up to the helm of 441 and turned the key to start her. The two 300 horsepower engines sprang into life with an enormous roar. The five soldiers at the back of the boat almost jumped out of their skins when the engine started. Alfie smiled. Somehow he thought they probably hadn't been expecting that, but then again, 441 had many secrets and had seen much action in her long and distinguished career as a World War II rescue launch.

How fitting that 441 should, once more, have soldiers on board and that she should, once more, be launching a rescue mission, albeit of an entirely different variety. Although 441 still bore the scars of the bullets that had been fired at her during the Second World War, as she attempted to rescue the downed pilots in the English Channel, Alfie was under no illusions that she may well be adding to those scars on this trip.

The soldiers on the deck were all stood to attention and looking at something on the quayside and so Alfie powered down the boat and knocked it into neutral, and went out to see who was there.

Standing on the quayside was the Head of the Ecuadorian Army, who had been so generous with his kindness, cooperation and the loan of his men. He saluted Alfie when he saw him. 'Good luck to you, Mr Parker,' he said, 'and to your amazing boat. Safe journey, wherever that may take you.' Alfie gestured a salute in response, and returned to the helm to guide 441 safely out of the harbour and on her way to the coordinates that he did not yet have, but he knew somebody that did.

Alfie pulled his mobile phone from his jacket pocket and pushed the number one, which he knew that Angela had programmed in, to connect him directly with her mobile. Other than boats and planes, the advancing age of technology was something that had rather passed Alfie by and he was always grateful for the odd short cut.

The irony was that whilst he had been able to rebuild 441 from scratch, including the shaping of the wood and the complete restoration of all its original parts, dialling a number on a mobile telephone was still something that he struggled with. The number rang twice and a familiar voice answered.

'You're there,' said Angela.

'I am indeed,' said Alfie. 'Under way, five friends on board, with a shed load of provisions and a destination that I am completely unaware of.'

'OK,' said Angela, 'get ready with the Sat Nav.'

Alfie stood poised over the Sat Nav, ready to put in the coordinates.

'And what if the Sat Nav stops working half way across?' asked Alfie.

'You can deal with it,' said Angela. 'Hang on, how many people did you say you had with you?'

'Five,' said Alfie.

'Good,' she said. 'Put one in charge, line four of them up in a particular order and give them each two numbers to remember. If the Sat Nav throws it out, then, hopefully, if you line them up and ask them to repeat the numbers, Evil will not have made them forget something which is not obviously related to their destination.'

'Clever clogs,' said Alfie.

'Jose,' he shouted over his shoulder and Jose appeared from the back of the boat. 'Can you bring your men in and line them up in height order.'

Jose raised an eyebrow as if to say, 'These strange English traditions'. He called to his men who appeared; Jose jabbered at them in Spanish and quickly assembled themselves into height order. They wore khaki uniforms, that looked different to those of the British army – their hats were squarer and the colour on the uniforms reflected the terrain of Ecuador, rather than of England.

'Now,' said Alfie, 'I'm going to read out eight numbers. Starting with the shortest, I want them to remember two, and then the next person, two, and then the next person and then the next person. Am I making myself clear?'

'Yes, Mr Parker,' said Jose, his eyebrows raised as if to say 'these strange English customs'.

'And please,' said Alfie. 'Stop calling me Mr Parker. My name is Alfie. Ready?'

Alfie put the phone to his ear again. 'OK, go,' he said.

And Angela started to read the numbers. As she read them, Alfie typed them into Sat Nav and, as each two numbers came through he repeated them to Jose, who allocated them to the man with the correct height.

'OK,' said Alfie, 'I'll read that back to you.' And he read back what he had programmed into Sat Nav. As he said the numbers, Jose translated and each of the soldiers nodded.

'Now your turn,' said Alfie. 'Get the men to read back their numbers, you translate.' And one by one the numbers were read back.

'OK,' said Alfie, 'I think we're as good as we ever will be. I am not sure what, if any, mobile signal we will get when we get closer to our destination.'

Angela said, 'I took the liberty of asking the Ecuadorian Government if they could provide you with a satellite phone. You should find that Jose has it on the boat somewhere.'

Alfie put his hand over the phone and looked at Jose. 'Satellite phone?'

'Yes, Mr Parker, I mean Alfie. I have the satellite phone.' Jose nodded enthusiastically and went to the storage section on the deck of 441.

'You think of everything,' said Alfie as Jose rooted around in the cupboard for the equipment.

'Flattery,' said Angela, 'will get you absolutely anywhere… Good luck.'

'Thank you,' said Alfie. 'On this particular occasion, I fear I might need it.'

Jack, Harry and Mr Darwin had managed to edge their way out of the tent and across to where the last embers of the camp fire were still smouldering.

'Now,' said Mr Darwin, 'if we can manage to twist round and I can hold my ropes over this hot piece of wood, there is a chance that I can burn through the rope and free us.'

'Won't you also burn your hand?' asked Jack.

Mr Darwin said, very solemnly, 'Master Jack, that would be a small price to pay in light of all that you have told me. What are two burnt hands when compared with my works never seeing the light of day?'

Mr Darwin managed to kick out one of the larger embers with his feet and the three of them shuffled round until they had managed to place Mr Darwin's hands over the sizzling ember.

He took a sharp intake of breath and Jack could tell that it was clearly hot and clearly hurting. For what seemed like an age, Mr Darwin held his hands over the burning embers and Jack could finally feel him start to wriggle his hands further.

'Are you all right?' asked Jack.

'Yes, Master Jack, I am absolutely fine,' said Mr Darwin. 'And all the better,' he said, as he pulled his hands round in front of him, 'for being able to move my hands!'

'Thank goodness,' muttered Harry.

Of course, they were still all entwined in a large rope around their chests and shoulders, which was keeping them all back to back, but it did not take Mr Darwin long to unfasten both Jack and Harry's hand ropes and then for the three of them to untangle themselves from the ropes around their chest and shoulders.

'Go and put your hands in cold water,' said Jack to Mr Darwin. And as he saw Mr Darwin start to hesitate, he said.

'Now! It will make it much better.'

Mr Darwin smiled at the thought that he was taking commands from a 13 year old, but did as he was instructed.

He walked towards the water's edge, which was now lapping up at where the camp was situated, and as he walked towards where he thought he could put his hands into the soothing waters, the waters suddenly subsided. He took a couple of steps forward, and the waters moved back again. He turned to Jack and Harry.

'The water, it seems to be going backwards,' said Mr Darwin in astonishment.

'Well,' said Jack, 'either we are about to have a tsunami or it means that we are triumphing over Evil and that the destruction of the island is being reversed.'

Suddenly there was a loud guffawing from behind the two boys and out from behind the tent stepped one of their captors. He was still a big man with a cutlass strapped to his waist. He was still unshaven and still very frightening looking.

'The worse thing is,' laughed the Buccaneer, 'is that we don't need to keep watch over you; we have our own alarm signal.' And he pointed to the subsiding water. 'As soon as the water started to recede, we knew that we had to come back through our Gate as we knew you were up to something.'

Mr Darwin looked at him with disdain. 'Well, it seems to me,' he said, 'that you are outnumbered. There are three of us and one of you.' It was at that point that about ten buccaneers emerged from behind the tents, arms folded, laughing. And as they started to come closer, they appeared to be getting bigger and bigger.

'Hold hands!' said Jack, and Mr Darwin looked at him is if he was completely mad.

'Master Jack, this is not the time ...'

'Just hold hands,' said Harry. 'Quickly! Think of good things.'

Mr Darwin frowned at them. Jack and Harry joined hands

and held out their free hands to Mr Darwin.

'Come on, Mr Darwin, you have to think of the good that you've done. If you don't then Evil will triumph,' said Jack.

Mr Darwin offered his hands, tentatively.

'Tell us something good that you've done,' said Jack. 'Quickly.'

'Two days ago, I found a giant tortoise that had managed to find its way onto its back,' he said. 'I turned it the right way up, and it went off about its business and appeared to be grateful.'

'Harry?' said Jack.

'I put my hands further into the fire so that Mr Darwin could break his ropes.'

Jack looked immediately at Harry's hands and could see that they were, indeed, red and scorched and felt hot to the touch.

'I did not pack all my clothes for half term when we went to Auntie Issie, so that Rosie could get in some more Princess Dresses,' said Jack.

As each of them told of the good that they had done, the size of the buccaneers started to reduce until, finally, they were no bigger than mere men. They were still huge and towered over Jack and Sam but they were just mere men and not giants.

'What kind of magic is this?' asked Mr Darwin.

'There's not enough time to explain,' said Jack. 'But we need to run for our lives. Harry, Mr Darwin, go behind me and across the rocks. Go now, please. I'll try and keep them at bay as much as possible.' Jack turned back towards the life size buccaneers and tried to stand up to his full height, which even then was only half of even the smallest of the buccaneers.

The buccaneers laughed loudly together. 'There is no one to help you, young Master Jack,' said the leader. 'Mr Darwin's shipmates are tied up in a cave where they will soon drown when the waters start to return. And how will you, a mere boy, keep us at bay?' There was more laughter from the buccaneers and one of them shouted from the back. 'Yeah,' he said, 'you and whose army?'

'Oh,' said Jack with a smile. 'Did I not mention the army?' He looked over the shoulders of the buccaneers.

'Oh, that old trick,' said the leader. 'Make us all look in another direction whilst you leg it. I don't think so.'

'Suit yourself,' said Jack, and shrugged his shoulders and started to walk off.

The buccaneer came charging towards Jack, pulling out his cutlass as he approached. 'I've had quite enough of you,' he said. And as he got almost within touching distance of Jack, there was a thud and the buccaneer landed at Jack's feet. There had been no shot and no apparent weapon used, but as he landed, Jack looked back behind him and, stood on a rise, was a distinguished looking gentleman in brightly coloured regalia and there, stood by his side, was Rosie. In the man's hand was a slingshot. Jack smiled with thanks and recognition.

As the other buccaneers turned to see what had brought down their great leader, there stepped into view not one, not two, but over forty brightly coloured warriors.

'Gentlemen,' said Jack with an unfaltering voice, 'let me introduce my army!'

Alfie pushed forward full throttle on 441 and they hurtled out into the ocean, following the Sat Nav. It was still showing the coordinates that Angela had given them but Alfie suspected that Evil may try and change them at some stage. So, every half an hour, he called in the Ecuadorian soldiers and lined them up in height order and asked them to recite the numbers. As they got further away from the mainland, he noticed that the Sat Nav was subtly adjusting the numbers to perhaps one or two degrees out and on each occasion that he discovered this, he re-set the Sat Nav to the correct coordinates and the boat changed direction very slightly.

The journey was pleasant, the sun was warm and occasionally Alfie would see a dolphin leap from the water, the water shining from its back. Often there followed many hundreds more, skimming the water in the sunshine. Overhead, frigate birds swooped and hovered, anxious to see if he had any food on board. They had been going at full pelt for about four hours when Alfie noticed the first small boat rowing towards them. It was filled with people and some belongings, including a bicycle and he pulled up alongside it, called over to Jose and asked him to ask the people in the boat where they had come from. There were six adults and five children, ranging in ages from a babe in arms to about 10. They all looked hot and as if they had left in a hurry. They had bundles of belongings in the bottom of the boat.

'From the islands, they are saying,' said Jose, looking perplexed. 'But that can't be right, there are no islands in this direction. They say that the islands are flooding and that their homes are gone.'

'How many people do they say are on the islands?' asked Alfie.

Jose translated. '400,' said Jose.

'400? We'll never get all of them in 441,' said Alfie, almost to himself.

Alfie got his mobile phone out and dialled Angela's number. There was no signal.

'OK,' said Alfie. 'Can we get the satellite phone out? As quick as you can.' Jose rushed to the back of the boat and pulled out a case. He opened it and removed the strange looking phone from its protective casing.

'Any idea how to use it?' asked Alfie.

Jose had a wry smile and raised one eyebrow. 'You tell me the number you need to dial,' he said. 'I will dial it.'

Alfie read out the number from his mobile. He hoped to goodness that there was a satellite overhead which could relay the message to Angela. The Pentagon had promised that they would ensure that there were sufficient satellites for the whole of his time here but he was always sceptical about such promises.

Jose paused for a minute or so and then nodded and handed the phone across to Alfie. 'It is ringing,' he said.

'Alfie,' said Angela answering immediately. 'Problem?'

'Possibly,' said Alfie. 'We've just found our first boatload of people from some islands; they say that they are being flooded.'

There was a chattering of Spanish and Jose interrupted. 'One of these people, he speaks English and he says to tell you that the islands have not gone completely but there is not much left and the animals are finding they have nowhere to go and there are not enough boats to get all the people off.'

Angela had heard this. 'I know that one or two of the islands were inhabited, but I had no idea that it was this many people.' Alfie of course had no knowledge of the islands or their inhabitants – Evil had seen to that by removing all memories of the Galapagos from him. But what he did realise was that people needed help.

'These people look a bit desperate,' he said.

'Leave it with me,' said Angela and disconnected the phone immediately.

CHAPTER NINE

Back in Lavender Lane, Angela turned to the rest of the room who were waiting with baited breath for news from Ecuador.

'It's not looking good,' she said. 'The islands are practically flooded and the inhabitants are trying to get away in small boats, the animals are in danger of drowning and there are not enough boats to evacuate everyone.'

The residents of Lavender Lane were crowded into the room and they all looked sombre. They knew that this meant one thing, that Jack and his young friends had probably failed. They glanced at Auntie Issie and Uncle Stanley, who would be impacted more than most by the news. They had a look of steely resolve on their faces.

Auntie Issie got to her feet. 'It's not over until the fat lady sings,' she said. 'In the meantime, we need to take all steps to save as much life as possible. Where's my mobile?'

The offices of Drucan in Southampton were as you would expect for the world's most prestigious ship builder, which had started with Samuel Drucan being awarded the first transatlantic steamship mail service in 1839. Winston Churchill always credited the Queen Matilda and the Queen Ann as shortening the Second World War as they were put into service carrying troops across the Channel. From the first Queen Ann to the most recent The Royal Adventurer, Queen Caroline and Queen Ann

2, Drucan was the one brand in cruising that was recognised throughout the world.

Their offices were spacious and modern, with a wonderful view across the Solent, the sea directly adjacent to Southampton and Portsmouth. Duncan Snugs, the President and Chief Executive, a tall, smart and softly spoken man, was just finalising the choices of wall colour for their newest ship, when his long suffering but greatly appreciated PA, Bella, knocked briefly and poked her head round the corner of his door.

'Sorry to disturb, Duncan. A bit of an emergency.'

'No problem,' said Duncan getting to his feet as the conversation was still going on around him. 'Gentlemen, ladies, please excuse me. I'll be back in a few minutes.' He strode quickly to the door and shut it behind him, still able to hear the voices behind the door reaching a loud crescendo of excitement behind him. He doubted that they had noticed he had left.

Duncan smiled at Bella. 'Is there genuinely an emergency?' he asked. 'Or were you just being kind, getting me out of that meeting? These arty types can get terribly involved. I know that they mean well but do I really need to be sat in on two hours of the colour of the carpets?'

Bella smiled. 'No, a genuine emergency,' and she handed Duncan the phone and went off to make a strong cup of tea for her boss.

The voice at the other end was one that Duncan recognised instantly and he was immediately alert, knowing that Issie would not have called him unless it was absolutely necessary.

After the usual pleasantries Issie lowered her voice to a very serious tone. 'Duncan,' she said and he knew that this was not going to be an ordinary request; it never was. Many of his friends and former colleagues rang him when they wanted a cheap deal or a better cabin. Issie rang him when she wanted something serious.

'You and I have been friends for many years, and I need to ask you a favour, and you will need to put your absolute faith and trust in me.' Duncan smiled. It was going to be a very interesting request.

'Sounds ominous, Issie,' said Duncan, knowing immediately that whatever she asked he would agree to; she was always true to her word.

'You don't know what I am about to ask,' she said.

'I know you are not looking for a cheap deal, Issie, let's put it that way,' and he listened intently, pen in hand making notes, asking the occasional question, frowning at intervals. It did not take long and then Duncan said quietly into the phone:

'Leave it with me, Issie.' And then he put the phone down.

He turned to Bella who handed him a cup of tea. 'Can you get Sophia on the telephone?' he asked and sat down in the nearest seat, unenthusiastic about rejoining the meeting.

Alfie had managed to pull all of the evacuees from the small boat into 441. They were a little dehydrated and shocked and Jose and his men were handing out cups of water and sweets. The children on board looked in amazement at the huge engines that they were sat next to. The adults peered into the cabin of 441 in surprise.

Jose and his colleagues had tied the small boat that their new visitors had arrived in to the back of 441 and Alfie fired up the engines again and, at a slightly slower speed, started heading towards the coordinates again, having double checked them again with his sized Ecuadorian soldiers. However, it was not long before they saw more little boats heading in their direction, all equally packed with people and goods, and one of them even appeared to have a giant tortoise on board, although Alfie suspected that that was probably more for food supply than out of a concern to preserve its genes.

'Jose,' he called. Jose came forward. 'We haven't got the capacity to pick everybody up, but what we do have is food and water and I know that help will be on its way. What we'll do is tie all the boats together and, as we find more, we'll bring them to the one central place, where they will have food and water, until help arrives.'

'But,' said Jose. 'Why would help arrive? Nobody knows these people are here and they don't know where they've come from.'

'Have faith, Jose,' said Alfie as he steered 441 towards the other small boats filled with people who were now waving their hands wildly to ensure that they attracted the attention of this small lifeline. Alfie mumbled under his breath, 'Lord knows, I'm trying to.'

It seemed that all the boats were heading in the same direction, and it was easy to persuade them all to come to one central location. There was no stampede, no attempt to board 441 and cause mass panic, just quiet thanks for the fact that they were all together and there was food and water. Luckily it was not too hot and for those who needed a little shelter they were able to come onboard 441 and sit in her cabin and use the facilities if needs be.

With a little manoeuvring, the strange assortment of small boats and craft were moored up alongside one another. Jose's men moved amongst the crafts to make sure that everyone was well and no one needed medical attention. There was much chattering going on between them and those that appeared to be escaping, and even with Alfie's rudimentary Spanish and his knowledge of French, he could understand that Jose's men were asking where these people had come from, and they were explaining that they had come from the Galapagos Islands, and Jose's men were shrugging their shoulders in no recognition of that destination and disbelief, saying that those islands did not exist.

The boat people explained that in recent months the number of visitors to the islands had become fewer and fewer and now no one came, that their stores had diminished, they had no fuel or food and that things had been getting desperate, even before the seas had started to close in.

Once Alfie was satisfied that everybody was well and had food and water, they arranged to tie all the small crafts together but to loosen 441 to enable her to continue to see if there was anything more that they could do until help arrived, if indeed it did arrive.

Jose had made sure that he had explained this to all the small boats so that they did not believe they were being deserted. They left water and food in each of the small crafts.

Alfie was just untying the last of the boats from the ropes hanging from 441 and checking that all of those who should be on board were and all of those who should have returned to their crafts had actually done so. He looked up and something on the horizon caught his attention. He thought perhaps he was imagining it, he had been out in the sun for a while, but then he saw it again and reached for the binoculars. He held them up to his eyes and looked again. He had not been imagining it. For there, on the horizon, coming full steam ahead, was an enormous cruise liner.

'Jose,' said Alfie. 'Flares, quickly!'

Jose dug down, underneath the provisions, and pulled out a box. Alfie quickly liberated the flare gun and inserted a flare.

'Tell the people not to be frightened,' he said. 'I'm about to let off a flare, and someone will be here to rescue us.'

He hesitated for a few minutes whilst Jose imparted that to all of those who could hear him, who, in turn, passed it along the line of the little boats, which were all tied together in a large pontoon.

When Alfie could see that the message had reached the very end of the line, he held up his flare gun and released the orange flare. This showed better in the daylight rather than the red one and he felt that this was an emergency rather than just a warning to the ship.

No sooner had he done it, when there was a loud foghorn blast coming from the direction of the ship, and it turned to ensure that it was sailing in exactly their direction. Those in the small boats who had not seen the ship approaching, certainly heard it, and eager heads turned in the direction of the approaching giant. As they saw it they were not afraid and instead a cheer went up from almost every man, woman and child who were sat bobbing on the ocean with their worldly possessions packed in underneath them.

It did not take long for the 150,000 tonne cruise liner to reach them and the closer it came, the more that Alfie was able to pick out some of its details. The red and white funnels, the 19 layers of decks with cabins and balconies, housing 2620 passengers. As she drew closer Alfie was able to make out the words, *The Royal Adventurer* written down her side, and to see the thousands of passengers who were lining the various decks, curious to see exactly what was going on. Alfie smiled; he knew now why Angela had been so certain they would be helped. Not for the first time the President and Chief Executive of Drucan had ridden to their collective rescue.

The huge form of the The Royal Adventurer came within 500 metres of the small flotilla of boats and then came to a complete halt. They were not in water that was too deep and Alfie could hear the rumble of the anchor chains as they launched their anchors to the bottom to secure the massive ship in its place. The engines were in neutral but were still ticking over. Immediately there was launched a small tender out of the side, which had been lowered down by a small winch from inside the bowels of The Royal Adventurer. It set a course directly towards 441 and Alfie watched as it approached.

Alfie could make out three figures in white: one woman and two men. He assumed that the taller of the men was probably the Captain; they all appeared to have various braiding adorning their shoulders, but it was harder to make out at a distance.

The tender got closer and the chatter from amongst all of the small boats tied together got louder and louder. Looking up, Alfie could see many of the passengers of The Royal Adventurer were still hanging over the railings and waving and pointing and many were taking pictures.

The tender pulled alongside 441 and, as it was much lower in the water than 441, Alfie looked over the railings down into the tender below.

'Alfie Parker,' he said, doing a mock salute to the gathered officers. He looked at the three of them in their white uniforms, expecting one of the men to step forward, but, instead, the small figure of a woman stepped forward.

'Hello, Mr Parker. I've heard a lot about you,' she said, her accent noticeable but not heavy – from somewhere in Scandinavia, Alfie concluded. 'My name is Captain Sophia Bergman, and I am the Captain of the The Royal Adventurer.'

Alfie tried hard not to let the surprise show on his face, as he realised that he really was behind the times. He was embarrassed that he had not even considered that she may have been the Captain; she was tiny next to her male colleagues. However, this was clearly a reaction that Captain Bergman was used to.

'Well, Captain,' Alfie said. 'I'm very grateful for your assistance.'

The Captain looked up and smiled warmly. 'I have no idea why we are here and no idea what we are expected to do when we are here, but when the boss calls me and asks me to divert to a location and says it's a matter of life and death, then that's what I'll do.'

Alfie smiled. 'Well,' he said, 'I think this is just the tip of the iceberg in terms of people fleeing from whatever it is behind them. Like you, I have no memory and no knowledge of what it is, for reasons that I can't even begin to explain to you. However, what I believe is that if we keep going in this direction, we will find many more people and, indeed, many animals that need rescuing. Is this something that you could help with?'

The Captain smiled again. 'We have already checked our records and we have five vets and fifteen doctors on board, in addition to our own medical staff. I think we can probably cope. We do have one of the biggest medical centres of any cruise ship. Is anyone hurt, do you know?'

'No,' said Alfie, balancing on the edge of the rails. 'It appears from what we've been told that it's more of a flood than anything else. Everyone is scared, hot and hungry, but they are not hurt.'

'Good,' said Captain Bergman. 'Well, in that case, let's get this lot on board and let's launch the tenders to see what else we can find.'

'If you don't mind,' said Alfie. 'Once you've got everybody on board, I'd quite like to go forward with 441 and my Ecuadorian escort.' He gestured to Jose and his colleagues who were stood at the other end of the boat.

The Captain smiled radiantly at them. 'Of course,' she said. 'Would you like to come aboard to freshen up or do you just want to get straight into it?' Alfie raised his eyebrows at Jose to ask him the same question and he in turn jabbered in Spanish at his four colleagues. After a few minutes of debate Jose turned back:

'We would rather go on, Alfie,' said Jose.

'Well,' said Alfie turning back to Captain Bergman. 'It would seem to us that things are happening fairly quickly, so I'd rather not waste any time, if you don't mind. We could do with some more fuel and water and perhaps a little more food?'

'Consider it done,' said Captain Bergman. 'We took the liberty of bringing fuel, water and food with us. We will transfer them across and then unhook the little boats, and we'll take care of them. You need to get on your way.'

As the stand-off continued with the buccaneers, George and his men, Rosie watched her brother stood, chest out and hands in a protective stance, sheltering Mr Darwin. She felt pride swell in her own chest as she watched her big brother being so brave.

'Jack!' she shouted, and went to run forward, but was held back by George's arm; she looked up and he shook his head as if to say: 'Now would not be the best time.'

Jack looked up and, almost bowing, he smiled and gave a half salute to Sam and to JJ, and rustled up his biggest and most encouraging smile for his baby sister.

'Are all of these people known to you?' asked Mr Darwin, under his breath, looking in the direction of Rosie, Sam and JJ.

'Some of them are, Mr Darwin,' said Jack. 'The small ones. The girl, she is my sister, and the other two, they are friends, Sam and JJ. The others I do not know but they appear to be friends.'

'Gracious!' said Mr Darwin. 'What on earth are they?' He said this slightly louder than he had meant to, but such was his surprise. He pointed to the two four legged creatures stood behind the humans, adorned with beads and multicoloured swathes of cloth.

'They,' laughed Jack, 'are my Aunt and Uncle's dogs, Molly and Charlie.'

'But there are no dogs on the island,' said Mr Darwin.

'No,' said Jack. 'They're not from the island. It's a long story and we probably need to try and get ourselves out of this mess before I tell it to you.' Jack kept his eyes on the buccaneers at all times. In the back of his mind there was something that he had learned recently that he thought might now be of assistance to him. And then it came to him and he smiled to himself. He turned to the unkempt men stood between him and his sister.

'Retreat now, buccaneers,' Jack said in his loudest voice, 'and you will come to no harm.'

The new leader looked at Jack and threw back his head, laughing loudly. '*You*,' he said, 'a mere child, will tell *me* to retreat. I don't think so. We've come to do a job and we will finish it.' And he looked menacingly at Mr Darwin.

Jack stepped closer to Mr Darwin, as did Harry. 'You will not succeed,' said Jack. 'Evil will never triumph over good. Go now and leave us be.'

And, at that stage, all of the buccaneers threw back their heads and started to laugh, and the laughter got louder and louder. Their leader looked at Jack in a menacing way. 'So, let me get this right. You children, a scientist and a bunch of people in brightly coloured clothes are going to stop us?'

Rosie stepped forward in indignation. 'Who is he calling a bunch of children?' she said.

Again, George held her back with his arm for the second time, and shook his head again. He pushed his spear into the ground and leant on it in a rather relaxed manner.

'I'll tell you what's going to happen,' said Jack, his voice even louder. Jack started to rub his left arm with his right and winced slightly as he did so, but he carried on: 'Mr Darwin and my friend, Harry and I, are going to walk over there to join our friends, and you will not lay a finger on us. If you do,' he said, 'I cannot be held responsible for the consequences.' Again, Jack rubbed his arm and then allowed it to hang down slightly by his side, indicating that he had injured it.

Jack saw his sister look at him and then at George; she looked worried.

There was more laughter and the leader of the buccaneers made a pretend bow, sweeping his hat from his head, and bowing graciously before Jack, as if to say: 'After you'.

Jack looked across at his sister and raised his eyebrows very slightly. She nodded. He looked at Sam and made the same gesture and got the same response. Sam understood even more than the others, but only because he had spent a lesson with Jack and Elias.

Finally, Jack looked across at JJ, beautiful in her multicoloured outfit, and raised his eyebrows, only slightly. She didn't nod back, she simply stood firm and a smile crossed her lips, and Jack knew that she, too, was ready.

'Right,' he whispered to Harry and Mr Darwin. 'We're going to walk across in the direction of my friends. Mr Darwin, I need you to stay on the opposite side to the buccaneers, so that I am between them and you.'

Mr Darwin looked down kindly at the small boy before him. 'Master Jack,' he said. 'It is I who should be protecting you and not the other way around. I see that you have injured your arm as well; you cannot possibly protect me.'

It was at that stage that Harry looked at Mr Darwin. 'No, Mr Darwin, in all of this, you are the most important person here. Jack and I will walk side by side and you must walk as far away from the buccaneers as possible. It's the only way that we can go, we are trapped here in this corner. We need to get past them, ' he said. 'Also, you will see that Rosie's new friends, they all have bows and arrows. They won't be able to use them if we are stood on the other side of the buccaneers, for fear of hitting us.'

It was at that stage that George uttered a few words that Jack did not understand, and many of his men pulled arrows from their quiver and knelt with the tips pointing towards the buccaneers, poised, ready to release them.

Jack clutched his left arm again and uttered words of pain. Rosie, JJ, Harry and Mr Darwin looked at him simultaneously with concern. The buccaneers looked with satisfaction, realising that their opponent was injured. Jack could see Rosie and Sam slowly pulling something from their robes. He watched as JJ quietly freed her new regalia to ensure that her legs could move freely. Her bow and arrows were laid down on the floor beside her.

'OK,' said Jack, quietly under his breath to Mr Darwin. 'Start walking very slowly please.'

And, as they started to walk towards George and his men, the buccaneers stepped forward in a menacing fashion, brandishing cutlasses and daggers. Their eyes were wild, like mad men.

Jack could hear the gentle lapping of water and turned briefly to see that where the seas had retreated previously, they were now starting to make their way back up towards the centre of the island.

'Evil must think it's winning,' said Jack, out loud, and the buccaneer laughed loudly again.

'We don't just *think* we're winning,' he said. 'We *are* winning and all of this will be destroyed. Grab them!' he shouted, and the buccaneers rushed forward towards Jack, focussing in on what they believed to be his injured arm. Before they had reached him, Rosie, Sam and JJ had run straight across and were stood side by side with Jack, and Harry also stepped in by his side. The dogs had thought about moving to join them but one command from Rosie to stay, and they had hunched down next to George and had not moved. Suddenly there was a stand-off.

'Move in behind us as far as possible,' said Jack to Mr Darwin.

'Uh,' Mr Darwin opened his mouth to say something.

'Don't argue with me, Mr Darwin. I don't wish to sound disrespectful, but you need to do as I say,' said Jack. Rosie's pride swelled even more.

Mr Darwin moved back as far as he could towards the sea, in behind Jack, Rosie, Sam and JJ.

'Right,' said Jack. 'If you want him, you come and get him,' he said to the buccaneers in his bravest voice. It was at that point that the buccaneers charged.

The first one reached Jack and went straight for his injured left arm. Jack was waiting for him and shot out his strong left arm and grabbed hold of the buccaneer's tunic. Before he knew what had happened, Jack had twisted his foot round the leg of the man, adjusted his weight and thrown the buccaneer into the sand.

'What the...' said the buccaneer, loudly, as he shook his head to work out which way up he was and how he had managed to end up on the ground. The buccaneer looked up and, stood over him, was one of George's men, bow and arrow in hand, poised, ready to fire an arrow at the buccaneer's head.

The buccaneer had been thinking about standing up, but, on seeing the welcome party from above, decided it was probably best to sit down and wait for further instructions.

However, Jack was already up and charging at the next buccaneer, head first. As the buccaneer approached, Jack, again, hooked his leg around that of the approaching mad man and, with ease, adjusted his weight and threw the man down into the sand. The buccaneer's cutlass fell into the sand and he spluttered as he landed face down, inhaling a large mouthful of sand as he had been running with his mouth open, shouting in a menacing way.

A few feet away, Rosie and Sam produced what they had been hiding in their cloaks, which were their handmade weapons. Although a little rough and ready, they were certainly sharp enough to do some serious harm if someone were to come into contact with them.

They picked out two of the buccaneers who were brandishing cutlasses and charged at them. Sam struck the cutlass with his weapon and the buccaneer pulled back, brandishing the cutlass over his head, as if he was going to smash it down on Sam's body. At that point, Rosie moved in, poking the buccaneer under the armpit with the end of her weapon, and such was the pain that he dropped his cutlass and screamed loudly, tripping backwards onto the sand. He regained his composure to find one of George's men standing over him, bow and arrow poised, ready to fire. He held up his hands in a gesture which said, 'I surrender'.

Jack looked up to see that JJ was surrounded by three buccaneers, all intent on capturing her and, rather than be concerned, Jack almost took a step back in order to enjoy what he knew was probably coming next.

Without losing her balance, JJ raised her left leg so that her foot was above her head. This was about level with the buccaneer's chin, and with a small but accurate flick, JJ floored the buccaneer with what was the boxing equivalent of a right hook.

This left two buccaneers facing her and as they both went to grab her, JJ launched at one of them, grabbing him around the shoulders, and, using him as an anchor point, launched up at the second buccaneer with both feet, catching him cleanly on the jaw, and he, too, fell to the sand.

JJ quickly dropped the buccaneer from her grasp, and the two stood facing one another. By now, he was aware that the danger was in the legs and had dropped his cutlass and was ready to grab at any leg that came his way. But JJ was too quick for him. She made a dummy move and he went to grab at the leg that he thought was moving towards his head, but JJ was then behind him and tripped the buccaneer from behind and the buccaneer landed on the sand face upwards. He was able to clearly see the now traditional welcome party of an arrow pointing directly down at his head and he raised his hands in surrender and did not try and get up.

Rosie and Sam were locked in combat with two of the larger buccaneers. They stood back to back, facing their attackers with their makeshift weapons, cutting and thrusting every time the cutlasses were brandished at them. As they poked and prodded with their makeshift weapons, which were sharp, if nothing else, they started to draw blood and could see that the buccaneers were in pain.

Almost at the same time, both Rosie's attacker and the buccaneer fighting Sam, started to move backwards and Rosie and Sam continued to push them to move backwards. Suddenly, both buccaneers tripped backwards into the sand. Sam and Rosie looked at each other in surprise and then looked again to discover that Molly and Charlie had moved behind both buccaneers as they had been moving backwards, and both had tripped over the multicoloured dogs. Molly and Charlie shot off as quickly as they had arrived. Again, both buccaneers looked up from their sandy landing to find a warrior with a bow and arrow pointing the tip of the arrow at their chest, and both of them simultaneously held up their hands and fell back into the sand, offering no further resistance.

In the meantime, Harry was engaged in hand to hand combat with one of the smaller buccaneers, as they pushed and shoved each other and fell to the ground and rolled one on top of the other. Eventually, the buccaneer was on top, pinning Harry down, with his knees on his arms, and he drew his cutlass from his belt. Harry knew that he was powerless to do anything about it and closed his eyes briefly to await his fate, only to hear a loud clunk, which caused him to open his eyes immediately. He felt the weight go from on top of him and, as he opened his eyes, he realised why. The buccaneer was completely unconscious, having been clouted on the head by a cooking pot. Harry looked up further and, stood over him, was none other than Mr Darwin, clutching the pot and smiling from ear to ear.

'Glad to be of assistance, Master Harry,' he said.

'Look out!' shouted Harry, as he saw, coming up behind Mr Darwin, another two buccaneers. Before he could react, the buccaneers grabbed him from behind and one swung Mr Darwin like a ragdoll up over his shoulder, and they turned and ran in the direction from which they had come. Harry lay there, unable to move quickly enough as he had the weight of the unconscious buccaneer on top of him and in any event he was outnumbered. He looked around wildly.

By this stage, the multicoloured warriors had joined in hand to hand fighting against the buccaneers. Jack was throwing them to the ground as if they were half their size, JJ was using many of them for her Taekwondo target practice, and Sam and Rosie continued to draw blood from any of the buccaneers that came within fencing distance of them.

However, everyone's attentions were suddenly distracted by Harry's cry; they almost stopped in their tracks. The buccaneers realised that the attention of their attackers had been distracted, and they shoulder barged their way into the middle of the fight. Although the buccaneers initially looked pleased with the ground that they had made up it took thirty seconds for George's warriors to pin them to the ground, arrows aimed at their heads. This meant that all of the remaining buccaneers were now disarmed, other than the ones who were making off with Charles Darwin thrown over their shoulder.

Watching these buccaneers disappear off into the distance, Jack recognised the danger immediately. 'Follow me!' shouted Jack, and the five children and two dogs set off down the sandy track in the direction of the buccaneers who were clutching Mr Darwin.

As Alfie approached the land, cautiously, in 441, he could see straight away that the islands were significantly smaller than they used to be. He could see the tops of bushes and small trees poking up through the salt water of the oceans, and he could also see small black dots all making their way up the remaining slopes. As 441 got closer to the land, he realised that what he had mistaken for black dots were, when seen through the binoculars, giant tortoises, all desperately trying to get away from the water's edge.

There were also, around the water's edge, small sea lions being helped through the waters by their mothers, obviously looking for rocks to land on, which had long since disappeared, and albatrosses swooping overhead, looking for their nests, which would have been on the tops of the rocks, many of which were now submerged beneath the waves.

The water was moving up the slope at a ferocious pace and Alfie realised quickly that he needed help. The Captain of The Royal Adventurer had left a shortwave radio on board 441 and Alfie picked it up.

'The Royal Adventurer, this is 441,' said Alfie, pressing the transmit button.

'The Royal Adventurer, come in 441,' said a man's voice from within the radio.

'The islands are disappearing fast,' said Alfie. 'We need help straight away, as many boats as you can muster. There are animals trapped on the island and they will drown.'

The voice came back through the radio. 'What kind of animals, 441? We have no knowledge of islands or their inhabitants. Please confirm.'

Alfie had forgotten that, of course, the memory banks of all of those involved would have been erased. He pressed the transmit button. 'Tortoises,' he said. 'Giant tortoises are the main victims. I think you will need at least four to six people in a boat to lift them. Also land iguanas; they are not dangerous. Just follow the direction which 441 went when I left you.'

'Roger that,' said the voice, and the radio went silent.

'Jose,' said Alfie, shouting back to the rear of 441. 'Get me in as close as you can and I'm going to jump on the land and take your four boys with me. We need to try and catch these tortoises as quickly as possible or they will all drown.'

'I understand, Alfie,' said Jose, and came running forward and took over at the helm.

441 inched in closer and closer towards where the waves were lapping against the island, being careful not to catch the engines on trees and other debris. When they were as close in as they could possibly get, Alfie hung a ladder over the back of 441 and climbed down, dropping into the water. The four Ecuadorian soldiers followed, and they waded, waist deep in warm Galapagos water, until they managed to get to the shore.

It was at that point that Alfie realised that, whilst he spoke no Spanish and the four Ecuadorians spoke no English, he guessed that the universal sign for rounding up tortoises was probably the same in any language, and he pointed at a tortoise, gave the thumbs up sign and all five of them moved towards it in unison. The tortoise immediately pulled its head and legs into its shell and each of them grabbed a corner and lifted the tortoise from the ground, and carried it up to a clear piece of land further up the slope. It was enormously heavy and so it took a while to manoeuvre it into position.

Quickly they moved a few rocks and boulders and pieces of scrub so that they had created a corral, and they set about finding and locating the giant tortoises into this as quickly as they possibly could, ready to move to the boats.

Within ten minutes Alfie noticed a flotilla of tenders and zodiacs approaching, all launched from The Royal Adventurer, each filled with volunteers from the ship. As they disgorged their occupants into the warm waters, they waded up the 'beach', rolled up their sleeves and got stuck in with the business of rescuing these unique animals.

And so it was that, as the waters lapped further up the islands that had been made so famous by Charles Darwin, as danger loomed for its inhabitants, with the help of one of Drucan's flagships which had seen action in the Falklands war, they now set about rescuing this unique population of giant tortoises and iguanas.

Tender after tender came from The Royal Adventurer. In each tender volunteered crew and passengers and back they came, time after time with these giant prehistoric creatures sitting in the bottom of the boat. Gently they lifted them into the belly of the great cruise liner to be nurtured by the vets and other passengers and into a room that had quickly been cleared but which now boasted fresh water at tortoise height and the entire stock of greenery that the ship possessed. There was obviously no lettuce though, this being poisonous to most tortoises.

As the tortoises arrived at The Royal Adventurer by small boat, they were deep in their shells and visibly traumatised. But they were quickly encouraged out by the small children on board The Royal Adventurer with their infectious caring and the sight of succulent green leaves and fresh water.

As Jack, Rosie, Sam, Harry and JJ ran along the sand in the direction of the buccaneers who had Mr Darwin, Rosie asked, in a breathless voice: 'Where do you think they're taking them?'

Harry said quickly: 'They are looking for the Evil Gateway. That is the only way that they can get back to their own world.'

'But is their Gate the same one as ours?' asked Jack.

'Absolutely not,' said Harry. 'Their Gate will be quite different to yours, and you will not be able to pass through it, nor they through yours.'

'Then, presumably, they can't take Mr Darwin through either?' asked Rosie.

'No,' said Harry. 'They can't, which means that they will try to kill him before they pass through.'

With that, all of the children increased their speed across the sand. Bounding behind them came Molly and Charlie, still adorned in their multicoloured coats.

'I hope we're not too late,' said Jack, as he glanced towards the lapping sea water, which appeared to be advancing at a frighteningly quick pace. It was clear that Evil believed it was winning and time was running out. Along the shoreline and across the rocks they went into the thicket and then the path stopped and divided.

'Which way?' asked Rosie, and Charlie and Molly immediately put their noses to the ground. They took two sniffs, they looked at each other and both of them went left.

'Are you sure?' said JJ coming to a halt. Jack and Rosie looked at her with the expression that said 'of course we're sure'.

And then, as they ran to the corner, those with weapons raising them in anticipation of trouble, they were stopped in their tracks. For as they rounded the corner and again had a full view of the ocean there, anchored so close that they could almost touch it, was the HMS Beagle.

It glimmered in the sunshine. Its sails billowed in the breeze, and it looked to all exactly as it should have, as a knight in shining armour.

'You *beauty*,' said Harry coming to an immediate halt.

The children stopped and quickly assessed what was going on before them. In the water, there were five or six small rowing boats with four or five sailors in each. The oarsmen were rowing against the waves which were trying to bring them ashore as there was no obvious place for them to land. The sailors had their muskets to their shoulders ready to fire. They were all dressed in the outfits that Jack would have expected from the HMS Beagle, well drilled sailors intent on saving the lives of their colleagues. In one of the boats stood the tall, regal figure of the Captain of the

Beagle, Captain Robert Fitzroy. Even Jack recognised him from
the pictures.

As they tried to aim their muskets, the waves were moving
the small rowing boats up and down as the waves lapped up
around the island so it was almost impossible to get a clear shot.
Captain Fitzroy bellowed at the top of his voice 'fire when safe
to do so' and the musket barrels waved up and down in the air as
his men struggled to control them. It was clear, standing on the
shore, that any help would come from the shore alone, no matter
how good the intentions of those in the small boats.

On the shoreline were the buccaneers, in a stand-off. Mr
Darwin had been thrown to the ground from his previous position
across the shoulders of one of the buccaneers, and, stood over him,
the buccaneer had his cutlass drawn and would have cheerfully
chopped Mr Darwin's head off if he had moved an inch. The
buccaneers had not seen the children at this stage, as the children
and the dogs were behind them. Jack gestured with his hand and
the other four and the dogs all ducked down behind a sand dune.

Jack called Charlie and Molly quietly and they came
immediately to him. One by one, he unhooked their brightly
coloured coats and beads. The dogs looked slightly disappointed
at this. 'We need stealth,' said Jack. 'And you look too conspicuous
wearing all of those colours.' He knew that the dogs understood
him, but just couldn't talk back. Their ears were alert and their
tongues hanging out, heads tilted slightly to one side.

Jack looked across at the dunes on the far side of the
buccaneers. He pointed and looked at the dogs: 'Away!' Jack said,
as he had seen his Aunt do. He pointed in the direction of the
sand dunes behind the buccaneers. The dogs looked at each other
and ran off immediately, around the back of the dunes, in the
direction of the far side, but out of sight.

'Right,' said Jack. He turned back to his band of fellow
warriors who all looked at him intently. 'JJ, have you still got the

bow and arrow?' JJ turned her back to Jack to display the bow and arrow, which were both slung across her back where she had picked them up after her most recent encounter with the first buccaneers. 'Other weapons?' he asked, and Sam and Rosie brandished their makeshift weapons.

'Right,' said Jack. 'Well I think our only chance is to come in behind them and to try and give Mr Darwin enough time to escape from 'cutlass man'.' Jack nodded his head in the general direction of the men holding Mr Darwin and they all looked, understanding the seriousness of the situation.

'But Jack,' said JJ. 'There isn't enough scrub and cover – they'll see us coming. The real danger is that the man with the cutlass will get to Mr Darwin before one of the Beagle crew can shoot him. If we can get the cutlass out of his hand, then that should give us enough time. Our only chance is with the bow and arrow.' She unhooked the bow and arrow from around her shoulder and held it in her hand, offering it to Jack. 'I have calculated where I need to be.' Her razor sharp intellect and mathematical brain had instantly worked out the best place for her to fire from.

Jack took the bow and arrow in his hand and hesitated. He thought for a moment and then held out the bow and arrow to give it back to her. He locked eyes with JJ and they exchanged a small smile and a nod.

'Right,' said JJ. 'I need to be as close in as possible and have a clear shot. I need you four to distract the buccaneers. You need to make sure that you are not in the firing line from the ship's crew if they open fire, and so follow where the dogs went around the back of dunes and across the other side. If you can distract them in that direction, it will give me a chance to get in place.'

JJ put her hand on Jack's shoulder. 'Be safe,' she said. 'I will not let you down.' She squeezed his shoulder and Jack felt his legs turn to jelly and his stomach turn somersaults. She smiled back and glanced at the crew bobbing in the water. 'Don't get caught in their crossfire,' she smiled and turned on her heels.

The buccaneers stood defiantly where they had dropped their prisoner; they laughed, knowing that if the Beagle crew fired, then whilst they might die, so too would Mr Darwin and their mission would be accomplished.

Jack, Rosie and Harry ducked down behind the dunes and headed off in the direction that the dogs had taken a few minutes earlier. They could hear raised voices coming from the shoreline, which was, they assumed, the stand-off between the crew of the Beagle and those holding Mr Darwin captive.

'I am the Captain of the HMS Beagle,' came a loud voice. 'And I insist that you hand back our scientist.' This was followed by laughter from the buccaneers and the children knew that they had to move quickly.

They reached the far side and slipped into the undergrowth. Rosie and Sam had shed their war colours and hoped that they were now as neutral as they possibly could be, to save them being spotted by the buccaneers. As they reached their vantage point in the dunes they realised that, lying in the grass in front of them, flat as pancakes, were Molly and Charlie, ears alert, waiting for their next instruction.

Jack lay down next to them in the undergrowth, looking down at the scene in front of him and he realised that it was now or never. The lapping waters were creeping faster than before across the shore and very soon the whole island would be engulfed. He knew that this meant that Evil sensed it was winning and, right at this moment in time, he had to agree with it.

Mr Darwin was in the hands of the buccaneers, who had a cutlass to his throat, and even the crew of the Beagle were powerless to prevent that from happening. His only hope lay in the hands of JJ and he had to do as he had promised his friend that he would, and to make the biggest distraction possible to give JJ the only hope of saving Mr Darwin's life, the life of the most influential scientist in the world. If they failed, this eminent scientist would disappear from the memories of the world forever. And he, his sister and their two friends would never go home.

Jack looked carefully and worked out that the buccaneers had nothing that could reach the children if they were to be fired or thrown, but simply had their cutlasses to rely on. He looked at the crew of the Beagle in their small craft, aiming muskets at those on the land. He hoped, in fact prayed, that the range of the musket rifle was not as far as Jack and that even if the crew of the Beagle were to take leave of their senses and to start firing at Jack, his sister and their friends, that it would not reach them or be so inaccurate due to the swell.

He saw the buccaneer standing behind Mr Darwin adjust his weight and lift his hand clutching the cutlass. Concluding that this was probably the last chance, Jack leapt to his feet and charged down the sandy slopes towards them, screaming at the top of his voice like a mad wailing banshee. The other children exchanged glances and, without asking to be invited, they, too, leapt to their feet and started down the shoreline towards the buccaneers.

Jack glanced towards the crew of the Beagle and noted that their sights and rifle angle had shifted in their direction. 'Don't shoot!' he shouted. 'We are friends, not foe.' And from ahead of him, he heard the familiar tone of Mr Darwin.

'He is right, Beagle. Do not shoot!' shouted Mr Darwin. 'Keep your rifles trained on the buccaneers. Do not let them escape.' Whilst more of aspiration than reality, Jack appreciated the sentiment.

Jack looked at the buccaneers, who were all watching him and his friends come down the pathway towards them. Jack glanced down. The only thing missing were the dogs and he concluded that they must have been spooked by all the shouting, and were still lying in the grass keeping guard, overlooking this extraordinary scene.

From the corner of his eye, Jack saw the shape directly ahead of him about 200 metres; he presumed this to be JJ, moving slowly through the undergrowth and dunes, closer and closer to the buccaneers to ensure that she had the best shot. Jack did not dare look at her directly, for fear of alerting the buccaneers to her presence.

Jack screamed louder and his noise was quickly followed by similar sounds from Sam and Harry. Rosie was next with a high pitched wailing that would deafen even the most hardened of buccaneers.

Over sand they ran, flailing their arms and screaming at the tops of their voices. Jack saw the buccaneers staring at them, and their attention starting to turn to them completely, without considering what else might be around them. Jack saw the buccaneer holding Mr Darwin lean down and lift Mr Darwin up by the scruff of his neck. The buccaneer raised the cutlass to the height of Mr Darwin's throat and, in theatrical style, held it out above his head before, as Jack assumed, he would draw it across the throat of Mr Darwin and all would be lost. The sea lapped quickly up the shoreline and Jack closed his eyes briefly, knowing that all was now lost.

Rosie saw this too, screamed, 'No!' at the top of her voice, and then, in slow motion, two things happened simultaneously.

From the long undergrowth behind Mr Darwin, leapt Charlie, clean off the ground from what appeared to be a standing start where he had crawled, and as he leapt through the air he grasped the cutlass-bearing arm of the buccaneer in this teeth, causing such shock that the buccaneer dropped the weapon and his other arm went slack and dropped Mr Darwin onto the sand.

The buccaneer searched blindly for his secondary knife along his belt and as he did, a single arrow flew through the air from 200 metres to his left and landed squarely in the chest of Mr

Darwin's captor and he dropped to the sand like a stone. Jack continued to run directly towards Mr Darwin and realised that the arrow had come from the bow of JJ and had landed with pinpoint accuracy.

The other buccaneers, who had stood behind Mr Darwin and his captor, moved forward in a concerted effort to grab Mr Darwin as their colleague fell to the ground, and as they did, the musket barrels cracked from the shore. Mr Darwin threw himself down onto the sand as flat as possible to avoid being hit by the musket balls and Jack, Sam, Harry and Rosie all did exactly the same. One or two of the buccaneers were hit, but none mortally and those that were still standing, raised their arms in surrender.

The first of the rowing boats came ashore quickly and out of it spilled five or six crew from the Beagle, who quickly moved amongst the buccaneers, relieving them of their cutlasses and knives.

The children slowly got to their feet and watched as, out of the undergrowth, came JJ, who was immediately embraced by Mr Darwin and then in turn, his fellow shipmates. Mr Darwin spoke quickly to the crew, explaining that others were held in caves which were likely to be flooded and that they needed to understand from the buccaneers where they were. He added that he hoped they would be co-operative if they valued their lives and the buccaneers, overhearing the conversation, took the hint and immediately blurted out the location of the remaining sailors.

Captain Fitzroy landed in his boat and walked purposely towards the prisoners. On seeing this impressive sailor, the buccaneers fell to their knees and placed their hands on their heads, indicating immediate surrender.

Jack, Rosie, Sam and Harry ran towards Mr Darwin and joined in the hugs and the congratulations. The captain of the Beagle shook hands with the children and laughed loudly. Everyone inspected the other, to make sure that they were well.

CHAPTER TEN

After all the congratulations, Rosie suddenly said, 'Where are the dogs?' Everyone stopped immediately.

'Molly, Charlie!' shouted Rosie. There was an eerie silence across the battlefield as Rosie ran out into the sand and called again. There was no reply and for the third time she called their names.

After what seemed forever, they all heard the faint whine that they immediately recognised as Molly's. 'Molly,' they called, trying to get her to repeat the noise so that they could locate her. There it was again. They followed it, moving aside the buccaneers and the ship's crew, until eventually they came across a buccaneer who had obviously been felled by a bullet from the crew of the Beagle, and it seemed that the noise was coming from beneath him.

'There she is,' said Jack. 'Quickly, quickly, get this man off her!' They could just make out the mottled grey tail of Molly. As they rolled the man to free her, the tail started to wag, not much, but enough to know that she was still alive. And as the man was rolled over, the circumstances in which Molly came to find herself under the injured buccaneer were immediately obvious.

For there she lay with her jaws neatly clasped around his right wrist, in which he was brandishing a large cutlass. As his body was liberated from on top of her, she released her grip and lay there for a minute or so.

Rosie went running over, tears streaming down her face. 'Molly, are you hurt?' Molly sat up, shook her head and her big ears stood alert. She got to her feet, a little wobbly, and then lifted her right paw and looked at Rosie.

'Have you got a hurty paw?' asked Rosie, and Molly sat down and lifted her paw even higher. 'You'd better come here then and I'll give you a big cuddle; it will make it better.' And there the two of them sat on the beach, cuddling, until a solitary bark stopped them all in their tracks.

Jack knew that Charlie had a number of barks for different occasions. An alarm bark, which was continuous and a polite bark to be let in from the garden, which was just once. This was a polite bark to say that he was locked out. The only problem was that Jack couldn't see immediately where Charlie was barking from. Then he remembered that the last occasion that he had seen Charlie had been as he leapt at the cutlass-wielding arm of the buccaneer who was about to kill Mr Darwin.

Jack ran back to where the man lay dead, an arrow through his chest, but there was no sign of Charlie. And then he saw the blood.

'Quickly, everybody,' he shouted. 'Charlie's been hurt,' and they followed the blood over the mound from which Charlie had launched his attack, and there, lying on the other side of the sandy rise, lay his Aunt's eldest Border Collie. He was covered in blood, but his eyes were alert and as he saw Jack approaching, he barked once and wagged his tail weakly.

'No!' shouted Jack, and ran towards the dog, but he was held back by a smart looking gentleman and Mr Darwin himself.

'Move aside, Master Jack,' said Mr Darwin. 'This is the ship's doctor and if anyone can help him, then he can.' Jack held back and was joined by his sister, JJ and Sam. They all hugged each other and then sank to the sand. Molly came running over the dune and they clasped her tightly to stop her interfering. She too lay in the sand watching as the two men knelt by her beloved Charlie. He seemed so very still. She whimpered slightly and

Rosie stroked her ears. Molly put her head down between her paws and closed her eyes as if she was saying a doggie prayer.

The children sat in silence as the doctor and Mr Darwin worked furiously. The doctor had brought with him his medical bag with many instruments and many, it appeared, were being utilised. There were bandages and dressings and all the time Charlie lay very still. Rosie was crying quietly and the others, who had been trying to put on a brave face, soon followed suit.

Around them the crew of the Beagle went about disarming and tying up the buccaneers, taking them back to their small boats and then back to the Beagle for appropriate punishment. Harry, having said 'Hello' to his friends from the ship, came and sat with the children in the sand and waited.

It was now early afternoon and the sunshine warmed their backs. One of the crew brought over a water bottle and they passed it amongst themselves drinking but saying nothing. Molly took a sip as it was offered to her but her eyes were fixed at all times on Charlie. Occasionally the children would stroke her fur and play with her ears, but, for once, she didn't acknowledge this but stared, steadfastly ahead of her, waiting for news.

After what seemed like days but was probably half an hour, Mr Darwin stood and straightened his back. He walked towards the children. They all examined his face to try and work out what he had to say to them, but he gave no hint. There was no sadness, and yet no joy.

He crouched in the sand beside them and stroked Molly's head. He looked at the children in turn. 'I will not lie,' he said. 'Charlie is gravely ill, but we have done all that we can. He has lost a lot of blood but we've stemmed the flow and he does not seem to have sustained any real damage from the cut to his shoulder. But our experience is with humans and not with dogs...' He paused and examined the young faces looking back at him. 'You have said to me, Master Jack, that you are not from this world and I have not thus far explored this with you, but what I would say is this: that if you have a means of returning to that world, where you may be more advanced than we are here, then you should do so and try and save your dog.'

Jack nodded solemnly and Rosie sobbed loudly.

Harry put his hand on Jack's shoulder. 'The Gate is not too far from here,' he said. 'We can carry him.'

Jack looked into the eyes of his young friend and then at the waters still lapping not far from them. 'But,' said Jack, 'the waters are still too high. The cave through which we entered will still be full of water. We would drown in trying to get through the Gate now and I do not know how long it will take before the waters recede.'

'The water will drop back quite quickly and I can help you,' said Harry. 'I cannot cross through the Gate, but I can help to carry Charlie. It will almost be easier to carry him through water than it will on the land. You know that he can be saved and we must try.'

Jack turned back to Mr Darwin and smiled. 'Mr Darwin, I think it would probably be best if I did not tell you where we came from. Suffice to say that when you come to write your scientific masterpieces, and your story of your journey on the Beagle, please do not mention your encounter with us. Go on and be the eminent scientist for which you are known and recognised. You will go on to say 'survival of the fittest' and Charlie will survive.'

Jack turned to the ship's doctor. 'Doctor Bynoe', he said, pleased that he had remembered the man's name from his research with the Collectors. 'Thank you for all your help in trying to save our dog. I hope that when Mr Darwin finds an opportune moment, he will reward you for your kindness.'

Sam stepped forward. 'Are we able to create some sort of stretcher for Charlie? We don't have far to go but we don't want him to be uncomfortable or hurt even further.' And, within minutes, the ship's crew had produced a small makeshift stretcher, made from wood and oars and canvas, onto which Charlie was carefully loaded, with Molly all the time fussing around him and sniffing and licking. He was still conscious and his eyes were fixed firmly on Jack, trusting eyes which said to Jack that he knew that Jack would save his life.

'I am a little confused,' said Jack, looking up along the shoreline, 'as to exactly where the Gate is. The landscape looks so different with the water so far up.'

'I know,' said Harry. 'I know where the Gate is.'

'But, how?' asked Jack. 'How could you know?'

'Because, I was waiting for you. I knew that you would come and I wanted to be able to help.' Harry looked down at the ground, embarrassed to admit that theirs was not a chance encounter.

They were walking side by side, heading along the coast towards the location of the Gate, Charlie being carefully and gently carried by the crew from the Beagle, the doctor and Mr Darwin trotting alongside to make sure that he was not being jolted or hurt.

Harry's face did not change in expression but he turned to Jack as they walked along: 'I would like you to do me one favour, Master Jack.'

'Anything,' said Jack. 'Just name it.'

Harry reached into his pocket and pulled out a small locket on a chain. He opened it up and inside was pressed a piece of lavender. Jack took it and examined it. It was beautifully made, probably from silver, very delicate. Jack could still make out the faint smell of lavender as he closed it.

'Where did you get this?' asked Jack.

'I can't explain,' said Harry. 'But please, give it to your mother when you see her.'

'But I can't,' said Jack. 'It is forbidden to take anything back from the other world. That's what they told me.'

Harry looked at him and their eyes locked. 'You do not need to worry, Master Jack; this comes from your world and not mine. Take it.' And he put it into Jack's hands and clasped Jack's fingers around it.

'Now,' he said, looking ahead. 'We are almost here. Let me go first and check it out,' and he left Jack stood on the shoreline, clasping the locket.

'What was that about?' asked Rosie, as she came up behind him.

'I don't know,' said Jack, 'I don't think we have time to worry about it at the moment – we need to try and get Charlie back.'

They had arrived at where the stream came down from the hillside which marked the route down towards the caves. Harry had already taken off his shoes and his shirt and had jumped into the water. He swam out a little way and then bobbed down, coming back up again within 30 seconds.

'The cave is here,' he said. 'If you look, you will see that it is diagonally down from the grass where the tortoises were eating and where the stream meets the land.'

The children looked and they could indeed make out the landmarks that they had first seen when they arrived.

'The cave that you arrived in was full of sea lions,' said Harry. 'They have now long gone and they will be further up the shoreline, but you should follow me under the water, down into where the Gate is and because you have succeeded in your task, the Gate will open and you will be allowed through.'

'But,' said Jack, 'originally the Gate was only supposed to allow me through, but the others, they followed without me knowing. How do we know that it will let us all back?'

Harry smiled. 'The Gate will let all of you who pass through back onto the other side. The only thing that I cannot say is where you will appear.'

Rosie looked at him in astonishment. 'You mean, we might not be back at Angela's house?'

Harry ruffled her hair a little. 'You might not but you will not be placed in danger. You may find yourselves returning not to the place that you started from, but to the place that you went to but in the right time parallel.'

'In other words,' said JJ, 'we could find ourselves on the Galapagos Islands but in the right century.'

'That is exactly right,' said Harry. 'Now hurry please. How is Molly with water?'

The others looked at each other and laughed. 'The biggest problem is keeping her out of it,' they said.

'That's fine,' said Harry. 'Come on Molly, this way.' Molly glanced at the children, nuzzled Charlie in his stretcher and leapt from the rocks into the water, doggy paddling all the way across to Harry.

'Now the rest of you,' said Harry. 'Quickly, then we will lower Charlie down and see how he is in the water. He is quite weak.'

All four children kicked off their shoes and were quickly in the water. 'Now,' said Harry. 'Let me show you where the cave is so that you will know which way to go and can go together.' He ducked down under the water and all of them quickly followed. Molly, on the surface of the water, realising that everybody had disappeared, ducked down and quickly swam after them.

The children swam down through the clear blue water along the path that they had come up on their arrival and down into the cave. Harry pointed to the open area which they all looked at and nodded and agreed that this was where they had fallen through the Gate, however many days ago it had been.

They all swam to the surface again, including Molly, who, by this stage, had decided that this was an exceptional game that she would probably have to play again, and preferably it should involve some sort of ball, as that was the only element of doggy fun that was currently missing.

When they reached the surface, some of the crew and the doctor had gently eased Charlie into the water, out of his make shift stretcher and he waited quietly on the surface for them. He was calm and his eyes stared into Jack's in complete trust. The water around was slightly red as the blood that had caked his fur soaked off in the warm salty water. Jack looked alarmed.

'Is he bleeding again?' asked Jack.

'No,' said the doctor. 'It is just the old blood that is washing off. I have stemmed the blood flow and the water will help with that. But you must get him away as soon as possible, in case the sharks take an interest.' Jack had not thought about sharks but the mention of them now gave him added urgency.

'OK, Charlie,' whispered Jack, holding his gaze. 'We need you to hold your breath and we are going to take you under the water and then we are going to be home.' Charlie licked the end of Jack's nose and moved his paw to touch Jack's arm. Jack looked up and the crew of the Beagle were all looking on from the banks solemnly. Captain Fitzroy had his hat off his head and held it across his chest.

'I will come down as far as I can,' said Harry. 'But I cannot cross through the Gate. I will help you with Charlie.' Harry turned to Jack, who was treading water. 'Goodbye my dear friend, I am proud of you like a brother,' he said and hugged Jack manfully.

Harry then turned to Rosie and did the same, only this time he whispered 'goodbye my dear friend, I am proud of you like a sister'. He shook hands with Sam and hugged JJ. 'Great shot,' he said with admiration and JJ smiled shyly.

Harry then turned back to the matter in hand: 'On my count of three we will all duck down and swim towards the Gate. Just follow me. One, two...' and Harry and Jack ducked down beneath the water; both had a hand on Charlie's collar and they slowly pulled him with them, gently, as they swam towards the Gate. Rosie and Sam followed with their hands on Molly's collar, with JJ bringing up the rear.

Jack had been worried that the Gate was quite far inside the cave, as it had seemed such a long way out when they had arrived but as they swam down, he could already see the bright light of the Gate and he knew that they would make it. His chest was getting tighter now and he knew that he could not stay underwater for too much longer. Jack looked at Charlie who had his eyes closed but looked serene. Harry slowed and released Charlie's collar, he made a salute to Jack, Rosie and their friends and in an instant had turned in the water and swam back towards the surface. Jack watched as he disappeared towards the light. He felt a sudden sense of loss.

Jack watched Harry go and then turned back towards the Gate. He looked at his sister and friends. They were all in a line before the bright light and exchanged glances. Jack did a thumbs up and they all reciprocated. Jack pointed to the Gate, held up three fingers, then two, then one and, gently pulling the dogs behind them, as one, they swam through the Gate.

CHAPTER ELEVEN

Alfie was supervising the departure of the latest tender, this time crammed full of land iguanas in hessian sacks, sat terrified and squirming in the bottom of the boat. Around them there were passengers and crew from The Royal Adventurer, all sat quietly, trying not to worry the little creatures even more, but prepared if they made a break for it.

All around Alfie the same activities were going on in other tenders from The Royal Adventurer, whether it was land iguanas, baby birds, or giant tortoises. One by one they were all being lifted from the island and taken to safety.

Alfie was satisfied that this tender was ready to go and as he helped push it into the deeper water, something in the water caught his eye. It caught his eye because it was different. It was not a turtle or a sea lion or a drowning tortoise, but there appeared to be a group and two of them were a strange colouration of black, white and brown. In an instant he knew exactly what it was.

'Jose!' he shouted. 'Over there! Quickly, rescue those children from the water.'

Jose grabbed the binoculars and looked in the direction to see four small human heads bobbing in the water and what looked like two dogs. He muttered something in Spanish and, leaping into the water, swam towards the group. As he reached them, he shouted back in English to Alfie, 'They say that their names are Jack, Rosie, Sam and JJ, and that they are in urgent need of a vet.'

Jose started to swim back towards 441, gently pulling what

Alfie realised was Charlie, his head being held out of the water but, otherwise, not seeming to be moving to any great extent. Molly, on the other hand, swam fast and furious next to the four children. Alfie jumped into the water and swam towards them.

As they reached 441, the makeshift crew lowered down a loading basket and Charlie was carefully placed into it and winched up. The children climbed the steep ladder hung over 441's side and went up and over and dropped onto the deck to the great surprise of the four Ecuadorian soldiers.

Alfie was the last up, having supervised the loading of Molly and as he arrived the children were surrounding Charlie who was lying fairly motionless in the middle of the deck. Alfie ran to him and felt for a pulse. There was one but it was weak. 'What happened?' he asked.

'Charlie was hit by a cutlass and has got a big cut and he's lost a lot of blood. Please save him, Mr Parker,' said Jack with pleading eyes.

'Don't worry,' said Alfie. 'I may not be able to, but I know somebody that can.' Even as he spoke, the engines of 441 roared into life, Jose now being entrusted to manoeuvre 441 away from its position near the island.

'Right,' Alfie said. 'Next stop, The Royal Adventurer.'

The children all looked at each other. 'But isn't that a cruise liner?' they asked almost as one.

'It certainly is,' he said. 'Equipped with five vets and fifteen doctors. I think by now they are probably fed up with giant tortoises and land iguanas, so dealing with a dehydrated Border Collie who has lost a lot of blood will be fairly much up their street.'

As 441 headed out towards the open sea the children watched in amazement at the fleet of tenders and inflatable boats heading to and from the island. Those heading back had tortoises and nests with eggs and squirming bags of creatures. Those heading towards the islands were empty.

As they rounded the corner of the island they saw for the first time the enormous shape of The Royal Adventurer, sat quietly in deeper water, whilst everyone else moved around her.

'Wow,' said Sam as all of the children looked out to where she lay.

As 441 hurtled towards the hull of The Royal Adventurer, Alfie radioed ahead to explain the situation. By the time they arrived, standing on the docking station were what Jack assumed were all five of the vets who were on board, and the area had been cleared of giant tortoises and land iguanas. There were also many people in white uniforms, who Jack assumed were the ship's crew. As they got closer, Jack realised that the white uniforms were by now a little grubby and he assumed that this was as a result of carrying tortoises and iguanas.

Alfie manoeuvred 441 alongside so that lots of gentle hands were able to help lift Charlie gently out of the boat and onto a stretcher, which appeared to be on wheels. There were nurses in uniform and Jack could only imagine that they had come from the sick bay. Charlie's eyes were watching Jack intently and Jack knew that he was still there and still strong.

The vet put a stethoscope to Charlie's heart. 'He's weak, but he's still alive,' he said. 'Let's get him to sick bay straight away.' And off they rushed with him before Jack could even get out of the boat.

The children were helped out, one by one, and Molly, who seemed unusually unenthusiastic about jumping from a small boat into an enormous great ship such as The Royal Adventurer, had to be lifted and passed across. However, once she was on the solid floor of The Royal Adventurer, she was much happier and started running about, sniffing and looking for her brother.

'Molly,' said Jack. 'Stay close please.' And Molly, realising that she couldn't just run off as and when she wanted, stuck to Jack's heel, as if she was glued there.

A lady in a cleaner, white outfit arrived and looked the children up and down. 'Are you English?' she asked.

'Yes we are,' said Rosie. 'Who are you?'

The woman's face softened slightly. 'I'm the Captain,' she said. 'And this is my ship.' She held out her small and delicate hand. 'I am Sophia Bergman, welcome aboard.'

'WOW!' said Sam. 'A lady Captain. That's amazing!'

'Yes,' said Captain Bergman. 'I think so too. Right then, I'm not even going to ask how you came to be in the waters off the island and what you are doing there with two Collie dogs, when there are no dogs on the island, but I think what you all need are some warm clothes and some food.'

The four children's eyes lit up at the thought of food, realising that a hard morning's fighting had meant that they were all ravenous again and without further comment they followed the Captain. They all had blankets around their shoulders and they were flanked by what Jack assumed were other officers of the boat, as they were all also in white.

'So,' said Jack to the Captain. 'You can remember about the islands then?'

The Captain looked at him slightly quizzically. 'Well of course I can. They're the Galapagos Islands; they're the most famous islands throughout the world. Why should I not remember them?'

And Jack just smiled. 'What has caused the flooding?' he asked.

'We think,' she said, 'that it is El Niño, where the waters warm and suddenly they swamp the small islands. It's happened before. We were just glad that we were able to be there to rescue as many of the creatures as possible, and certainly the guests are having fun.' She nodded in the direction of one of the larger reception rooms and there were a number of children with giant tortoises. They were being supervised but they were clearly enjoying these giant creatures, who were being fed watercress by the handful.

'The worst seems to be over,' she said. 'The waters are receding now and we hope that we will be able to put everybody back fairly soon. Now, into the lift, please.' She pointed to the banks of lifts and they all traipsed into the lift one by one, squidging as they walked with bare feet which were still soaked from their swim through the Gate. The other officers did not follow.

Rosie looked at her brother and tugged his arm slightly. 'I'm really hungry, Jack,' she said. 'But they're not going to try and serve us tortoise are they?'

The Captain laughed when she heard this. 'Don't worry, young lady,' she said. 'We're fresh out of tortoise now. I think we might be able to rustle you up a nice sausage and chips.'

'Really?' said Rosie. 'What, proper sausages? Proper chips? I can't remember the last time I had a proper meal.'

Captain Bergman pressed a button and they appeared to go up in the lift forever. Jack thought perhaps this was one of the Gate's tricks, like Charlie and the Chocolate factory, and they were going to fly out through the roof. He was almost disappointed when it came to a halt and they emerged in a carpeted corridor which did not look as if it would do well from having four wet children's feet walking on it, but nobody said anything to the contrary, and so they all moved out of the lift and then stopped and waited for their next instructions.

'Stay here,' said the Captain. 'I'll go and sort out with the chef about food.'

Jack felt Molly nuzzle against his legs and she whinnied slightly. 'Don't worry, Molly,' he said. 'There'll be food for dogs as well. You like sausages don't you?' Molly's ears perked up.

JJ got down on her knees and looked Molly in the eyes. 'Don't worry, Molly,' she said. 'Charlie's getting the best possible care.'

'What are we going to tell them?' asked Sam quietly.

Jack looked at him quizzically. 'I didn't really think of that,' he said. 'I suppose they're going to want to know how we came to be here and what we were doing and why we are here without parents or adult supervision. OK, leave any discussions to me.'

The Captain reappeared. 'Right,' she said. 'We're in luck. They are just putting out the afternoon tea buffet, so once we have got you some dry clothes you can come in and help yourselves. Chef is on standby for four sausage and chips though.' Just as she spoke, the other lift arrived with a 'ting' and the children looked up to see a kindly lady clutching a pile of what appeared to be clothes.

'Right,' said the Captain. 'Before you go into the dining room, help yourselves. There should be sweatshirts and tee-shirts and tracksuit bottoms and clean underwear. You can go across to the toilets over there and put everything on and see me back in the buffet in a couple of minutes.'

The children grabbed the pile of clothes, finding things that would probably fit them. There were some tee-shirts with pictures of the ship on and some with pictures of far flung places, all in bright colours. Molly followed Rosie and JJ into the ladies' toilet, almost as if she realised that she was indeed a girl. The boys went into the gentlemen's toilet with their pile.

The Captain had done well: there was something that fitted everybody, and, within minutes, at the thought of proper food, they were all back, clothed and ready to meet her at the entrance to the buffet.

'Now, just remember,' said the Captain, 'if you haven't eaten much, try and resist the temptation of filling your plates as full as you can. You do, after all, only have little tummies.' They all nodded solemnly, including Molly, who didn't really understand what was being said to her, but felt she should nod as well.

'Now the only thing is,' she said, 'I'm not sure about the dog in the dining room. I think that probably breaches all sorts of health and safety rules.'

Rosie looked at her and said, 'If Molly doesn't come, then we don't come.' And all four of them stood resolutely with their arms folded.

'OK,' said the Captain. 'Just this once, and you tell no one.' She smiled and the door to the restaurant was opened, and before them was a feast for sore eyes. On table after table there were cakes and sandwiches, meats, sausage rolls, salmon, bread, and that was just the starters.

Jack took a small plate at first but, having viewed everything that was on offer, decided that in fact a significantly larger plate was probably needed and went back to start again.

'Don't forget,' said Jack. 'Don't give Molly chicken bones – she'll choke.'

'Jack, I know,' said Rosie. 'I'm not stupid.' And with four plates piled high with food, and a fifth for Molly, which was kindly carried by the Captain, they moved to a table in the empty restaurant and sat down. The Captain watched as all four of them ate in silence as if they had never eaten before.

Once the first plate had been devoured, a chef appeared with four plates containing sausage and chips. The chef glanced at Molly, sat quietly tucking into smoked salmon. He looked at the Captain who shrugged as if to say 'what can I say' and the chef smiled and left them to it.

Molly was then enjoying chasing the scotch egg around the carpet, trying to get her mouth round it. 'I think I might need to cut that up for her,' said the Captain thoughtfully, and Jack nodded, his mouth much too full with chips to even contemplate saying anything, as he knew that his mother would be extremely cross.

The Captain lifted Molly's plate up and cut up everything that she possibly could and placed it back on the floor for Molly, who gratefully wolfed it down, and looked longingly at the buffet again, licking her lips.

'I think that means she wants some more,' said Rosie. 'That's what she does at home with Auntie Issie.'

'That's not a problem,' said the Captain. 'I'll get her some more.' And off she went, not too proud to refill the plate of a hungry young border collie who had appeared mysteriously on her ship.

As the Captain surveyed the buffet with Molly stuck close to her heels, almost indicating what she would quite like to try next, the children spoke in hushed tones.

'I'm going to tell them that we were out fishing with a family friend and that our rowing boat became detached and eventually sank,' Jack said.

The others looked at him as if to say, 'They're never going to believe that.'

'It's the best I can do,' he said. 'I just hope that Alfie will be on board soon and be able to protect us from any questions.'

The Captain returned to the table with another plate of food for Molly. She looked at them all as they ate. 'What were you doing in the water?' she asked.

All four children indicated that they had much too much in their mouths to be able to answer that particular question at that time, but that they would do so as soon as they had finished the entire plate.

'Don't worry,' laughed the Captain, 'I understand.'

And, mouthful after mouthful, the children ate, hoping to avoid the questions. Eventually, the silence was broken by the Captain's radio springing to life. She was asked to confirm her location, and she confirmed that she was in the buffet restaurant, feeding the children. The voice on the other end explained that someone would be there shortly.

Jack went visibly pale. 'It's bad news about Charlie, isn't it,' he said.

The Captain patted his hand. 'Be positive,' she said. 'He is in the best possible place and will have the best possible care. If we can save him, we will.'

Within five minutes the children heard the swinging doors to the restaurant open and in walked Alfie, together with a tall, very serious looking gentleman, who was wearing shorts and sandals with socks and a tee-shirt and, over that, a white coat. He approached them solemnly and all four children put down their knives and forks and watched him as he walked towards them. It was only as he was within five feet of their table, that a small smile crossed his lips.

'Ladies and Gentlemen,' he said. 'I am Noah Nolan, a vet and also a guest on the ship. I am pleased to confirm that your dog Charlie will be fine.'

The children leapt up in unison and cheered and Molly barked, which surprised the visitor a great deal, as he had not been expecting to see a dog in the dining room.

'He is very weak,' the vet said. 'But he will make a full recovery. He just needs peace and quiet and rest.'

'Good luck with that one,' said Alfie. 'He's a Border Collie.'

'We have sedated him a little to try and keep him calm whilst his body regenerates,' said the kindly gentleman. 'He was very lucky as, if you had not brought him here so quickly, I am not sure that we would have been able to save him.'

Rosie looked at Alfie. 'Thank you, Mr Parker,' she said. 'Thank you for saving Charlie's life.' And she ran towards him and gave him a huge hug, and just as Alfie was embarrassed by the first one, came a wave, as each child ran at him and hugged him to thank him for his fast-thinking in getting Charlie to help as quickly as he had.

'So,' said the Captain, 'I was just talking to the children about how they came to be in the waters off the island.'

Alfie looked at the four children, who all stared at him wide-eyed. They were not quite sure what he was going to say. 'I can answer that one,' said Alfie. 'They were out fishing with friends of ours and their boat was tied to the back. The knot could not have been tight enough, as the next time our friends looked, the dingy was missing. They radioed me to come and help look for them. I think the dogs must have jumped in and pierced it, giving a slow puncture. They were only trying to save the children and probably ended up causing the damage in the first place.'

Molly made a whining noise as if to say that she was not that happy about taking the blame and Alfie looked at her as if to say, 'You be quiet, this is all for your own good!'

'Well,' said the Captain. 'You really did have a lucky escape. Especially with you having five soldiers from the Ecuadorian army on board. But you might have mentioned, Mr Parker, when we saw you, that you had lost a boat with four children and two dogs, as we might have made an additional effort to look for them.' She looked at Alfie with a look that said, 'I'm not entirely sure that I believe you, but now is not the time or the place'. And, at that stage, her radio sprung to life again.

This time, the voice at the other end requested the Captain to please pick up the telephone, as there was an urgent call for her.

'Can't it wait?' asked the Captain.

'Err, no, Captain. I don't think this particular call can wait. I really do think you need to take it,' said the voice at the other end of the radio.

The Captain raised her eyebrows, but walked across to the nearest telephone and picked it up.

'Captain Bergman here,' she said.

'Standby for the call,' said the person at the other end. 'It's....' there was a pause as if the person could not quite believe it themselves. 'It is the President of the United States.'

Before the Captain could say anything to the person putting

the call through, to the effect that somebody must have been having a serious joke somewhere, a voice was on the other end of the line.

'Captain Bergman?' asked the soft American tones on the other end of the telephone.

'Yes, Mr President.'

Everyone looked up from the table at that point with surprise and then at each other. Alfie exchanged looks with the children which they knew meant 'say nothing'.

'I'm just calling to let you know that I am immensely grateful for the rescue of these four children and the two precious dogs. They belong to friends of mine. I am indebted to you, Captain, and I wanted to let you know that Air Force One is currently en route to Ecuador to collect all of them and to return them home. For reasons that I cannot go into, it is important that no details are provided to anybody about the children or the dogs. I will deal with all of the officials but please mention nothing to the crew or the rest of your passengers other than the fact that they were rescued. Do we understand each other, Captain?'

'Yes, Mr President,' said the Captain. 'I understand completely. I understand from Mr Parker that they were in a fishing boat that came loose and now, luckily, they have been rescued.'

'That's entirely correct,' said the President. 'Now, I understand that there are certain people on board who have saved the life of the dog, Charlie.'

'Yes, Mr President, and in fact, one of them, Mr Nolan, is with me now.'

'Good,' he said. 'Put him on please.'

The Captain handed the phone across to a bemused looking vet, who was stood in his shorts and sandals. 'Um, the President of the United States would like a word.'

The vet looked at her with an expression that said 'very funny' but when she did not smile back he realised she was serious. He took the phone and said, 'Noah Nolan here.'

The vet raised his eyebrows at the Captain, as if to say, 'is this for real?' and the Captain nodded, to explain that, yes it was. As the children watched his face carefully it gently broke into a very wide grin and he looked almost bashful. 'Thank you, Mr President,' he said on more than one occasion.

'Now,' said the President. 'I would like to speak to the young man, known as Jack.'

The vet placed his hand over the receiver, so as to mask his words. 'The President would like to speak to Jack,' he said.

'That's me,' said Jack, pushing back his chair.

'Do you think we're in trouble?' asked Rosie.

'No,' said Sam. 'I'm sure they would have said if we were in trouble.'

'Yes,' said JJ. 'I'm sure they would have said.'

But they all watched intently as Jack moved towards the phone. The vet handed it across and Jack stood as straight as he could, with his shoulders back, and took a deep breath. 'Mr President,' he said. 'This is Jack.'

'Jack, young man,' came the voice from the other end of the phone, 'I knew from the moment that I saw you that you were a man of great courage and integrity. The world is very grateful to you and to your sister and two friends.'

'Thank you, Mr President. The dogs as well. You won't forget the dogs will you?'

'Of course not,' said the President. 'I know that this was a team effort and you will all be rewarded.'

'We don't need rewards,' said Jack. He turned his back slightly so that those at the table could not hear what he said. 'It's enough to know that we have done what was asked of us.'

'Well,' said the President, 'I'm sending Air Force One, my private personal plane, to collect you all and take you back to England.'

'The dogs as well?' said Jack.

'Well, yes, of course, the dogs,' said the President.

'But I was just worried,' said Jack and hesitated, 'that we're in a different country now and what about quarantine and rabies, and things like that?'

'Don't you worry, Jack,' said the President. 'If the President of the United States cannot sort a small matter of two dogs returning to England, then I should not be in the job. You have my word. Goodbye, Jack. I hope that our paths will cross again.'

'Me too,' said Jack, and put the phone down. He stopped for a few seconds. Looking at the telephone, wondering if that had just happened and then turned back to his sister and their friends. Alfie and Mr Nolan had sat down at the table by this stage.

'Can we see Charlie now?' Jack asked and Rosie leapt to her feet.

'Yes! Can we see Charlie?' And they all looked pleadingly at Mr Nolan.

Molly sat in front of him and pawed his leg in the way that she does when she wants something.

'OK,' he said. 'But only for a very short time. He's very weak and he needs his rest.' And, with that, the children took their last mouthfuls of food, wiped their mouths with their napkins, jumped down from their seats and followed the vet from the dining room.

'If you don't mind,' said Alfie. 'I'll stay here and have a bite or two to eat. All this rescuing has made me quite hungry.'

'I will stay with you as well,' said the Captain, 'and keep you company. Children, you go with Mr Nolan, he'll take you to where Charlie is and then someone will show you your cabins until we can get you to the mainland.'

They followed Mr Nolan out into the corridor and down in the lift. This time they seemed to go even further down than before and when the doors opened, the walls were very white, and there was a slight smell of antiseptic in the air.

The vet knocked on one of the doors off the long corridor and a voice said, 'Come in,' and he opened it. There, lying on a small bed, only a few inches off the ground, with bandages on his shoulder and a drip attached to his front paw, was Charlie. His eyes sparkled when he saw who was there.

'Charlie!' shouted Rosie.

'Now, not too loud,' said the vet. 'I've told you he needs his rest and we can't have him excited.'

Charlie's tail started to wag underneath the blanket, which was covering half of his body.

'Charlie,' said Rosie, and ran towards him, flinging her arms around his neck. He lifted his head a little off the pillow and licked her face.

Jack stood in front of him and their eyes met. 'Thank you, Charlie,' said Jack. 'You saved all of our lives.' And Charlie let out a small, hardly audible, little bark and wagged his tail.

At that point, Molly poked her head round Jack's legs, so she was almost nose to nose with her brother. She whined and whinnied a little and wagged her tail. They obviously said everything that they needed to in doggy language and Charlie put his head back onto his bed.

'Right, children. Charlie must rest now. Come on, I'll get somebody to show you to your cabins,' said Mr Nolan, spinning round in his sandals and leading the way out.

A smartly dressed member of the ship's crew appeared beside the vet. He looked at Molly. 'I'm afraid that the dog will have to stay in the kennels that we have on board,' said the quite serious looking man.

Jack pulled himself up to his full height and stepped forward. 'First of all,' he said, 'this is not just a 'dog', this is Molly, and you should be extremely grateful to her for everything that she has done. The second thing is that Molly will not be staying in kennels; she has never been in a kennel in her life and she is not starting now.'

The other three stepped forward, so that they were shoulder to shoulder with Jack. By this time, Molly's ears had been laid flat on the top of her head and she had scampered round so that she was on the other side of Charlie's stretcher, lying down with her head on his back legs, ears flat.

'I'm happy to discuss this with the Captain,' said Jack. 'But this is not negotiable.'

The crew member looked at the vet, who shrugged, as if to say, 'Nothing I can do about it'.

'Give me a few minutes,' he said, and disappeared. He shut the door behind him but they could hear his voice, as the crew member was obviously using the telephone out in the corridor. 'But, Captain,' he was saying, 'what about the rules?' There was silence, as he obviously listened to the response. 'Yes, Ma'am, I completely understand. It will be done immediately. But what if it needs to go to the toilet?'

The response that had come back from the Captain was obviously fairly similar to the response of Jack, namely that this was not an 'it' but this was indeed, Molly, an extremely important dog.

'Apologies, Captain,' said the crew member. 'I meant Molly, not 'it'. Yes, I completely understand. I'll deal with this immediately.'

The children were half listening at the door and when they heard the footsteps back along the carpet, they immediately went back to fussing Charlie and Molly. The door opened and the crew member appeared. 'Right,' he said, 'I have spoken to the Captain and she has agreed that the ... apologies, Molly, can stay in your cabin, but she has asked please that you do not take her around the ship, because that will cause a few problems with the other guests.

'Outside your cabin, you have an area with astroturf and the Captain has asked if you could make sure that you clean up after...' he hesitated, remembering Molly's name, so as not to make the same mistake yet again, '... so that when Molly needs to go to the toilet.'

Rosie looked at him and folded her arms. 'We are responsible dog owners,' she said, and Jack had to try hard not to smile, as he remembered that this was an expression that Auntie Issie used quite a lot when talking to people that she met out on walks.

'Yes, of course,' said the crew member. 'No, no, I didn't mean to imply anything to the contrary. It's just I'm passing on what the Captain says.'

'We understand,' said Sam. 'And please don't worry. We will make sure that we look after Molly and that she isn't a nuisance.'

'In which case,' said the crew member, 'you had better follow me.'

Back into the lift and this time they went up. When the doors opened, the carpet was much brighter with a deeper pile and the children all looked at one another, as they had expected that they would be in a small room with bunk beds at the bottom of the ship and room for Molly to lie with one of them. It was therefore to their amazement when the crew member, who by now they had understood was called Albie, slid a card into a door and led them into what could only be described as a small palace. There was a large lounge and two bedrooms off it and a huge balcony which appeared to run along most of the ship. There were two wonderful bathrooms, and a huge television in most of the rooms.

'This is for us?' asked Jack in amazement.

Albie smiled. 'The Captain took pity on you. This is the Presidential Suite. There was nobody staying, so we thought it would probably be the quietest and safest place to put you.'

'Wow!' said JJ, as she jumped on the bed with her bottom and then lay flat on the beautiful soft duvet. 'I just realised that I am quite tired,' she said.

'Me too,' said Rosie, sitting next to her. 'I can't remember when we last had a proper night's sleep.'

'Oh, it was up with George...' Sam started to explain when they had last had a good night's sleep, but realised that saying so in front of Albie was probably not the best idea, as they did not want to have to explain everything and, indeed, they didn't really understand it themselves.

'And out here,' said Albie, pointing to the windows of the cabin, 'is your balcony. You have extra space, including the astroturf for Molly.' He looked at Molly to acknowledge her. Molly looked back, big ears alert, and smiled in that doggy way that only Molly can do.

He pulled down the latch and slid across the doors to the balcony, and they all stepped through into the sunshine. As they hung over the rail, they could see all the little boats and the tenders from the ship.

'What are they all doing now?' asked Jack. 'Are they still bringing animals from the islands?'

'No,' said Albie. 'Apparently, the flood waters have subsided significantly and so all the boats are taking the animals back. Here,' he said, 'use these binoculars,' and handed Jack a set from inside the door. Jack focused and could see in each of the little boats was at least one and generally two giant tortoises. Mainly they were right inside their shells, which is what tortoises do when they are frightened, but one or two of them seemed brave enough to have their head and even their legs out.

In some of the tenders from the ship, there were some of the older children, who were there with watercress, coaxing the tortoises out of their shells so that they could stroke them and take pictures, being careful not to fuss them too much but just trying to build a bond with these enormous creatures.

Some of the tenders had large cages and boxes which appeared to be filled with land iguanas, all being repatriated back to the island. There were large birds' nests with eggs still in them, and enormous birds flying over those boats containing the nests, clearly with a worried mother and father bird keeping a careful eye on their brood.

'What about the local people?' asked JJ. 'Have they lost everything?'

'Many of them have had their homes flooded, but we have sent word to the mainland and the ships are already on their way with food and fresh water and building materials. They should be here very soon to help the islanders rebuild their homes and to make sure that they are in proper sheltered accommodation until then.'

'Was anyone hurt?' asked Rosie.

Albie smiled. 'Apparently not,' he said. 'A couple of broken bones and a few cuts, dehydration and heat stroke but nothing serious. The hospital downstairs has patched them up and they are all on their way back.'

At this point, there was a tap on the door to their cabin. 'I'll see who that is,' said Albie, and emerged back on the balcony in the presence of Alfie. Molly wagged her tail at him and sat at his feet adoringly. He leant down and gave her a little stroke.

'I thought I'd come and see how you are settling in,' he said.

'I'll leave you to it, then,' said Albie, and leaving the keys to the room, which consisted of square plastic credit card sized keys, he bid them farewell and left.

Alfie walked out onto the balcony to see what the children were looking at.

'They're all going home,' said Jack.

'They are indeed,' said Alfie. 'And the reason that they have a home to go to is because of you.' He looked down at Molly. 'And of course Molly and Charlie.'

'What happens to us?' asked Sam.

'Well,' said Alfie. 'The plan is that we will all go back to the Ecuadorian mainland and, from there, the President has very kindly lent you Air Force One to take you back to the UK.'

'But,' said JJ, 'we've been away for a few days – my Aunt and Uncle will be frantic.'

Alfie smiled. 'Do not worry, young lady,' he said. 'The way in which the Gate works, time will essentially stand still for those back in Lavender Lane and the families that you have left behind. Once you are safely back at Homegarth, then time will start again. So, for you, it feels as if you've been away for many days, but if I were to ring Angela, she would think that you had been gone a matter of minutes.'

'That's very clever,' said Rosie. 'So we could be gone for weeks and nobody would notice.' She looked at Jack and smiled, and he smiled back.

'Don't even think about it,' said Alfie. 'The chances of you four going through the Gate again are slim to non-existent. We still have no idea why the Gate allowed you all through, including the dogs, but it's not something we intend to try and replicate.'

The children looked crestfallen. 'You've had a big adventure,' said Alfie. 'And you have helped to save the world. You can be very proud of that. You need to recover from this adventure first. Now, I suggest that you all rest. Supper will be at 7pm, and we think that, by that stage, we would probably have managed to repatriate most of the animals and birds to the island, so we will be setting sail around 11pm, back to Ecuador.'

Jack looked quizzically. 'What do the people on board think has happened? Who do they think that we are?'

'Oh, don't worry about that,' said Alfie. 'The Captain has told everybody that you were here on holiday and that your boat capsized, and we are therefore taking you back to Ecuador to put you on a flight.'

'And the dogs? How do we explain away the dogs?' asked Jack.

'Oh well,' said Alfie. 'Everyone's been told that the dogs are heroes; they helped to keep you afloat when your boat capsized.'

'What if somebody wants to interview us?' asked Sam. 'What if the Press think that it's such a great story?'

'Oh, don't worry about that,' said Alfie. 'We have ways and means of ensuring that the Press have no interest at all. We will try and keep you as far away from the rest of the guests as possible whilst we are on the boat and we can arrange for your meals to be served in your cabin.'

'It's called 'Presidential Suite',' said Rosie proudly. 'That's what Albie told us. Does that mean that we are presidents?'

'Quite right,' said Alfie. 'The Presidential Suite for the President's heroes. Anyway, you can have your supper here, and we should be back in Ecuador at some stage tomorrow, so that you can all have a good night's sleep. But you might like to go and use the swimming pool or go to the cinema. Just don't take Molly with you, will you?' Molly's ears flattened again.

'But Molly will need some exercise,' said Jack. 'We can't leave her locked up in the room all day.'

'Oh, don't worry about that,' said Alfie. 'There are other dogs on board and there is an exercise area up on the top deck, so we can arrange to take her up there and she can play with the other dogs, and just come back here to sleep. Now, I'm not going to be on board because I'm going to be in 441 and we'll be racing you back to the mainland.'

'Can we come too?' asked Sam.

'Sadly not,' said Alfie. 'I already have five members of the Ecuadorian Army on board and we're going to have to go pretty fast to keep up with The Royal Adventurer, so I'd rather that you stayed on board here and enjoyed their facilities until we get back to the mainland. Now, I'll leave you to it and I'll see you for supper at 7 o'clock. I'll come here.'

That night they feasted on an amazing supper brought to the presidential suite, washed down with ginger beer and lemonade and by 9pm they were all tucked up in bed, Molly lying between the two girls, sound asleep. Alfie looked at them all and smiled, switched out the light and went back to his own bunk for a good night's sleep before tomorrow's long ride back to Ecuador. 441 had been refuelled and its water tanks replenished.

She had been hosed down so that all trace of tortoise and iguana had been washed away and the five soldiers were showered, rested and ready to head back. They had been offered the option of riding back on The Royal Adventurer but the thought of travelling home in this historic craft again was too tempting. However, the Captain had arranged for them all to have Royal Adventurer T shirts for them and their whole families to take home as souvenirs to thank them for their part in the rescue.

The Royal Adventurer glided effortlessly through the water and the children, stood on the very top deck near to the bridge, with special permission of the Captain, were able to watch as she was carefully manoeuvred into position alongside the jetty, using the very powerful water jets and engines. As they watched in awe Jack asked:

'Don't you have tugs anymore?'

'Well,' said Captain Bergman. 'Sometimes we do, but now the ships are designed so well that we can manoeuvre them very easily and can bring them into position alongside the quay. There are some harbours where we have to have tugs because it's too dangerous, but this isn't one of them.'

Many of the passengers were out on the decks, waving and cheering to those who were hundreds of feet below on the quayside.

Jack looked across and stood next to him were his sister, his good friend, Sam, and JJ. They were still all dressed in clothes from the ship's shop and looked remarkably smart, all things considered. Lying between them was Molly, her head between her paws as she didn't really like the motion of being at sea or the vibration. They had a makeshift lead attached to her collar. This wasn't to stop her running off but was just for show in case any of the passengers were concerned that there was a dog loose on board.

'Right,' said the Captain, 'we're almost there. We're going to let you off directly onto the quayside to stop any fuss, and so I think we need to go down and collect Charlie.'

The faces of all four children lit up and Molly looked up with her ears alert and looked happier than she had been since the ship had started its engines and moved off from the Galapagos.

Below them they could see two long black cars, both flying two flags – the yellow, blue and red stripes of Ecuador and the red, white and blue of the United States, or the Stars and Stripes as it was known around the world.

They got into the lift outside the bridge, and within a few minutes were back in the antiseptic smelling medical centre. They had already been to see Charlie first thing that morning to make sure that his recovery continued to be good. As they walked through the door, they looked at Charlie's bed and Rosie gasped. It was empty.

Jack's eyes welled up with tears. 'Where's Charlie?' he asked.

Molly's ears went flat and ran towards the bed, trying to look under it and behind it for her beloved Charlie.

'Fear not,' said Noah Nolan from the other room. 'Charlie is alive and well, we are just sorting him out now.' And, from around the corner, came a slightly wobbly Charlie, recently brushed, sporting a large ribbon round his collar. Molly dashed towards him in that 'bottom first' subservient manner that she did with Charlie and he pulled at her ears until she squealed.

The two dogs touched noses, then there was a small whinny that went between them.

'Well,' said Mr Nolan, 'we couldn't really have him carried out of here could we. He's still a little sore and he is on some drugs that will make him slightly sleepy, but he should be fine.'

The children descended upon Charlie and hugged and kissed him and he sat down and enjoyed the fuss.

'Right then,' said the Captain. 'Does everybody have everything?'

Jack put his hand into his pocket and behind the zip he could feel the small locket and chain. He would obviously have to explain to Alfie at some stage that he had lost the pack with everything in it and also have to explain to his father that he had lost the glorch, but what mattered was that his sister and his friends and his Aunt's beloved dogs had all come back from their great adventure safely, and that was much more important than 'stuff'.

They walked slowly into the lift to make sure that Charlie could keep up, and down they went in the Charlie and the Chocolate Factory lift, right to the bottom this time. As the doors opened, they could see that the gangway had been put up against the side of the ship and the door was now open, so that they could exit straight onto the dockside next to them. No-one else was getting off that day, although there were plenty of stores already being loaded back on to The Royal Adventurer, to make up for all those they had left behind on the islands.

Waiting for them by the entrance to the gangway were many of the ship's crew, in their formal uniforms, and, standing in front of them all, was Albie, who smiled as he saw the children and dogs approaching. He knelt down on one knee and looked Molly in the eye. 'Will you forgive me for forgetting your name?' he said, and Molly licked the end of his nose.

'Good,' he said. 'I have a present for you,' and he produced
from behind his back a multicoloured bow, similar to that that
Charlie was wearing. 'A special bow for a special dog,' he said. At
which point, Charlie came over and sat directly next to his sister.
Albie moved his face across in front of Charlie's. 'Get well soon,
Charlie,' he said, and he too got a lick on the nose.

Alfie appeared from up the gangway, and he looked at each
child in turn. 'Time to go home, everybody,' he said. He turned
to the Captain. 'Captain Bergman, thank you again for your
hospitality and kindness and for bending the rules slightly.' He
looked down at Molly. She flattened her ears. 'I hope that we did
not take advantage of your hospitality.'

'On the contrary, Mr Parker,' said the Captain. 'We would
never have known that they were there.'

Rosie giggled and whispered to her brother, 'Except when
Molly barked at the seagulls of course.'

'Shhhhsh,' said Jack. 'It was only once or twice.'

'You are always welcome on board my ship, Mr Parker, you
and the children. And, indeed, the dogs,' said the Captain.

Stood next to her was Mr Nolan. 'Say thank you,' said Jack as
he shook his hand in a grown up way. Charlie walked over and sat
at the vet's feet. He held up a paw, as if to shake his saviour by the
hand.

The vet crouched down on his haunches and looked at
Charlie. 'Farewell my friend, keep safe.' Charlie licked his nose,
and then Molly joined in as well, as an extra thank you for saving
her brother, until eventually the vet was knocked backwards onto
the floor as both dogs nuzzled and licked him in the only way
they knew to say thank you to a human.

Then it was the children's turn to say goodbye. Each of them
hugged the vet for the second time in two days. 'Thank you, Mr
Nolan,' said Rosie. 'Thank you for saving our dog.'

'It has been a pleasure and a privilege,' said the vet. 'However, I will very much enjoy going back to being a passenger on this ship. Have a safe trip home.'

Next, it was the turn of the Captain, with all four children gathered around her, hugging her round the waist in thanks. She looked like a mother hen with her brood around her. 'Thank you,' they all said. 'Thank you for rescuing us and the dogs and all the animals off the island.'

The Captain smiled. 'I'm not entirely sure that I shall ever know what this was all about,' she said. 'However, it has been a privilege meeting you all.'

'There is one thing I keep meaning to ask,' said Jack. 'How you knew to be there at exactly that time? Were you just passing?'

The Captain smiled. 'You have some very influential friends. We had what I think is known in the English language, as a 'tip off' that we needed to be there.'

With that, the children proceeded down the line of the ship's company, hugging each one of them, to say thank you. Grown men and women were visibly moved by the display of affection, and as the children passed along the line, each adult wiped away a small tear.

They got to the end of the line, turned back and whistled to the two dogs. 'Come on then!' Molly bounded and Charlie hobbled slightly towards the entrance. They turned back for one last time and waved at the assembled ship's officers, and out into the bright sunlight they walked across the bridge that forged between the quayside and this massive ship.

It was at that stage that they noticed a contingent of what appeared to be American soldiers stood on the quayside. As the children emerged, the soldiers stood to attention and the tallest one, with what appeared to be the most decorations, looked directly at the children. 'With the compliments of the President of the United States,' he said. 'We are tasked with bringing you safely to the airfield and Air Force One is at your disposal.'

Charlie and Molly poked their heads round from behind the children's legs and the officer smiled. 'Yes, that is all of you, including the dogs. This is Dr Peter Beale, who is the most senior vet in the whole of the USA. He will accompany you on your trip. However,' he hesitated, 'I understand that we will not be going straight home to the United Kingdom, but we have a small diversion to make, as there is still a holiday to be had.' He smiled and the soldiers parted to reveal Jack and Rosie's beloved parents. They were dressed casually in light coloured chinos and summer shirts, both with hats and sunglasses but unmistakably their parents.

'Mum! Dad!' they cried, and launched themselves at their parents, reaching them about waist height and almost knocking both of them off their feet. 'How did you know we'd be here?'

'Well,' Grace said, 'there we were hanging about the garden feeling very sorry that the two of you were not there with us and watching the news every hour to see if there was any chance you could join us, when the phone rang.' Her husband James stepped in to take up the story. 'The man on the other end told us he was the President of the USA and we obviously laughed but it turned out that he was being serious,' he said, making a face as if to say that this had been quite embarrassing. 'He said that he had made arrangements to get you home for your holidays and that if we came to the quayside in Ecuador today then we could pick you up.'

Grace stepped in, 'And then he said that he had arranged transport for us and there we were waiting at La Paz airport when Air Force One flew in and we were ushered aboard like a couple of pop stars.' She laughed, having obviously enjoyed the experience. She hugged her two children even closer. 'And here we are…'

Charlie let out one bark, which is what he did when he

was either happy or frightened, at which point a massive cheer erupted from the sides of the ship, and Jack and Rosie looked back to see that practically every free railing around the ship was occupied by either a crew member or a passenger, all of whom were cheering and clapping and whistling.

The four children took a step back, looked at the waving crowds and waved back.

'Thank you, everybody,' shouted Jack. 'Thank you for helping. Thank you for bringing us home safely.' They waved frantically.

There was a polite cough behind them and the Chief Officer from Air Force One, politely enquired if they had any luggage.

'No, sir,' said Sam. 'This is us, this is all we have, the clothes we stand up in.' They all laughed. It was at that stage that Jack remembered that that was not quite right. That he did have something that he had not started out with. He also remembered that he had lost the glorch that his Dad had made and given to him. But he also realised he had not even introduced his two friends who were hovering in the background.

'Oh, I'm sorry,' said Jack. 'I'm being very rude. Let me introduce my friends. This is Sam.'

'Hello Sam,' said James. 'You must go to the School as well.'

Sam looked at Jack in a slightly embarrassed way. 'No,' he said. 'I'm hoping to go to the School, but I have not been selected yet.'

Jack smiled. 'Of course he'll be going. Anyone that can beat my sister at fencing deserves a place in our School.'

James and Grace laughed, glad to see that the healthy rivalry between their two children had not deteriorated, despite their great adventures.

'And this is my friend, JJ,' said Rosie. She introduced JJ, who held out a long slim hand and smiled broadly.

'It's a pleasure to meet you, Mr and Mrs Simmons,' she

said. 'I've heard a great deal about you and about your many adventures. I have to say I'm very jealous.'

James raised an eyebrow, impressed immediately by the charm of his daughter's friend. 'So, you must be in Jack's year?' asked James.

'That's right, Mr Simmons,' said JJ. 'Jack and I are in the same year and it has been a great privilege.'

Jack could feel himself getting redder and redder. James looked at his son and raised an eyebrow. Jack could tell that even his own father was impressed by this.

'And these two, you certainly know,' said Jack. Charlie and Molly came bounding up to say hello to their extended family.

James examined the shaved area around Charlie's shoulder, where he now sported a variety of sutures and bandages. 'You have been in the wars, old boy, haven't you? I'm not sure that Auntie Issie's going to be very impressed, us sending you back looking like this.' Charlie licked his nose. 'Molly-Moo,' said James, as he cuddled the little bundle of fluff upside down on her back, legs in the air, enjoying her tummy being rubbed. 'It's so lovely to see you.'

'They saved our lives, Dad.'

'I know,' said James. 'But you can tell us all about it on the plane. In the meantime, I think there are certain Air Force One officers who would quite like to get this show on the road.' He gestured towards the very official officers stood behind them.

'Now, say goodbye to your public, all of you,' said Grace, and the four children and two dogs turned back towards the ship. By this stage, the Captain could be seen outside the bridge, and all of her crew were lined up, hats off, to wave farewell to their short-term guests.

'Thank you, The Royal Adventurer,' shouted Jack, and at that point the cheers of the crowd were drowned by the deafening foghorn of the ship as it saluted the children.

It was at this stage that Alfie appeared and James and Grace greeted him with hugs and kisses. 'Thank you, Alfie,' they said quietly.

'You have nothing to thank me for,' he said. 'This was all of their own doing.'

'Yes,' said Grace, 'and I shall be having some words with my sister next time I speak about how the situation came about in the first place.'

Alfie smiled, 'They are four very brave children,' he said. 'They acted selflessly. Don't be too hard on her.'

Grace smiled, 'Never,' she said. 'They are back safely now and that's all that counts.'

Jack pulled at his father's shirt and James bent down so that Jack could speak quietly to his father.

'Dad, I'm afraid I've lost the glorch,' he whispered.

James smiled. 'I've made you another one already. Some things are more important than stuff.'

At that stage Alfie's phone rang and he stepped away to answer it. Angela's voice was on the other end. 'Alfie, the seas are returning to normal, the Gate will be closing soon and you know what will happen then. We need them to be back safe and sound in surroundings they will recognise,' she said quickly, knowing they did not have much time.

'Grace and James are here,' said Alfie. 'Air Force One will drop them in Bolivia and then bring the other two and the dogs home...' He paused. 'Can they get home, how is the volcano?'

He suddenly had a horrible thought that he would not be able to get Sam and JJ back home before the Gate closed. 'No problem,' said Angela. 'The volcano stopped yesterday, all flights resuming. You probably have 24 hours?'

'Plenty,' said Alfie glancing across at the children. 'I have arranged for 441 to be repatriated to the UK. I am leaving Jose in charge; he knows what he is doing. I will fly back on Air Force

One with the others. Got to go,' said Alfie as he saw that everyone was moving off in the direction of the cars.

The two large stretched limos moved up closer and into the first went Grace, James, Jack and Rosie together with Charlie and Molly. The immaculately dressed chauffeurs did not bat an eyelid as the border collies jumped into the back of the white carpeted limousines. It was almost as if this happened every day of the week. Alfie followed with Sam and JJ and the two vehicles slipped out of the dockside and onto the main road, heading towards the airport.

Air Force One stood there immaculate and gleaming on the runway. Around it, a cordon of security and defences. The limos pulled up to the steps which stood up against the entrance to the aircraft and each of them in turn climbed the short way up to the aircraft entrance, with the exception of Charlie, who was clearly finding the stairs quite difficult with his injuries, and, without a word, a burly American Marine lifted him up as if he were made of paper, and carried him gently to the top of the steps.

'Make yourself at home,' said the gentleman inside the door. 'I am your Captain and the plane is entirely at your disposal. In the fridge you'll find Coca Cola and lemonade. A light lunch will be served after we take off as the flight to Bolivia is only a short one. We have constructed a special dog bowl for our canine guests so that they can drink water without spilling it when we are taking off and landing. All they need to do is to suck in this tube here,' he said, pointing. The dogs looked at each other in a knowing way and Charlie approached it with caution. He put his mouth round the edge and sucked slightly, and jumped backwards as the water sprayed. Everybody laughed. Molly had a go and exactly the same thing happened to her, but they soon got the hang of it.

'We have also brought along with us some canine restraints for take-off and landing,' said the Captain. 'We hope that this will not cause Charlie too much distress with his injuries, but it is important that he is strapped in when we are in the air.' And with that, two of the crew members led Charlie and Molly to their beanbag seated area and proceeded to strap them in. They were very gentle with Charlie and he did not appear to be in too much distress.

The children picked their seats and buckled in. 'Are there any in-flight movies we can watch?' asked Rosie.

The Captain smiled. 'Luckily for you, young lady, we have to take the President's children and grandchildren around the globe, so each of you have in your seat your own personal entertainment system, with as many movies as you can possibly want, including all of those that have just been released this week.'

'Wow!' said Sam.

'But before you do,' said James, 'we want to hear all about your adventures. Let's take off, have something to eat and then we can talk. We're going to go via Bolivia to drop us off and then Air Force One will take you back to the UK, where you will be met and taken home. Are you happy with that or would you prefer me to accompany you back to the UK?' asked James.

'No thank you, Mr Simmons,' said JJ. 'We'll be absolutely fine.'

'Good,' he said. 'Let's sit back and relax.'

Alfie looked across at the excited faces of the children as the engines roared and the enormous plane turned to taxi to the runway. He was not worried what the children told their parents on the trip to Bolivia because he knew that as soon as the Gate was closed, all memories of their adventures would disappear, from everyone except the History Keepers. Whilst he too was anxious to hear what had gone on he knew that he was the only one who would remember what they said, but even he would have to wait until he got back to Lavender Lane.

Back in Lavender Lane, the History Keepers watched as the last rays of light disappeared from the Gate and it shut firmly with a definite 'click'.

Alfie sighed. He was tired after his long flight home and slightly worried whether 441 would be arriving back in one piece, but he knew that Jose would be travelling with her and Jose would be joining them for a few days' rest and recuperation in Lavender Lane – all visas compliments of the President of the United States.

'Well,' said Angela, 'I guess all of the children's memories of this little adventure will now disappear. It is a shame really, they did so well.'

Issie sat down at the table and cupped her hands around the cup of coffee in front of her. 'Until they come back to Lavender Lane,' she said. 'Then they will remember everything. We cannot keep them away forever.'

Stanley looked at the rest of the room. Benjamin and Melissa looked deep in thought, Adam was studying his coffee intently and Ella and Max were sat motionless. Michael and Martha were fiddling around making more coffee, under the careful direction of Cameron. Nobody said anything.

'Well,' said Cameron, 'there is another option…'

Everyone glanced up at him. He paused and looked at the assembled group.

'I know that we have very strict rules on History Keepers but these children have proved themselves. The Gate has let them through so it clearly thinks that they are worthy.'

'But…' interrupted Adam. 'They are children!'

Alfie may have been tired but he was not too tired to respond. 'These children,' he said, 'are brave, clever, resourceful and compassionate…' It was at that point that Molly and Charlie, equally as tired from their flight, settled in next to his feet, in approval.

'They deserve to join our ranks. They have proved themselves ten times over when all was almost lost.' He paused and looked at the others. In turn they nodded.

'Well,' said Angela, 'then that settles it. With immediate effect, Jack, Rosie, Sam and JJ are now officially History Keepers. Whilst they will not remember anything of their adventure until they come back to Lavender Lane, when they return we will invest them officially.'

And everyone else raised a coffee cup to toast this.

Jack awoke to the smell of freshly laundered sheets. He could feel the warm breeze on his face and could hear the familiar chattering of tropical birds wafting through the window. He opened his eyes slowly, trying to remember exactly where he was and then he did. It was half term and he was at home in Bolivia, of course. How could he possibly forget his most favourite place in the whole world?

He was conscious of having had the strangest of dreams. Dragons, giants, ships and planes. He put it down to jet lag.

He heard the sound of small feet muffled by socks on the marble floor and looked up to see Rosie stood in the doorway. Her hair was sticking out and her pyjamas slightly skewed, and she still had sleep in her eyes. She yawned loudly.

'It's really weird, Jack, we are in Bolivia and I don't remember getting here,' she said. 'Have I been asleep for a long time?'

Jack sat up and looked around him. 'I didn't think we'd be able to come,' he said. 'I thought that the volcano ash had stopped all flights.'

It was at that stage that their mother Grace appeared around the corner with a tray on which she had piled all of their favourite fruits, added hot buttered toast for Rosie, muffins for Jack and freshly squeezed papaya juice, which she knew that they both loved.

'You're quite right, Jack,' she said. 'The volcano did stop the flights but then, as quickly as it had started, the volcano stopped. You got the night flight out of London yesterday, and you both arrived absolutely exhausted.'

'Where are our cases?' asked Jack.

'Sadly, they did not make it. We are expecting them to follow,' said his mother. 'It seems the disruption in the whole system has meant that whilst they could get people around, they couldn't quite manage the luggage at the same time, or at least not your luggage. So, if you had wanted Max to bring home the case from a Uruguayan businessman, or a French ballerina, I understand that that could have been arranged – they were all at the airport but yours were not.' They all laughed.

'So, all you have are the clothes that you arrived in,' she said, and gestured to the chair. 'I have to say I don't remember buying you any of them, I assume that Auntie Issie must have given you The Royal Adventurer T-shirts from her last cruise. Luckily for you, you were coming home, and so there are plenty of things for you to wear.'

'I had the strangest dream,' said Jack.

'Me too,' said Rosie. And with that they both sat down on Jack's bed to devour their breakfast.

Back in Brighthaven, Sam awoke to the gentle tapping on his door. 'Come in,' he said, propping himself up on his elbows. Around the door poked the rather sheepish looking face of his father.

'You've been asleep a long time, Sam,' he said. 'I was starting to worry.'

'I must have been very tired,' said Sam. 'It was probably our visit to the School.'

'That's what I wanted to talk to you about,' said his father. 'Are you up for a chat before I go to work?'

Sam looked at the clock. It was 10am. 'But you're late already, Dad. You should have been gone hours ago.'

'I know, I know,' said his father. 'But some things are more important.' He looked even more sheepish and Sam was not sure he had seen him like this before. He was suddenly worried that his father may be ill? Before he could ask however, his father continued.

'I behaved like a buffoon at the School the other day, and I wanted to apologise to you personally. I've been thinking about it for a few days. I do rely too much on technology and I don't spend enough time with you or your mother. I wanted to tell you that personally, and to say that I will try harder, and that I think that the School would be the perfect place for you, and I will support you 100% if that's what you want to do. I can get you extra tuition, anything you need to get you in there.' He started to ramble, and Sam looked at him with a sympathetic smile. He knew that it would have taken a lot for his father to say this.

'Dad, I don't need extra tuition. It's not about academics. The School is about me and if I am the right sort of person.'

His father held up his hand to stop Sam. 'You're right, you're right,' he said. 'I'm doing it again aren't I? Interfering, thinking I know best.' He sat down on the edge of Sam's bed. 'I'd like to do something to say sorry.'

'You don't have to apologise, Dad,' said Sam. 'I know you mean well, and you want the best for us as a family. I do want to go to the School and I very much hope that they will want me, but I can't influence that. What will be will be.'

'Am I forgiven?' asked his father.

'You don't need to be forgiven for anything, Dad, but if it makes you feel better, you are forgiven.'

Just at that point, his father's mobile phone started to ring and he was about to answer it when he looked at Sam and stopped. He smiled, mischievously, and took the phone from his pocket and threw it straight out through the open window, and started to laugh. His laugh was infectious that Sam started to laugh too.

'I hope that didn't hit the cat!' said Sam.

'I hope it didn't hit your Mother!' said his father. 'With any luck, it landed in the pond,' laughed Mr Bailey-Knox.

'Now,' he reached into his jacket pocket. 'How about this?' He pulled out a piece of paper and Sam read it.

'Dear Sam, tomorrow morning at 11am, you, me and your Mother are going on the Eurostar to Paris, where we will visit the Louvre and see the Mona Lisa, as you have always wanted to do, and we are then going to spend two days in Disneyland Paris. I know it's hard being an only child sometimes, and therefore if you would like to bring a friend, he would be more than welcome.'

Sam read it and looked at his father, incredulously. 'Is this for real?' he said. 'What, we're actually going to Paris, and to Disneyland?'

'Yep,' said his Dad. 'And all electronic devices will be left safely back here, I have told the office I am completely uncontactable and I promise that I will not attempt to replace them or sneak them with me. We're just going to go off and have some fun. Now,' he said, 'who would you like to bring with you?'

'Oh my gosh!' said Sam. 'Well, either Jack, Rosie or JJ,' he said, and then stopped.

His father looked at him, 'They're friends that I haven't heard you mention before,' he said.

'No,' said Sam. 'Um, you remember Jack from the School, and his sister Rosie, who I fenced with on the first day of half term?'

'Oh, yes, of course,' said his Dad. 'But you've only known them a matter of days. I wouldn't have said that they were special friends of yours. What about some of the people from your current school?'

'I don't know, Dad. It seems really funny, but it's as if I've known the three of them for a long time. I would very much like to invite one of them to come with me.'

'Well I believe,' said his father, 'that Jack and Rosie were off to Bolivia to spend the half term holiday with their parents now that the volcanic ash has stopped.'

'Of course,' said Sam. 'I had completely forgotten.'

'Do you know where JJ lives?'

'She has an Aunt who lives in town,' said Sam. 'I think that's what she said.'

'Well, even if we did know where that was, we can't really just bowl up and ask her if she would like to come to Paris for a few days,' said Sam's father sympathetically. 'That would look a little odd.'

'I suppose,' said Sam. 'I'll try and think of someone, Dad, and thank you. It's very, very kind. Even if I can't find someone, it would be lovely to go with you and Mum.' His father let out a sigh of relief, as if he finally felt as if he had done something right.

Sam lay back in bed. He had the most overwhelming sensation that something had happened that he couldn't quite remember and he couldn't quite understand why he felt such an affinity to three people whom he had only met a matter of days beforehand.

Sam climbed out of bed, put his dressing gown on and went downstairs. His Mother was in the kitchen. 'Hello, darling,' she said, looking up as he arrived in the kitchen. 'I'm just making you a lovely breakfast.'

The television was on in the background and it was the news. The reporter was showing footage from an island which appeared to have been severely affected by flood. 'And, curiously,' said the announcer, 'almost as quickly as it arrived, the floods receded, leaving its inhabitants to rebuild their lives. Luckily, due to the quick reactions of the crew and passengers of the Drucan flagship The Royal Adventurer, it is believed that all of the giant tortoises were saved from drowning.' And they proceeded to show a number of photographs of tenders from the The Royal Adventurer with giant tortoises in the bottom being rowed back and forth to the cruise liner and then cut to an interview with Duncan Snugs, Chief Executive and President of Drucan. He explained how they had been happy to help.

Sam stared at the screen for a while. Something in the back of his mind was stirring a memory that he couldn't quite grab hold of. 'Thanks, Mum, I'm starving,' he said absentmindedly.

Sam was just tucking into hot buttered toast and bagels with smoked salmon when the doorbell rang. He looked at his mother, who looked at him equally quizzically. 'You're not expecting anyone are you, Sam?'

'I don't think so,' said Sam. 'It must be a delivery.'

He could hear his mother go out into the corridor and open the front door. There was a conversation that ensued, and two minutes later his mother appeared. 'You have a visitor,' she said and stood aside. There, in the doorway, was JJ. She smiled broadly.

'JJ!' said Sam leaping to his feet. 'How did you...?'

'I remembered where you lived from when I came over with Rosie and Jack on the first day of half term. I wanted to come across and ask if you wanted to do anything over half term. I'm a bit bored really, I'm staying with my Aunt and I don't really know anybody in the area. But I'm afraid I don't fence...' she said apologetically.

'No but you are a great shot and the best at taekwondo,' blurted out Sam, not sure how he knew this, but he did. He looked at the floor slightly embarrassed.

'Of course,' he said. 'It would be fantastic. I mean, would you like to go to Paris?'

JJ looked at him in a slightly odd way, is if to say, 'You are joking, aren't you?'

'Sorry?' she said eventually.

'Paris. Mum and Dad want to take me to Paris but they have also said that I could bring a friend and I wondered if you would like to come? Have you got a passport?'

'Yes,' she said. 'Of course.'

'Good, well that's settled then,' said Sam.

'Wait a minute,' said his mother sensibly, holding up her hand as if to suggest that everything needed to slow down slightly. 'We'll have to clear this with JJ's Aunt and Uncle to make sure that they are happy. I mean, we could be anyone really, couldn't we?' She laughed nervously and Sam and JJ looked at her quizzically.

Sam's mother took a deep breath and smiled. 'JJ, why don't you sit down. Would you like some breakfast? Let's have a chat about this and then perhaps we can go across and see your Aunt a little later on.'

'Thank you,' said JJ, and pulled up a seat beside Sam. Together they sat and ate toast, drank juice and coffee and talked like two old friends who had known each other for years.

Out in the hall, Sam's Mother was on the telephone to his father. 'Yes,' she said in hushed tones. 'It is quite extraordinary. They have only met briefly yet the two of them are acting as if they are very old friends. She's a very nice girl and very well mannered...' Her husband cut in and she listened. 'The two of them would absolutely love her to come to Paris...uhuh...' she listened further. 'OK,' she said eventually, 'thank you Gerald, I will sort it out.'

Jack had had a long hot shower and wrapped himself up in his freshly laundered fluffy dressing gown and his slippers. He breathed in the smell of freshly laundered clothes and looked around at his bedroom, happy to be amongst such familiarity.

He started looking for some clean clothes to wear in the drawers of his dressing table and, to get to them, he had to move the clothes that he had arrived in the previous evening. As he picked them up and moved them from the back of the chair, he heard a 'clunk' as something small fell out of a pocket and landed on the tiled floor.

He got down on his hands and knees and eventually found it underneath his dressing table. It was a small silver locket on a chain and when he opened it up, inside was a pressed piece of lavender. He turned it over and over but could find no inscriptions and no indication as to where it had come from. He thought, then, that perhaps it had been on the dressing table, left there by his mother or one of the domestic staff that helped her keep the house looking so beautiful.

Jack placed the locket carefully on the dressing table and carried on looking for clothes to wear in the drawers. Finding something suitable he struggled into them, then combed his hair, ate another piece of mango and, picking up the locket in his hand, he went off in search of his mother.

The floors were marbled and cool and all of the windows were open, letting in the early morning breeze. The air was warm and welcoming. Jack skipped down the stairs and, not finding his mother in the kitchen, went out through the open back door to the beautifully tended gardens. There he found his mother, wandering thoughtfully along, brushing her hands against the lavender as she did.

'Mum,' Jack shouted and Grace turned and smiled at her son.

How grown up he looked now, broad shouldered just like his father. She instinctively opened her arms and he flung his arms around her and hugged his mother tightly.

When they had both hugged hard, Jack stepped back and held out his hand: 'I think you might have left this in my room.' His mother held out her hand and into her outstretched palm Jack placed the small silver locket.

Grace stared at it for a moment and then at Jack. 'Where did you get this, darling?' she asked gently, breathing steadily, not wanting to give away the surprise and shock that she felt holding this precious thing in her hands, after all these years.

'I moved my clothes and it fell to the floor,' he said. 'I think I brushed it off the dressing table, I don't think it was in my pockets.' Grace studied her son's innocent face very carefully and knew that he genuinely had no idea what it was he had in his hand or indeed where it had come from.

'You are absolutely right, darling,' said Grace with a smile and a bright laugh. 'I must have left it on your dressing table when I helped put you to bed last night. Thank you for returning it to me, Jack, I can't tell you how much this means to me.' Her fist clenched around the small little silver locket. 'Now go and brush your teeth,' she said in true mother like style and Jack turned around and bounded back towards the kitchen door.

Grace stood for a while and watched her son disappear from view. Eventually she opened her fingers and looked closely at the locket. She went to open it but she knew what she would find inside – a small but perfectly preserved piece of lavender. Nevertheless she clicked it open and gasped. And then, she carefully closed the small locket and brought it up to her lips and planted a kiss on it.

The last time that she had seen this locket, had been when she had said goodbye to Jack's brother Harry, following his accident all of those years ago. She and James had agreed that something that they treasured would be buried with him, and they had put in a piece of lavender because it was Harry's favourite thing to do, running through the gardens, his fingers trailing through the lavender bushes, releasing the scent.

And now, she held it in her hand and knew that it was a sign. She knew that Harry would never be returned to them but she knew that he was out there somewhere watching over them. She did not understand how or why but she knew that he was there and this was his way of letting her know.

Grace tightened her fingers around the small locket and smiled. 'Thank you,' she said to no-one in particular and somehow she knew that the strange dreams that Rosie and Jack had had were probably much more than that. She had had them herself sometimes, a feeling as if there had been great adventures that she could not quite remember.

But Grace did not feel afraid for her children; she felt proud. Proud of Jack and Rosie. Proud of Harry. He had found a way to send her a message and he had undoubtedly been very much part of any great adventure; that was the sort of boy he had always been.

She felt a tear well up in her eyes, not of sadness but of pride. She tucked the little locket into her pocket and turned back towards the house, determined to give Jack and Rosie the best half term holiday of their lives.

CHAPTER TWELVE

It was September and the School was alive with students arriving from all corners of the globe.

'Stop running,' came the bellow of Mr Warren from his viewpoint out of his first floor office window, as gaggles of children moved back and forward carrying books and clothes, cuddly animals and pictures.

Parked outside Jack's boarding house was a large Volvo estate, with its boot open. Jack watched as the driver emerged from around the back with a large suitcase and Jack immediately recognised the burly figure of Mr Bailey-Knox.

Jack leapt to his feet and flew outside to meet him. 'Mr Bailey-Knox,' he shouted and the large man looked up and a broad smile crossed his face.

'Why, young master Jack,' he called out and putting the case down he strode purposely across to greet Jack, hand held out firmly. 'How wonderful to see you again,' he said and really sounded like he meant it.

'No problems getting in this time then?' asked Jack with a wry smile, thinking that perhaps he was pushing his luck slightly. Jack knew that Sam had got into the School; they had stayed in close touch with one another since the spring and Jack had given Sam as much help as he could to get him through the selection week. It had paid off and two weeks later Sam had written to Jack to say that he would be joining the School in the September term.

'None whatsoever,' said Mr Bailey-Knox proudly. 'Indeed I did not even have to hand in any equipment,' he said defiantly and

Jack looked at him suspiciously.

'Nothing?' asked Jack. 'Not even a phone?'

Mr Bailey-Knox threw back his head and laughed and for the first time Jack saw that he was much more relaxed and slimmer; he looked like a man who was enjoying life. 'No,' he said. 'Not even a phone. You see, Master Jack, our chance encounter changed my life.' He looked serious for a moment. 'I realised that I was not working myself to death because I enjoyed it, but because I felt that I had to. And once we knew Sam had got into the School I realised that there were no fees to pay and so we sat down as a family and decided what we really wanted to do.'

Jack was truly intrigued by this stage. He knew from Sam what had been going on but was very interested to hear it from his father's point of view.

'My family have always been farmers and my father was very elderly and despairing that there was no-one left to run the family farm. He was going to sell it but we all agreed that this was what we really wanted to do, so we sold our house in Brighthaven and moved back to Suffolk – built an extension on the house for my Dad and started to remind myself about being a farmer again.'

Jack smiled; he was genuinely pleased for them all. At that point Mrs Bailey-Knox appeared from inside the building, with Sam right behind her. She looked relaxed in smart chinos and a long sleeved shirt and jacket, with long black boots. Sam and Jack embraced and Mrs Bailey-Knox smiled warmly at Jack.

'I have just been telling young Master Simmons what a profound effect he has had on our lives,' laughed Mr Bailey-Knox.

'Did you mention George?' asked Sam, almost disappointed that his father had let the cat out of the bag.

'Certainly not,' said Mr Bailey-Knox, indignant that his son would think that he had given away his son's big surprise to his friend. Sam grinned broadly and let out a little whistle. There was movement in the back of the Volvo and out from the back jumped a small black, brown and white fur ball.

'Sit,' said Sam with authority and the fur ball sat obediently on the pavement. 'Come here,' commanded Sam and sank to his knees and the fur ball raced over and leapt into his arms.

'This,' said Sam proudly, holding up the ball of fur to his friend, 'is George.' George licked Jack's face obediently. The name struck a chord in Jack's heart but he did not know why.

'We bought him to round up the sheep, and I am training him,' said Sam proudly. George wagged his tail at the mention of sheep.

'He is gorgeous,' said Jack, very jealous all of a sudden. 'Won't you miss him?'

'We will take good care of him whilst Sam is away,' said Mrs Bailey-Knox. 'Perhaps you would like to come and spend a half term with us and see how he is developing?'

'And Rosie and JJ of course!' said Sam, just as the two girls came walking around the corner.

'We have loads of room on the farm and you would really like my Grandad.' Sam put George down on the floor and the squeals from Rosie told him that she had seen him and she knelt down and held out her arms and the little bundle ran towards her and Rosie swept George up into her arms.

The girls came over and said hello to Mr and Mrs Bailey-Knox. JJ was well known to them after their amazing few days in Paris in the spring and had been a regular visitor as an additional mentor to Sam in his quest to get into the School.

'I am just arranging for you all to come and stay with us one half term,' said Sam and the other three smiled broadly and George barked excitedly.

'Perhaps,' said Jack cautiously 'we could have some great adventures...' He watched as Sam, Rosie and JJ looked at him with a look that told him that they too remembered something in the same way that he did.

There was a pause and then they all stood together, shoulder to shoulder and smiled at each other.

'Yes,' said JJ. 'I look forward to great adventures.'

And so it was sealed. The four of them stood as one, not knowing that they represented the new generation of History Keepers, not knowing that this was not the end of their adventures... but just the start.

9 781910 223024